HOSTAGE

MAY 17

CH

HOSTAGE

A NOVEL

KRISTINA OHLSSON

Translated by Marlaine Delargy

EMILY BESTLER BOOKS

—

WASHINGTON SQUARE PRESS

NEW YORK   LONDON   TORONTO   SYDNEY   NEW DELHI

EMILY
BESTLER
BOOKS

WASHINGTON SQUARE PRESS
An Imprint of Simon & Schuster, Inc.
1230 Avenue of the Americas
New York, NY 10020

Copyright © 2012 by Kristina Ohlsson

English language translation © 2014 by Marlaine Delargy

Originally published in Swedish in 2012 as *Paradisoffer*. Published by agreement with Salomonsson Agency.

First Emily Bestler Books/Washington Square Press paperback edition November 2015

EMILY BESTLER BOOKS / WASHINGTON SQUARE PRESS and colophons are trademarks of Simon & Schuster, Inc.

For information about special discounts for bulk purchases, please contact Simon & Schuster Special Sales at 1-866-506-1949 or business@simonandschuster.com.

The Simon & Schuster Speakers Bureau can bring authors to your live event. For more information, or to book an event, contact the Simon & Schuster Speakers Bureau at 1-866-248-3049 or visit our website at www.simonspeakers.com.

Interior design by Akasha Archer

Manufactured in the United States of America

10   9   8   7   6   5   4   3   2   1

Library of Congress Cataloging-in-Publication Data

Ohlsson, Kristina, date.
  [Piratförlaget. English]
Hostage : a novel / by Kristina Ohlsson.
  pages cm
"Marlaine Delargy has translated works by many writers"—Verso title page.
Originally published as Paradisoffer (Stockholm : Piratförlaget, 2012).
I. Delargy, Marlaine, translator. II. Title.
PT9877.25.H57P3713 2015
839.73'8—dc23   2014040177

ISBN 978-1-4767-3403-3
ISBN 978-1-4767-3405-7 (ebook)

HOSTAGE

Washington, DC, USA

It is early evening as Flight 573 heads toward the USA. An endless network of runways stretches into the distance beyond the control tower where Bruce Johnson is waiting for news. The room is silent, and he scarcely notices that he is holding his breath. They still don't know if the plane will be given permission to land.

Bruce can see police cars and other emergency vehicles lined up next to one of the runways. A whole fleet of ambulances and fire engines. No one knows how this drama will end. Whether the whole thing will go disastrously wrong. He can't see the men from the armed-response unit, dressed all in black, but Bruce knows they are waiting in the darkness with their guns at the ready. A thought passes through his mind:

We shoot the hostage. That's rule number one.

He doesn't know where that thought just came from. Shooting the hostage has never been a rule. No one in the FBI would ever think or act according to such a counterproductive principle. Rule number one is that we never, under any circumstances, negotiate with terrorists.

And that applies right here and now. Their refusal to compromise has guided their actions ever since the plane took off from Arlanda Airport just outside Stockholm, a city that Bruce has wanted to visit for a long time. But he doesn't really believe he will ever get there. Why would someone like him ever travel to Sweden?

The plane is a 1989 jumbo jet. It is carrying over four hundred passengers. Now it has run out of fuel, and the pilot is begging for permission to land.

Bruce isn't sure what is going to happen next. He is still waiting for instructions from his boss. In Sweden, it must be almost eleven thirty at night. Bruce knows what a lack of sleep can do to a person, and he is keeping that in mind. No doubt his colleagues in Stockholm are thinking along the same lines, but they have been left with no choice. During all the hours that have passed, he has been in touch with the same group of people in Sweden; it has been too intense to bring in replacements. Someone mentioned something about the light in Sweden, the fact that the sun is up for such a long time in the summer, and therefore, the Swedes sleep less, even when it is autumn, as it is now. Perhaps that's true.

No other planes are using the airspace above the airport. All incoming flights have been diverted to other cities, and all outgoing flights have had to delay their departure times. The media have been banned from the complex, but Bruce knows that they will be on-site: far away, beyond the perimeter fence, using telephoto lenses that enable them to see all the way to China, snapping one blurred image after another.

The sound of the telephone ringing makes him jump. It's his boss.

"They've made a decision. It's bad news."

Bruce puts down the phone and reaches for another handset. He sits there, holding it in his hand for a few moments, before keying in the number he now knows by heart, then waits for Eden to pick up.

The sentence has been passed—the plane will not reach its destination.

They have opted for the rule that did not exist.

The hostage will die.

One day earlier

Monday, October 10, 2011

1

Stockholm, 12:27

Once innocence was lost, it could never be regained.

He had thought this on countless occasions. As far as Sweden was concerned, it had begun with the assassination attempt at Drottninggatan right in the middle of the Christmas-shopping rush in Stockholm. Sweden had its first suicide bomber, and the shock waves spread throughout the whole country. What next? Would Sweden become one of those countries whose citizens dared not venture out for fear of terrorist attacks?

No one had been more worried than the prime minister.

"How do we learn to live with this?" he had asked over a glass of cognac late one night in Rosenbad, the government offices in the city center.

There was no clear answer to that.

The consequences had been devastating. Not from a material point of view—physical things could be repaired. However, many emotional and moral values had been shattered. As the newly appointed minister for justice, he had been astonished to see the shaken individuals demanding new laws in order to make society safer, and had treated them with caution. The government party that opposed immigration capitalized on the situation and made one statement after another.

"We have to take a firm approach on the issue of terrorism," the foreign secretary had said when the government met for the first time after the attack.

As if she were the only one who realized this.

They had all looked hopefully at the new minister for justice, who had taken up his post only weeks after the terrorist attack in Stockholm.

Muhammed Haddad.

Sometimes he wondered if they had known what was to come, and had handpicked him for the post. As an alibi. As the only person who could take necessary action without anyone being able to call him a racist. Sweden's first Muslim minister for justice. A newcomer to the party who had never met any opposition during his short career. Sometimes it sickened him. He knew that he was given preferential treatment because of his ethnic and religious background. Not that he didn't deserve his success. He had been a brilliant lawyer, and had realized at an early stage that he wanted to devote himself to criminal law. His clients had dubbed him the miracle worker. He wasn't satisfied with winning; he also demanded redress. He had been fifteen years old when he came to Sweden; now he was forty-five and knew that he would never return to his homeland, Lebanon.

His secretary knocked and stuck her head around the door.

"Säpo called. They'll be here in half an hour."

He had been expecting the call. The security service, known as Säpo, wanted to discuss a high-security matter, and Muhammed had made it clear that he wished to take the meeting in person, even though this was not common practice.

"How many of them are coming?"

"Three."

"And Eden Lundell?"

"She's coming, too."

Muhammed felt calmer. "Show them into the large conference room. Tell the others we'll meet there five minutes beforehand."

2

12:32

"I need to go soon. There's a meeting I have to attend."

Fredrika Bergman looked at her watch, then at her former boss, who was sitting opposite her.

Alex Recht shrugged.

"No problem, we'll have a longer catch-up some other time."

She smiled at him warmly.

"I'd really like that."

One of the disadvantages of no longer working at Police HQ in Kungsholmen was the lack of decent places for lunch. At the moment, they were in a mediocre Asian restaurant on Drottninggatan. Alex's choice, not hers.

"Next time, you can decide where we meet," Alex said, as if he could read her mind.

Which he could. Fredrika was rarely good at hiding her feelings.

"There aren't that many places to choose from."

She pushed away her plate. The meeting was due to begin in half an hour, and she ought to be back fifteen minutes beforehand. She tried to interpret the silence that had descended over their table. Perhaps they had already dealt with everything there was to say— straightforward matters that couldn't possibly lead to unnecessarily painful discussions. They had talked about Alex's new job with the National Bureau of Investigation. About how much Fredrika was enjoying her temporary post with the Justice Department. About her year on maternity leave in New York with her second child, Isak; Spencer, her husband, had been given a research post there.

"You should have told us you were getting married—we would have come along," Alex said for the second or third time.

Fredrika shifted uncomfortably on her chair.

"We got married in secret. Even my parents weren't there."

Her mother still hadn't forgiven her.

"They didn't try to recruit you in the USA?" Alex said with a wry smile.

"Who? NYPD?"

He nodded.

"No, unfortunately. That really would have been a challenge."

"I was there on a course once. The Yanks are like everybody else. Good at some things, bad at others."

Fredrika couldn't comment on that point. She hadn't worked for one single hour during her time in New York. Her entire existence had revolved around the two children, and on the task of getting Spencer back on his feet. Nothing had been the same since a student had accused him of rape two years ago. When they discovered that Fredrika was expecting their second child, they had initially agreed that a termination was the only way out.

"We can't cope with another child," Spencer had said.

"It's not the right time," Fredrika had agreed.

Then they had gazed at one another for a long time.

"We're keeping it," Spencer said.

"That's exactly how I feel," Fredrika said.

· · ·

Alex put down his coffee cup with a clatter.

"I thought you'd come back. To the police."

"You mean after New York?"

"Yes."

The noise of the other diners suddenly seemed intrusive.

Forgive me, she wanted to say. Forgive me for making you wait, even though I knew I had no intention of coming back.

But not one word passed her lips.

"On the other hand, I understand that you couldn't turn down a job with the Justice Department," Alex said. "It's not every day you get an offer like that."

It wasn't an offer. I went after the bloody job, because I knew that my soul would rot if I came back to Kungsholmen.

Fredrika pushed back a strand of hair from her face.

"That's true."

There was nothing more to say. After the case involving the writer who refused to speak and the graves in Midsommarkransen that Alex and his team had investigated in the spring of 2009, everything had started to fall apart. When Margareta Berlin, the head of human resources, had called Alex into her office to tell him that the special unit he had led for the past few years was to be dissolved, the news was far from unexpected. The team was running on empty, and Alex was putting all his energy into his relationship with Diana Trolle, the new woman in his life, while Fredrika had fallen pregnant.

"Have you heard from Peder?"

Alex gave a start when he heard Peder's name.

"No—how about you?"

She shook her head sadly.

"Not since he cleared his office. But I did hear . . . that he wasn't doing too well."

"I heard the same." Alex cleared his throat. "I bumped into Ylva last week. She told me a bit about how things had been."

Fredrika tried to imagine the hell Peder was living through, but it was impossible. She didn't know how many times she had tried, but it was always equally difficult.

Some things just don't heal. However hard we fight.

She knew that Alex had a different view of the situation: he felt that Peder ought to pull himself together and move on. Which was why she hadn't mentioned it before.

"He's got to stop behaving as if he has a monopoly on grief," Alex said, using the same words as he always did when they attempted to talk about what had happened. "He's not the only one who's lost someone close."

Alex had lost his wife, Lena, to cancer, so he knew the dark depths of grief. But it seemed to Fredrika that there were essential differences between losing someone to cancer and having a brother murdered by a ruthless killer.

"I don't think Peder's in a state where he can make decisions about how he's feeling," she said, choosing her words with care. "His grief has become an illness."

"But he's asked for help, and he's been given help. And he's still no better."

They fell silent, reluctant to pursue the discussion. They knew that if they did, they would end up falling out, as usual.

"I really do have to make a move."

Fredrika started to gather up her things. Handbag, scarf, jacket.

"You know I'll always keep the door open for you."

She stopped in midmovement, thinking that no, she hadn't actually known that at all.

"Thanks."

"You were one of the best, Fredrika."

Her cheeks grew hot and her vision was suddenly blurred.

Alex looked as if he was about to say something else, but she put a stop to that by getting to her feet. They left the restaurant together and, in the middle of Drottninggatan, Alex held out his arms and gave her a hug.

"I miss you, too," Fredrika whispered.

Then they went their separate ways.

• • •

Detective Inspector Alex Recht had a distinguished career behind him. He had spent many years in the police service, with considerable success. In 2007, his efforts had been rewarded: he was asked to form a special investigation team. It would be small, but would bring together the most competent individuals. Additional resources would be available when necessary. Alex had started by recruiting the relatively young but driven Peder Rydh; he had proved to be a talented and conscientious investigator, but his temperament could be volatile, and his judgment was sometimes flawed. With hindsight, Alex had asked himself if he was partly to blame for the tragedy that had occurred two years ago, resulting in Peder's dismissal from the police service. He didn't think so. It had been a terrible case, and the price had been high for all those involved.

But no one had paid a higher price than Peder's brother, Jimmy.

Alex knew he shouldn't brood on the case that had cost him so much. Following Peder's sudden departure from the team, things had gone downhill fast. Fredrika Bergman, the only member of the team who hadn't been handpicked by Alex, had lost her spark, and when she then became pregnant with her second child, it seemed to Alex that she somehow disappeared from active duty.

He was the first to admit that he hadn't liked her initially. Fredrika was an academic, a civilian investigator with no real aptitude or interest in the job. For a long time, Alex had tried to circumvent her, giving her the simplest tasks he could find. Until one day he realized that he was wrong. In fact, she had a considerable aptitude for the job. However, her lack of interest was still a problem. Alex could see that she wasn't happy within the organization, and there wasn't a great deal he could do to change things. The impetus had to come from her, and one day she turned a corner. When the case of Rebecca Trolle's dismembered body landed on Alex's desk, Fredrika came back early from her maternity leave. The team had reached its zenith that spring. They had never been better.

Alex picked up his coffee cup and went along to the kitchen for a refill. He had a new job with the National Bureau of Investigation. A good job in a good team. Interesting cases related to serious organized crime. However, he couldn't help missing the life he used to have. Before everything fell apart. Lunch with Fredrika had merely served to remind him of everything he had lost.

He wasn't stupid; he realized that Fredrika had applied for the post with the Justice Department because she wanted to get away. It was hard to criticize her for making that choice. She was a conscientious and hardworking individual, and people like that always get restless. Alex wasn't sure what her actual role was within the department; he knew that she had a certain amount of contact with the security service, but he hadn't delved any further.

He had other things to think about.

People he had lost, in different ways.

"You can't keep going over it all like this," Diana had said only the day before. "You've got to put what has happened behind you."

Diana Trolle.

He would have been lost without her. She knew just as well as he did what real grief felt like, how painful it could be. Sometimes he wasn't sure whether they would have fallen in love if they hadn't been united by a sense of despair.

Grief.

Loss.

Pain.

He had known that they existed, that they had to be taken into account. Being crushed was just part of life. Or was it? He felt a fresh wave of irritation when he thought about Peder. Why the hell couldn't he just pull himself together? Why couldn't he deal with the trauma in a different way, rather than making himself unhappy all the time?

If only Peder had handled things better, he could have kept his job and carried on working with Alex and Fredrika. Because when it came down to it, that was what Alex found so upsetting: he had lost a close colleague, someone he had enjoyed working with. And even though he knew it wasn't fair, he found that very hard to forgive.

Alex's train of thought was interrupted as his boss stuck his head around the door.

"Bomb threat," he said. "Came in just now."

"I'm on it," Alex said, getting to his feet.

A bomb threat. Buildings destroyed, human beings blown to pieces. An evil act in its purest form.

A short while later, he was fully up to speed. Not one but four bomb threats, targeting different places in Stockholm. Including Rosenbad, the government building.

Alex couldn't understand it.

Four bombs. What the hell was this about?

3

12:32

Where did all this anger come from?

Eden Lundell had no idea. As the head of the security service's counterterrorism unit, she was expected to have a clear grasp of every case that passed through her hands, but she often found it extremely difficult to follow the thought processes that lay behind the actions of certain individuals.

Right now there were a number of issues that merited closer attention, and Eden had to prioritize. Resources were limited, and she wanted to see results. Patience was a quality she had lacked all her life, and things hadn't improved since she had come to work for Säpo.

If only they understood the origins, the source of this rage.

The rage that made young people turn their backs on respect for life, and resort to violence in order to bring about the changes they thought were necessary. To commit acts of terrorism. Eden had asked herself many times what could possibly make her cross that line, make her take up arms and fight against people living in the same country as her, with no evidence of antipathy.

What would drive me to commit the worst sin of all?

She had reached the conclusion that the love she felt for her family might be just such a trigger. If they were threatened or affected by misfortune in some way.

God forbid that such a thing should ever happen, because then I will lay waste the castle of my enemy.

But the anger that Eden encountered through her work didn't seem to have a personal background. The hatred took root within young people for a completely different reason. It was impossible to point to one single factor that could explain the whole phenomenon, however hard they looked for it.

Eden was systematically going through the latest pile of material in one of the cases on her desk. It was depressingly thin. The original information was unequivocal: the suspects were financing acts of terrorism in Colombia. But this source could not be used in court and, therefore, Säpo had to get hold of their own information in order to confirm what they already knew, which hopefully would then lead to a successful prosecution.

All too often, the intelligence said one thing and the evidence another, always with the same result. The prosecution would lose in court, or even before the case got there. The authorities would end up looking weak and incompetent, and as if they were constantly persecuting innocent individuals who had done nothing whatsoever to deserve the attentions of the security service.

Eden couldn't understand why there was always the same fuss. Her years with the National Bureau of Investigation hadn't exactly been a catalog of successful investigations, but that kind of thing aroused far less interest from the public and the media. However, since the terrorist attack in Stockholm, Eden felt that a great deal had changed. Expectations were higher. If they hadn't won the latest case in the crown court, their everyday working lives would have been much more challenging.

There was a knock on Eden's door, and Sebastian, the unit's head of analysis, walked in. Eden pushed the papers on her desk across to him.

"What do you think?"

"Exactly what I've been saying for the last few weeks. We're not going to come up with anything else on these guys. Let it go."

Eden nodded thoughtfully. "And what about the money we know they're sending to terrorist organizations in South America?"

Sebastian shrugged. "We can't win 'em all."

Eden tossed the papers into the cabinet and slammed the door shut. The case was history as soon as it disappeared from view. She would focus on Zakaria Khelifi instead—the man who had been freed by the court, while his friends were sent down.

"When are we due at the Justice Department?"

"In half an hour. I thought we could walk."

That sounded like a good idea. Eden could have a cigarette on the way and think about what she could say to make the minister for justice realize that the government must expel the Algerian Zakaria Khelifi from the country.

Given all the information they had, and the fact that the Immigration Court of Appeal had gone along with their view, it shouldn't be particularly difficult. And once Khelifi had left the country, they could finally draw a line under Operation Paradise.

• • •

The meeting was held in one of the department's more discreet rooms. The minister for justice was present, along with the secretary of state, a political expert, and a handful of civil servants who were involved. Fredrika Bergman was part of this latter group. Säpo had come to Rosenbad to put forward what they referred to as a security issue. They wanted a foreign citizen's residence permit revoked, on the grounds that the man could become a serious threat to national security. The case had gone from the Immigration Board to the Immigration Court of Appeal, and now it had ended up with the government.

Fredrika couldn't help reflecting on the way they were seated at the table: the Justice Department on one side, Säpo on the other. All the representatives from Säpo had introduced themselves with some kind of title underlining their authority: head of department, head of analysis, and Eden Lundell, head of the counterterrorism unit. She smelled of cigarette smoke; she must be around six feet tall, and her hair was a shade of honey blond that Fredrika refused to believe was her natural color. The smell of smoke was surprising; Eden looked too fresh to be a smoker.

"Let's make a start," the minister said. "We've got half an hour."

The head of analysis placed a laptop on the table and started it up. Eden reached over and attached the computer to a cable.

"Could you switch on the projector?" she said to Fredrika.

Her voice was husky, and she spoke with an accent that Fredrika couldn't quite place. She had long, slender fingers with short, un-varnished nails. If she had let them grow and painted them red, she could have picked up any man she wanted in a bar. Fredrika noticed a ring on Eden's left hand. She was either married or engaged. That was just as much of a surprise as the cigarette smoke.

"Of course," Fredrika said, starting up the projector on the ceiling with two clicks.

The head of analysis began his presentation. The first image appeared on the screen. Blue background, Säpo's logo on the right. Small white dots in different formations. The heading was straight-forward: The Case of Zakaria Khelifi.

Next image. Background.

Eden took over.

"As you all know, Zakaria Khelifi was the subject of a case in which the court ruled last week. The prosecutor was aiming for a conviction on the grounds of preparing to commit an act of terror-ism, but Khelifi was acquitted and released."

The head of department, who was sitting next to Eden and was obviously her boss, coughed discreetly. Eden went on, "However, in the case involving Khelifi, we did manage to secure convictions on the same charge for two other North African nationals. We were able to prove that they had spent the months before their arrest preparing a major attack which was to be directed at the Swedish parliament. We found an explosive device that was virtually complete, and the means to make at least two more. We believe that the attack was to be carried out during the key debate on immigration and integration, which has been talked about for such a long time but has not yet taken place."

"Tomorrow," the minister said. "It's scheduled for tomorrow morning."

Fredrika went cold all over whenever the immigration-and-integration debate was mentioned. It was something that no one really wanted, apart from those who were racists. Had the debate been the target of the two men who had just been convicted? If that was the case, then they must have been ready and waiting for the most perfect and most spectacular opportunity to strike, because the debate had only been under discussion for a few weeks.

"We think the two men were acting alone. All of our intelligence points in that direction, and we see no reason to revise that assessment. Therefore, we have not raised the question of increased security in the parliament building; that includes tomorrow's debate. Apart from what has been planned already, of course. We have coordinated with our colleagues in the police, and they have put rigorous security measures in place in order to ensure that the debate can proceed peacefully."

Of course, Fredrika thought. Even when you were using the fabric of democracy in order to try to abolish it, you had the support of the forces of law and order.

The head of department interrupted Eden's presentation.

"The successful outcome in court with regard to the two men was very welcome, as far as we are concerned. It was important for Säpo to be able to avert a terrorist attack. We are told all too often that we do too little or too much, too early or too late."

Fredrika understood what he was talking about. When Säpo took a case to court but failed to secure a conviction, they were often heavily criticized, particularly in those instances when an arrest didn't even lead to prosecution. She had often reflected on the delicate balancing act the Swedish security services had to maintain, and she had wondered whether she herself would have been able to carry out such a thankless task.

Then came Drottninggatan, and the wind changed. Those same journalists who had often claimed that the security services sometimes overstepped the mark now thought that far too little was being done. The man who blew himself up on Drottninggatan had been on Facebook, for God's sake, so why hadn't Säpo known about him?

Who wants a society where Säpo monitors everyone on Facebook? Fredrika had asked herself. Quite a lot of people, apparently.

Eden carried on talking. Fredrika wondered what the head of analysis was there for. To carry the laptop around, perhaps?

"The two perpetrators who were convicted last week were acting alone, but we have identified several collaborators close to them," Eden said. "Zakaria Khelifi is one of those collaborators."

She pointed to the picture of Zakaria on the screen.

"He was the only one on whom we didn't have sufficient evidence for an arrest and prosecution."

The minister for justice tilted his head to one side.

"I think we should regard it as a positive point that it takes a considerable amount of evidence to secure a conviction, in other crimes as well as terrorism."

"Of course."

Silence.

"Zakaria Khelifi," Eden said. "That's why we're here."

Everyone was listening.

4

13:12

"Zakaria Khelifi came to Sweden from Algeria in 2008. He was an asylum seeker, and claimed that he was being persecuted by a notorious family because he had been seeing the daughter of the family, and had happened to get her pregnant before they married. According to Zakaria, his wife had been murdered by her own relatives.

"During the spring, we received several indications suggesting that further groups were planning terrorist attacks on targets in Sweden, and that these attacks were connected with similar cases in other European countries. We felt that it was possible to take this information seriously in only one of the Swedish cases."

New image: three small photographs of men whom Fredrika recognized from the media—the two men who had been convicted in court, and Zakaria Khelifi, who had been acquitted.

"To begin with, there was no sign of Zakaria Khelifi in our investigation, but then he started to be seen more and more often in the company of the main suspects. On one occasion, thanks to telephone surveillance, we heard one of the men say, 'You can go and pick up the item we talked about yesterday,' at which point Khelifi went and collected a package containing substances that we were later able to establish were part of the explosive device constructed by the main suspects."

"Zakaria Khelifi said in court that he didn't know what the package contained," the secretary of state added.

"Indeed he did, but, in the surveillance footage, he seemed very nervous when he went into the shop to collect it. He looked around several times while he was carrying it to his car, and he was dripping with sweat by the time he got in and drove away. We should also mention that, under interrogation, one of the main suspects named Khelifi as one of their collaborators."

"A statement which Ellis later retracted, I believe?" the minister for justice said.

"Yes, and that surprised us. Before the trial began, he had been very clear in his description of Khelifi's role, insisting that Khelifi had been a great help. We have no idea why Ellis backtracked when the prosecutor questioned him, to be honest. We've tried to find out whether he was threatened in some way, but he refuses to answer our questions. He just keeps saying that he mixed up different names and different people and, unfortunately, said the wrong thing. But none of us believes that. Ellis was telling the truth during the interrogation, and he lied in court."

The minister listened in silence as Eden continued talking.

"It turns out that this wasn't the first time Khelifi had been associated with individuals suspected of terrorist crimes. We have subsequently discovered that he came up during a preliminary investigation back in 2009, the year he was given a residence permit. We were following up on a number of people that we suspected of financing terrorist activity overseas, but unfortunately, we had to drop the case, as we were unable to prove that a crime had been committed."

New image.

Fredrika and the others looked at it attentively.

"We found Khelifi's contact details through secret phone surveillance—mapping phone traffic. There were several numbers that we were unable to identify, but one of them later turned out to belong to Khelifi. We then noticed that Khelifi's number *also* cropped up in connection with another operation that we had launched after the terrorist threats in France earlier this year."

The minister for justice looked troubled. "He was involved in those as well?"

"We don't know for sure. But we do know that before the attack, he had been in contact with one of the perpetrators who was convicted in the French courts last spring. Although, at that time, we had yet to realize who the phone number belonged to, as I said."

Fredrika was curious. Phone tapping and surveillance could take an investigation a long way; she had seen it happen in virtually every case she had been involved in during her time with the police. You just had to work out how everything hung together, which wasn't always easy.

"What did Zakaria Khelifi say when you asked about his phone contacts?" she asked. "The ones linked to previous investigations?"

"He said the phone belonged to someone else at the time," Eden replied. "He said he only bought it in February or March 2011."

"Can you disprove that?" the secretary of state asked.

"No, but we don't need to. He couldn't tell us exactly when he bought the phone, or who from, or how much he paid. It was obviously something he came up with after the event."

"I see," said the minister for justice, who was keen to move on. "So, Zakaria Khelifi was acquitted in court. And now you want us to revoke his residence permit?"

"Yes. In view of the facts we have presented here today, we are asking you to revoke Zakaria Khelifi's permanent residence permit so that he can be taken into custody and sent home to Algeria. He has cropped up in three preliminary investigations and operations, he was named by Ellis during interrogation, and he obviously helped the two perpetrators with their preparations."

The minister for justice leaned back in his chair.

"Are there any obstacles to implementing this course of action, or is it possible for him to go home?"

"According to the Immigration Court of Appeal, there is no reason why he can't be deported. The Algerian authorities have not been involved in our work, and they have no reason to seek him out. He is therefore not at risk of torture or the death penalty."

The secretary of state joined in the discussion. "And what about the reasons why he was given permission to stay here in the first place?"

"No longer applicable," Eden said. "The father and brother of his ex-wife died in a road-traffic accident some time ago. We believe that the remaining family members are no longer interested in punishing him."

Fredrika didn't say a word. This was a whole new world to her.

"How does this guy make a living?" the minister wanted to know.

"He's worked as a youth leader."

Fredrika remembered how he had been portrayed in the media: the nice guy who worked with young people and had difficulty finding a way into Swedish society. Zakaria Khelifi had learned to speak fluent Swedish, and was in many ways an excellent role model. A youth leader who was helping terrorists at the same time. Fredrika found it difficult to reconcile these two contradictory images.

The legs of the minister's chair scraped against the parquet floor as he moved.

"And what is this going to look like in the media?" he said. "Zakaria Khelifi has just been acquitted on two separate counts in court, and yet both Säpo and the government decide to send him home."

"What's the alternative?" Eden asked. "Let him stay here? Keep him under surveillance? Risk a situation where he becomes an icon for young people in the suburbs with an immigrant background? An icon who could inspire others to join the armed struggle? We can do that, of course. But in that case, both the government and Säpo will be guilty of dereliction of duty, because it is our responsibility to ensure that those who could constitute a security threat do not have the opportunity to establish themselves in this country."

She shook her head and continued: "We can't risk that kind of domino effect; we have to be clear and make an example of Khelifi. And even if the odd journalist writes a negative article, the message to those who seek to join people like Zakaria Khelifi will be crystal clear: you don't fuck with Swedish democracy."

The minister for justice appeared to be deep in thought, and Fredrika wondered what Eden's background was. Her rhetoric was not Swedish, and it looked as if her head of department was embarrassed by the way she had spoken.

Nobody said anything, and suddenly a brief ringtone sliced through the silence.

"Sorry, I forgot to switch it off," Eden said, taking her cell phone out of her pocket.

Eden's colleagues were staring at her. Everyone was expected to turn off their phone.

But Eden didn't seem to care what anyone thought. Her attention was focused on the phone in her hand; she read the message she had just received, then said:

"Apparently, there have been a number of bomb threats against targets in Stockholm. One of those targets is Rosenbad."

Less than a minute later, the meeting was over, and Säpo had disappeared from the room as if by magic.

5

13:35

There was a time when Alex Recht had wanted nothing more than a post within Säpo. But many felt they were called and few were chosen. Year after year, Alex waited for the magical phone call that would change his life, the voice that would say he was wanted and welcome, that he was one of those who would be allowed through the portals.

Eventually, they did call. It was a Sunday, and Alex and Lena were busy repainting the fence. They called, and even though they didn't say who they were, Alex knew. He was given a time and place for a meeting. He arrived five minutes late and informed them that he wasn't interested. By that time, he had gotten to know several people who worked within the organization, and he thought they looked bored to death by the whole thing. He didn't actually say that during the meeting but talked about how much he was enjoying his present post, and how much he wanted to remain in what was referred to as the open side of the police.

"Well, you can always go back," said the Säpo representative.

But Alex wasn't so sure about that. If he started working for Säpo, there was a risk that he would stay there. And the idea didn't appeal to him one little bit.

Once you had rejected Säpo, they never came back. Not that he was waiting for it to happen, but as the years went by and Alex gained a reputation as one of Sweden's leading investigators, he thought they would contact him again. They didn't. Perhaps they sensed that he still wasn't interested.

Alex was sitting quietly in his office, thinking hard. Four bomb threats against different targets in inner-city Stockholm. First of all, someone had phoned and said the target was the Royal Library in Humlegården. Then another call came in, this time about the Central Station. Then the Åhlén's department store. And finally, Rosenbad, the government building, which meant that Säpo were automatically drawn in. According to Alex's boss, they would be in touch with him as soon as they had completed their own assessment.

The situation required an immediate response. Alex felt instinctively that the whole thing was nothing more than a hoax; someone was bored and had decided to make false bomb threats in order to cause havoc. At the same time, they had to be careful. Sweden couldn't cope with any more acts of terrorism, and it certainly couldn't cope with any mistakes on the part of the police.

According to the caller, the first bomb would explode at five o'clock that afternoon, the next at five fifteen, the third at five thirty, and the fourth at five forty-five. It wasn't clear which target would be attacked first, and no reason was given for the threat.

The only thing they knew for certain was that at five o'clock in the afternoon all the targeted locations would be crowded with people.

They had tried to trace the calls, but they had all been made using unregistered pay-as-you-go SIM cards and different cell phones. The person who called had used some kind of voice distortion, which made Alex raise his eyebrows; it was very unusual, almost ridiculous, really. He hadn't heard such rubbish since the 1980s.

He was sure that the same person had made all four calls, even though they had come from different phones, but just to be on the safe side, he requested a rapid analysis of the cell phone tower links to see where the calls had been made. They had come in at intervals of fewer than three minutes, so it ought to be possible to tell if it was the same person who had made all four calls.

The phone on Alex's desk rang; he picked it up and heard a husky female voice.

"Eden Lundell from Säpo; I'm calling about the bomb threats. I got your name and number from Hjärpe."

Hjärpe was Alex's boss. If he had been informed, then everything was as it should be. It sounded as if Eden Lundell was out-doors, because the line was crackling.

"I was expecting to hear from you," Alex said. "How can I help?"

Säpo, so near and yet so far. Their offices were inside police HQ, and yet they were a world of their own.

"We need to meet. Can you come over to us?"

Alex couldn't recall ever having worked with Säpo in this way. Of course he knew that they had collaborated with the police on major incidents, such as the murder of Anna Lindh, the foreign secretary, outside the NK department store, but he had never been involved.

He told Eden Lundell he was on his way.

"Great, I'll come down and meet you."

"I'll be there in five minutes."

"Make it ten. I'm just on my way back from a meeting at Rosen-bad."

• • •

It just wasn't acceptable for someone to make a bomb threat against Rosenbad on the day before parliament gathered to debate the issues surrounding immigration and integration. Particularly as it was less than an hour since Eden Lundell had sat there and personally assured Sweden's minister for justice that there was no need for in-creased security during the debate.

"It's not necessarily anything serious," the head of analysis said when Eden caught up with him by the lifts as she was on her way down to collect Alex Recht.

She had dashed into her office and dropped off her handbag when she got back from the meeting at the Justice Department. From a suspected terrorist to suspected bomb threats. The world was not an attractive place for someone who had Eden's job.

"Can we take the risk?"

Sebastian looked unhappy. "No," he said. "No, we can't."

Eden pushed the elevator call button impatiently. "There's going to be hell to pay when we evacuate both the Central Station and Rosenbad."

Sebastian nodded in agreement. "But nobody will thank us if we don't bother, and let everyone die instead."

Eden laughed. "You're not wrong there." Her expression grew serious. As the elevator doors slid open, she turned to Sebastian. "Why Rosenbad? I mean, the debate is taking place elsewhere, in the parliament building. And it's tomorrow, not today."

"Because this isn't about the debate."

"So what is it about?"

"I have no idea. Maybe somebody was bored. Maybe they just want to test the system."

Eden stepped into the elevator and held the doors to stop them closing. "By the way, Alex Recht—do you know anything about him?"

"He's like you."

"A woman?"

"A legend."

Eden allowed the doors to close.

• • •

It was Fredrika Bergman's job to assess the political grounds for deporting Zakaria Khelifi. In plain language, this meant making sure that it wasn't a repeat of the Egyptian fiasco. How she was supposed to achieve this wasn't at all clear, but if she failed, many heads would roll. She couldn't stop thinking about the bomb threats Eden had mentioned before the meeting broke up so abruptly. She wondered whether Alex was working on them.

Not that it mattered. She and Alex were no longer colleagues; she had other duties.

With her head in her hands, she sat and read through Zakaria Khelifi's application for asylum.

He had met the love of his life in the spring of 2006. She wasn't from the family into which his father thought he ought to marry, but his father decided to allow the marriage to take place. According to Zakaria, he had given them his blessing and wished them every happiness.

So far, so good. To begin with, the girl's parents had also been favorably disposed toward the young couple's romance. Zakaria came from a decent family, he had studied at university for several years, and he expected to get a good job. His girlfriend was also university-educated. They were both intending to carry on working after they got married. The girl had asked her mother if she would help out with taking care of any possible grandchildren in the future, and her mother had agreed.

But as so often in the past, there was no happy ending to this particular fairy tale. Suddenly the girl's father decided that he wanted his daughter to marry the son of a business acquaintance instead. At the very least he insisted she should take a break from her relationship with Zakaria and give this new man a chance. The girl refused, which led to violent family quarrels. According to Zakaria, the young couple eventually ran away and settled in a different part of the country, where they found it difficult to find work and to make ends meet.

At this point the girl discovered she was pregnant. Zakaria Khelifi had told the Immigration Board they were both happy about the child, but at the same time they were afraid that people would find out they had started a family before they were married. Therefore, they got married very quickly. Unfortunately, somehow the rumor that the girl had gotten pregnant while she was still single reached the ears of her parents. That was the beginning of a nightmare that ended when Zakaria's wife died in a car accident halfway through her pregnancy.

Zakaria Khelifi claimed that his wife's eldest brother called him and told him that the car accident had been arranged, and that they would deal with Zakaria, too, as soon as the opportunity arose. So-called honor killings were not uncommon in many places around the world, including Algeria on occasion. Zakaria left the country a week or so later.

And now, just a few years down the line, he had ended up in the middle of Säpo's latest terrorist investigation, and they wanted him deported—in spite of the fact that he had a legally binding judgment granting him permanent residence in Sweden. He also had a steady job and a girlfriend. The state had far-reaching powers when it came to handling threats against national security.

Fredrika tried not to feel uneasy. Deporting someone who had previously been deemed to have grounds for asylum was a serious measure, with radical consequences for the individual. Surely Säpo would exercise extreme caution when taking such a step? The statistics supported this view; cases like that of Zakaria Khelifi were exceptionally rare.

At the same time, it was impossible to ignore the context that had given rise to this particular case.

Over the past decade, the fear of international terrorism had become overwhelming. And that fear gave legitimacy to countermeasures which would otherwise have been less clear-cut. How could you make sure that no innocent party got caught in the crossfire? You had to have the courage to ask such questions, even if they had been asked many times before. The authorities always faced the dilemma of possibly punishing innocent people, irrespective of the type of criminal behavior involved. But when it came to terrorism, the issue became even more important. The consequences of making the wrong call could be catastrophic.

She had been fascinated by Säpo's presentation. Very little of the content or delivery had surprised her; since she started working for the police, she had often thought that Säpo's reputation for drama was undeserved. Perhaps it was their own fault. In spite of the fact that there had been a stated policy of transparency for several years, at times, Fredrika still couldn't see why they didn't do more to explain their actions.

One of her colleagues knocked on the door. "The phones are red hot."

"Because of the bomb threats?"

"Yes. They want to know if the government is taking the threats seriously, and if there's a link to the recent terrorism convictions. Or to tomorrow's parliamentary debate."

Fredrika sincerely hoped not.

And yet she could see it all so clearly. How one problem led to another, like concentric ripples spreading out across the water.

If this was the start of something new, there was good reason to wonder how it would end.

6

14:01

They gathered in one of Säpo's conference rooms. Eden Lundell chaired the meeting, which included investigators, analysts, and Alex Recht from the police. Alex reported on the results of his own brief inquiries: four unregistered pay-as-you-go SIM cards. The same person had probably made all four calls, but that was all they knew at the moment.

"When will you find out where the calls came from?" Eden asked.

The case of Zakaria Khelifi was already long gone. The here and now was what mattered; four bomb threats, four potential targets.

"Within the next few hours," Alex replied.

The situation was critical. Decisions had to be made immediately. If they were taking the threats seriously, they had to act soon.

Eden had taken an immediate liking to Alex, which was very unusual for her. She was normally very cautious about opening up to people she didn't know, but it was different with Alex Recht. Sebastian had said he was like her; perhaps there was some truth in that.

"What steps would you want to take?" Eden asked Alex. "Setting aside the threat to Rosenbad, how would you handle this?"

Alex frowned. That was another thing Eden liked about him; he thought before he spoke, in spite of the urgency of the situation. Panicking rarely helped, and it annoyed Eden that so few people she had met during her career understood such a simple premise.

"I don't like the fact that the threats mentioned specific times. Nor do I like the fact that they came in through four separate phone calls, and that voice distortion was used. And I don't understand why someone would go for targets as diverse as the Royal Library and Åhlén's department store."

"So what's your conclusion?" Sebastian asked.

Alex looked at him. "That we need to evacuate all the locations immediately, and if nothing happens, we simply lift the restrictions."

"I agree," Eden said.

She gestured toward one of her colleagues. "Do it—evacuate all four locations. Try to handle it discreetly."

Alex smiled at her. "Unfortunately I don't think all the discretion in the world will do any good. There's going to be a hell of a fuss."

"That can't be helped."

Sebastian raised his hand to indicate that he had something to say.

"Yes?" Eden said.

"You don't think this could be a diversionary tactic?"

"What do you mean?"

"At nine thirty tomorrow morning, parliament will open the most controversial debate of the year. And we have just decided to dedicate all our resources to investigating no less than four bomb threats targeting completely different locations."

Rain was hammering against the windowpane behind Eden, but she hardly noticed it. How could she have missed something so obvious?

"Parliament," Alex said. "It's not my call, but don't you think they should cancel the debate? Or at least postpone it until we know what this is all about?"

Sebastian placed a hand on Eden's arm.

"I agree. An hour ago, we said that we didn't think tomorrow's debate merited increased security arrangements, but now our assessment has changed. That means the debate should be canceled or postponed."

Eden moved her arm away.

"That's GD's decision. All we can do is supply the information and make decisions."

Säpo's general director was always known within the organization as GD. Everyone knew his name was Buster, but he was only
ever referred to as GD.

"Of course."

Eden glanced at the clock. Time was passing much too quickly.
She wished she could put her finger on the hands and stop them
from moving.

● ● ●

The decision to evacuate the four targeted locations was made just
fifteen minutes later by the commanding officer of the Stockholm
city police, together with the general director of Säpo. The city police
would handle the practical arrangements and ensure that the buildings were emptied. Alex could feel his pulse rate increasing as he ran
back to his office along the corridor.

Peder Rydh would have loved this, he thought. And Fredrika
would have been the one reminding us to stop and think.

The four bomb threats overshadowed every other news item.
The journalists had a hundred questions, but the police had no answers. In the shadow of the tumult that followed the evacuation of
the four locations, there was a brief interval during which the police
were able to evacuate the parliament building as well, and search the
whole place with sniffer dogs. Just after four o'clock, the press caught
up with the story, and parliament was besieged with reporters.

The big question was whether to advise the postponement of
the debate. Eden Lundell was right; it wasn't her decision. It was an
issue for other branches of Säpo to consider, and Alex assumed that
it would then be up to the director to make a recommendation. But
what did Alex know—after all, he had once turned down the opportunity to work within the country's most secret security service. They
had no evidence whatsoever to suggest that the threat was actually
directed at parliament, even though it was tempting to jump to that
conclusion.

Alex couldn't stop thinking about Eden Lundell. He had heard
her name before, but they had never met. How was that possible?

How could she have been working for the National Bureau of Investigation for several years without their bumping into one another?

Eden was not a police officer, but she had gone through the formal leadership program, and had far better qualifications than most. It was clear that she had no objection to getting her hands dirty. She wasn't the classic desk jockey who avoided the practical aspects of the job and buried herself in admin. Eden Lundell had real presence, and Alex caught himself thinking that he would really like to work with her.

He went straight up to his office, picked up his jacket, and went out again. He didn't want to sit there wondering what was going on, he wanted to be on the spot. His boss looked surprised when Alex stopped by and said that he was on his way to parliament. It wasn't about the need to control things, it was simply a desire to be in the thick of the action. And to try to understand what was going on.

One of the squad cars was parked on Polhemsgatan. Alex unlocked the door and climbed in. It was pouring, and he got soaked even though he hurried.

As he glanced in the rearview mirror, he saw Eden scurry past; she ran across Polhemsgatan to a car parked a little way down the street. Was she going to parliament as well? If so, she could travel with Alex. But Eden was fast. She was already in the car and had started the engine. Alex didn't move. Perhaps she wasn't going to parliament at all, but to another meeting.

When Eden drove away, Alex was still sitting behind the wheel. They were the ones who had assumed that parliament was a target for the person who had made the threats. They were the ones who had created this sense of confusion. As he turned the key, he couldn't help wondering if that had, in fact, been the aim: to cause havoc.

7

16:03

It was obvious that the bomb threats had frightened people. Fredrika Bergman and her colleagues in the Justice Department who had offices in Rosenbad were evacuated along with everyone else. Fredrika slipped her documents into her bag and was given a temporary workstation in the Foreign Office building on Fredsgatan, where she would continue to work on Zakaria Khelifi's case. She was acutely aware of the anxiety engendered by the threats, and spoke to several of her colleagues on the phone. No one had heard anything new, no one had any idea what it was all about.

She felt restless as she turned her attention to Khelifi's case. She made one call after another, getting in touch with the Immigration Board, the Immigration Supreme Court, and the police. There was nothing to add as far as Khelifi was concerned. He would have to leave the country. Zakaria Khelifi would serve as an example of what happened if you challenged democracy and an open society. As the idiot who had just made four separate bomb threats had done.

Fredrika couldn't settle. Why did she never enjoy her job? Why did she constantly wish she was somewhere else, doing something different? There had been times when she had thought she would never find job satisfaction in her life. The pursuit of happiness had subsided since the birth of her children. They assuaged her hunger in a way that felt secure, enabling her to grow as a person. She ran her finger over the photograph of her son. So like his father. She hoped that Spencer would live for many years to come, so that the child wouldn't lose his father when he was too young.

Thinking about Spencer's age often made her feel stressed, so she made an effort and focused on the computer. She read several articles about the bomb threats that had paralyzed the whole of inner-city Stockholm in less than an hour.

His name cropped up in the middle of one piece. Alex Recht.

Detective Inspector Alex Recht was not prepared to comment on the National Bureau of Investigation's view of the bomb threats that have been received, but he stated that all necessary measures have been taken, and that the Stockholm city police and Säpo are working closely together.

A longing that Fredrika had been unaware of suddenly sprang to life. Alex Recht was one of the best bosses she had ever had, far superior to any other team leader she had known.

Without thinking about what she was doing, she reached out and picked up her cell phone. Alex answered at the third ring.

"Things are pretty difficult right now, Fredrika."

"I realize that. I just wanted to . . ."

What did she want? What had she been thinking when she called him? Nothing at all.

"You wanted some information about the bomb threats?"

"Yes."

Her voice was so weak, his so decisive.

"I don't really know what to say. It's a bit chaotic around here at the moment. Bombs all over the city, for God's sake."

The line crackled; it sounded as if he was outdoors, in a windy spot somewhere. She looked out of the window. The usual weather for this time of year: rain. And yet, just hearing his voice made her feel safe. If Alex was dealing with the bomb threats, then things were bound to turn out okay.

"And what about parliament?"

"We can't be sure yet, but it's possible that someone might have made the threats in order to keep us busy elsewhere while they attack the parliament building."

"Bloody hell."

"Exactly. If that's the plan, then I have to say we're facing a dangerous scenario."

Fredrika looked at her screen.

"This will be grist to the mill of the antiforeigner brigade—the debate has just been canceled."

"It hasn't been canceled," Alex said. "But it might be postponed. The speaker was furious when Säpo spoke to him. He insisted the debate must go ahead tomorrow, at any price. The cost of canceling would be incalculable."

The speaker was best known for two things: his quick temper and his warmth. Fredrika didn't know anyone who disliked him, regardless of which party they belonged to.

"I have to go," Alex said.

"Call me if . . . anything happens. Or if . . ."

She heard a sharp intake of breath at the other end of the line.

"Are you missing us? The police, I mean?"

Was she?

"No, no, I'm really happy here in the Justice Department. Up to my ears in papers and reports. Just what I like."

"I thought we'd decided that you were like the rest of us, someone who wanted to be out in the field."

When she didn't reply, Alex said, "Take care of yourself; I'll speak to you soon."

He ended the call, and Fredrika put down her phone. It was ten to five. The first bomb would soon explode.

● ● ●

The rain made Eden Lundell's hair curl and extinguished her cigarette. Bloody weather. She threw away the cigarette and walked into the foyer of the parliament building.

"I'm sorry, you can't come in here," said the uniformed police officer on the door.

Eden took out her ID and he stepped aside. The other officers followed her with their eyes as she swept past. Sebastian had looked at her as if she was crazy when she told him where she was going.

"You're the boss," he said. "You're not expected to go out on this kind of thing."

He meant well, and his tone of voice was the one Eden had noticed other parents using when they talked to their children. She herself had always spoken to her children the same way she spoke to everyone else—as if they were adults.

"I couldn't care less what people expect."

Sebastian started to look annoyed.

"If you're going out, you should at least have someone with you. One of my analysts, for example."

Eden had been unable to hide her contempt for his suggestion.

"You mean one of your so-called Arabists?"

She could have bitten her tongue, but the words were already out. And Sebastian, who of course was loyal to his colleagues, had hit the roof.

"You have absolutely no right to say such a thing! I really don't know—"

"Correct," Eden said, raising her voice. "You don't know anything. And that really doesn't matter, Sebastian. But in that case, you have to let those of us with the necessary experience go out and do the job properly. I have to know what I'm talking about when I see GD later."

It had been an unnecessary confrontation. Eden worked well with Sebastian, and yet she had felt it necessary to trample all over him *and* his analysts. So-called Arabists. By that she meant those who started their CV with the claim that they had studied Arabic for several years, and yet were incapable of running a simple meeting with Arab speakers without the assistance of an interpreter. That had nothing to do with their analytical skills, of course. Generally speaking, Sebastian's team was highly qualified. By no means had all of them studied Arabic, and those who had didn't do so in order to learn to communicate in the language. Shit. She would definitely have to apologize later. If Sebastian took the matter further, it would look bad.

The argument went out of her mind. She had to focus on parliament now.

It struck her that the Swedish parliament was housed in a very boring building. Not like their British or French counterparts.

Or the Israeli parliament.

The Knesset in Jerusalem was a joy in its simplicity, a reminder of how young the Israeli state was, and yet what a long history it had. If her husband, Mikael, had gotten his way, he and Eden would have moved there along with her parents. But Eden couldn't think of anywhere she would be less happy to bring up her children, and that clinched the argument. If the Jewish member of the family didn't want to emigrate, then everyone else stayed at home, too.

She soon spotted Alex. He was talking to a man whom Eden assumed was a police officer. Alex raised a hand in greeting when he saw her.

"So you couldn't stay away either?" she said.

Alex looked embarrassed.

"I like to keep an eye on things."

"Me, too. Have they found anything?"

"Nothing. But they've only just started."

Eden gazed around. Police everywhere. No doubt the situation was exactly the same at the Central Station and the Royal Library. And at Åhlén's and Rosenbad.

It was a strange choice of locations.

Mikael called, wanting to know where she was.

"What's going on?" he said.

The priest calling his private source for advice. The thought appealed to Eden.

"We don't know," she said, turning away from Alex.

"Should I be worried?"

"What? No, no. Mikael, this is really nothing to worry about."

"Are you sure? I've been watching the news. It's crazy out there."

Eden didn't know what he was talking about. She told him she had to go, and ended the call.

"My husband," she said briefly to Alex, who hadn't asked who the call was from.

"Is he a police officer too?"

"A priest."

Alex looked as if he was about to burst out laughing, but he managed to control himself.

"I know," Eden said. "I don't look like someone who's married to a priest."

She tugged at her wet hair, trying to make it lie down. A uniformed officer came over to them.

"There are huge numbers of people out on the streets."

So that was what Mikael had meant.

"Doing what?"

"Well, there are all the people we've turned out of the various locations, plus the rubberneckers who've come to see what's going on."

Eden could feel her frustration growing. Four bomb threats, plus the evacuation of parliament just to be on the safe side. One word passed through her mind: *idiotic.* This was an idiotic exercise.

"This is nothing," she said firmly to Alex. "It's a bluff. The bomb threats, parliament, the whole thing. This is just someone who wants to wind us up. Cause havoc. And take a look around. It's hard to say that he or she hasn't succeeded."

Alex scratched his head.

"It's too soon to be sure that it's just a bluff. We need to hold our nerve."

Eden looked at her watch.

"It's gone five o'clock, and evidently no bomb has gone off so far. Nothing is going to happen at five fifteen or five thirty either," she said.

"Let's wait and see," Alex replied.

If Eden was right, Stockholm would still be intact when the hands on the clock had passed five forty-five.

8

19:10

The crisis came and went. By six o'clock, no bombs had gone off, and as far as parliament was concerned, Säpo were continuing to search the building, but didn't expect to find anything. The speaker announced that the debate on immigration and integration would take place as planned the following morning.

The Central Station and Åhlén's department store opened their doors to the public just after seven and, at about the same time, it was decided that employees at the Royal Library and Rosenbad could return to their offices if they needed to make up the working hours they had lost.

Fredrika Bergman stayed on in the Foreign Office building on Fredsgatan after the end of the working day; she didn't want to go home until the issue of the bomb threats was resolved.

Then suddenly the danger was past. The story of the mysterious bomb threats lived on in news bulletins all over the country, but nowhere else. Fredrika picked up her jacket and bag and went home.

• • •

That night she lay awake in the darkened bedroom, gazing at Spencer.

"What's the matter?" he asked without lifting his head from the pillow.

"Nothing. I'm just happy to see you."

She sensed a smile on his face.

"Aha."

Was he looking older these days? She edged closer. Sometimes she thought she could see new lines and wrinkles on his face every day, and that made her panic. She didn't want Spencer to age any more quickly than he had done over the past few years. He was twenty-five years older than she was; she couldn't bear it if the gap grew any wider.

She caressed his forehead, saw him close his eyes. He would fall asleep at any moment, as he always did when they had made love even though it was very late. There had been a time in their lives when their relationship couldn't be exposed to the light of day; they had been able to meet only in the evenings and at night. In those days it was never too late for sex, and they were never too tired.

But now . . .

After two children and a period of turbulence caused by Spencer's separation from his wife, plus the chaos that followed when he was falsely accused of raping a student, things were very different. Most of the time they were both perfectly happy sitting side by side on the sofa and falling asleep in front of some mindless TV program.

It was hard to admit it but, unfortunately, Spencer wasn't the only one who had aged. For example, Fredrika couldn't remember the last time she had been really drunk. Was it at a deadly boring reception that one of Spencer's colleagues had given in New York? She couldn't remember.

"What are you thinking about?" Spencer asked.

"The last time I was drunk."

He opened his eyes. "Okay . . ."

"Have we gotten old and boring?"

"I don't think we'll ever be boring, but I'm afraid we're never going to be younger either."

Fredrika burst out laughing.

"You're a wise man, Spencer."

"Indeed I am."

He reached out and pulled her close, hugging her tightly.

I will love you forever.

Fredrika found his hand, kissed his fingers. Her lips brushed against the ring he had received when he gained his doctorate; he wore it next to his wedding ring. She had been unable to hold back the tears when they got married. During all the years they had been lovers, she had never once thought that they would be a proper couple. Not once. And now he was both the father of her children and her husband. The only issue that remained was their surname. Fredrika flatly refused to take the name Lagergren, and of course the conservative Spencer didn't want to be called Bergman.

"What does it matter what you're called?" Spencer had said. "Can't you just drop your maiden name?"

"Darling Spencer, you could just as easily drop your name!"

At that point the discussion usually came to an end, and they decided it didn't matter what they were called.

After all, we share everything else.

Fredrika stroked Spencer's wedding ring and suddenly realized she was thinking about Eden Lundell. For some reason she had been surprised to discover that Eden was married. It didn't fit in with her persona, which was hard and uncompromising. Almost as if she ate small children for breakfast, as the secretary of state had said when they were leaving the conference room.

"You don't fuck with Swedish democracy," Eden had said. That was no doubt true, but was that really what Zakaria Khelifi had been doing? There was no better way of fucking with democracy than by making people afraid, Fredrika knew that much. It frightened her that following various terror attacks, people were starting to become less critical of laws that went against the principle of integrity. It was almost as if integrity was a luxury that could be afforded only under certain circumstances.

No doubt, Eden had a high level of integrity. Eden, who had honey-colored hair and smelled of cigarette smoke. Eden, who had the longest legs Fredrika had ever seen, and who looked as if she had just been to war, in spite of the fact that she was wearing a skirt suit.

Some crimes could not be expiated. And it would be both stupid and dangerous to take unnecessary risks when both Säpo and the government had a legal obligation to protect the country's security. The decision on the case of Zakaria Khelifi had been formally approved at six o'clock, and a few hours later, Säpo would have picked him up. By now he would be sitting in a custody cell.

Fredrika had never dealt with so-called security issues before, nor had she come across the term when she was working for the police. Eden Lundell had given her their cards when they left, but Fredrika didn't feel comfortable calling any of them. Particularly Eden.

When Spencer had fallen asleep, Fredrika picked up a handout on security issues that a colleague had put together. It confirmed what she had already read on Säpo's website:

It was Säpo's job to ensure that Sweden didn't become a refuge for individuals who could constitute a danger to the country's security. It was their role to look at the background, contacts, and activities of a foreign national—in Sweden or overseas—and to determine if the individual in question could pose a security risk. The most common grounds for suspicion were linked to terrorism, but they could also involve espionage on the part of refugees. The organization looked to the future; they were concerned not only with who did or did not constitute a threat, but also who *might possibly* constitute a threat. However they were supposed to know that . . .

Fredrika couldn't shake off a feeling of unease. Just a few hours ago, inner-city Stockholm had been paralyzed by false bomb threats delivered over the phone. Threats that coincided with the major immigration debate in parliament. Which in turn coincided with the conviction of two young men for preparing to commit an act of terrorism, with severe sentences being handed down.

There is absolutely no way that this has all happened by chance, Fredrika thought.

Every fiber of her being was telling her that something was wrong.

The bomb threats were a smoke screen. Anything else was out of the question. But what could they expect instead?

9

21:35

It was nine thirty by the time Eden Lundell smoked her last cigarette of the day. She had just gotten home from work and had a quick puff, hidden behind the garage wall. If the neighbors saw her, they would think she'd started drinking in secret, not that she couldn't stand Mikael going on about how upset he was that she was still smoking.

Just before she left the office she had had a call from Alex Recht, who had heard from one of his subordinates about where the bomb threats had originated.

"All the phones were linked to towers close to Arlanda. The last call was definitely made from inside the airport complex itself."

Eden walked toward the house. Now they had a location, which meant that the answer to the questions who? and why? couldn't be far away.

The windows at the front of the house were in darkness when Eden put her key in the lock. She glanced around instinctively before she closed the door behind her, double-locked it, and set the alarm. She just couldn't understand people who didn't take care of their own home, their own safety.

She heard Mikael's footsteps coming down the stairs as she was taking off her coat. It smelled faintly of cigarette smoke. Shit. She quickly walked toward him, wanting to get away from the treacherous aroma.

She held her breath as he kissed her cheek, but it didn't quite work. Her hair smelled of smoke as well.

"Have you been smoking?"

The house was silent. Diana was asleep, and Alex Recht was alone in his office. The intensity of his working day had made it impossible to sleep; he felt wide awake. Diana's lovely smile shone out at him from a photograph on his desk.

The children had accepted Diana right away. His daughter had wept when he finally managed to come out with the fact that he had met someone.

"I'm really, really happy for you," she had said.

Alex got a lump in his throat when he remembered her words. And he still felt like crying when he thought about Lena, the mother of his children, the woman with whom he had thought he would spend the rest of his life. But we don't always get what we want. Things don't always turn out the way we expect. He knew that now, and he had to fight to stop himself from being destroyed by the fear of losing everything all over again. Lena was still with him. In a photograph with the children. Taken during the last summer of her life.

If you just glanced at the picture, you couldn't see that anything was wrong. You didn't notice Lena's tired eyes, or how much weight she had lost. And you didn't see the shadow of fear on the face of both his son and daughter. His daughter was smiling as usual, but Alex knew what she looked like when she was happy, and what she looked like when she wasn't. In the photograph, she looked positively devastated.

And his son. With his hair standing on end as if he were a teenager, and an expression so angry that it made Alex shudder. They had never been able to communicate, not without falling out and starting to yell at one another. At one time, Alex had thought he would be closer to his son than his daughter, but it turned out he was wrong.

Alex focused on his job instead. None of the bomb threats had been genuine. No one had been hurt. And yet he still felt on edge.

Four bomb threats. Not one, not two, not three, but four. Aimed at different locations in inner-city Stockholm that took a huge amount of resources to evacuate and search. They had thought it might be an attempt to divert their attention from something much worse, but that hadn't happened either. The whole thing had begun and ended with four bomb threats, made by someone in the vicinity of Arlanda, using voice distortion.

Arlanda. What the hell was the link between the bomb threats and the country's biggest airport?

Tuesday, October 11, 2011

10

Flight 573, 09:03

It had been a chaotic morning. For a while it had looked as if Erik was going to be late for work. First of all, the bus to the commuter train was late. Then the train to Central Station was late as well, which meant he missed the Arlanda Express he had been hoping to catch. When he eventually left on the next train, it had to travel at a reduced speed due to an earlier accident.

Erik tried not to feel stressed, but beads of sweat broke through along his hairline, and his palms were damp. He was going to have to run to the plane, which was hardly appropriate for a responsible copilot. Among other things—including a patch of dried baby food on his uniform.

He had been delighted to get a job so quickly. Hard work and a natural aptitude for the profession went a long way, as it turned out. And the opportunity had been there. Very few of the other pilots were as young as Erik. He felt his stomach flip over with a sudden attack of nerves.

What if I don't deliver? What if I'm not good enough?

His cell phone rang when the train had almost reached the south platform at Arlanda.

"I'll be there in a minute," he said.

And he was.

The train slowed down and Erik hit the ground running. Claudia called; she just wanted to hear his voice one last time before they parted. In an hour or so, she and their son would be on a plane to South America, heading off to visit Claudia's parents. Erik was on the flight to New York, and he would then follow them for a much-needed holiday. They would eat late in the evening, drink wine, and dance long into the night. Lie in bed in the morning. Claudia's mother would take care of their little boy, give them a break. In Erik's opinion, they were doing the child a favor. It was hard work being the parent of a toddler; sometimes it was so hard that Erik would have given his right arm just to sleep through one single night. Therefore, it had to be good for both the parent and child if they had a rest from one another occasionally.

That had to mean fewer arguments and a stronger bond.

The security checks had increased and grown far more stringent in recent years. Erik couldn't help thinking some of them were unnecessary. As long as people were allowed to carry several liters of alcohol on board, there was little point in X-raying their hand luggage and asking them to remove items such as nail scissors.

Erik was allowed to go to the front of the line for the X-ray machines. The security guard gave him a nod of recognition.

"Running late?"

"Too bloody right."

They did their best to speed up the process. It was only a question of minutes, then he would be on his way. Erik placed his bag on the conveyor belt and walked through the metal detector. Picked up his bag and ran.

He could see his colleague in the distance. Karim Sassi, a man Claudia had once referred to as "the most handsome man she had ever seen." With a certain amount of reluctance, Erik had to admit that Karim looked good. He was six foot four, dark, and charismatic. The main thing that made Karim Sassi so attractive was his cheerful expression and the energy radiating from his brown eyes. "Eyes you could drown in," Claudia had commented, before Erik stated firmly that he didn't want to hear any more about how fantastic his colleague was.

But to tell the truth, Erik really liked Karim. They had worked together for several months and knew each other well by this stage. They had even started spending some time together outside work; Erik hoped their friendship would deepen, because he enjoyed Karim's company.

Karim was facing the window, but Erik could see his profile. Tense jawline, eyes half closed. Always equally focused before a flight. He would never dream of having a couple of drinks and falling asleep, like certain other pilots.

Erik covered the last few yards at top speed.

"I thought I was going to have to fly without a copilot today," Karim said.

"The bus was late so I missed the commuter train. And then the Arlanda Express was delayed as well."

Karim looked annoyed but made no further comment on Erik's timekeeping.

"Let's go," he said.

Erik couldn't stop himself. He wasn't that bloody late!

"Has something happened?"

Karim ran a hand through his unruly black hair.

"No, I just like everything to be in order. And I've had a report that a severe storm is due to come in over the East Coast of the US during the day."

"Damn. Could that cause us problems with landing?"

"It looks that way. But I've asked for additional fuel so that we can stay in the air for a few hours if necessary. Or divert elsewhere."

"How many extra hours did you request?"

"Five."

Karim turned away from Erik and headed toward the aircraft.

• • •

They took off at nine thirty, exactly as planned.

The sky was different above the clouds. Clearer. An endless space where there were no problems. Erik knew why he had become a pilot. To be a part of all this. Something bigger than himself. The very idea made his head spin. Just knowing that he was thirty thousand feet above the surface of the earth right now got the adrenaline pumping.

I will never get tired of this.

The cockpit doorbell rang. Karim glanced at the monitor to see who wanted to come in. It was Fatima, one of the flight attendants.

She rang again. Karim pressed the button to release the lock; Fatima came in and closed the door behind her.

Her face was ashen. Erik had never liked that expression, but now he realized that was because he had never before seen anyone whose face had lost all its color. Her lips were so pale they looked bloodless.

"I found this in the toilet," she said, handing Karim a folded piece of paper.

Karim opened it and began to read.

"What does it say?" Erik asked.

"They're threatening to blow up the plane," Fatima said.

"What? Who's threatening to blow up the plane?"

Fatima didn't answer.

"Where did you find this?" Karim asked.

"In the toilet in first class. When I went to check if there was enough toilet paper."

"Have any of the passengers seen it?"

"I've no idea. But I don't think so—they would have said something."

Erik spoke up: "We've just turned off the sign telling them to fasten their seat belts; how many of them would have had time to go to the toilet?"

"Not very many," Fatima whispered.

"More like none," Erik said. "Can I see what it says?"

There were only a few lines written on the piece of paper. Erik passed it back to Karim, trying to stop his hand from trembling.

"How the hell did it get in the toilet?" he asked.

"It must have been there when we took off," Fatima replied.

"But who could have put it there?"

"Perhaps someone was asked to leave it in there. Someone who had access to the plane."

Erik didn't understand. He didn't understand why this particular flight had to be dragged into some kind of bomb threat, and he didn't understand how the piece of paper had got into the toilet. If they were lucky, the whole thing would turn out to be a really bad joke. If they weren't, then it was a serious threat, and in that case none of them knew if they would live to see tomorrow.

"What do we do now, Karim?" he asked.

Karim read the note again. Or rather he looked at the words, his gaze sweeping across the paper, back and forth.

"We have to do as they say."

Erik stared at him.

"Do as they say?"

"But that's impossible," Fatima said.

"And what's the alternative? It specifically states that they will blow the plane to pieces if we don't follow their instructions."

"How would they know?" Fatima said.

Absurd. It was absurd. The whole thing. Erik tried to gather his thoughts.

"If the threat is genuine, and according to security regulations we have to act as if it is, then we ought to follow the instructions," he said. "Obviously. But we have to call air-traffic control and SAS to ask for help on how to proceed. And we need to tell them what the message says. I mean, it's clearly not aimed at us."

The message is not aimed at us, we are the hostages.

For the first time, Erik felt afraid. Something else occurred to him.

"What if one of the passengers left the note in the toilet?" he said slowly.

"Yes?"

"That means he or she is still on the plane, monitoring our actions."

Fatima stood there with her arms wrapped around her and leaned—or slumped—against the wall. If she started to cry, Erik would lose all respect for her. But she didn't.

"Did you show this to anyone else on the crew?" Erik asked.

"No."

"Keep it to yourself for the time being," Karim said. "We'll call ATC and tell them what's happened, then we'll decide how to proceed."

Fatima straightened up.

"I'd better get back."

She left the cockpit and slammed the door shut behind her.

Karim put on his headset and called Arlanda.

"This is Karim Sassi, the captain on Flight 573. We have received a bomb threat; it was written on a piece of paper and left in one of the toilets on board. The content is as follows: 'Unless the USA shuts down Tennyson Cottage immediately, this plane will be blown up. The same applies unless the Swedish government revokes its decision to deport a man by the name of Zakaria Khelifi. If the plane attempts to land before these decisions have been made and implemented, it will be blown up.' As captain, I am instructed to fly the plane for as long as the fuel lasts. That's the time the two governments have in which to act. They will determine how this ends. When the fuel runs out, the time runs out."

11

The control tower received the information from Flight 573 just after the plane had taken off. It was immediately passed on to the central communications office at the National Bureau of Investigation, RKC, to SAS, and to the Transport Agency. The National Bureau of Investigation was still working on the bomb threats made the previous day, targeting locations in central Stockholm, but the message was given top priority. For the second time in twenty-four hours, Alex Recht was sitting there with a bomb threat on his desk.

He could hardly believe his eyes as he read the memo from RKC.

A Boeing 747 that had taken off from Arlanda twenty minutes ago had received a bomb threat, and was therefore classified as hijacked, indirectly. The captain had contacted air-traffic control and informed them of the situation.

In the light of the previous day's events, the threat must be taken seriously. Alex had read the morning papers and knew who Zakaria Khelifi was. Apparently, Säpo had taken him into custody and were going to deport him. That was the extent of Alex's knowledge.

After speaking to his boss, he called Eden Lundell.

"This Zakaria Khelifi is one of yours, isn't he?"

"That's right."

Eden had already received a copy of the memo, and was in a meeting with one of her deputies. She promised to call Alex back.

He spent the next few minutes going through the key details of the message. The plane had taken off with plenty of fuel. There were a couple of empty seats in first class, but otherwise it was full. There was a crew of ten, including the captain and copilot. When the plane ran out of fuel, time was going to be up for the Swedish and US governments.

Alex could understand the demand that had been made of the Swedish government, but what the hell was Tennyson Cottage? Eden probably knew the answer to that question. During his years in the police force, Alex had dealt with a number of bomb threats aimed at planes on their way to or from Sweden, but they had never turned out to be anything but a hoax.

Could this one be different? Was there a danger that there really was a bomb on board Flight 573? If that was the case, it meant that someone had checked in a bag containing explosives, and was now sitting among the passengers. Unless the bomb had been smuggled into someone else's luggage, which Alex thought was highly improbable. The most likely scenario was that there was no bomb on board.

Alex's boss appeared.

"We have to go down and brief the government. Or rather you, not we," Hjärpe said.

"Nobody's done that yet?"

"They know about the bomb threat, but not the details. We wanted to assimilate all the information we had first of all. I've called and told them we're on our way. We need to get a move on—it's only a matter of time before the press gets hold of this."

Alex got ready to head for the government offices yet again.

"Who's providing me with backup? We don't know anything."

"You're going in with Säpo. Let them do the talking. All we know is what's in the note."

"And what are our recommendations?"

"That we wait and see what happens. I mean, what are they supposed to do? Just let this Khelifi go?"

Alex and his boss headed for the elevators.

"Have we been in direct contact with the captain of the plane?" Alex asked.

A shadow passed over Hjärpe's face.

"Not yet. In a situation like this, the captain has a significant level of authority. We can make suggestions, but at the end of the day he's the one who decides what to do."

"I'd advise him to dump the fuel and make an emergency landing."

Hjärpe muttered something unintelligible, then stood next to Alex in silence as they waited for the elevator to arrive. He suddenly placed a hand on Alex's shoulder.

"I have to say that I admire your professionalism in this situation. By the time I realized how things stood, I'd already given you the job. If you don't feel you can handle it, that's fine—I want you to know that I can easily pass it on to someone else."

The elevator arrived and the doors opened.

"What are you talking about?" Alex said as he stepped inside, escaping from Hjärpe's hand.

His boss looked completely stunned.

"I thought they'd told you. They said they were going to tell you."

"Tell me what? Who was supposed to tell me what?"

Speaking very quietly, Hjärpe uttered the very last words that Alex wanted to hear.

"Alex, your son is the copilot on that plane."

• • •

Without being given any further information, Fredrika Bergman was called to a meeting at the prime minister's office. Representatives from the Justice Department and the Foreign Office would also be there. And the police. Nobody was prepared to say what had happened, but the meeting was urgent and it was essential that Fredrika attend.

Things were more or less back to normal at Rosenbad following the bomb threats, but it was obvious that the previous day had been something different. People were scurrying around all over the place. Everyone seemed to be on the way to somewhere else; no one was sitting at their desk.

The atmosphere in the room where the meeting was to take place was noticeably tense. Fredrika said hello to her colleagues from the Foreign Office and the PM's office, and looped her handbag over the back of a chair. A light drizzle was still falling outside.

Fredrika looked around and spotted two familiar faces: Eden Lundell from Säpo, and Alex Recht. They were standing side by side, with their heads close together. Did they know one another? Alex noticed Fredrika and nodded to her.

"Nice to see you again so soon."

He didn't mean that. His face was distorted in a grimace; he looked angry and upset.

You can't keep any secrets from me.

"Do you know Eden?"

"Yes, we met yesterday."

They shook hands, and Fredrika thought that Eden's grip was one of the firmest she had ever felt. She could smell cigarette smoke today as well. And Eden wasn't smiling. She looked as if she would really like Fredrika to go away so that she could be alone with Alex.

"Fredrika and I used to work together," Alex explained. "She was part of my special investigation team."

Eden looked surprised.

"I would never have guessed you were a police officer," she said to Fredrika.

"She's not," Alex replied. "She's a criminologist. And a highly skilled investigator."

Fredrika blushed. She would never have thought that Alex knew what she had studied at university. Not that he wasn't interested, but he did have a tendency to mix up different academic disciplines.

Alex's words softened Eden's expression.

"Good to have someone with your background on board right now," she said.

The secretary of state cleared his throat. "Perhaps we could make a start?"

They sat down around the table.

"We have received another bomb threat," Eden began. "This time the target is a plane that recently took off from Arlanda, heading for New York."

The silence around the table was palpable.

"The terms are crystal clear. The hijackers have made two demands that must be met. Meanwhile, the plane is not allowed to land; if it attempts to do so, it will be blown up. In other words, they are saying that there is a bomb on board."

"But what *is* all this?" the secretary of state asked, sounding like a child.

"All we know is that one of the flight attendants found the bomb threat written on a piece of paper in one of the toilets," Eden said. "How it got there is of course of great interest to all of us, but at the moment we have no information on that point. It could have been put there by one of the passengers, or a member of the crew. The prosecutor has decided to launch a preliminary investigation, and we are currently trying to persuade SAS to provide us with a list of passengers, and of the crew members on board, so that we can compare them with our own databases to see if we find any matches."

"So that hasn't been done yet?" the secretary of state said.

"No. But we're expecting a quick turnaround. We're also working on the specific demands made in the note. One is directed at the US government, and calls for the closure of Tennyson Cottage."

"What's that?" Fredrika asked.

"An American detention facility in Afghanistan," Eden explained. "It's relatively unknown, so it's not at all clear how the person who made the threat could be familiar with the place. We have already made contact with our American colleagues. It's important that we're all on the same page in our dealings with the American side. I assume you'll take care of communications with the political leadership over there?"

"Yes," the cabinet secretary from the Foreign Office replied.

"Good."

Eden turned to Fredrika and the secretary of state.

"There is a further demand, this time aimed at the Swedish government. It concerns the matter we discussed during yesterday's meeting: Zakaria Khelifi."

The secretary of state folded his arms; Fredrika had noticed that he often did this when he felt under pressure.

"Whoever made the threat is calling for his immediate release, and for the restoration of his residence permit."

The atmosphere in the room was oppressive.

"Had you been expecting this?" the secretary of state asked, much to Fredrika's surprise.

"No, of course not," Eden said, unable to hide her irritation. "And I must add that we don't know if this is another hoax."

"Hard to say, isn't it?" the cabinet secretary said.

Eden's eyes narrowed.

"I don't think this kind of discussion is particularly helpful."

"True," the secretary of state said. "So what's our next move?"

"My suggestion is that we start talking to our respective American colleagues. Säpo will also try to establish direct contact with the captain of the plane in order to find out what his intentions are. Personally, I would prefer to see him go for an emergency landing as soon as possible, but bearing in mind the way in which the threat is expressed, and that we still don't know if it's genuine, or if one of the perpetrators is on board, I daren't make that recommendation at the moment."

"How much time do we have?" the secretary of state asked.

Fredrika saw Eden and Alex exchange glances. Alex looked deeply distressed.

Eden explained what the note had said about how much time the two governments had to meet their demands: when the fuel ran out, their time was up.

"Oh, my God," the cabinet secretary said, covering his mouth with his hand.

"I must point out once again that we don't know whether this is a threat we need to take seriously, but I can say that Säpo are extremely concerned," Eden said.

Fredrika hesitated for a moment, then asked a question.

"You didn't say how long we've got. How long will the fuel last?"

Eden bit her lip.

"We have just over thirteen hours, starting from now. Then the plane will crash, unless it's allowed to land."

12

10:45

Tennyson Cottage. A dark corner of the earth where dubious activities took place.

Eden Lundell hadn't wanted to say too much about it during the meeting, but she knew exactly what it was. An American so-called secret detention facility in Afghanistan, close to the Pakistani border. Notorious to those who had been there, unknown to everyone else. The turnover of inmates was low. Most of those who ended up there were suspected terrorists who had been captured in Pakistan, and who were then moved on through the system after a period in Tennyson Cottage. In the past, they had been flown to Guantánamo, but now they were taken to other facilities. The Americans had never confirmed it, but Eden suspected that there had been fatalities among the inmates.

Eden hadn't had anything to do with Tennyson Cottage herself, but she had heard the name mentioned when she was working in London.

They gathered in one of the larger operational meeting rooms: Eden, Sebastian, whom she still hadn't apologized to, and a number of investigators and analysts. A total of twelve people were seated around the table. Only one of them wasn't wearing a black suit, and that was Eden. She was wearing a blue pinstripe suit by Hugo Boss. As she often said to Mikael, "Authority doesn't come for free."

And Mikael would usually reply, "Particularly when it stinks of smoke."

Eden had to bite her lip to stop herself from laughing. One day, she would make her husband happy by stubbing out her very last cigarette. But not today.

When everyone had settled down, Eden opened the meeting. She didn't waste any time but got straight down to what she considered to be the key question as far as Säpo was concerned.

"Why has Zakaria Khelifi come up in this context? Who would do such a thing with the aim of helping him? Is it his current girlfriend? A friend? A group of activists?"

"Or a terrorist group," someone said.

"Or a terrorist group," Eden repeated. "And secondly, why is Tennyson Cottage mentioned? What's the connection with Khelifi?"

"Does there have to be a connection?" Sebastian asked. "It could be someone who just wants to kill two birds with one stone, so to speak."

"True," Eden said, grateful for Sebastian's contribution. "That could of course be the case. But then the question remains: how does this person know about Tennyson Cottage? I mean, it's not particularly well known."

One of the investigators raised his hand.

"I think you can find it if you do an Internet search. Well, I know you can. I just tried it myself."

"I did the same thing," Sebastian said. "But there weren't many matches—only a handful. It doesn't seem like a place you would just come across unless you knew what you were looking for."

"Which takes us back to square one," Eden said. "How did the person or persons who made the threat know about Tennyson Cottage?"

Was this the right angle of attack? Eden was doubtful. She was finding it difficult to work out how to react to the two different demands contained in the note. Was Tennyson Cottage the most important thing for the hijacker or hijackers, or was it Zakaria Khelifi? Why decide to challenge two governments rather than just one? Surely whoever it was must realize that the USA would never accept a hostage situation. They didn't negotiate with terrorists, and there was no way they would shut down Tennyson Cottage during the time it took a jumbo jet to use up its fuel.

As far as Zakaria Khelifi was concerned, Eden thought the same applied. The Swedish government was not going to revise its decision because of a bomb threat. If they did, it would open the floodgates for a surge of hostage situations and bomb threats. Besides which, they still didn't know if this was a hoax, and that bothered Eden more than anything else.

"Let's just ignore the demands for a while and focus on the actual threat instead," she said. "The bomb that's supposed to be on the plane. What does Arlanda say, first of all?"

"I've been in touch with them," one of the investigators said. "They reckon it's virtually impossible to smuggle a bomb on board these days, either in hand luggage or in baggage that's been checked in. At least with flights that have the USA as their final destination."

"Because the Americans insist that everything has to be X-rayed?"

"Exactly. Every single thing is X-rayed."

"And what do they do if they see something suspicious in baggage that's been checked in? Do they open it? I can think of countless occasions when people have been asked to open their hand luggage to show what they're carrying, but I've never heard of anyone having to open a suitcase after it's been checked in. And most people lock their cases these days, so what happens then? Do they break them open? I can't recall ever seeing that either."

Sebastian broke in, sounding slightly impatient.

"Isn't this exactly what this kind of threat is aiming to achieve?"

"What do you mean?"

"They want us to sit here trying to guess whether or not there really is a bomb. The fact that we can't be sure makes the answer irrelevant, because we can't afford to take the risk. Therefore, it's not a good idea to mess with people who threaten a plane that's actually in the air."

Eden nodded thoughtfully. "We can compare this situation with the threats we dealt with yesterday. We were given times and locations for four bombs; we were able to get there, evacuate each location, and carry out a search for any possible explosives. In the case of a plane that's already in the air, with the threat that it will be blown up if it tries to land, that's impossible. Even if we sent one of the crew down into the hold to search the baggage, it would be impossible. There are far too many bags to go through, and they don't have the necessary equipment."

"This claim that the plane will be blown up if it comes in to land tells us something else," Sebastian said.

"Yes," Eden agreed. "So far, not one word has leaked out to the press, so in order for whoever has made the threat to know if the plane lands . . ."

". . . at least one of them has to be on board. Or they have a contact on board," Sebastian finished.

Eden thought for a moment. It was the perfect threat. The police and the government would need nerves of steel if they were going to defy the hijackers and hope that the whole thing was nothing more than a bluff, that there was no bomb.

"If the person who left the note in the toilet is still on board, then that person believes they will be able to leave the plane without being recognized and stopped by the police. And they're counting on the fact that they won't have to blow the plane to pieces, because then the person in question would die, too. Of course, it's possible that he or she might be prepared to die for the cause, but perhaps it's not the most credible scenario."

"Which raises another question," one of the investigators said. "How does the person behind all this think he or she is going to communicate with us, find out if their demands have been met?"

"Through the media," Sebastian said.

"But the media don't have the story."

"Not yet, but it's only a matter of time. There's no chance that there won't be a leak from somewhere—Arlanda, SAS, the police, or the government office. Or the Americans, for that matter."

"So the person behind all this thinks that he'll be able to read about it if Zakaria Khelifi is released and allowed to stay here, and if the Americans close down Tennyson Cottage."

"I think that must be the case," Eden said. "No one has tried to make direct contact either with us or the Americans."

She clasped her hands in her lap, which was something she often did when she was thinking.

"We don't know if there is a bomb on board, but most indications would suggest that this is unlikely. Nor do we know if the person behind the threat is on board the plane, but as the note was found in the toilet, that is a reasonable assumption."

She leaned back and went on:

"What we do know, however, is that the news has not yet reached the mass media. We also know that the perpetrators have chosen not to contact us directly."

The others waited.

"What are you getting at?" Sebastian asked.

"We could try to effect an emergency landing in secret, and evacuate the passengers and crew before the news gets out."

"Are you crazy? And risk everyone's life?"

Eden pursed her lips.

"Just think about it. If there really is a bomb on board, the perpetrators must have made extensive preparations in order to get it there. They must also realize that if the plane is blown up, airports all over Europe and the USA will revise their security procedures so that it will become even more difficult to take a bomb on board. In other words, they will never get another chance. Therefore, as far as they are concerned, it's essential that everything works this time. Blowing up the plane just because we try for an emergency landing makes no sense at all to me."

The door of the meeting room opened and closed as someone realized they were in the wrong place.

"So you think that if we try to bring the plane down, we'll find out if whoever is behind the threat is serious, and whether one of them is sitting on the plane, or has some other way of knowing what's happening on board?"

"Exactly. I believe that if we try to bring the plane down, even if there is a bomb on board, the plane won't be blown up. I think the person behind the threat will make himself or herself known, and will remind us that we're not sticking to the rules."

"And what do we do then?"

"Then obviously we don't defy the hijackers, we take the plane back up again. What do you think?"

The others exchanged glances.

"What would the view of the police be? They have more experience with this kind of thing," said the investigator who had spoken earlier.

"I'll talk to Alex Recht as soon as we're done here," Eden said. "Then we can speak directly to the captain on the plane."

She thought to herself that in the future she wanted Alex at these meetings. The situation was critical; there was no time to go through everything twice.

"By the way, have we spoken to Khelifi about this?" the investigator asked.

"Not yet," Eden replied.

She looked at her colleagues.

"So what do you say? If the National Bureau of Investigation is with us, do you agree that we should try for an emergency landing?"

Everyone nodded.

"Good," Eden said.

"Just one thing," Sebastian said.

"What?"

"Remind the pilot not to dump the fuel, otherwise we've lost the chance of taking the plane back up again."

13

Flight 573

Erik Recht was thinking about his son more than anything else.

He really felt as if the boy had arrived several years too early. As his father pointed out, that was the downside of getting together with a woman who was ten years older than him.

"I don't want to wait any longer," Claudia had said. "If I do, we might not be able to have children at all."

What could he say to that? Not a thing. Claudia was almost forty. If he said he wasn't ready, he would come across as being childish. And if he came across as being childish, she would leave him. So they had a baby.

"Isn't it all a bit quick?" his father had said at the time.

Erik didn't answer that kind of question. They had never been able to communicate with one another—not when Erik was a teenager and out of control, and not since then. It was as if those damned teenage years had created a barrier between them, and neither of them was capable of ignoring it. The years went by, but Erik knew that his father still regarded him as unreliable, in spite of the fact that he had now been with the same woman for several years. In spite of the fact that he had completed his training as a pilot and got a permanent post with SAS.

What was the point in trying if you were never told that you were good enough?

"You've got a lot to be proud of," his sister had said the last time they met up. "Think about all the things you've achieved. You've lived abroad, for example. Lots of people dream of living your life."

The words had cooled Erik's overheated temperament. There

were those who would have liked a part of his life. That was good enough. Erik couldn't be responsible for the fact that his father wished things were different.

In Erik's current situation, as copilot on a plane that had been hijacked, he began to wish that his relationship with his father had been different. He even caught himself longing to hear Alex's voice. It carried with it a stability that Erik himself had never been able to conjure up. And the sound of his father's voice made him feel safe.

Erik's thoughts returned to his own son.

He wasn't going to bloody well leave his son when he was still just a baby!

He glanced over at Karim. He was miles away; he almost looked as if he was in another world.

"We've got to get ourselves out of this," Erik said.

Karim's tense features hardened.

"We will."

In order to reinforce what he had said, Erik went on:

"We have to think about our families."

Only then did Karim turn and look at him.

"Believe me, I'm thinking of nothing else."

14

Stockholm, 11:00

Erik was born on a Sunday. Alex remembered it well, because Lena's labor pains had started while they were having Sunday lunch with Alex's parents. When it was all over, Lena said it had felt as if she was pushing out a baby that was lying across the womb, as if he was resisting, refusing to come out. The image of his son lying the wrong way around had haunted Alex all his life. That was how he thought of Erik—not flexible and accommodating like his sister, but constantly hot-tempered and determined to negotiate:

"If you do this for me, then I'll do that for you."

Lena had said that their son lacked direction, but Alex had seen only defiance. It wasn't that he didn't love Erik—he did, but he couldn't ever remember feeling particularly close to him. The trip to South America a few years earlier had worked miracles. The journey had proved to Erik that Alex was genuinely interested in what he was doing, that he wanted to be a part of his life. It had made things easier. During the weeks he spent in South America, father and son had had conversations that Alex would never have thought possible.

Then Erik had moved back to Sweden. Alex couldn't work out how it had happened, but suddenly everything went downhill again. Lena's death weighed heavily on both of them, of course, but there were other factors that also had a bearing on their relationship. Erik made one dubious choice after another. Like training to be a pilot, for example, at a time when so many pilots were being laid off, and hardly any new appointments were being made. Sometimes Alex thought that if it hadn't been for his overt skepticism about his son's choice of profession, Erik would never have managed to push himself and secure a permanent post.

And if he hadn't been a pilot, he wouldn't be sitting on that bloody plane right now. If it wasn't for his son, Alex wouldn't have been particularly stressed out by the bomb threat. Instead, he would have said they needed to have nerves of steel, that it was unreasonable to think there was actually a bomb on board, and that they should wait for further instructions from the hijackers. He would also have been curious to see what the government was intending to do.

He had promised Hjärpe that he would act professionally without getting personally involved, but they both knew this was highly unlikely. Therefore, the responsibility for handling the situation had been discreetly passed on to another investigator in Alex's department. That was fine by Alex; as long as he knew what was going on, he was satisfied.

Fredrika Bergman called him and got straight to the point.

"How's it going? With the plane, I mean."

Why was she asking that? They'd just been at the same meeting at Rosenbad. He had nothing new to tell her.

"I'm going over to Säpo in a little while," Alex said. "Nothing has been decided yet. What kind of signals are you picking up at your end?"

"We've got a meeting with the minister shortly. I'll know more after that."

Alex wished she was working for him instead; he needed her right now.

"Perhaps we can have a chat later, after our meetings?" he said.

If you tell me something, then I'll tell you something.

"Good idea," Fredrika said.

He was about to end the call when he realized there was something else on her mind. How well did you know someone when you could tell how she was feeling just from her breathing?

Fredrika lowered her voice.

"There's something else I need to tell you," she said. "But it has to stay between us. At all costs."

"Absolutely."

Alex had no hesitation in accepting those conditions when they came from Fredrika.

"It's about Zakaria Khelifi, the man who's named in the note from the hijackers."

"What about him?"

He heard the hesitation in her voice.

"I don't know, Alex. But I don't like this case. I'm the one who's dealing with it, and . . . I just don't have a good feeling about it."

"You don't usually let your feelings influence your decisions."

"No, but this time I don't have any logical arguments to back up what I want to say. I've read Säpo's statement and I was there when they went through everything, but now this has happened . . . Suddenly it all feels very flimsy. What if we're wrong?"

Alex could picture her so clearly, with that anxious expression, the depth of emotion in those eyes.

"Hang on, you're new to this job," he said. "There must be someone else who's familiar with the case and can decide whether it's flimsy or not?"

"Of course. Several of my colleagues have read through the notes, and I haven't heard a reaction from anyone else. They assume that Säpo know what they're talking about, that they wouldn't take a step like this unless it was essential."

"And you don't feel the same about Säpo?"

"Of course I do. I'm just saying that now that we're in this situation, I'm not sure if I really believe the judgment stands up."

"What are you trying to say?"

Alex thought there was a brief second's hesitation before Fredrika spoke, but he could have been wrong.

"What I'm trying to say is that it's not out of the question that a misjudgment might have been made in the case of Zakaria Khelifi. In which case, it's not impossible that someone out there knows he's innocent, and is doing everything they can to make sure he can stay here."

"Even if that means risking the lives of four hundred people?"

"I think so," Fredrika said. "After all, desperation has driven people to do far worse things, wouldn't you say?"

• • •

She regretted her words as soon as she put down the phone. Alex must think she was crazy, that she sympathized with the terrorists. At the same time, she knew she couldn't live with herself if she didn't pass on her doubts in time.

Because I think there is something wrong with the Zakaria Khelifi case.

Fredrika knew what she would have done if she had still been with the police. She would have rushed out into the autumn chill and started talking to those around Zakaria Khelifi. Tried to gauge their mood, to assess how the people around him reacted to the accusations of involvement in terrorism. But Fredrika didn't work for the police anymore; instead, she was sitting behind a desk in the Justice Department.

"You're so incredibly successful," a friend had said to her just a few days earlier. "The Justice Department—have you any idea how many people would give anything for a job like that?"

Why would anyone want her job? All she did was push paper around. It was a job that made no difference whatsoever to one single person on this earth. Apart from Zakaria Khelifi, perhaps.

For what must have been the twentieth time that morning, Fredrika pulled out his file. She summarized Säpo's information to herself. He, or rather his telephone number, had cropped up during a preliminary investigation back in 2009. Then he came up in the operation following the death threats against prominent figures in France. And finally, he came up again in the investigation during which he was arrested and charged. There was now proof that he had helped the perpetrators to collect packages containing substances that they had later used to produce a bomb. Furthermore, Säpo added that Zakaria Khelifi had been identified by Ellis, one of the perpetrators, as a person who had assisted them.

Fredrika went over the issue again and again. She would be attending a briefing with the minister for justice very soon. Did she have any objections that she could raise during the meeting?

Not really.

What should she say? The same as she had said to Alex—that she had a feeling something was wrong? It would be stupid to imagine that the minister for justice would be impressed by such a feeble argument. There was sufficient evidence to regard Zakaria Khelifi as a security threat. If it had been any other crime apart from terrorism, she wouldn't have hesitated for a second when it came to his guilt. And if she wanted to raise the issue of how security matters were handled as a matter of principle, she would have to wait for a better opportunity.

Alex was right; she was behaving neither rationally nor professionally. Who was she to start questioning procedures that had doubtless been in place for decades? If everyone else thought the rules were in order and that Zakaria Khelifi's case had been assessed correctly, then why should she start asking questions?

Säpo's work seemed very familiar, yet at the same time it was a million miles from the police work Fredrika had been involved in as part of Alex's team. Säpo dealt with cases where only a small number were ever convicted, but far more were suspects. They often had information that couldn't be brought up in a public forum, which made it difficult to move forward in certain instances. How frustrating must that be on a daily basis?

Fredrika decided it was time to back off. She wasn't getting anywhere. If she wanted to raise the issue, she had to come up with new information. God knows how she was going to do that.

Once she had made the decision, she felt much calmer. The meeting with the minister took place shortly afterward.

"I've spoken to the PM," Muhammed Haddad said. "We're in agreement; we refuse to meet the hijackers' demands. If we do, we'll end up with one bomb threat for every single person we decide to deport, and we can't have that. However, we are wondering how we're going to communicate with the hijackers to inform them of our standpoint."

"That's a matter for the police," the secretary of state said.

"I realize that, but we have to bear in mind that the threat was left on the plane, and therefore it was up to the crew to deal with it. The hijackers did not choose to contact the police directly, which suggests that we might be able to work out a communication strategy of our own. They might even be expecting it."

"What did the Americans say?" Fredrika asked.

"They went crazy, of course," said the secretary of state, who had evidently been involved in the discussion. "The Foreign Office is dealing with communications, but they expect support from us with ongoing updates. We have spoken to both the State Department and the Department of Homeland Security, and they in turn have spoken to just about everybody you can think of—the CIA, FBI, NSA, the lot. Säpo are dealing with those contacts from the Swedish side, by the way."

It was obvious that the secretary of state was enjoying being in the center of things. Fredrika was sure he got a hard-on just from saying CIA. Pathetic.

She glanced at her watch. The plane had been in the air for less than two hours. There was still plenty of fuel in the tank.

The minister for justice was very clear. The government had no intention of revising its decision on the deportation of Zakaria Khelifi. Hearing him speak made Fredrika feel safe. Muhammed Haddad was known for his calm approach and his intelligence, but above all, he was not remotely interested in individual glory. If he thought the government had made a mistake in revoking Khelifi's residence permit, he wouldn't hesitate to admit that he had been wrong.

But Zakaria Khelifi was only half the solution. The hijackers had also asked for the closure of a detention facility known as Tennyson Cottage. A so-called secret jail.

The chances of the Americans shutting down a place like that in order to meet the demands of a hijacker were nonexistent.

15

Washington, DC, 05:02

At 09:30 Swedish time, a jumbo jet had taken off from Arlanda Airport in Stockholm. Half an hour later, the pilot had called the control tower and informed them that a bomb threat had been found in one of the plane's toilets. The message that landed on Bruce Johnson's desk didn't contain a great deal of information, but it was more than enough.

The plane's final destination was New York.

There were American citizens on board.

And the threat was addressed directly to the United States government.

"If the Swedes don't get the fact that we're going to sort this out together, we'll just walk all over them," the director of the FBI had said when he got a call at four o'clock in the morning US time, and was given the news.

He had then put Bruce's boss in charge of dealing with the hijacked plane, and the boss in turn had handed operational responsibility to Bruce.

It was now five o'clock in the morning, and Bruce was on his second cup of coffee. The FBI worked around the clock, but there weren't many people in the office yet. He had already been in touch with his counterpart in the CIA, and had also spoken to several different departments that were involved. It would be a few hours before everyone was in, but once they were, it would be all-out war. At the moment, it looked as if the FBI would carry the main responsibility, but as the plane wasn't yet in American airspace, it could be argued that this was an external threat approaching the borders of the USA, and should therefore fall within the remit of the defense service.

Bruce wasn't interested in arguments of that kind. If everyone just stuck to their own job and did what they were best at, their joint operations were usually successful.

He wasn't particularly impressed with the information he had received from Sweden. He hadn't seen a list of passengers or crew members. Nor had he been given any details about the Swedes' assessment of how likely it was that there might be a bomb in the baggage hold or in the cabin itself.

Bruce was far from convinced that there really was a bomb; however, he was certain that the hijackers were serious. The reason for this was that Tennyson Cottage had been mentioned.

Tennyson Cottage was one of the CIA's facilities, and not something with which the FBI would concern itself under any circumstances, but that didn't mean Bruce didn't know about the place and its brief history. Guantánamo had become too controversial, too complicated, and by this stage, Bruce knew hardly anyone who didn't want to shut down the goddamn place and forget it ever existed. But that wasn't the way things worked, and everyone knew it. One person who had become particularly conscious of the problem was the president, who had made it an election issue in 2008. You had to wonder what kind of advisers the guy must have had; a high school student could have worked out that trying to shut down Guantánamo was going to be hell.

But why would a place like Tennyson Cottage turn up in a bomb threat written in Swedish, which also gave the name of a person that the Swedish security service believed was involved in terrorism? Bruce was very dubious about the whole thing, to say the least. Tennyson Cottage wasn't like Guantánamo; it wasn't well known and it wasn't talked about. He believed the name had leaked out in some context, and that it was possible to find it on the Internet, but you had to know what you were looking for.

Therefore, the fact that the hijackers had mentioned Tennyson Cottage said something about them. The only question was what that might be. Had Swedish citizens ever been held there? Bruce didn't think so, but he would have to check with the CIA. He knew that Säpo had been in touch with the CIA, and that it was therefore entirely possible that Säpo knew more than the FBI right now, but if that was the case, things had to change.

Bruce had made a note of the person he had spoken to: Eden Lundell. Her English was so good that Bruce had felt compelled to ask if she originally came from an English-speaking country. It transpired that her mother was British, and that Eden had lived in London for many years.

There was something familiar about both Eden's name and her half-British background, but for the life of him, Bruce couldn't remember where he had come across her before. Eventually he went to see a colleague who might be able to help.

"Eden Lundell, used to live in England. Have we worked with her? Why does her name sound so familiar?"

His colleague grinned. "We certainly do know who she is," he said.

And Bruce suddenly remembered the story they had heard from the Brits a few years ago. *How the hell had she managed to become the boss of the Swedish counterterrorism operation?* Didn't the Swedes realize what a risk she constituted?

Tennyson Cottage. That was what Bruce had to focus on, not how Säpo recruited its personnel. How could the hijacker or hijackers possibly know about Tennyson Cottage? And why was it important to them that Tennyson Cottage of all places should be shut down?

If they could find the answers to those questions, they would soon be on the trail of whoever was behind the hijacking.

16

Stockholm, 11:22

They met in Säpo's HQ once again. This time, Alex Recht got to see more of the counterterrorism unit. If he hadn't known, he would never have guessed that he was just a stone's throw from his own office. A huge number of internal walls had been knocked down to create vast open-plan offices, with tall screens marking out the different workstations. The windows were just as depressingly small as in the building where the National Bureau of Investigation operated, but the ceiling height had been raised and the walls were painted white. The floor was newly laid, and the computers were much more up-to-date than the ones Alex was used to. Most of the staff seemed to have at least two monitors on their desks; some had three. Several glass cubes dotted around the office served as modern meeting rooms, combining the maximum amount of light with maximum soundproofing. In some of the cubes, huge screens displayed maps, pictures of a range of individuals, and detailed summaries of information.

"Impressive," Alex said.

"Thanks; our analysts are responsible for those rooms, which also serve as our operational offices. It's important that we have all the information at hand when we're discussing a particular issue. The screens have been invaluable in that respect."

"I can well believe it," Alex said, mainly for the sake of having something to say.

Säpo looked like a film set for an American crime thriller, which wasn't quite what he had been expecting. He was also surprised by the dress code; all the men were wearing dark suits, and so were most of the women. Those who weren't in trouser suits wore a skirt suit or a dress. Alex felt out of place in his dark trousers and sports jacket.

As Eden led the way through the open-plan office, they passed a man who was on the phone, speaking loudly in French.

"You don't use interpreters here?" Alex asked.

"On certain occasions, but as a rule we expect our staff to speak at least one language in addition to Swedish and English. Many are fluent in four or five."

She smiled at Alex. "How many languages do you speak?"

"One. Two if you count English, but I'm not that good."

"In that case, perhaps it's just as well that you were assigned to this particular job so that you can get some practice," Eden said. "Coffee?"

The coffee machine looked like a spaceship.

"No thanks," Alex said, not wanting to reveal that he was a technophobe as well as a poor linguist.

But Eden saw through him and handed him a cup anyway.

"Press here and here, et voilà!"

He peered into the cup.

"Amazing," he said.

"We live and learn," Eden replied. "This way."

One of the smaller, more discreet glass cubes turned out to be Eden's office. She closed the door behind them.

"As I understand it, you're sharing responsibility for this case with a colleague," Eden said.

"Yes, but he's gone to another meeting," Alex said. "With the Criminal Intelligence Service. We decided I would come and see you."

Alex had no idea what the purpose of the other meeting might be, and was glad that he was seeing Eden instead.

"Excuse me for asking, but is there a reason why there are two of you in charge now? Because you had sole responsibility to begin with, didn't you?"

The coffee was hot and felt as if it was scalding his throat on the way down.

"My son is the copilot on the hijacked plane. We didn't realize that at first. I never know which flights he's on."

We don't speak very often, he wanted to add, but felt it was too personal.

Eden sat down at her desk and gazed at Alex.

"I understand," she said.

She rifled through a pile of papers in front of her and extracted a document.

"Oh, yes, it's on here," she said. "Erik Recht is your son?"

"Yes."

Alex drank some more coffee, which was still too bloody hot.

Someone knocked on the door. Eden looked up as it opened.

"SAS have just sent over the lists of passengers and crew. We're running them through our internal databases, and should have a result within a few minutes. I'll take a closer look at any matches that might come up, see if they look interesting, and I'll get back to you as soon as I know."

"Brilliant!" Eden said, bringing both hands down on the surface of her desk.

The door closed.

"Which databases will you be running the names through?" Alex asked.

"All of them. Every database and every register, then we'll see if we find anything useful. I mean, we might get a match, but if it's a speeding offense it's of no interest."

Alex understood; they were looking for connections with serious crime.

"I mentioned our suggestion on the phone," Eden said. "Did you have time to talk to your colleagues about it?"

He had. It had been a brief discussion, because no one could come up with anything better.

"We agree that it would be a good idea to contact the captain and suggest an emergency landing."

"Good. I've spoken to SAS, who have stayed in touch with the captain, and he hasn't proposed anything else. So if he doesn't have any ideas of his own, he ought to go for ours."

Alex hoped so. He had been pleased to see that Karim Sassi was the captain. They had met at a birthday party at Erik's, and Karim had made a very good impression. Steady, as Diana had put it. Reassuring. And sensible. A lovely wife and delightful children. He didn't seem to drift off, as Erik was in the habit of doing.

Drifting off. Is that what you're doing now, Erik?

"By the way," Alex said. "We were talking about the relatives of the crew members. Should they be informed?"

"Not yet. We're keeping the lid on this for as long as possible, at least until we've tried to bring about an emergency landing. If this gets out it could seriously jeopardize their safety."

Alex nodded; he knew Eden was right. At the same time, he said a quiet prayer that everything would go well. It would look appalling if the worst came to the worst, if the plane was blown up and none of the relatives of the passengers or crew had been informed of what was going on.

That just couldn't happen. Not under any circumstances.

If the plane was blown up, Alex's life would be over. He had to take a deep breath, get some air.

"Alex?"

"I'm okay."

"Nobody would blame you if you decided to . . ."

"I said I was okay."

His tone was sharper than he had intended, but he couldn't bear the thought of being excluded from the case at this stage.

"Nobody would withhold information from you," Eden said. "Just so you know. If you took a step back you would still have the number of my direct line, and you could call me whenever you wanted to."

He could see that she meant what she said, but he had no intention of taking a step back. He wasn't like Peder, who had allowed his entire life to be destroyed just because he didn't know how to keep his feelings in check.

"Thanks, but I'm staying put."

"Fine."

She picked up the phone and keyed in a number.

"We're going to make the call now," she said. "Do you want to be here?"

She hardly had time to put the phone down before the door flew open. A man of about fifty came in. He was tall and looked fit, and the only thing that made Alex think he was fifty were the lines on his face. They shook hands.

"Alex Recht."

"Dennis."

No surname, just a first name.

"Dennis is the head of the investigation unit here at Säpo," Eden explained.

Dennis sat down next to Alex.

"What's the plan?"

"If we call SAS, they will put us through to the plane. Don't ask me how—it's already passed over both Sweden and Norway."

"Where's it going to land?"

"We've spoken to the Norwegians, and they're happy to accept the plane if the pilot turns back."

Eden picked up the phone again and keyed in a number that she had written down on a piece of paper. She switched to speakerphone and put down the receiver. After three rings the call was answered, then redirected.

Erik, Alex thought.

17

11:45

But it was Karim Sassi who answered, not Erik. Of course. It was obvious that the officer in charge would answer when the police called.

Eden introduced herself, and explained that Alex and Dennis were listening in. Karim's responses were brief, but the line was clear and they had no difficulty in hearing what he said.

"What's the atmosphere like on board?" Eden asked.

"Same as usual."

Eden frowned.

"I'm sorry?"

"Nobody knows what's happening except the crew."

"Okay, let me rephrase the question. What's the atmosphere like among the crew?"

There was a rushing sound on the line.

"We're fine."

"Nobody has gone to pieces?" Dennis said.

"No."

"Good," Eden said.

She clicked on her computer as she carried on speaking.

"What's your course at the moment?"

"We're still on autopilot, on course for New York."

Alex hadn't thought about that. Should they still be heading for the USA, or would it be a good idea to stay away?

"You haven't considered an alternative route, in view of what has happened?" Eden said.

"No."

"But you had requested extra fuel before you took off?"

"Yes. Storms are forecast for New York."

"How many hours are we talking about?" Dennis asked, wanting to double check the information they had been given earlier.

"I have enough fuel for just under twelve more hours."

Alex felt his blood pressure plummet. Twelve hours wasn't very long for two governments to accede to two impossible demands.

"Karim, you're doing brilliantly," Eden said. "We have a suggestion that we would like to put to you, and we would ask you to think it over."

There was something impressive about the hierarchy that now became apparent; Alex hadn't thought about it before. Eden Lundell, one of Säpo's most senior representatives, was calling the pilot of an SAS plane and making a suggestion. Not giving an order or a directive, but making a suggestion. Because while he was at the controls of Flight 573, Karim Sassi alone was king.

"Are you listening?" Eden said when Karim didn't reply.

"I'm listening."

And Eden began to explain.

●   ●   ●

"No," Karim Sassi said.

Time stood still inside the glass cube. Alex asked himself whether they could have foreseen Karim's reaction, but he thought not. It was entirely unexpected.

"No?" Eden said.

"The answer is no. I am not prepared to go against the hijackers' instructions and bring down the plane. I would be jeopardizing the safety of everyone on board."

Alex saw Eden swallow hard. She rested her elbows on the desk and put her head in her hands. When she looked up her expression was dark. She wasn't used to being contradicted.

"Karim, listen to me." It was clear that she was having to make a real effort not to sound angry. "We share your concerns, but as I said there are a number of logical arguments which suggest that the hijackers would have far too much to lose by blowing up the plane in midair. It takes time to land, and that would give the hijackers the chance to protest. In which case you just take the plane back up again."

A scraping noise came from the speaker.

"I'm not doing it," Karim said. "What happens if one of the hijackers is on board, and panics? We might end up with a hostage situation. Someone could get hurt. We have no idea what we might trigger."

"But at least we would know if there really is a hijacker and a genuine threat," Dennis said.

They heard another voice in the background. Erik. Alex felt his heartbeat increase. Without realizing what he was doing he leaned forward in his chair, as if trying to hear better. They waited as Karim and Erik spoke to one another. It wasn't possible to hear what they were saying, but Alex could tell from his son's tone of voice that he was wound up. Erik had always been quick to flare up, to sound agitated, but this time Alex had to admit that he had every reason to behave that way.

Eventually, Karim came back on the line.

"I am the captain of this plane. And I am not going to make any attempt at an emergency landing, particularly in view of the fact that I can't dump the fuel, which we are all agreed is out of the question."

Eden chose her words with care.

"We totally respect the fact that you alone are in command," she said. "But how are you intending to resolve this situation?"

"What do you mean?"

"I mean exactly what I say. If you don't intend to attempt an emergency landing, what's your plan?"

"What's *my* plan? It's not my fucking responsibility to sort this out!"

For the first time, Karim sounded really angry. "It's *your* responsibility, either by finding the idiots who are behind this, or by cooperating with the hijackers and doing exactly as they say. My only task is to keep the plane in the air until it's all over."

Then he ended the call.

Eden looked at Dennis and Alex.

"Shit," Dennis said.

"Although he does have a point," Alex said.

The others stared at him, as if he had gone mad.

"There are three ways of resolving this," Alex said. "Number one, we manage to land the plane and get everyone off without the hijackers noticing. Number two, both governments meet the demands of the hijackers. Or number three, we find the perpetrators behind the hijacking. And that might be the only achievable solution."

"And an emergency landing isn't the obvious option?"

"To us, yes. But evidently not to Karim Sassi."

"Can we force him to cooperate?" Dennis said.

"I've no idea," Eden replied. "We'll have to call SAS and check. It seems strange if we don't have clear jurisdiction over an individual pilot."

Dennis got to his feet.

"I'll go and find out."

When he had closed the door behind him, Alex turned to Eden.

"If Karim says no, then I'm afraid we'll have to accept it."

"Me, too."

"So what's the alternative?"

"Would it help if you spoke to him? Does he know you? Does he know you're Erik's father?"

Alex shook his head; he couldn't imagine it would be any easier for him to get through to Karim.

"It wouldn't make any difference," he said.

Eden linked her hands behind her head and stared into space.

"If we don't neutralize the threat by landing the plane, then we either have to meet the hijackers' demands or identify the perpetrators before the fuel runs out, as you said. And to be frank, there isn't a cat in hell's chance of either the Swedish or American governments giving in."

It was an accurate assessment, so Alex raised no objections.

"In that case, we have to find whoever kicked off this entire circus," he said.

They sat in silence for a while.

"There is one consolation," Eden said.

Alex raised an eyebrow. "Is there?"

"I really don't believe there's a bomb on board that plane."

After almost thirty years with the police, Alex had learned that a case could take the most unexpected turns. He ran his fingers over the pink scar tissue on his hands. He had made mistakes on more than one occasion, and had once burned his hands badly as a result.

"I'm not quite so convinced," he said. "We have to be prepared for any eventuality, particularly as we don't even understand everything about the message that was left on the plane."

"What do you mean?"

"Exactly what I say. For example, we don't know how Tennyson Cottage comes into all this. And what's the connection with Zakaria Khelifi?"

Eden was about to answer when Sebastian yanked open the door of her office.

"Bad news. The press have started calling; someone has leaked the hijack story."

"Shit," Eden said. "We could have done with more time."

"I know," Sebastian said. "But if you come over to my office, I've got something to show you that's even worse. We've just got a match on one of the names from the lists. And it looks bad. Really bad."

18

Flight 573

Why couldn't they agree? Erik and Karim had had a frank and vociferous row about the call from Säpo and their suggestion of an emergency landing. Erik couldn't understand why Karim was so vehemently opposed to the idea that he wasn't even prepared to discuss it. He had stated his position very clearly to Erik: the plane was staying in the air, in accordance with the hijackers' instructions. Under no circumstances would he attempt to land until their demands had been met.

"For fuck's sake!" Erik had yelled. "Don't you realize that's not going to happen? There isn't a sensible government anywhere in the world that would go along with such demands!"

But Karim wasn't listening. Or he didn't care. Erik was seething with suppressed rage. Karim's behavior was totally unacceptable. It was completely unreasonable.

Wherever Erik looked, all he could see was the sky, extending into infinity beyond the plane. This usually gave him a sense of peace, but right now he was almost scared out of his wits at the thought of being at a height of thirty thousand feet. They had seen several other aircraft in the distance, on their way to different destinations. Erik wished he was on board any one of them. He just wanted to be anywhere but on a plane that someone was threatening to blow up.

What if this was the day when he was going to die?

Erik had a pragmatic view of death. As his grandfather used to say, death was the only certainty in life. It might come when you were old, or when you were young. As Erik's mother had been. Erik had always thought of her as young, even though she had been almost fifty-five. Being young wasn't just about age; it was in the soul. Erik's father had always been old, ever since Erik was a child.

He watched as Karim wiped his forehead, over and over again. Karim had barely said a word since they received the threat. Unlike Erik, he didn't seem to feel the need to talk about the situation in which they found themselves. He just kept on staring straight ahead.

They had agreed not to tell the passengers about the threat. It would only create chaos and despair, and make the crew's job even harder. However, every member of the crew had been discreetly informed by Fatima, who had found the note. They had had a lot of questions, and the anxiety level was high. It had been decided that Fatima would be the link between cockpit and crew, which Erik and Karim thought was a good idea. The fact that the crew had many questions was understandable, but unfortunately there were no answers. The plane had been hijacked, and no one knew how the drama would end.

Erik didn't know Fatima all that well; they had worked together only a few times in the past. She was a pretty girl, and seemed clever. Tall and dark. She had the loveliest cheekbones Erik had ever seen on a woman. If he had been single he would have asked her out for a glass of wine. But he wasn't single, so he hadn't bothered to find out whether she was seeing anyone. Erik had messed up a lot of things in his life, but never his relationships. He had never been unfaithful to any of the girls he had gone out with. That kind of crap didn't interest him. Going astray was one thing, betrayal was something else altogether. And he just wouldn't do it.

He turned to Karim. Tried again: "What do you think the police are going to do if you refuse to land?"

Karim shrugged. "What can they do? We're sitting on a jumbo jet with four hundred passengers, flying at thirty thousand feet. If they want us to come down, they need to start delivering."

Erik attempted to reason with him.

"If they meet the hijackers' demands, they would lay themselves open to a horrific future, where it becomes worth hijacking a plane or taking hostages in order for terrorists to get what they want. We have to resolve this in some other way."

Fresh beads of sweat broke out on Karim's forehead.

"There is no other way," he said.

Erik didn't know what to say, so he turned away from Karim and looked out at the sky instead. How did Karim know that there was no alternative to meeting the hijackers' demands?

19

Stockholm, 12:01

Less than ten minutes had passed since the minister for justice, Muhammed Haddad, had been given the latest update, and he was sitting alone in his office. Collaborating with the Americans was never easy. Washington seemed to find it difficult to share its assessment of the situation and its expertise. As a consequence, Muhammed found himself responding in the same way. The secretary of state hadn't quite known how to handle his American colleagues; Muhammed had made it very clear that he expected the secretary of state to keep them on a tight rein. Whether that was going to resolve the issue was another matter.

But the Americans weren't the only problem. A short while ago the news about the bomb threat had exploded in the media. It was obvious that the press didn't really know what angle to take. A threat had been directed at Swedish interests for the second time in as many days, and in the first instance it had clearly been a false alarm. Did that mean this was another hoax?

Muhammed wished he knew the answer to that question.

The press secretary stuck his head around the door:

"We've discussed the format for the press conference, and it won't work unless you're there to back up the PM. We're starting in fifteen minutes."

Muhammed felt a surge of irritation.

"What the hell is the point of my being there?"

The press secretary looked surprised.

"Has no one spoken to you? It's all over the papers."

"Thank you, I've seen it."

"I mean the whole thing. Not just that there's a bomb threat, but the plane's destination and the hijackers' demands."

Right from the start they had known that there was something wrong about this business with the plane, but only now was Muhammed beginning to grasp the extent of the problems facing him.

"How did that happen?" he said. "How can someone have leaked the specific demands of the hijackers?"

The press secretary shrugged.

"I haven't got time to think about that right now. It could be anybody."

"Wrong," Muhammed said. "Only a few people in each organization know that Zakaria Khelifi and Tennyson Cottage were mentioned in the note."

"That's usually enough for things to reach the journalists," the press secretary said nonchalantly. "Besides, it doesn't necessarily mean the leak has come from the government or the police. It could just as easily be Arlanda or the airline."

They would never know. The only thing they knew for certain about leaks was that you could never find the source, often because attempting to track them down would be illegal, but also because it simply wasn't worth the trouble.

"So you want me to attend the press conference just to answer questions about Zakaria Khelifi and why we intend to deport him?"

"Yes."

Muhammed shoved his hands into his trouser pockets and gazed out of the window. A colleague had once said the he looked like John F. Kennedy when he stood there like that. "Slightly darker, that's all." It was crap, of course, but pretty cool. A Kennedy from Lebanon.

"No," he said, still with his back to the press secretary.

"No?"

"It would be wrong to bring me in. We have nothing to add to what has already been said about Khelifi. We're not going to get stressed and start making mistakes. The prime minister has called a press conference to inform them that we have received the threat, and that we do not negotiate with terrorists, but will seek other ways in which to resolve the situation. He has *not* called a press conference to discuss whether there are reasons to reconsider our decision with regard to the deportation of Zakaria Khelifi."

Muhammed turned around.

"Wouldn't you agree?"

"I'll speak to the PM right away."

And then he was alone again. As he had been so many times in the past.

Muhammed sat down at the big conference table in the middle of the room. He knew what his role was. Many good people had held the post of minister for justice before him, and they had all left some kind of impression.

Muhammed had often thought that his own range of choices was much smaller. He was predestined to leave one impression, and one alone: as the tough minister who took a hard line against the extremists who espoused violence.

Violence bred violence. Most people were agreed on that. However, many seemed to believe that it was acceptable to go to any lengths in all other areas, which also involved encroaching on the physical freedom of the individual. He constantly heard calls for an increase in CCTV surveillance, more police involvement in social media. The police had to be where the terrorists were, that was the recurring argument. Words that would have been unthinkable before terrorism showed its face in Scandinavia. Now that everyone knew what it looked like, it was as if the general public had lost both its head and its judgment.

But Muhammed, who was born and raised in Lebanon, had a different perception of what terrorism was, and what should really be feared. No one who had spent their whole life in Sweden and was younger than sixty-five had ever lain awake at night waiting for a bombing raid from a neighboring country. Or feared a civil war. Or seen members of their family imprisoned simply for expressing the wrong opinions in public.

The Swedes didn't know the meaning of fear. They thought fear was what they felt when their luggage arrived three hours late on a trip to the Canaries, or when energy prices went up. Muhammed ran his hands over the smooth surface of the desk. There were days and occasions when he felt Swedish. But he would never live his whole life feeling that way. And he wouldn't want to either.

His thoughts returned to Zakaria Khelifi. He had every confidence in Säpo. It was extremely rare for them to raise an objection to the Immigration Office's decision to grant someone a residence permit. And for them to make a request as they had done in the case of Khelifi, revoking a permit that had already been granted, was virtually unknown. This told Muhammed that there was something different about Zakaria Khelifi, and to ignore the country's security service under such circumstances would be no less than a breach of his professional duty.

However, Muhammed had another idea, and the more he thought about it, the more it appealed to him. He went over to his desk and called Fredrika Bergman. He asked her to come up to his office, then he called Fredrika's boss and asked him to do the same.

Muhammed glanced at the clock on the wall. The major parliamentary debate on immigration and integration was over, and he had devoted hardly any of his time to it. He realized it was spiteful. Those who criticized immigration could point to no less than two recent guilty verdicts in court, which was very unpleasant ammunition they could arm themselves with if they wished to kill off Sweden's long tradition of a generous immigration policy.

If Muhammed had not been expecting Fredrika and her boss, he would have done something that he had not done for several years: he would have gotten down on his knees and prayed for his brothers and sisters. If the government agreed to reduce immigration, to make it more difficult for refugees—as Muhammed himself had once been—to come to Sweden, could he remain in his post as minister for justice?

The answer to that question was no. If they closed Sweden's borders, then Muhammed would step down, because if the anti-immigration elements won, Muhammed would have lost everything he believed in. And that would mean that he could no longer see a future as a politician in Sweden.

But these were major issues. Right now Muhammed must do his duty as minister for justice. In the name of democracy, meeting the demands of the hijackers was out of the question. He knew that the US government shared that view.

In which case, the only options were to attempt an emergency landing, or to find those who had set this atrocious plan in motion, before disaster struck. With every passing minute Muhammed was less and less convinced that they would succeed.

20

12:01

A match with the database that looked really bad.

That was what Sebastian had said, and Eden feared the worst.

They met in one of the operational conference rooms. Sebastian and one of his analysts went through what they had found out so far. Eden realized that Sebastian was still angry about her comment on his colleagues, and wondered if Alex had picked up on the awkward atmosphere in the room. She didn't think so. He had nothing to compare it with; he had no way of knowing what was a good or bad atmosphere in their normal working day. But Eden could feel the coldness emanating from Sebastian just as palpably as if he had placed an icy hand on the back of her neck. Fortunately he chose to maintain a pleasant facade in front of Alex.

If only she could have lit a cigarette. It enabled her to think so much better. She ought to get something to eat as well. She would have to send one of her assistants out for a salad later.

"What have you found?"

All her life she had been told that she was too impatient, so she made an effort to sound neutral.

The screen behind Sebastian flashed into life.

"A remarkable connection between yesterday's bomb threats and the threat on the plane, to say the least; this is the last thing we want."

A list of telephone numbers with various lines between them appeared on the screen. Four were in red.

"Yesterday's bomb threats came from these four numbers. As you know they belong to unregistered pay-as-you-go SIM cards and cannot be traced to specific users or subscribers. However, we were able to check whether there had been any other traffic to or from these phones. And there had. Three of the phones don't appear to have been used before, but two calls had been made from the fourth phone, which was used to make the last bomb threat. One call was made this morning, one yesterday evening."

Sebastian pointed to one of the numbers that was highlighted in yellow.

"To this number. A private cell phone number, according to our inquiries. It belongs to Karim Sassi."

One colleague after another passed by outside the glass cube, but Eden couldn't take her eyes off the numbers on the screen.

Karim Sassi.

The captain of Flight 573 had been in touch with whoever had made bomb threats against four different locations in Stockholm.

It couldn't be true, for fuck's sake.

"And what does this mean?"

It was a rhetorical question; as she spoke, it sounded as if she was thinking out loud.

"Hang on," Sebastian said. "There's more. Karim also called the same number both yesterday and this morning."

Eden felt the waves of adrenaline surging through her body. She didn't need to turn and look at Alex to know that he was also fired up by what he had just heard—she could feel it in her bones. The hunt united them, they were the same creatures, they had just been born at different times.

"Were they long calls?" Alex asked.

"The call to Karim this morning lasted for approximately twelve minutes; the others are all between two and three minutes."

"Did Karim make the first call yesterday, or was he the recipient?" Eden said.

"The call was made to him, then he called back," Sebastian said.

"So our esteemed captain has been in touch with the person or persons who called in with the bomb threat against Rosenbad yesterday. Rosenbad was the final target, wasn't it?"

"It was," Alex confirmed.

"That's too many calls to be a coincidence," Eden said.

"I'd say it's too few," Sebastian said. "If there were a thousand calls to different numbers listed on this phone, you could argue that Karim Sassi's had come up by chance. But there aren't a thousand calls, and there's just one number. And it belongs to Karim Sassi."

"Is Karim's phone switched on at the moment?" Alex said.

"No, it's off. We tried to call but it went straight to voicemail. We're assuming he has it with him on board."

Eden thought through what she had just been told. She agreed with Sebastian—it couldn't possibly be a coincidence, but she wasn't sure what conclusions she could draw. Did the contact between Karim's cell phone and the unknown phone mean that he had been involved in the previous day's threats, and was therefore probably also involved in the threat against the plane he was now flying? Or did it mean something else?

"Could Karim have been threatened on a personal level?" Alex wondered. "Is that why he doesn't want to land the plane?"

That was also a possibility that couldn't be ruled out, of course, and it could explain a great deal that currently seemed incomprehensible.

"But in that case, why did he board the plane?" Sebastian said.

"Good question," Eden replied.

"Could we ask him over the phone?" Alex said.

Or would such a conversation do more harm than good?

"I'm not sure," Eden said. "But I think the answer is no, we can't."

"Because if he is involved, then we'd be giving away what we know."

"Exactly."

Alex pushed one hand into his trouser pocket.

"We ought to be able to speak to his family, to his wife," he said. "The whole story is out there anyway, so I think that's something we have to do in any case."

He had hardly finished speaking before he realized what he was saying.

"Bloody hell," he said, leaping to his feet.

Eden understood immediately.

"Your son's family," she said, looking worried. "You haven't spoken to them yet."

"I didn't even think about them until I started talking about Karim's family. I need to speak to Erik's sister. And to Diana, my partner."

He looked very unhappy.

"Erik's family is on a plane to South America," he said. "I won't be able to reach them until they've landed."

"Go and call the people you can reach right away," Eden said. "And you're right, we have to speak to Karim's family, too."

"We're also setting up a crisis line for the relatives of the four hundred passengers," Sebastian said with a sigh. "I spoke to the Foreign Office and the Justice Department earlier, but apparently, it's the police who are expected to deal with this. The Information Office has already set up an exchange and issued a direct number."

Eden gave him a grateful look as Alex slipped out of the room.

"We have to move on, and fast," Eden said. "Alex is right, we'll start with a visit to Karim's home. I'd like you to go as soon as Alex gets back."

She glanced at Dennis, the head of the investigation unit.

Sebastian indicated that he had something to say.

"There's something else."

Eden looked at him.

"We called all the phones that were used to make the four bomb threats yesterday. They're all switched on."

"I'm sorry?"

"It's true. We've managed to trace them through the phone towers, and it appears that all four phones are in the same place. Inside the airport complex. We've got teams on the way there now to try and find them."

How was it possible that someone who had made a point of making each call on a different phone that couldn't be traced had then left the phones switched on, enabling the police to find them? Eden didn't know what to think. Either they were dealing with an amateur, or someone who was careless. Or else, they were heading straight into a trap, meticulously rigged by someone who was holding four hundred passengers hostage.

21

Washington, DC, 06:05

It was morning, but still dark outside. Bruce was wishing he'd had more sleep during the night. If he'd known he was going to be up so goddamn early, he would have sent Daisy home much sooner. Daisy with the long legs. The woman he couldn't live with, couldn't live without. A classic crap relationship, in other words.

One of the secretaries came into his office.

"They're here."

Bruce gathered up his papers and quickly made his way to the conference room on the ground floor, where four CIA agents were waiting for him. The resources allocated to counterterrorism measures had increased significantly within the FBI in recent years, and the same was true of the CIA. Bruce wished he'd brought some backup along when he saw how many agents had turned up from the other organization. It made the Bureau appear inferior.

He steeled himself. He knew that the CIA had information he needed, and he had no intention of giving up until he'd gotten it out of them.

The CIA agents sat down in a row along one side of the table. Pitching up at this meeting alone had definitely been a mistake.

"Thanks for coming on such short notice," Bruce said, sitting down.

"No problem. I hardly need to say that we're just as worried about all this as you are."

The man who spoke occupied one of the middle seats. He had an air of natural authority within the group, and Bruce knew he was the one who had been nominated to speak on behalf of them all. Bruce thought they had met once before; was his name—or was he known as—Green? If he remembered correctly, he was one of the heads of the CIA's international counterterrorism unit.

"Of course."

"The fact is, before we do anything we need to have a discussion about which of us actually has the responsibility for this issue."

Fuck. Bruce felt a surge of anger. His boss would take him apart for having put himself in such an obviously inferior position.

"As we see it, according to the information we have received, the FBI has the lead on this matter."

The man opposite smiled.

"That's strange, because we feel the CIA has the lead. At least as long as the plane is outside US airspace."

He had a point, and Bruce knew it.

"That doesn't change a thing. The plane's intended destination is New York, which is, as you know, US territory. And therefore the responsibility of the FBI."

The CIA was legally banned from operating on US soil; they hardly needed reminding of that fact.

"Let's not argue about this right now," Green said. "I understood from your message that you had some questions about Tennyson Cottage."

"That's right. As you know, Tennyson Cottage is named in the bomb threat that was found on the plane. Needless to say, I'm wondering how the person who wrote the note could possibly know about Tennyson Cottage, and secondly, what it has to do with Zakaria Khelifi."

Green sat in silence for a moment, his plump forehead deeply furrowed.

"I must be honest and admit that we can't answer either of your questions. Which is incredibly embarrassing, of course, but true nonetheless."

"You must be able to give me something to work on," Bruce said. "Names, dates, telephone numbers, anything at all with a Swedish connection."

Green exchanged a few muttered words with the colleague on his left. Unbelievable. Bruce realized that none of the others was going to speak during the meeting. Green was in charge, and that was the end of it.

"As I'm sure you understand, Tennyson Cottage is part of the most sensitive, and therefore the most secret, element of our operations. With all the rumors about torture and waterboarding over the past few years, places like Tennyson Cottage are simply not up for discussion. It's out of the question."

"I'm afraid it's too late for that," Bruce said. "Tennyson Cottage has already been leaked to the media. It's only a question of time before some journalist sits down and googles the name, and finds the meager amount of information available on the Internet. It's enough for them to work out what kind of place it is."

"Exactly," Green said. "Which is why we need to lie low, restrict the dissemination of information about what goes on there to the fewest people possible."

Bruce didn't have the energy to carry on being diplomatic. It was getting him nowhere in any case.

"And I'm not part of this restricted group?"

"Let's not get upset for no reason. Naturally we will cooperate with the FBI as necessary."

They were sitting in a sandpit, digging big holes with little spades and harsh words.

Green leaned across the table.

"I will give you what you need. But not a word to the Swedes. Any information they receive will come from us. Is that clear?"

Bruce nodded.

"Tennyson Cottage is one of our newer institutions," Green went on. "It's only been operating for just over three years. We've kept it as a limited facility; we didn't want to make it too big or too well known. You could say that some of the really difficult cases ended up there. High-ranking members of Al Qaeda, when we want them to start talking."

Start talking.

Bruce knew what that meant. And he was one of those who

didn't like it. Torture belonged back in the Dark Ages. Besides which, it was pointless. You couldn't rely on information that was forced out of someone with the help of electric shocks or waterboarding or similar methods. However, he didn't share his views with Green, otherwise the meeting would have been over before it had even started.

"It's hardly one of our most important detention facilities, but it has served its purpose with a certain amount of success. A total of approximately fifty detainees have been held there. We have tried to limit the numbers. No more than fifteen at a time, and no one has stayed longer than six months."

"You just pumped them for what they knew, then moved them on?"

"That was the idea, and that's how it worked. Of the fifty or so who have been there, forty-five were taken care of in a more permanent way; some were sent back to Pakistan, where they were handed over to our Pakistani colleagues, and some were dealt with in other ways. What has happened to them is actually of little interest; the important thing is that since their sojourn in Tennyson Cottage, they have had extremely limited opportunities to pass on their experiences to anyone else."

Bruce made a huge effort to remain neutral. He had met enough CIA agents to know that far from all of them shared Green's grotesque view of how the so-called war on terror would be won, which was why he was always equally surprised when he did come across someone like Green. Bruce also knew that it wasn't only the US government that had held a positive view of the use of torture to a certain extent. An astonishingly large number of the world's democracies believed that under certain circumstances, torture could be both useful and justified.

"But a small number have been released?"

"A very small number. Just two, to be precise."

"I thought you said that around fifty detainees had been held in Tennyson Cottage, and that forty-five had been moved on to other institutions?"

Green was fiddling with the pen he was holding in one hand.

"We lost a couple. Quite unintentionally, I can assure you. But that's what happened. One of them had a heart attack. Another suffered from epilepsy. I mean, we had no way of knowing that. They found him dead one morning. It was a fucking tragedy—that guy had a hell of a lot to tell us."

Bruce felt sick as he watched the pen in Green's hands. It was as if he couldn't bear to sit still. And as if the words spilling out of him meant jack shit to him.

"The ones who were actually released—could they have talked about Tennyson Cottage?"

"One of them actually did. There is an article—*just one article*—on the Internet where the place is mentioned by name. The father of one of the guys turned to the media to cry his eyes out over the damage that had been done to his son. Their names were protected in the article, but of course we realized who they were."

Green grinned at his colleagues and they grinned back. Bruce knew they had no choice. You didn't go against someone like Green, not unless you were prepared to ditch your entire career.

"Where was he from, this guy who spoke to the press?"

Bruce had seen the piece but couldn't remember any details.

"He didn't speak to them himself, it was his father. He was from Morocco; he'd traveled a long way to attend training camps in Pakistan."

"But he had no connection with Sweden or Khelifi?"

"Not as far as we know."

Bruce thought for a moment. Zakaria Khelifi also came from North Africa, but it was a tenuous link. Khelifi was Algerian, the other guy was Moroccan. Why should they know one another?

"Listen to me," Green said, attempting to look trustworthy. "Of course it's up to you how you choose to allocate your time, but if I were you I'd drop this idea of trying to find a connection between Zakaria Khelifi and Tennyson Cottage. Khelifi has never set foot in the place, nor has anyone he knows. Whoever wrote that note has simply bundled together two things that have nothing to do with one another."

"In which case, it's still interesting that the person in question chose to focus on Tennyson Cottage, which is practically unknown."

"Exactly. And we're working flat out on that angle, believe me. As I explained, there are very few people who have something to say about Tennyson Cottage, so it shouldn't be too difficult to flush out whoever decided to use it in that note."

"Of course, it could just be someone who had read the article," Bruce said. "And got real mad."

Green shook his head decisively.

"Have you seen it? Tennyson Cottage is only mentioned in passing. The stupid fucker who wrote it had no idea what a scoop he had, right there in front of his nose."

Green had a point. Bruce's interpretation of the piece had been exactly the same. Tennyson Cottage was mentioned, but nothing more. It wasn't enough to motivate a reaction like this. Unless, of course, the threat was 90 percent about Khelifi, with Tennyson Cottage as the icing on the top. In that case, the article could well have provided the perfect inspiration.

"We don't know what's more important to the hijacker," he said to Green. "Tennyson Cottage or Khelifi."

"No, we don't," Green replied.

Then the conversation was over. Green had nothing else to say, and Bruce had no more questions. He wanted the names of those who had been held in Tennyson Cottage, but Green was only prepared to give him the two who had been released. That would have to do for now.

"By the way, what happened to the other guy who was released?" Bruce said. "The one who didn't feature in the newspaper article?"

"You could say he's living a quiet life. Don't you worry about him."

Bruce gathered up his things and got ready to leave the room. But none of the CIA agents on the other side of the table moved.

"Now that we've finished talking about Tennyson Cottage, we can discuss another matter that has come to our attention," Green said.

Bruce stopped in midmovement.

"What's this about?"

"The commanding officer on board Flight 573, Karim Sassi."

"What about him?"

"We believe he's working with the terrorists who have threatened the plane."

22

Stockholm, 12:15

As this was the first time the minister for justice himself had contacted Fredrika directly, she hurried along to his office. She had seen the news reports on the Internet, and she was scared. The whole story was out there. She still hadn't heard from Alex about how the attempt at an emergency landing had gone. Was it even a possibility now that the whole world was following developments minute by minute? Who knew who was hiding among the sea of people? Perhaps this was exactly what the hijackers wanted—for the media to start reporting so that they would have an insight into what was going on.

Spencer called.

"Has the world gone mad?"

"It seems that way, doesn't it?"

"When do you think you'll be home tonight?"

"I've no idea. I mean, I'm not with the police anymore, so it shouldn't be too late."

"Shall I pick the kids up from nursery anyway?"

"That would be great."

Kids at nursery, a ring on her finger, how quickly had that happened? Not a day went by without Fredrika thinking about it. Spencer didn't seem at all inclined to such musings.

"I thought we could have Indian takeout," he said.

"Sounds like a good idea. Listen, I have to go. I'll call you later."

Fredrika said hello to the minister's secretary and knocked on Muhammed Haddad's door. Her boss was already sitting at the conference table with Haddad.

"Thank you for coming so quickly. Please sit down," the minister said. "I don't think I need to explain how frustrating and alarming I find this whole situation."

Indeed he didn't.

"Apart from the fact that it's extremely worrying to know that four hundred Swedish and American citizens are trapped on board an SAS plane at thirty thousand feet, it concerns me that those of us still on the ground are having difficulty in coordinating our efforts."

Fredrika listened without knowing where this conversation was heading.

"It has come to my attention that we are having some problems with our American colleagues, who want to take and give nothing in return, and I also feel that our interaction with the police could be improved. We have several hours of intensive work ahead of us, whatever happens, and to be honest I'm not happy that we're communicating with the police and Säpo only via the telephone and isolated meetings."

The minister for justice turned to Fredrika.

"I want someone on the spot with the police, someone who can act as liaison officer between the government and the police, and who can report directly to the press secretary and government officials. And to me, obviously. What would you say if I asked you to be that person?"

Fredrika blinked.

"Me?"

"You were handpicked from the applicants for your current post to deal with security matters here at the Justice Department, among other things. You know the police setup inside out. I can't think of a more suitable candidate for the role. Your background gives you a legitimacy that none of the rest of us would have."

"And Säpo?"

"I'll make sure that you have access to the areas and information you need. What do you say?"

There wasn't one iota of hesitation in Fredrika's mind.

"I say yes."

And that was it. Fredrika Bergman was—temporarily—on her way back to the police.

· · ·

With a feeling that she had stepped back in time two years, Fredrika walked into Alex's office less than an hour later. It wasn't the same office, but it was the same Alex.

"Back again," he said.

"It's only temporary."

"I'll believe that when I see it."

She remained standing. Her handbag slid off her shoulder and she heard it land on the floor with a thud.

"Sit down," Alex said. "Säpo and I have just discussed the allocation of the most urgent tasks; we've worked out what they're going to do and what the National Bureau of Investigation will do. I'm heading out to try to get hold of Karim Sassi's family, along with an investigator from Säpo. Do you want to come?"

Fredrika was confused.

"I don't know. I don't think I'm here to go out and about with you."

"So why are you here?" Alex sounded annoyed.

"Well, I'm supposed to act as a kind of liaison officer, make sure the communication channels between the police and the government office are kept open so that we don't end up out of the loop. It's important that we're updated on a regular basis."

"So what are you going to do? Just sit here?"

She swallowed. "I'll come with you."

Alex looked pleased.

"I just need to call in and see what Säpo is up to," Fredrika added.

"I've just come from there—I can give you the latest," Alex said.

Fredrika got up and followed Alex out of the room, the sight of his broad back making her feel safe. The corridor on which the National Bureau of Investigation was located looked just like every other corridor in Police HQ, and it smelled the same, too. Coffee. Always coffee.

"Does it feel good to be back?"

"Alex, I'm not back. I'm just here because of the hijacking."

He didn't say anything—he didn't need to. She could tell exactly what he was thinking: that she was fooling herself and everyone around her. That she belonged in the police.

God knows where I belong, Fredrika thought. Everywhere and nowhere.

She was suddenly overwhelmed by memories of the year in New York. Endless days spent pushing her son's buggy up and down the streets of Manhattan, thinking she was the luckiest woman in the world. It had been good for them to get away. Spencer had had the chance to grow, to heal after everything that had gone wrong. He was only a few years away from retirement age, but he had made it clear to both Fredrika and his superiors that he intended to carry on working. For a long time.

The underground garage was just the same; several stories deep, the air full of cold and exhaust fumes. She didn't like being down there, and got in the car as quickly as she could. Alex explained why they were going to speak to Karim's family, and the color drained from Fredrika's face.

"Hang on a minute—are you telling me you think the captain is involved in this whole business?"

"We don't think anything and we know virtually nothing," Alex replied. "But from what we've seen, Karim Sassi has been in contact with one of the cell phones that was used to make the bomb threats in Stockholm yesterday. And that's why we want to talk to his family, find out whether they noticed if he seemed tense or was behaving oddly before this trip."

"Can't you ask him straight out? Over the phone?"

Alex maneuvered the car out of the cramped garage.

"And risk a situation where he feels pressurized, and does something really stupid? We don't actually know if he is involved. But if he is, then I don't like the idea of discussing it over the phone."

He was right, of course. It was a nightmare for all concerned if Karim was part of the plan. If the terrorists had the pilot on their side, then they didn't need bombs.

"If the worst comes to the worst," Fredrika said slowly. "If we find out that Karim really is a part of what's going on . . ."

She fell silent.

"Yes?"

"What then? Could you call Erik and ask him to take over the controls, if that's the case?"

She could see that the same thought had occurred to Alex.

"I don't know. If we do end up facing that situation, I'm afraid they would take me off the case. After what happened with Peder."

Fredrika knew exactly what he meant. Peder's actions two years ago when he shot dead the man who had murdered his brother had led to a major internal investigation. There had been endless discussions about what could have been done differently. How could the tragedy have been avoided? Because it was a tragedy, there was no other way of looking at it. Peder had lost his job, and the police had lost a valued colleague. Fredrika hadn't given much thought to what the world had lost through Peder's crime; from what she had heard, the man he had shot would be missed by no one.

Unlike everyone on board Flight 573.

Going to Karim Sassi's house seemed like a good idea. What, if anything, had this married father with young children gotten himself into? What was he hiding, this man who carried the responsibility for the lives of over four hundred people?

No crime could be planned and carried out without a single person realizing what was going on.

If Karim was mixed up in the hijack, they would soon know about it.

23

13:00

They couldn't put it off any longer. It was time to go over to the cells and talk to Zakaria Khelifi. Eden Lundell knew he had been told that an entire jumbo jet had been hijacked in his honor.

She hated the fact that a plane was under threat rather than a terrestrial target. The situation was slipping through her fingers, and there wasn't a thing she could do to change that. And the time she had at her disposal was disappearing fast.

The press hadn't revealed exactly which flight was involved, which meant that virtually every single individual with a relative who was currently on board a plane was calling the police to find out if the person they knew was at risk. Eden just couldn't understand how responsible adults could behave in that way. The newspapers had made it absolutely clear that the hijacked plane was on its way to the USA, so why would someone whose relative was on the way to Lanzarote call the police?

Sebastian had gently suggested that she should be a little more self-critical. They had decided against confirming the story in the mass media, which had led to increased speculation.

"We have to give them something," he said.

"Like what?"

"Anything at all. Confirm that there has been a threat, at least. That it definitely involves a flight to the USA and nowhere else. We don't have to be any more specific than that."

The police and Foreign Office phone lines were jammed. Eden had refused to release the passenger lists, which meant that those who called didn't get an answer to their questions. It wouldn't work for long, but it would have to do for the time being.

Eden wanted to question Khelifi herself, or Zakaria as she usually thought of him, and there were several people who objected to that particular suggestion. Her own head of department was very clear about what a stupid idea it was.

"Eden, someone in your position doesn't conduct an interrogation."

"Since when?"

"Since always. You need to leave this to one of Dennis's team."

Eden informed Dennis, the head of investigation, that she would be happy to take one of his team along with her, but that she absolutely intended to be there. She heard her boss sigh behind her as she left his office.

But Eden didn't care. She knew when she wanted something, and she knew how to get it. Alex Recht and Fredrika Bergman had just gone to talk to Karim Sassi's family, and Säpo were going to speak to Zakaria Khelifi at the same time; after all, he was the protagonist in the drama.

Eden couldn't help thinking about Fredrika. She had seen the way Alex looked at her, and thought she could sense something akin to desire. It wasn't necessarily sexual; it could just as easily be material or intellectual, and Eden felt that Alex's desire tended toward the intellectual. Strange. She couldn't understand why Fredrika and Alex worked so well together when they were so different.

One of the investigators met her in the custody block. Eden wanted to interview Zakaria in his cell. Shake him up a bit.

A guard led them to the cell and unlocked the heavy door. Khelifi sat up on his bed as soon as Eden walked in, with the investigator following two steps behind.

Eden made the introductions and pulled up a chair. She sat down and left her colleague standing; he would soon realize that he was surplus to requirements in any case.

She could see that Zakaria was wondering why she was there. High-ranking officials from Säpo were rarely, if ever, involved in interviews, but Eden wasn't like everyone else.

"I would like answers to a few questions," she began. "You have very little to gain by failing to cooperate. Okay?"

Zakaria was pale, and the green T-shirt he was wearing made him look seasick. His expression was the same one she had seen on the faces of so many others in his situation. Provoked. Angry. Unavoidable emotions for someone who had seen his life's work smashed to pieces.

"I've got nothing to do with the plane that's been hijacked."

Eden took out her cigarettes.

"Would you like one?"

She saw her colleague open his mouth and close it again. Zakaria hesitated for a second, then took a cigarette. Eden didn't hesitate at all. She took one for herself then lit both.

"Let me explain," she said, discreetly blowing smoke over her shoulder. "It doesn't matter whether you're involved in the hijack or not; you might still know something that's important to us."

Zakaria shuffled backward on his bed, puffing greedily on his cigarette. He tapped the ash into an empty coffee cup, and Eden automatically did the same.

"I'm going to die if you send me back to Algeria," he said.

There was no hint of a plea in his voice. His words were a statement, a simple transfer of information.

"Our assessment of the situation is different," Eden said.

Zakaria leaned his head against the wall.

"In that case, you're crazy."

Eden was sitting with her legs crossed as usual. The cigarette felt as familiar between her fingers as the weight of her handbag over her shoulder.

"We'll take the responsibility for our decision," she said.

"To protect national security?"

"Something like that."

She stubbed out her cigarette.

"Listen to me, Zakaria. Right now, several hundred people are being held hostage on a plane thirty thousand feet up in the air. We have reason to believe that the person who is behind all this is on board that plane. And we believe there is a risk that this will end in tragedy."

She looked out of the small window. It was just possible to sense the gray, overcast sky outside.

"And the really bad news as far as you're concerned is that it won't make any difference. You're going home, Zakaria. I was informed just an hour ago that the government will not revise its decision. It cannot and will not negotiate with terrorists. If you want to stay in Sweden, you'll have to offer us something better than a hostage scenario."

Zakaria burst out furiously: "How many times do I have to tell you, this is nothing to do with me!"

Eden shrugged.

"As I've already said, it doesn't make any difference. What I'm trying to explain to you is that if some close friend or relative of yours is sitting on that plane, then that person is risking death or a lengthy prison sentence for nothing. So you would be doing them a great service by cooperating with us."

"That's the second time you've mentioned cooperating," Zakaria said.

"And I shall carry on mentioning it," Eden said. "It's a good idea."

Zakaria dropped his cigarette into the coffee cup. "What's in it for me?"

"That's something we can discuss, of course. Have you any idea who might be behind this mess?"

Zakaria shook his head. "I haven't a clue. I don't know anyone who's capable of something like this. I don't move in that kind of circle."

"Oh, please," Eden said. "We've already dealt with all that. You've seen our surveillance footage, heard our phone tap material. You know that we know who your friends are."

Zakaria stared at Eden, then burst out laughing. But his eyes were full of sorrow.

"You are fucking unbelievable. You sit there with your stupid photograph and leap to conclusions that put every conspiracy theory about Elvis in the shade. You have nothing, *nothing* that proves I was involved in planning a terrorist attack with Hassan and Ellis."

"I think I have a great deal," Eden said. "Not only did you collect that package . . ."

"I've told you, I didn't know what was in it!"

". . . but your friend Ellis was kind enough to tell us that you were involved."

The look Zakaria gave her was poisonous.

"Just think about it," Eden said, leaning toward Zakaria. "You could make the difference between life and death for several hundred people. If you're really not like Ellis and Hassan, you shouldn't have any objections to helping us in our investigation. Who could be behind this?"

Zakaria scratched his head. He looked tired. When he glanced up and met Eden's gaze, she felt sorry for him for the first time.

"I don't know anything about this. Nothing at all."

And she believed him.

Shit.

She sat still for a little while longer. Her colleague didn't move either; he seemed to have accepted his role.

Zakaria took a deep breath. "You have to listen to me," he said, pleading with her for the first time. "I am not involved in any form of terrorism. I know you were able to link my phone to previous investigations, but as I've said a hundred times, that phone didn't belong to me back then."

Eden knew that had been his defense, but it didn't really change anything.

"But you wouldn't tell us whose phone it was, who you bought it from. And in court, you suddenly said that you didn't remember the name of the person who sold it to you, or when you bought it. In which case, surely you have to understand that your story isn't very convincing?"

Zakaria said nothing.

"I presume you still don't remember where you got your cell phone from?"

Eden straightened up. Of course he wasn't going to answer a

question like that; it was all lies. Zakaria had no credibility left on this particular point; he had changed his story about the phone so many times that it was impossible to take him seriously, whatever he said.

Still he didn't speak; clearly the pleading was over for now.

"No? Okay. You don't remember, and I don't have time to guess."

Eden got to her feet.

"Whenever you come up with the name of someone you think could be involved in the hijack, just tell the guard and he'll arrange for one of us to come down and see you."

She put the chair back in the corner.

"Thanks for the chat."

"Thanks for the cigarette."

"You're welcome," Eden said, and left the cell, with her colleague trailing behind her.

24

13:15

"I thought someone from Säpo was supposed to be coming with us?" Fredrika said as they were driving along Sankt Eriksgatan toward Torsgatan.

They were on their way to Solna, where Karim lived.

"Apparently, he's traveling in his own car," Alex replied.

They headed along Torsgatan toward the Solna Bridge and passed the Northern Station area, which had been transformed into a gigantic building site. There was talk of thousands of new homes and offices, but for most people the final outcome seemed very distant. So far there was no sign of any construction, just a whole lot of dust.

"What's your impression of Säpo?"

Fredrika couldn't help feeling curious. The people she had met at the two meetings she had attended so far had looked much as she had expected: well dressed and talented. Eden Lundell was different, however; she was too colorful, too obvious. There was nothing discreet about Eden's appearance, and yet it seemed to Fredrika that she didn't give away anything of herself.

"They've surprised me," Alex said. "I thought they'd be grayer, more boring."

"Why?"

"I've had several colleagues who've moved across to Säpo over the years, and none of them has looked exactly full of the joys of spring. Admittedly, they've all said they were happy in their new post, in spite of the fact that everything was so bloody secretive, but I could tell that things weren't right somehow. Eventually, one of them got drunk at a party and told me the truth—that he would never have stayed if the money hadn't been so good. Although he did seem to be doing a particularly boring job, and I'm sure a lot of them enjoy their work. Eden certainly seems to."

Fredrika shuddered. A boring job was the worst thing in the world. She also had friends and former colleagues who had moved over to Säpo, and had reached approximately the same conclusion as Alex. Not enough happened at Säpo, however bizarre that might sound, to make it worth applying for a post there.

Alex slowed down; they had arrived.

Karim Sassi lived in a house at the end of a terrace. Fredrika noticed that most of the windows lacked curtains, but there were large potted plants in several of them. She could see that the small garden at the front of the house was well cared for, even though autumn had come early and mercilessly killed off everything that was pretty and flourishing in the borders.

They got out and were walking toward the front door just as another car appeared and parked behind Alex. A tall, dark man got out, raising a hand in greeting.

"No one home?" he asked.

"We don't know yet," Alex replied.

"I can't see any lights," Fredrika said.

The house was in darkness. She pulled her jacket more tightly around her; why did it always have to be so cold?

Alex rang the bell, and the shrill sound made them all jump. No one came, and Alex tried again.

The guy from Säpo shook his head.

"There's no one in," he said. He went down the steps and started peering in through the windows.

Alex followed him, but Fredrika waited at the bottom of the steps. She was too short to be able to see in properly.

This was a very pleasant area. Quiet. Plenty of greenery. Spencer, who had spent the whole of his adult life living in houses, had begun to question their decision to live in an apartment in the city center. The children needed a garden, he said. But Fredrika thought it was more about Spencer's own needs, about his identity.

You can't fool me, my darling.

Fredrika would rather stick pins in her eyes than live outside the city.

"If you can find a house in the middle of town, then I'll move," she had said.

They hadn't really discussed the matter since then.

Alex and the guy from Säpo had finished inspecting the house. No one was home, it was as simple as that.

"I suppose the kids are in school and the wife is at work," Alex concluded.

But Fredrika had a feeling there was more to it. The house had a deserted air about it, and she wondered if the family had actually gone away.

"Don't we have a phone number for the wife?" she asked. "We could call her instead."

"We checked, but we couldn't find anything," Alex said. "That's why we had to waste time driving over here. We don't even have a landline number."

As they headed back toward the cars, they saw a young woman with a buggy approaching Karim's house. She looked worried, and slowed down before stopping a few yards away.

Alex went to meet her, and introduced himself and his colleagues. Fredrika thought he had a disarming manner when he spoke to people he didn't know, whereas she had a tendency to become more rigid, getting stuck in her professional role in a way that failed to inspire trust.

The woman told them she was a close friend of the Sassi family.

"I live over there," she said, pointing. "We usually keep an eye on the mail when one of us is away; I was just coming to empty their mailbox."

So they had gone away. Fredrika felt a stab of disappointment, and she could see that Alex felt the same. Their colleague from Säpo remained expressionless.

"Has something happened?" the woman asked. "With the police being here, I mean."

She looked even more worried as she went on.

"Well, I mean, of course something's happened; such a lot seems to have gone on, both yesterday and today. It's all very upsetting, what with this plane being hijacked and everything."

Strangely enough, she didn't seem to have made a connection between the police's visit to Karim's house and the plane she had just mentioned, Fredrika thought. If they were such good friends that they took care of each other's mail, then she must know that Karim was a pilot.

"We need to get hold of Karim's wife," Alex said. "It's nothing serious, we'd just like to ask her one or two questions. I don't suppose you have her contact details?"

The neighbor started rummaging in her handbag.

"Yes, I've got her cell phone number here. She usually keeps her phone switched on even when she's in Denmark."

"Denmark?"

"Her parents live there; she was born and raised in Copenhagen."

"I see. Will she be there for long?"

"They left this morning, and I think they're staying all week."

So they wouldn't be able to see her face-to-face for several days, but that didn't matter; they would have to call her instead.

We only have hours in any case.

Fredrika had to remind herself that this investigation had a time limit unlike any other. She pictured the plane as she silently worked out how much fuel was being used up every minute, every hour. How could they possibly fix this in time?

"You haven't noticed anything unusual in the neighborhood over the last few days?" Alex asked casually.

The woman shook her head.

"No, I can't say I have."

"Good," Alex said. "In that case, I'm sure everything's fine."

He made a note of the cell phone number and thanked the woman for her help.

As they were just about to walk away, she suddenly said, "Actually, there was something."

It was always the same. There was usually something to remember if you just thought about it.

"Tell me," Alex said.

"I don't know if this is of any interest to you, but when I came over to pick up the key this morning, I saw Karim's youngest daughter talking to a girl I didn't recognize."

"It wasn't another mother from somewhere around here?"

"No, I don't think so, but I have to confess that I can't really tell you much about what she looked like. She was leaning forward, facing away from me. Karim's daughter was playing in the front garden, and the door was open. This girl was standing on the pavement, talking to the child over the fence. I wouldn't have thought anything of it if the little girl hadn't gotten so upset."

Fredrika could see that Alex was digesting what he had heard. Could this have something to do with the investigation, or was it just an unrelated incident?

"Why did she get upset?"

"I don't know. She suddenly raised her voice—Karim's daughter, I mean. I didn't really hear what she said."

"Was Karim home at the time?"

"No, he'd already left for work."

"What happened next?"

"Karim's daughter ran back inside, and the girl walked away."

Fredrika pictured the scene. The child in the garden and the girl on the street. The child running indoors, the girl walking away. Perhaps the child had annoyed the girl? Thrown something at her as she was passing by?

A nonevent that had no place in the investigation.

The frustration was growing. Nothing would be more dangerous than if they started wasting time chasing ghosts.

25

13:16

Buster Hansson, the general director of Säpo, had two problems. The first involved the unfortunate plane hijacking, of course, which looked as though it was going to be a much more long-drawn-out saga than he had first thought. And the second problem involved Eden Lundell.

Eden Lundell.

What a bloody name. Apparently, Eden was a common Jewish girl's name, but Buster had never heard it before. The woman was as pretty as a picture, but she had a style and an attitude that had already started to get on Buster's nerves.

There had been some doubt about whether it was possible to appoint a Jewess as the head of counterterrorism in Sweden. What signals would it send when they were working with other countries' security services, particularly when it came to the Middle East? It had been decided at an early stage that Eden would attend as few meetings as possible. After all, she was the head of the unit, and as such would not normally be involved in working parties. Of course, it was impossible to keep Eden away from international contacts altogether. For example, within the CTG, the EU's intelligence group on counterterrorism, Eden had to play her part. Within the EU her background was less of an issue; the French might possibly raise an eyebrow, but Buster couldn't have cared less about that.

What he did care about was the fact that the head of MI5 had requested a meeting with Buster in order to discuss one of his "latest recruits." He had called Buster personally, and had said little over the phone. Eden's name had not been mentioned during the conversation, but Buster was still convinced that she was the person his British colleague wanted to talk about.

The call from MI5 had been surprising in more ways than one. First of all, that kind of direct contact at the highest level was unusual, and secondly it had been made very clear that the information the head of MI5 intended to pass on to Buster must be kept within as limited a circle as possible, and that he therefore didn't want anyone else at their meeting. Thirdly, he had asked for their conversation to be off the record.

Admittedly, Buster hadn't been head of Säpo for very long, but he found it difficult to imagine that this kind of arrangement was normal. He glanced at his watch; it was almost time. He had asked his secretary to make room in his calendar for a "special activity" and had booked one of the less popular conference rooms. Buster Hansson leaned back on his chair. He didn't like the sound of this. Not one little bit.

· · ·

Fifteen minutes after the agreed time, the head of MI5 called from his cell phone.

"My apologies," he said. "Where can we meet?"

Buster took the elevator down to the ground floor to meet his visitor at the entrance to Polhemsgatan 30. A former general director of Säpo had taken the initiative and commissioned the construction of a new HQ, which would be ready in 2013. It was much needed. The organization had outgrown its current accommodation long ago. The move would bring a fresh start, and would be worthy of a national security service.

Buster led the head of MI5 to the dullest and most discreet conference room. Ugly but functional. His colleague looked around.

"I don't think I've been in here before," he said.

I don't suppose you have, Buster thought.

"Coffee? Tea? Or would you prefer water?"

Buster's wife had always said he wasn't a good host, and she was probably right. He couldn't find any snacks in the small pantry adjoining the conference room; his visitor said yes to coffee and no to everything else.

They sat down facing one another. Buster wanted to get this over with as quickly as possible, but his counterpart didn't appear to be in any hurry. He looked a little unsure of himself, as if he was having last-minute doubts about the wisdom of requesting this meeting.

"You've been busy lately," he said eventually.

"You could say that," Buster replied. "But things have turned out well."

"I must congratulate you on the recent convictions; I had a feeling that Operation Paradise would be a great success. Just as several other European operations were at the same time."

"Thanks."

The Englishman finished his coffee and pushed away his cup.

"Eden Lundell," he said.

"Yes?"

"Your latest recruit. A real shooting star, and another reason to offer my congratulations."

For some reason, this comment didn't seem quite as sincere as the first, but Buster chose not to say anything.

"As I'm sure you know, Eden worked for us for a number of years."

"I'm aware of that. I also recall that we contacted you to ask for references. You had nothing but positive things to say about her."

"Absolutely," the head of MI5 agreed. "Eden was one of the very best; she could have gone far with us if she'd stayed."

"But she chose to move to Sweden with her husband," Buster said.

He knew Eden's story by heart. She was married to Mikael Lundell, a pastor who had worked for the Swedish church in London. That was how they had gotten to know one another and become a couple. Mikael's post in London was temporary; sooner or later he would have to return home to Sweden. It made no difference to Eden; she had been born in Stockholm to a British mother who was also Jewish. Her father was Swedish and a Christian, at least on paper. If Buster remembered rightly, he had converted when he moved to Tel Aviv with Eden's mother. The family had lived in Stockholm first of all, then London. They had moved to Israel some years ago.

"A wise decision," the head of MI5 said, referring to Eden's move to Stockholm with Mikael. "She's not the kind of woman who could cope with a long-distance relationship."

Buster had no idea whether that was true or not. His impression of Eden was that she was driven and full of grit and determination.

"But there were also other reasons why Eden left the UK," the head of MI5 said.

"Oh?"

"She was fired."

The Englishman's expression was inscrutable.

"I'm sorry?" Buster said.

"She was fired."

The anger came from nowhere. Who the hell did this British toffee-nosed snob think he was, asking for an informal meeting, then coming out with information that Buster should have been given several months ago?

"We discovered by chance that she had been in contact with one of Mossad's nondeclared information officers in London. At first, we thought she had been the subject of a recruitment attempt, but then we realized that they knew one another. Once we started mapping her activities, we also realized that she had been in touch with another Mossad operative. And then, of course, there were all those trips to Israel."

Buster had a drink of water. He swallowed hard. He didn't know what to say.

"But her parents live in Israel."

"Correct. But we followed her once, and she met up with her parents on only one occasion, over dinner. The rest of the time she was on her own or with Israelis we were unable to identify."

"Perhaps they were just friends of hers?" Buster could hear how unconvincing that sounded. "So you fired her because you thought she was a double agent—you thought she was working for Mossad?" he added.

"Yes."

"And you failed to pass on this information to us?"

"We had no choice, and for that we apologize. We couldn't risk a situation where Eden might find out that we know about her double game."

"But if you fired her, surely she must have realized that you knew?"

"I don't think so. She was actually fired for another mistake she made in the course of duty. It was serious enough to lead to her dismissal."

"And what was that about?"

"I'm afraid I can't tell you."

"But you would still call her one of the very best?"

"Yes."

Buster tried to process the information.

"Let me summarize what you've just said. Eden has been seen with suspected Mossad operatives. She has traveled to Israel on a number of occasions for reasons other than to spend time with her parents. She has not been confronted with this information, and has therefore not been given the opportunity to explain herself. So it could all be perfectly innocent, but we don't know that."

The head of MI5 smiled for the first time since the meeting had begun.

"That could be true, of course. But personally, I'm convinced that Eden is playing a double game, which makes her a dangerous colleague."

"And what do you expect me to do now? I have to pass on what you've told me."

"Of course. Hopefully, you will be more successful than we were."

"Didn't you give it to your counterespionage team?"

"Yes, but there wasn't enough evidence. It would have cost too much to confront Eden with what we had until we could work out why Mossad would want to recruit one of our agents."

An organization like Mossad really didn't need any particular reason, Buster thought. In his opinion, their Israeli colleagues were among the most ruthless in the world. Ruthless, but good.

The Englishman scratched his head.

"We didn't really give Eden much thought once she'd left us.

After all, it was three years ago. She came to work for the police here in Sweden, didn't she?"

Buster responded with a quiet yes. Eden Lundell had been regarded as one of the most strategic recruits for several decades within the police service. With a degree in international law from Cambridge and her background in MI5, she was an absolute dream. In addition she was a gifted linguist, and was fluent in Russian, French, and Italian as well as English and Swedish. She had also completed two years' military service in the British army. Buster knew that every intelligence service in Sweden had tried to recruit Eden when she arrived in Stockholm, but she had made it very clear that she wasn't interested. She was tired of that closed, secretive world; she wanted to work within a more open environment. She had spent some time as a consultant within the Defense Department but had found the work extremely boring. She had then moved to the National Bureau of Investigation, where she reorganized virtually every aspect of intelligence gathering before she left.

Buster recalled what the head of the NCU had said when he was asked to provide a reference:

"Eden is no ordinary woman—she's a force of nature. And I'll never forgive you if you recruit her."

They hadn't spoken since.

The mere thought that a suspected Israeli agent had been the architect behind the most sweeping reorganization of the National Bureau of Investigation in twenty years . . . Buster could taste the fear. This was the worst possible news.

"Anyway," the head of MI5 said. "I've done what I came to do. I don't care what you do with the information. And let me reiterate how sorry I am that I didn't say anything before. I'm actually in Stockholm on another matter, but when I heard about the hijacking I realized that we couldn't keep quiet any longer."

He took a folder out of his briefcase and handed it to Buster.

"Pictures of Eden's contacts and the information we have on them. Not a great deal, as you can see."

"How have these Israeli operatives been behaving since Eden left the UK? Have they approached any of your other employees?"

"Not as far as we're aware. And believe me, we've been keeping a close eye on them since we found out about them."

The fact that the Israelis hadn't turned to anyone else in Eden's absence worried Buster. Did that mean she was irreplaceable?

Oh, Eden, my expectations of you were never anything less than unreasonable.

"One of the operatives returned to Israel a year ago," the Englishman said. "We didn't hear anything of him after that. Until yesterday."

Buster gave a start.

"Yesterday?"

"We received new information indicating that he had returned to Europe."

The head of MI5 took the folder out of Buster's hands, opened it, and removed a photograph, which he placed on the table.

"Efraim Kiel. Forty-five years old, lived in the UK for four years, and prior to that in Spain for three years."

"And now?"

"Now it's exactly six hours since he entered Sweden. Who knows what he's doing here?"

26

13:45

Neither of them spoke on the way back to Säpo. Eden Lundell walked fast, thinking about the cell phone that Zakaria Khelifi insisted had belonged to someone else when Säpo linked it to their inquiries.

If the story about the phone was his alibi, why didn't he just give them the name of the previous owner? Was it because he was lying, or because he was guilty, regardless of who the phone had belonged to?

Eden went straight to her office. There was a risk, or a chance, that Zakaria was both lying and telling the truth. He could be lying when he said that he didn't remember when he had bought the phone or from whom, but he could be telling the truth when he said that it hadn't belonged to him during 2009 and 2010. In which case, he was lying to protect someone. Someone he either loved or feared to the extent that he was prepared to risk imprisonment or deportation to Algeria rather than give that person's name to the police. Or perhaps it was someone he sympathized with for other reasons.

Eden opened Zakaria's file on the computer. Operation Paradise had reached its final phase by the time she took up her post; all she knew about it was what she had read or been told. According to Zakaria, he had parents and two sisters back in Algeria. A Swedish girlfriend in Stockholm—Maria. Eden remembered seeing the transcript of an interview with her. She had seemed sensible, and had answered the questions truthfully. But they had only been together for a year. Eden didn't believe the phone had belonged to her, although she couldn't be sure. Apart from his family in Algeria and his girlfriend in Sweden, there were few people who were close to Zakaria. He had two friends that he often hung out with; neither of them had ever been the subject of an investigation by Säpo. Could one of them have bought the phone, or sold it to Zakaria?

Eden twirled a strand of hair around her finger.

They had so little time.

In her mind's eye she could see that bloody plane zooming through the sky, passing over oceans and continents, constantly moving on but with nowhere to go.

She called Sebastian.

"Can you get someone to check the phone traffic to and from Zakaria's cell phone again?"

"You mean one of my so-called Arabists?"

Eden suppressed a sigh. She couldn't cope with an argument right now; she just didn't have the patience.

"I'm really sorry I said that."

"Glad to hear it."

And that was the end of that. For the time being, at least.

"We need lists of all his calls," she said. "Check the calls he made, and whether it looks as if there's a change at some point, and he starts calling completely different people."

She could hear Sebastian tapping away on his keyboard.

"You believe him? You believe he didn't own the phone before 2011, as he kept on saying?"

Eden's eyes were itching. Bloody contact lenses.

"I don't know," she said truthfully. "I just want to make sure we haven't missed something. Even if it turns out that the phone did belong to someone else, which I don't believe, I'm still not sure that would necessarily make Zakaria a better person."

She ended the call and turned her attention back to the file in front of her.

If Zakaria's phone had been someone else's at the time when Säpo linked it to their preliminary investigations, then they had to come up with a way of tracking down that person, even if Zakaria refused to give them a name. And—more importantly—they had to find out if he or she had anything to do with the hijacking.

• • •

From not having set foot in Police HQ for over a year, in the space of a few hours, Fredrika Bergman had managed to acquire a workstation within both Säpo and the National Bureau of Investigation. When she and Alex got back from Solna, they went straight up to the counterterrorism unit, where they found Eden alone in her office.

"I heard what happened," she said. "It's lucky the neighbor happened to be passing just when you were there."

"We spoke to Karim's wife on the way back," Alex said. "She's staying with her parents in Copenhagen. She was shocked when she heard about the hijacking. She's coming back to Stockholm tonight, if possible."

"What had he said to her?" Eden asked.

"Nothing, really. Everything was perfectly normal this morning, according to his wife. Karim didn't seem stressed or anxious. We didn't mention the fact that we think he might be involved; we just asked her a few questions in general terms."

"And how has he seemed recently? Has she noticed anything different about him?"

"No, not that she could remember."

"What about the girl on the street, the one the neighbor saw? Did Karim's wife know her?"

"She'd heard about her from her daughter, of course, but she didn't know who she was. She didn't see her. To be honest, I don't think the girl on the street is of any interest to us."

Eden gazed at someone who happened to be passing by outside the glass cube. There were far too many things that didn't seem to be of any interest.

"He refuses to contemplate an emergency landing. And he's been in contact with one of the phones that was used to make a bomb threat yesterday," she summarized. "I wouldn't want to be sitting on that plane with Karim as the pilot."

Fredrika glanced at Alex. He was pale, and she knew what was haunting him. The idea of losing his son when he had already lost his wife must be unbearable. She suppressed the impulse to reach out and touch him.

"I'm so sorry," Eden said, having realized that what she had just said wasn't particularly helpful. "That was clumsy of me."

"It's fine," Alex said, but anyone could see that it wasn't.

"Have we spoken to the airline about the possibility of giving Karim direct orders?" Fredrika asked.

"Yes," Eden said. "In a case like this, it's unusual to force the captain into a course of action that he hasn't chosen for himself. He and he alone is regarded as the best person to decide what to do with the plane in the event of a hijacking."

"But if the captain himself is responsible for the hijacking, then surely that should put things in a different light?" Alex said.

"Sounds reasonable," Eden agreed. "But if the captain is the hijacker, then I think it's foolish to believe that he's going to take orders from the police."

Fredrika could see that Alex was starting to get agitated.

"We have to get in touch with Erik," he said. "He's the copilot, and he's just as capable as Karim of landing the plane."

"And how's that going to happen?" Eden said. "Is he going to knock Karim down first? I know the copilot's role is to take over the plane if the captain shows signs of unreliability, but I don't think that rule applies in this case. Karim is not going to hand over to Erik voluntarily."

She got up and came around the desk to join Alex and Fredrika. In her high heels she was taller than Alex.

"We've got to be clever now," she said. "Because we don't have much time. At the moment we haven't got enough evidence to call Erik secretly and ask him to put Karim out of action and land the plane himself. That would look like complete insanity if it got out, particularly if it all went wrong."

If it all went wrong.

If everyone on board died.

If they had to inform all those desperate people who were calling the police right now, wanting to know if their relatives were on that plane . . . if they had to inform all those people that the plane had gone down, and that their loved ones were at the bottom of the Atlantic.

Fredrika shuddered.

"If Karim is involved, it would explain something else," she said. "How the note got into the toilet."

"That occurred to me as well," Eden said.

They were interrupted by Sebastian, who yanked the door open without knocking.

"That was quick," Eden said. "Have you already finished working through the list of calls?"

"What list?" Alex wanted to know.

Eden waved away his question.

"It's about the bomb threats that were made yesterday," Sebastian said.

Fredrika could see that Eden was disappointed, and wondered what she had been hoping for. She thought she would have enjoyed working with Sebastian; he seemed calmer than Eden, less spiky and more amenable.

"You know our guys went out to Arlanda to look for the four phones that were used to make the bomb threats?"

"The phones someone had forgotten to switch off, which meant they could still be located," Eden said with a nod.

"Airport security helped them to search. It took seconds. They found all four in a garbage can in the multistory garage next to the domestic flights terminal."

Alex leaned back cautiously against one of the glass walls.

"And the voice distorter?"

"No sign. But we've got the phones, and forensics have secured fingerprints. The phones were new; they found prints belonging to just one person, and on only one of the phones."

"One person's prints on one phone?"

"That's right."

"And do we have a match?"

"No. But judging by the size of the prints, it seems unlikely that they were made by a woman."

Eden burst out laughing.

"I don't want to be rude, but I'm afraid no one was expecting you to find anything other than a man's prints on those phones!"

Was that true? Fredrika wondered. From a statistical point of view, a man was more likely than a woman to be behind serious violent crime, but that didn't mean it couldn't be a woman. She remembered the case she and Alex had worked on a few years ago: a priest and his wife had been murdered, and nothing had turned out to be the way they had first thought.

"We have to find out if they're Karim Sassi's prints," Eden said.

"How do we do that?"

"Call the prosecutor. We need permission to go into their house and lift prints for comparison."

Fredrika suddenly thought of something.

"His car is at the airport. His wife mentioned it."

"Excellent. Call her and get the registration number—forget the house for now."

"I don't think so."

Alex's voice sounded deeper than usual.

"We don't have time to put together some jigsaw puzzle and play guessing games," he said. "I suggest we go to the prosecutor and get a search warrant. I want to go back to Solna and turn Karim Sassi's house upside down. We need a breakthrough, and we need it now."

For a second, Fredrika was afraid that Eden would launch a counterattack, put Alex in his place for taking the lead in her office. But she didn't, because she knew he was right.

"Let's do that," she said. "Let's ask for a search warrant right now."

27

14:30

Alex headed back to Solna while Fredrika stayed behind at Säpo. Eden had found her a workstation in the open-plan office. She would only need it for one day. No longer. One day—after that the plane would have run out of fuel and the drama in the skies would be over.

Fredrika felt a knot of fear in her stomach. Hundreds of people trapped on board a plane that wasn't allowed to land. A plane that could plunge to earth or be destroyed by a bomb in the baggage hold.

Their options were limited. They could go for an emergency landing. Meet the hijackers' demands. Or find whoever was behind the threat, thus freeing the passengers and crew. They hadn't managed to come up with any alternative courses of action. And if it turned out that Karim Sassi was involved, they had no options at all, because in that case it wouldn't matter if they identified his fellow perpetrators on the ground; Karim Sassi would still have the power to determine the fate of Flight 573.

Unless they could get Alex's son, Erik, to intervene. It was only a question of time before they had to decide whether that was how they were going to save the plane. If Karim Sassi was involved, then Fredrika was more convinced than ever that there was no bomb on board. It had no obvious function if the captain was part of the plot.

She sat down at the computer to read through some of the newspaper articles. The PM's press conference had turned into a fiasco. The journalists refused to accept that he had no answers to their questions, but Fredrika thought he had at least managed to convey the most important point: the Swedish government did not negotiate with terrorists. They would not be reviewing the decision to revoke

Zakaria Khelifi's residence permit. If the hijackers wanted to have a discussion about this, they were welcome to get in touch, but so far no one had claimed responsibility for the threat.

Fredrika moved on to the American press to check out their angle on the story. It was certainly just as big on the other side of the pond, no doubt about it. Of the 437 passengers on board the plane, 151 were apparently US citizens. This was news to Fredrika; the US authorities must have leaked the figure. Twenty-two of these belonged to a junior soccer team who had traveled to Sweden to play a friendly against Bromma Boys' team.

The US citizens came from no fewer than ten states. The issue would occupy many members of Congress during the day. Fredrika could well imagine the political pressure that was rapidly building up in Washington, which would inevitably lead to loud demands for someone to *do something*. A favorite expression in the US. If someone died, if kids were getting too fat, if gas became too expensive, the cry went up: *do something*. Anything. At any price. The ability to take action had a strange intrinsic value in the USA.

On the other hand, that same ability had an equally strange lack of value in Sweden. Fredrika had never made any secret of the fact that she loved the USA and the American success ethic, the belief that anything was possible. She often found it difficult to swallow the European and Swedish smugness, the blind faith in their own social model. The year she had spent in New York hadn't diminished her enthusiasm; the Americans had a fire within them, and it created energy.

There were certain dates that people would always remember. Fredrika's parents and their friends knew exactly where they were and what they were doing on the day they heard that President Kennedy had been shot, and the same applied to the day they found out that Olof Palme had been assassinated.

And then, of course, there was 9/11. Fredrika knew exactly where she had been on that day: on holiday with Spencer. They had spent the whole afternoon in the hotel, unable to tear themselves away from the TV. The images of the Twin Towers collapsing were etched on her memory and could never be erased. Those majestic buildings came down at a speed that was reminiscent of a Hollywood film, with the proviso that Hollywood probably wouldn't have made quite such a good job of it.

The fear Fredrika had felt afterward had little to do with the terrorists behind the attack, and a great deal to do with the fact that the US president at the time was so ill-equipped to lead a country, in every possible respect. Who knew what he might do, what crazy ideas might pass through that man's mind?

The answer to that question came almost immediately. First, Afghanistan. Then, Iraq. And so many outrages in the hunt for the terrorists along the way that it was no longer possible to count them. It was a war that could not be won, and millions of people all over the world paid the price for the insanity of it all.

Fredrika called her boss and passed on the latest developments in the investigation. She was careful to play down the possibility of Karim's involvement; it would be better to tell him when they knew exactly what the situation was. She hoped that Alex and his colleagues would be discreet when they went into Karim's house; if the news that the police were searching Karim Sassi's house spread around the neighborhood, it wouldn't be long before everyone knew the police suspected that the captain was involved, which would make everything much more difficult. On a positive note, the press hadn't been told which specific flight was under threat, even if they had worked out that there weren't very many to choose from.

The hijacking was like nothing else Fredrika had ever worked on. It had been staged in a way which worried her and made her think. There were so many coincidences. For example, Karim Sassi just happened to be flying to New York the day after Säpo brought in Zakaria Khelifi. Was that by chance, or had he requested that particular flight?

She went over to Eden to ask whether they had checked with Karim's employer.

"According to SAS, the flight to New York was part of Karim's normal schedule; he's known about it for at least two months," Eden said.

"So he hasn't swapped flights or shifts with anyone?"

"Apparently not. I'm starting to wonder whether the esteemed Mr. Karim Sassi has been planning this for a long time."

"But that doesn't seem likely," Fredrika said. "The government only made a decision on Zakaria Khelifi yesterday."

"That's true. However, the date of the court hearing has been known since the beginning of August, which means it wasn't difficult to work out roughly when the verdict would be delivered. Perhaps whoever was so committed to Khelifi's case would have taken similar action if he had been convicted. The fact that it's happened as a result of the government's decision instead might not matter to whoever is behind this."

Fredrika thought for a moment. On the one hand, everything to do with the hijack seemed very carefully planned, while on the other, there was something impulsive about it.

"How are things looking in the mass media?" Eden asked.

"Terrible. We need to confirm which flight is involved very soon."

"I know, I know."

Fredrika sighed.

"It's not that the reports are lacking in detail. Whoever leaked the story seems to have kept nothing back apart from the flight number and departure time. Everything else is out there—the demands, the fact that the note was taped to the wall in one of the toilets—"

Eden stopped what she was doing.

"What did you say?"

"I just said the media reports were very detailed."

"No, you said the note that was found in the toilet was taped to the wall."

Fredrika nodded.

"You don't understand," Eden said. "I haven't heard anyone mention that the note was taped to the wall. Have you?"

Fredrika thought about it, and slowly realized what she had just said.

"No."

Eden leaped to her feet and ran past Fredrika.

"Come on." She shot through the open-plan office at lightning speed.

"Where did you see it?"

"It's in several papers."

Eden found Sebastian and told him what Fredrika had read. He had no idea that the note had allegedly been taped to the toilet wall.

"Which newspaper had the story first?" Eden asked.

"None of them. I think TT carried the news before anyone else."

"I'll call SAS and see if they knew about this."

Eden took out her cell phone and disappeared, leaving Fredrika with Sebastian as he clicked through various newspapers on his computer.

"Same everywhere," he said. "Doesn't make sense."

Eden came back; Fredrika could tell that she had received worrying news.

"SAS were just as surprised as we were. They called the plane and received confirmation that the story is true; the flight attendant found the note taped to the toilet wall. But at no point in their communication with the control tower has the crew said anything beyond the fact that it was found in the toilet."

She fell silent as the import of what she was saying sank in: the only person who knew that the note had been taped to the wall was on board the plane.

"Which means we know that the person who leaked the story to the media did not work for the police, the government, or the airport authority," Eden concluded.

"Are we saying that someone called from the plane and tipped off TT? That can't be right," Sebastian said.

"I agree, but let's check it out," Eden said. "Because if it wasn't someone on the plane, then it was someone on the ground. Which in turn means that that person is alarmingly well informed about details they couldn't possibly know unless they had been in contact with a member of the crew, or were actually involved in putting the note in place."

28

14:45

There were so many rules that suddenly seemed unimportant. Speed limits, for example. Alex Recht couldn't ever remember driving as fast as he did on the way to Solna.

Could this be his hundredth house search? Or more? He wasn't sure, but one thing he did know was that it was never pleasant, walking into the house of a person he didn't know and turning the place upside down. With as little fuss as possible, he went around to see the neighbor he had spoken to earlier and borrowed the key. Later, he would call Karim's wife and tell her what they had done so that she wouldn't think they'd had burglars.

Alex and four officers from Säpo quickly went through the house, carefully and methodically. Wardrobes and chests of drawers, desk and kitchen. All the computers in the house were removed and would be sent to Kungsholmen, where the technicians were waiting for them. With practiced hands Alex worked his way through one room after another. He didn't know what he was looking for, just that when he saw it he would know immediately if it felt right.

He was alone in Karim Sassi's bedroom. He looked under the bed and inside the wardrobes. Nothing. He yanked back the duvet and felt all over the sheets and mattress. Nothing.

"Have you found anything?" one of the Säpo officers shouted from downstairs.

"Not a thing."

He sat down on the bed. Looked around the room. It was cozy. Not smart or modern, just cozy. Soft colors for the curtains and cushions, toning in with the pale yellow walls. Almost like a summer cottage. A small number of pictures adorned the walls, and there were several family photos on a shelf.

Alex stood up to take a closer look. He recognized both Karim and his wife. The children were younger than he had thought. He picked up one of the framed photographs and held it for a moment. Several years ago, he and Fredrika had gone out to a deserted summerhouse on the island of Ekerö, searching for clues in a case that had proved to be one of the most complex they had ever faced. Framed family photographs had been a major element in solving the mystery.

Karim Sassi was also a mystery. Alex was becoming more and more convinced that he was a part of the problem rather than the solution, but for the life of him he couldn't understand what could have motivated Karim to do what he was doing now.

Alex ran his fingers around the frame. Removed the back and took out the photograph. Nothing; no clues. He grabbed another photograph and repeated the same procedure. No joy. There was no stopping him now, he had to check every single one. But his efforts were in vain. Feeling slightly embarrassed, he put the photographs back on the shelf where he had found them and went downstairs.

"How's it going?" he asked one of his colleagues. A police officer was a police officer and always a colleague. Even if he did work for Säpo.

"We've found fuck-all."

Alex glanced over the floor and walls of the living room, his expression grim. There was nothing for them here. Feeling frustrated he went into the hallway, through the kitchen, and ended up back in the living room.

The family seemed to enjoy reading. Large bookcases ran from floor to ceiling, covering two entire walls. Two officers were busy going through them, checking to see if there was anything useful behind the long rows of books.

"No secret compartment?" Alex joked.

"No."

He went over to a section that the others hadn't gotten around to yet. He pulled out a few of the books, peered behind them, put them back. He carried on systematically searching the rest of the shelf in the same way.

Suddenly he noticed a book that was lying on top of a row. It could be no more than a coincidence, but Alex no longer believed in that kind of thing. He picked it up and read the small gold lettering:

"*King Arthur—Idylls of the King* by Alfred Lord Tennyson."

The book weighed next to nothing, and he could feel his hands trembling.

Tennyson.

No way was this a coincidence.

Cautiously, he opened it and flicked through the first few pages. And discovered that someone had cut out a square hole inside the book. The most classic secret compartment of all. Alex looked with curiosity at what someone had hidden.

A photograph. It was obviously several years old, but Alex recognized both men. One was Karim Sassi, and he was with a man whose picture Alex had seen in the papers.

Zakaria Khelifi.

• • •

A small part of Eden Lundell was dubious as she headed back to the custody block to see Zakaria Khelifi, this time with a copy of the photograph that Alex had sent her from his phone. However, she was mostly sure she was doing the right thing. The fact that Flight 573 was speeding toward destruction simplified a decision that would otherwise have been difficult to make.

Zakaria was sitting on his bed reading when Eden walked in. She had the photograph in her hand, and no cigarettes this time. She didn't bother pulling up a chair, but simply placed the picture on Zakaria's knee.

"I can see that the man on the left is you," she said. "Who's the other guy?"

Zakaria picked it up and examined it carefully.

"Where did you find this?"

He sounded bewildered, as if he couldn't work out what he was looking at.

"That's irrelevant," Eden said. "Answer the question. Who is the man on the right?"

She knew it was Karim Sassi, but she wanted to hear Zakaria say it.

"It was such a long time ago," he said.

He spoke quietly, unable to tear his eyes away from the picture.

"When was it taken?"

"It must have been 2002. I was here that summer."

Eden couldn't remember hearing that Zakaria had been in Sweden before he entered the country seeking asylum.

"You were here in 2002?"

Zakaria would have been barely twenty back then.

He nodded.

"I was granted a visa to visit my uncle. He was working at an Ericsson factory in Kista."

That could be checked, but Eden had no reason to disbelieve what Zakaria said.

"How long were you here?"

"Eight weeks. My parents wanted me to have a different kind of summer holiday that year."

He passed the picture back to Eden, as if he wanted to get rid of it.

"Who is he?" she said.

Zakaria picked up the book he had put aside when Eden came in.

"His name is Karim."

"Surname?"

"Sassi, I think."

"How did you meet?"

"His mother worked at the Ericsson factory, too."

Eden decided to sit down after all.

"Have you had any contact with this man while you've been living in Sweden?"

Zakaria realized that Eden was going nowhere, and closed his book.

"No, I haven't seen him since 2002."

"And you're sure of that?"

Zakaria looked annoyed, and opened the book again.

"Of course I am."

"You don't know what this Karim Sassi is doing nowadays?"

"No idea. When we met that summer he used to say he wanted to be a pilot, but that's just the kind of thing you say, isn't it? I mean, who hasn't wanted to be a pilot at some stage?"

Me, Eden thought. I wanted to run a circus.

Mind you, she had been ten years old at the time, not twenty. She was going to become the manager of an enormous circus and take it all over Europe. Her heart suddenly felt hollow. The life she lived was a long way from the circus.

She handed the picture back to Zakaria.

"This is really, really important. Zakaria, I have to know: are you absolutely certain that you haven't seen Karim Sassi since you moved to Sweden?"

She wanted him to say no, to change his mind and start talking. She wanted a breakthrough, and she wanted it now. But Zakaria refused to deliver. He wouldn't even look at her.

"I know who I see and who I don't see. I haven't seen Karim Sassi since that summer all those years ago."

A summer when Zakaria had stayed with his uncle, who knew Karim's mother. That was something they would have to look into, but Eden was worried that it wouldn't be enough. Time was passing so quickly, and she could feel the ground trembling beneath her feet. They couldn't just carry on digging, they had to start taking action. Somehow.

She left Zakaria and went back to the counterterrorism unit. Karim knew Zakaria. They didn't really need to know any more. Karim Sassi, the captain of Flight 573, was implicated in the hijacking.

The worst possible scenario.

But there was more to come. Dennis caught up with her.

"We've found Karim Sassi's fingerprints on one of the phones," he said.

There. They didn't need any more on Sassi. The fact that he had been involved in the previous day's bomb threats was now beyond all reasonable doubt. If he had been on the ground, Eden would have had him brought in for questioning.

But that wasn't an option.

"Call the CIA," she said. "I want to know how far they've gotten."

29

Washington, DC, 08:45

The sun was shining down on the capital city that was regarded as one of the most influential in the world. Bruce Johnson took Green from the CIA along with him and went to see his boss, who had finally deigned to turn up. The chief looked less than pleased to see Green, but Bruce took no notice. They had to discuss the information that had been passed on to Bruce just hours ago, turning the whole investigation on its head before it had even gotten under way properly. There were indications that Captain Karim Sassi, the commander of Flight 573, was working with the terrorists. It couldn't get much worse.

Bruce had been completely floored as he tried to understand what the captain's involvement might mean. He loathed Green for spending so long sitting in the meeting before coming out with the information that so fundamentally upended every other theory they had been working on. Why hadn't Green told him about Sassi as soon as he walked through the door, for fuck's sake?

"So Karim Sassi is working with the terrorists?" the chief said, having found it extremely difficult to assimilate the information the first time he heard it.

"According to our sources, that seems to be the case. Karim Sassi is part of the group that implemented this plan, and personally placed the note containing the bomb threat on the plane. And Sassi has been given a supplementary order that is not stated in the note," Green said.

"Which is?"

"If the Swedish and American governments do not accede to the hijackers' demands, Sassi will crash the plane into the Capitol Building. Here in Washington."

Bruce's mouth went dry. He could see that the chief had lost his composure for a moment.

"Therefore, it is pointless to try to work out who is behind this mess, which the Swedes seem to believe is the way forward. It won't make any difference. The key player is sitting at the controls, and he's not going to land that plane unless he hears that the hijackers' demands have been met. Which isn't going to happen, as we know."

Where had they gotten this information from?

"Why hasn't the FBI been told this?"

"We're telling you now. And it changes things, wouldn't you agree?"

"To say the least. But I'm asking you again—why didn't you pass this on before?"

It was Green's turn to look annoyed.

"Because there was no reason to do so."

But Bruce's boss had more questions, and Bruce knew that he was worried. This new information meant that Flight 573 was no longer regarded as part of an armed attack on the United States, and therefore became entirely the responsibility of the CIA and the US Department of Defense.

The FBI would be marginalized.

"What's your plan of action?" Bruce's boss asked Green.

"It's very simple. The plane will not be allowed to land on US soil under any circumstances. When it gets close to US airspace we will contact the captain and tell him to change course. If he fails to comply, we will ask our supreme commander to approve the necessary measures."

The supreme commander was the president of the United States.

"You're escalating the issue to the White House? Why?"

"I'm happy to answer that question, but this stays between us until further notice. We will inform the Swedes as and when necessary."

He paused and waited for Bruce's boss to accept this condition, which he did.

The Swedes would be kept out of the picture for the time being.

"Okay," Green said. "We're elevating this to the White House so that we can do what was not done on 9/11. We have to prevent another attack on American interests."

Bruce's boss looked puzzled.

"And how are you going to do that?" he said in a voice that exuded weariness.

Green didn't reply at first.

Nor did he need to, because in the silence that followed, Bruce realized how the CIA were planning to deal with Flight 573.

"It's never going to arrive, is it?" he said.

Green's face took on the determined expression Bruce had seen so often in those who regarded their desk job as a theater of war.

"Exactly," he said. "It will never reach either Washington or New York. Not if the president does what we want, and believe me, he will."

30

Flight 573

They were flying across Canada now. Earlier, they had passed over Iceland and Greenland. Erik Recht had always wanted to visit Iceland, to bathe in its warm springs and ride Icelandic horses. Claudia would love it. She always enjoyed traveling abroad, discovering the world.

They still had so much to see.

The story of their hijacked plane had evidently been leaked to the media; the police had informed them of this fact. That changed things. Attempting an emergency landing no longer seemed like such a good idea, now that the press were following the plane's journey to New York. That was another thing Erik had tried to bring up with Karim: they ought to change course, stay away from US airspace. The Americans had a different view on the best way to deal with terrorists. There was a serious risk that the plane would get an extremely brutal reception if they ended up within the jurisdiction of the American authorities.

Erik excused himself and left the cockpit to go to the toilet. He had to get away from Karim for a while, try to gather his thoughts in peace. He also wanted to try to get hold of his father, ask for advice. Without Karim overhearing the conversation.

Outside the cockpit, he ran straight into Fatima, the flight attendant who had found the note.

"We have a problem," she said, moving toward the door to indicate that she wanted to discuss the matter in the cockpit.

"We have a number of problems," Erik said, gently putting his hand under her arm. "Come with me."

The toilets in first class were empty. Erik hesitated for a second, then opened one of the doors and went inside, pulling Fatima along with him. She looked as if she was about to protest, but then gave in.

"What's this about?" she said when Erik had closed and locked the door.

These ridiculous little toilets. Erik had tried to have sex on a plane only once, when he and Claudia flew to Sweden for the first time. He had been so nervous about going home that when Claudia had giggled and suggested that they should try joining the mile-high club, he had immediately gotten to his feet and headed for the toilets, with Claudia trailing along behind him. The cubicle was tiny and smelly, and it took almost ten minutes before they found a position that worked. By that time the flight attendant had noticed that the toilet had been engaged for some time, and started knocking on the door. It had been really bad sex, but an entertaining experience on the whole. And it had made Erik considerably less nervous.

Fatima was not Claudia. They were far too close together inside the cubicle. Erik thought about climbing onto the toilet seat, but then he would bang his head on the ceiling. Instead, they remained standing by the sink, chest to chest.

"You first," Erik said.

"Several crew members have noticed that some of the passengers are fiddling with their cell phones. When we point out that they're not allowed to make calls or use the Internet on board, they say they're just listening to music. But of course we already know that many passengers simply disregard those rules, and they're doing the same thing today."

"So you're afraid one of them will use their phone and find out what's happened?"

"Yes."

"It's not a problem, you know that. At thirty thousand feet, the phones connect to a hundred networks at the same time, which is why they don't work. Only the satellite phones in first-class seats would work at this altitude, but no one ever really uses those anyway. Too expensive, poor connection quality, and on an older plane like this, some of them might not even work anymore."

Admittedly, there was always a margin of error in that particular argument, as Erik well knew. There would be chaos if the news that the plane had been hijacked spread among the passengers. On the other hand, Erik was convinced that the flight was going to be considerably longer than the passengers were expecting, so they were going to have to make some kind of announcement anyway in order to explain the delay. And inform everyone that they might not arrive at all. He made a decision.

"Keep moving up and down the aisles, keep having a go at people. Remind them of the regulations, tell them it's dangerous to have their phones switched on."

Fatima looked uneasy.

"We'll deal with that problem if and when it arises," Erik said.

"Okay. But you said we had a number of problems?"

Yes, Erik thought. Our captain has gone crazy.

He searched for the words that would best express what he was thinking.

"Have you noticed anything odd about Karim?"

"No, I don't think so. Then again, I've hardly spoken to him since we took off. We bumped into one another outside the toilets just before we started boarding the passengers; he seemed a bit stressed, but he was perfectly pleasant."

Erik raised his eyebrows.

"You bumped into him outside the toilets? Before we let the passengers on board?"

"Yes, what's strange about that? I expect he's like everyone else—he has to go to the toilet now and again."

Erik couldn't hold back any longer.

"*Was it the same toilet where you found the note containing the bomb threat?*"

He had to stop himself from shaking Fatima.

"What the hell are you suggesting?"

Fatima moved back a step, away from Erik, and bumped into the door. She put her hand on the lock.

"I'm not suggesting anything—just answer the question."

He had frightened her, and that wasn't good. But he had to know, because during the past hour, Erik had become increasingly con-

vinced that Karim could be involved in what had happened. He had
to know whether Karim was the person who had left that note in the
toilet.

"I don't know."

He could see that she was telling the truth.

"I just assumed he'd been to the toilet, since that was where we
met. I don't know which one it was, but it doesn't matter. You can't
seriously believe that Karim, of all people, would be a part of all this?
He's a *good* person, Erik!"

Erik leaned back against the wall. He was so bloody tired. Already.

"I don't know," he said. "I just don't know. But he's not himself.
He's not behaving rationally, he's making the wrong decisions."

Fatima moved a step closer to Erik; she was no longer so afraid
of him.

"For God's sake, that doesn't necessarily mean that he has anything to do with the hijacking! Something could have happened at
home, or whatever. Something that's stressing him out, making him
anxious, and this terrible situation just makes him feel worse."

Erik heard what she said, but her words had no effect.

"We know one another, Karim and I," he said. "We hang out together. Our families spend time together. And I know there's something else on his mind."

Fatima reached out and stroked Erik's arm.

"In that case, you need to talk to him. Tell him there's no room
for personal problems, if he can't see that for himself. Talk to him.
Tell him what's on your mind."

Tell him what's on your mind. How would that work? If Karim
was involved, he was hardly going to want to discuss it with Erik.

In fact, several things were bothering Erik.

"He requested extra fuel before we took off. What if he did that
because he knew what was going to happen, knew we were going to
need more flying hours?"

"You mean he made up the fact that there's going to be bad
weather in New York? Oh, come on, Erik!"

Erik felt a sudden spurt of anger.

"Of course he didn't fucking make it up, we get weather reports! What concerns me is the amount of extra fuel he asked for. Five extra flying hours is far more than we usually request."

Fatima knew that, too, but she simply shook her head. "You're imagining things," she said. "That's all."

"I'm going to call my father," Erik said. "From one of the empty seats in first class—I can use the phone in the armrest. He's a police officer, and apparently he's working on the hijacking."

Fatima grabbed his arm.

"You're going to ring your father and tell him you think the captain of the plane is involved in the bomb threat? Erik, do you realize what you're saying? You'll be putting Karim in a really difficult position, if you do that. You'll be putting *all* of us in a really difficult position. Dangerous, in fact."

Perhaps she was right. Perhaps he was being too hasty. The toilet suddenly felt very small; he had to get out of there.

"Speak to Karim first," Fatima said. "Then you can decide whether you still want to call your father."

Erik thought for a moment, then made his decision. He would do as she said.

31

Stockholm, 15:45

The hours were passing quickly. Too quickly. And so far they had no idea how they were going to prevent the disaster that was moving closer and closer by the minute. By this stage no one really believed that the problem would be solved before the plane reached New York. Instead they were all thanking the weather gods for the predicted storm, and Karim Sassi's decision to request extra fuel. Fredrika Bergman wondered what he would have done if it hadn't been for the grim forecast. Would he still have asked for more fuel, or would he have simply taken off with only enough for the estimated flight time?

Fredrika, Alex, and Eden were on their way to a Säpo conference room where they were due to meet CIA agents. Fredrika had several male friends who would have sold their own children for the opportunity of meeting someone who worked for the CIA, but she wasn't quite so easily impressed. The current image of the organization was far too tainted by the reports of outrages which had followed in the wake of the war on terror.

The Americans were already waiting. Inconspicuous men whom Fredrika would barely have noticed on the street. On closer inspection, they all looked very much alike. Same height, same hair color, same haircut. When they shook hands, she noticed that they did so with the same level of firmness. Strong, but not so firm that it became unpleasant.

Eden hadn't been very keen on the idea of allowing Fredrika and Alex to attend the meeting, because they would be discussing sensitive intelligence. The Americans might feel inhibited if outsiders came along. It was decided that Fredrika and Alex would be there for the first part of the meeting while Karim Sassi was under consideration. Then they would have to leave, because Eden and the CIA agents would be moving on to another matter that Eden wasn't prepared to go into.

They had only just sat down when one of the CIA agents said, "Good to put a face to the name, Eden. Up to now, we've only spoken on the phone."

Eden smiled and said that it was good to meet him, too.

"Didn't you used to work in the UK? For the British Intelligence Service?"

Eden's smile became rather strained, but she didn't react as strongly as Fredrika might have done.

"That's right."

"I think we spoke back then, too."

"Perhaps we did."

"We're very familiar with your name, let me tell you."

It could have been meant as a compliment, but Fredrika could see that it wasn't. She noticed that Eden had reached the same conclusion. Slowly she put down her notepad and stared at the man who had spoken to her.

It looked as if she was trying to tell him something. *Not now.*

Eden won, because one of the other Americans took over and thanked Säpo for calling the meeting. They were all curious to hear what the Swedish investigation had come up with so far.

"We're happy to share everything we have, but with the proviso that the exchange is mutual, of course."

"No problem."

After two seconds Fredrika realized that there was nothing straightforward about this transaction. Intelligence was a world of its own. Nowhere else was it so true that knowledge was power. And knowledge was something to be bargained over.

However, Eden refused to play second fiddle, and the discussions were tough. Gradually she revealed what they knew about Karim Sassi, while at the same time she tried to milk the Americans for the information they had.

The CIA were very interested in Sassi.

"Have you spoken to his mother and Zakaria Khelifi's uncle about the time when Khelifi knew Sassi back in 2002?" they asked Eden after she had told them about her interview with Zakaria.

"Not yet."

Fredrika knew that they had gotten hold of both of them, and would be questioning them after the meeting with the CIA.

"Is Karim Sassi the only person on the plane that came up as a match on your database?"

To Fredrika's surprise, Eden said, "No."

Fredrika could see that this was news to Alex as well.

"Just before we came down here, I was told that we had a match on two other names," Eden said.

"Passengers or crew?"

"Passengers. Two Swedish citizens who figured in an investigation a few years ago. We've heard nothing of them since, and the case is closed. Therefore, we don't regard these matches as being of interest."

"We'd like to know what the investigation was about, and we'd also like the names of the two passengers."

"No," Eden said.

"No?"

"Tell me what you have instead."

The CIA agents looked at one another, and the one on the far right started talking.

"We also believe that Karim Sassi is the person on board who could be linked to the hijacking."

"And how did you reach that conclusion?"

"Unfortunately, I can't tell you that."

"You have information that suggests Karim Sassi is a terrorist, but you can't tell me where it came from?"

"That's the problem. It's not our own information, which means there are issues when it comes to passing it on."

The third-country rule. A security service must be certain that any information it decided to share would not be passed on. Although she didn't have any proof, Fredrika suspected there were many occasions on which this rule was disregarded.

"I understand that," Eden said. "But as we have so little time in this case, I expect you to go back to whoever you are working with, and to request permission to share that information with us. Anything else is unacceptable."

The man who had just spoken sank back in his seat. Fredrika felt naive as she realized that the whole thing was nothing more than a charade. They had already decided to pass on all the information they had, as long as they got something in exchange.

"So what about those two passengers you mentioned, the ones whose names had come up in a preliminary investigation?"

Eden got to her feet; she had probably seen through the Americans' tactics long before Fredrika.

"It's obvious we're not going to get any further with this. Thank you for taking the time to come here."

Her maneuver rattled the CIA agents.

"Hey, hang on a minute . . ."

"No, you hang on."

Fredrika would never have guessed that Eden was capable of shouting the way she did now. A woman who raised her voice could easily come across as hysterical or coarse, but that definitely didn't apply to Eden, who in spite of her femininity looked mentally stronger than anyone else in the room.

"Four hundred Swedish and American citizens are trapped on a plane with a captain who is very probably involved in a plot that could kill them all. If that's not enough to secure full cooperation, then I have no fucking intention of sitting here bargaining with you."

She remained standing for a full thirty seconds after she had finished speaking, then one of the Americans broke the silence.

"I apologize for the misunderstanding which seems to have arisen. Naturally, we will share with you all the information we can. Perhaps you'd like to sit down again?"

He waved his hand in a gesture that was more pleading than authoritative.

Eden sat down. Two strands of hair fell down over her face, but she didn't bother to brush them aside.

"The information comes from Germany."

"Germany?"

Eden couldn't hide her surprise.

"We received it from the Germans last week."

Time stood still in the room. Pink blotches appeared on Eden's cheeks.

"*Last week?* Are you saying you knew this was going to happen a week ago? And you didn't tell us?"

Now it was the CIA agent's turn to get angry.

"Of course not! What the fuck are you suggesting? Last week, we were told that a plane would be hijacked, that a bomb threat would be left on a plane that was already in the air. It would take off from a European airport, and there would be American citizens on board. According to the original intelligence, demands would be made only of the US government. Tennyson Cottage was explicitly mentioned. And the captain would be involved, and would be given special instructions."

"But neither you nor the Germans thought it would be a good idea to pass this on to us or other European security services?"

Eden sounded shocked.

"Since the whole thing appeared to be directed at American interests, we saw no reason to alert you at that point. Besides which, the hijacking wasn't supposed to happen until later—November, according to the informer. And the message came via email."

"Via email?"

"Exactly, and it was anonymous. So as you can understand, it wasn't given a particularly high priority, either by us or the Germans."

"Didn't they try to trace the email?"

"Of course, but it was impossible. They couldn't identify the IP number of the computer that had been used to send the message."

These damned, indispensable computers. Eden couldn't imagine a world without them, but at the same time she couldn't help wishing it wasn't so easy for criminals to use them for their own ends.

The American sighed wearily.

"To be honest, if Tennyson Cottage hadn't been mentioned, we wouldn't have taken any notice of this at all. We can't focus on every threat that circulates in the miasma of intelligence."

Eden nodded in agreement.

"But what about Karim Sassi? You said the email mentioned him, too."

"He wasn't named, it just said that the pilot would be a part of the plot. When we spoke to the Germans this morning, they said they'd had no further messages from whoever sent the first one."

Fredrika assumed that the person who had sent the message must have had considerable insight into the planned hijacking; otherwise, he or she wouldn't have had such detailed knowledge. However, she and Alex were outside the ongoing discussion, so she didn't say anything.

The CIA agent went on:

"There was one more thing."

"Which is?"

"Apparently, the pilot has been given an order which was not included in the note found on the plane. He must not change course, but must carry on heading for American airspace. If or when he is informed that the two governments refuse to meet the demands of the hijackers, he will crash the plane into the Capitol Building in Washington, DC."

Anything but that, Fredrika thought.

It was over.

That was the only conclusion she could reach. There was no way the Americans would allow such a thing to happen if they could prevent it. But how would they do it?

It was Eden who put the question into words.

"And what plans do you have to avoid that particular scenario?"

"We'll come back to that at a later stage, if you don't mind."

Later. As if they had all the time in the world.

Eden tried another question.

"What's your assessment of the reliability of this information?"

"It's hard to say, but given the accuracy of so much of the rest of the message, it's reasonable to assume that this is also on the nail. In any case it would be extremely difficult to refrain from acting on it."

Another nod from Eden, but no more questions.

She made a few rapid notes, then turned to Alex and Fredrika.

"Thank you, I think that concludes the part of the meeting that involves you."

She spoke in English to ensure that their American guests understood. Alex and Fredrika immediately got to their feet, like schoolchildren, thanked everyone for allowing them to attend, and left the room.

· · ·

"What a strange world they operate in," Alex said when they were back in the corridor leading to Police HQ.

Fredrika couldn't help but agree. People in dark suits traveling all over the globe to exchange fragmented information that would then be put together to form a whole, and would eventually make the world a safer place. If everything worked as it should. Which it rarely seemed to do.

"I don't think they put all their cards on the table," she said.

"Me neither. I suppose that's part of the strategy, keeping a spare card up your sleeve in case you end up having to negotiate."

"But what's the point in this case?" Fredrika wondered. "I can't see that they have anything whatsoever to gain by behaving like that, when we're facing a situation that for obvious reasons has to be resolved within the next few hours."

She glanced at Alex and saw that his face had lost its color.

"It will all work out," she said, placing a hand on his back.

Although there are no guarantees—there never are.

He stopped at the door leading to the National Bureau of Investigation's offices.

"I don't know what I'll do if I lose Erik as well. First Lena and now Erik—I just couldn't bear it."

She stood behind him, frozen in midmovement. There was nothing she could say, but she tried anyway.

"We'll bring the plane down safely, Alex."

"*But how?* We have to contact Erik, get him to take over. My God, if Karim is even considering crashing straight into the Capitol, he's even crazier than any of us thought."

"Don't think like that. You have to believe this will all work out. We'll do what you said and contact Erik. But not right now. Not in the middle of the investigation."

Alex turned around.

"Fredrika, it's a matter of hours. What are we supposed to investigate that could buy us more time?"

"I'm not sure, but we keep on finding out new things that move us forward. Go and talk to Karim's mother. Ask her about the book you found and Karim's relationship with Khelifi. Then maybe we can get in touch with Erik."

But how are we going to do that? she asked herself. Erik was sitting less than three feet away from Karim; how could they speak to him without Karim knowing? And how could Erik take command of the plane? Was he supposed to kill Karim with his bare hands?

Alex didn't say anything; he simply yanked open the door and trudged along to his office.

"Are you coming with me to see Karim's mother?" he asked Fredrika.

"I don't know; I really ought to stay here so that the government office can get hold of me if necessary."

"What the hell for? They can reach you on your cell phone just as easily."

"I thought someone from Säpo was supposed to be going with you?"

"I couldn't give a shit," Alex said. "I'll call them before we go and tell them we're on our way. If they want to come they can use their own car."

Fredrika went into her temporary office and picked up her jacket. It was becoming increasingly difficult to dispute the view that Karim Sassi was part of the terrorist plot behind the bomb threat to Flight 573. What Fredrika couldn't work out was why.

Why would a man like Karim Sassi get behind the controls of a plane full of passengers and head straight for disaster? And what did he have to do with Zakaria Khelifi and a place called Tennyson Cottage?

There had to be a connection somewhere that they hadn't yet found.

And there had to be someone who could tell them where they should look.

32

16:15

Eden Lundell was more worried than she was prepared to admit. How could they have ended up in a situation like this? Everything would have been so much easier if only they had had an opponent to negotiate with, to reason with. And Zakaria Khelifi appeared to be oblivious to everything that had happened.

GD had told her that the groundwork had already been done when she took over an operation connected with several other cases of preparing to commit an act of terrorism all over Europe. They had broken up a terrorist cell in Stockholm, thus preventing a major attack that would have claimed many lives. The evidence was secured and the suspects were arrested. The prosecutor had no doubt that convictions would follow, and he was quite right.

Except in the case of Zakaria Khelifi, and now Eden was starting to wonder what exactly was going on there. Just before she went to meet the Americans, Sebastian had spoken to her. They had gone through the lists of calls once again, and it looked as if Zakaria could well be telling the truth when he said that the phone had belonged to someone else. The contacts were largely different during the period when Zakaria insisted the phone had not been his; Sebastian had even found a date which constituted a kind of dividing line.

"If the phone did belong to someone else, then we can at least assume that they knew one another. They have several mutual acquaintances," he said.

This business of the phone had been difficult right from the start. Zakaria used several cell phones: one for work, one personal, one that belonged to his girlfriend.

Eden wanted to reexamine all their previous assumptions about Zakaria, simply to reassure herself that the case against him was solid. The evidence against him had been rather more sparse, and of course this became all too clear when the verdicts were delivered. If they had gotten it wrong, then Eden wanted to know before the day was over. By which she meant before midnight.

But right now she was sitting in a meeting with the CIA. She had intended to ask them some questions about Tennyson Cottage, but that could wait. First of all, she wanted to hear more about the German connection, then she would bring up Zakaria Khelifi once more.

"You said that a German identified Karim."

"No, we said that an email had been sent to the German intelligence service."

Same difference. There was a connection with Germany, and that country had cropped up several times on Zakaria's phone during the period when it might not have been his.

"Do you think that the group behind this, or elements of that group, could be in Germany?"

"We don't know. But obviously, Germany is of interest under the circumstances, even if we can't see a direct link to the rest of the case at this stage."

Eden told them about Zakaria's German contacts; the CIA agents listened and made notes.

"I'll get in touch with the Germans straight after this meeting," Eden said.

"Of course. Unless they get hold of you first. Now that the hijacking is public knowledge, they will probably want to talk to you about the email."

Eden thought so, too. One of the Americans summarized:

"So an unknown person has stated that Karim is involved in the hijacking. Karim has met Zakaria Khelifi in the past. Zakaria Khelifi has been in contact with individuals in Germany."

Eden moved on:

"And Tennyson Cottage? How does that fit into all this?"

It happened so fast that she almost missed it, but she just noticed the men on the other side of the table exchange glances before replying.

"We don't know."

"No? No one with a link to Sweden—or Germany—has been held there?"

"No."

Closed faces told Eden that she wasn't going to get any further with Tennyson Cottage.

"Tell us more about Zakaria Khelifi," one of the Americans said.

But Eden had reached her limit when it came to things she was prepared to discuss with the CIA. Karim Sassi was obviously of interest to both sides, but if they weren't going to talk about Tennyson Cottage, then Eden wasn't going to talk about Zakaria. Then she remembered that she had one more card to play.

"I mentioned that we found a photograph of Zakaria Khelifi and Karim Sassi at Karim's house."

The men opposite straightened up, eager to listen carefully to what she had to say.

"Did I tell you that we found it inside a book by Alfred Lord Tennyson?"

That hit the mark. The Americans were lost for words, and that was all Eden needed to know. She definitely had something they wanted.

"But I'm sure that's just a bizarre coincidence, isn't it?"

The fish was hooked; all she had to do was reel it in.

"I doubt it," one of the Americans said.

"Really?"

She played it cool, leaning back on her chair with her legs crossed. She might have been imagining things, but she thought her questions about Tennyson were making them nervous.

What is it you're not telling me?

"I swear we have nothing that explains why Tennyson Cottage has cropped up in the middle of this mess."

She didn't believe him. Once, and only once, Eden had failed to expose a liar when she was standing face-to-face with him. It had been an expensive mistake, and one she would not be making again. Ever.

"You don't have anything on Karim Sassi that you're keeping quiet about? Something that explains his interest in Tennyson?"

"No, no, and no again. What about you? Did you find anything related to Tennyson Cottage?"

"No."

She would have lied if necessary. She was a better player than them. One of the best in her field, in fact. Her boss back in the UK had told her that this particular quality would take her further than any other.

He had been right. It had saved her marriage, among other things.

Have you met someone else, Eden? Have you?

You're the only one for me, Mikael. I swear.

They had reached an impasse. If the CIA wanted to know more, Eden would be happy to meet them at any time of the day or night, as long as they promised to share information of their own. She thought she had made her point, loud and clear.

She brought the meeting to an end and took out her phone to call someone to escort her guests out of the building. But first she turned to her American colleagues.

"I need lists of personal details," she said.

"What lists?"

"Lists of those who have been held in Tennyson Cottage. I want to run them against our Swedish records to see if I can find a link to Khelifi."

She knew they would refuse but wanted to ask the question anyway.

"You must realize that's an unreasonable request."

"Then at least I want the names of those who've been released—surely there must be a few?"

"Once again, you have to trust us. There is no link between Khelifi and Tennyson Cottage."

Eden didn't reply. It was obvious that there had to be some common denominator between Khelifi and Tennyson. The only question was whether they would find it in time to avert a catastrophe. Someone was sitting on the truth, and that person had to start talking. Time was running out fast.

33

16:18

The media coverage was fragmented. It was as if the journalists didn't know what to focus on. The previous day's bomb threats. The hijacking. Or the parliamentary debate on immigration and integration. Buster Hansson, general director of Säpo, couldn't help thinking that if it hadn't been for the guilty verdicts in the terrorist cases, along with everything else that had happened in the last two days, the debate wouldn't have attracted half as much attention. He had avoided watching the live broadcast from the chamber. The far right had a following wind. They were becoming increasingly daring in the way they spoke and in the position they adopted, and were making increasingly bold demands when it came to the reduction, if not the complete cessation, of immigration. And then, of course, they referred to the acts of terrorism that had shaken Scandinavia, and asked: "Is this the way we want things to be?"

Buster Hansson had always been surprised that people couldn't count. He had made this discovery at an early stage in his career. Immigrants were indisputably overrepresented in the crime statistics. There was, in fact, a clear correlation between being part of a less privileged stratum of society, and being overrepresented in the crime statistics. Immigrants who lived in the Östermalm district of Stockholm featured no more heavily than people who had not been born overseas, or whose parents fell into that category. Therefore, the problem was not that immigrants were immigrants, but that regardless of an immigrant's background, as soon as they arrived in Sweden, they were banished to the periphery of society. And once they ended up there, it was easier to go astray in life.

During his time as secretary of state, Buster had given countless lectures on the subject. Those on the periphery of society were more likely to turn to crime than those who lived a more comfortable life. And since immigrants were more overrepresented than Swedes in the lowest stratum of society, then . . . Buster didn't have the strength to follow the chain of thought through to its conclusion; he had been there far too often, without ever coming up with anything new. There could be only one conclusion—immigration itself was not harmful. What was harmful was failing to give people any hope for the future.

However, he was by no means as certain that the international terrorism that had now reached Scandinavia could be explained in the same way. The men who had recently been convicted were young and driven, and had made a living running their own businesses. They earned good money, and had lived in Sweden all their lives. Their parents had been part of the group of Swedes born overseas who had made a great success of their life in Sweden. So the frustration must come from a different source other than the usual criminality.

Eden Lundell had often asked where all this anger came from, and Buster thought it was a good question. How come those with their origins in the Levant, for example, wanted to commit acts of terrorism in Europe because European soldiers were fighting in Afghanistan? And even if you accepted that as an explanation, how could anyone convince themselves that it was okay to carry out a suicide bombing on a street full of civilians who have never set foot in Afghanistan, and who probably didn't even have an opinion on the subject?

To Buster it was important not to mix up understanding an incident and justifying it. If he didn't have the courage to comprehend what might explain a particular action, then he was doomed to fail in his task.

Ensuring the safety of Sweden was not the same as keeping Sweden Swedish. Whatever the hell "Swedish" was supposed to mean.

His musings were interrupted by the arrival of Henrik Theander, head of counterespionage.

"You said it was urgent," Henrik said as he sat down.

Buster hesitated briefly, then decided he had no choice—he couldn't just ignore what he had been told about Eden by MI5. He quickly summarized the information he had received from his British colleague.

"Bloody hell," Henrik said when Buster had finished.

Buster could see that Henrik was badly shaken. It was obvious that something had to be done. But what?

"What do we really think about all this?" Henrik Theander asked. "Do we believe Eden is an Israeli spy?"

Buster spread his arms wide.

"She was always a bit too good to be true, wasn't she?"

"What's the situation with this Mossad agent who has entered the country?"

"I'd like you to put him under surveillance right away," Buster said. "He's staying at the Diplomat Hotel. If he approaches Eden, we need to know about it."

"No problem."

"And I want you to take over this case with immediate effect," Buster said.

It was hard to think of a worse time to expose the head of the counterterrorism unit as a spy for a foreign power. On the other hand, it was a good thing that Eden had been working for Säpo for only a few months.

Henrik gave a humorless laugh.

"That must be some kind of record," he said. "I mean, Eden has only just started."

"I don't understand what the Brits were thinking," Buster said. "Letting us recruit a potentially lethal woman to one of the most sensitive posts in the country. That's seriously poor judgment."

"True, but we don't know if their assumptions are correct."

"No, and we have to cling onto that, and hope she isn't a spy. Hope the Brits got rid of their strongest card for no reason."

"But didn't you say that she was actually fired for some other reason, some mistake she made?"

"Exactly," Buster said. "But he refused to tell me anything whatsoever about that."

He had decided to inform no one except the head of counterespionage. One or two investigators within the unit would probably have to be brought in, but Buster was happy to leave that up to Henrik.

"Should we pull her out right away? As a preventative measure?"

"I've thought about that, but Eden would get suspicious if we did something like that. When it comes down to it she prefers working in the field, close to the action. She actually made that a condition when we recruited her; she wasn't prepared to sit in meetings and deal with admin all the time."

"Which is also worth noting," Henrik said. "In the light of what we've just been told, I'm not at all happy that she wants to be 'close to the action.'"

Buster was supposed to be able to handle this kind of problem with a high degree of professionalism. But to be honest, he wasn't at all sure what to do. He almost wished the Brits hadn't told him anything about it.

"By the way, how's it going with the hijacking?" Henrik asked. "Are you getting anywhere?"

Buster suppressed a sigh.

"Eden's running the whole thing. She and Sebastian are due to report back to me as soon as they know more."

Henrik crossed his legs.

"In that case, let's hope Eden can sort this out."

"Absolutely," Buster replied. "Anything other than total success is unthinkable."

Deep down, he was wondering whether in this particular respect it was an advantage or a disadvantage if the head of counterterrorism was a Mossad agent.

34

16:20

Not so very long ago, Fredrika Bergman's civilian background had made it difficult for her to fit in with the police. Her colleagues had questioned the fact that she lacked police training, and suggested that she didn't have the necessary qualities to bring to the table. She had called their bluff and won the game. The idea that an investigator had to look a certain way was no more than a myth. The *assignment* itself was the important thing. The assignment had to come first. If only people would follow that basic principle, then everything would be so much easier.

Sitting in the car with Alex on the way to see Karim Sassi's mother, Fredrika thought that Eden Lundell and her colleagues were facing an undertaking which was unimaginably more difficult.

Protecting national security.

Every failure led to an outcry. The Swedish people demanded zero tolerance; no crime that seriously threatened the country's safety should be committed under any circumstances. The thought of what it would mean if the same demands were made of the section of the police authority where she had worked made her head spin.

No bank robberies.

No rapes.

No murders.

A Technicolor dream. Completely unattainable. A total absence of criminality would require such an oppressive police force that no one would want to go on living.

After the terrorist attack in Stockholm in 2010, nothing had frightened Fredrika more than the immediate calls for Säpo and the government to take decisive action against terrorism.

Decisive action.

With his back to the wall, the general director of Säpo had tried to get people to understand what they were asking for. A controlled society where everything that was written on Facebook was scrutinized, and where the private sphere virtually ceased to exist. A society in which Säpo would need to increase by several thousand percent in order to have the capacity to deal with all the information coming in. Fredrika thought he had won that debate; he had done a good job. People agreed with him—no thank you, they didn't want a controlled society.

Someone had mentioned the miasma of intelligence. After only a few hours working with Säpo, Fredrika thought she was beginning to understand what that meant. All those little snippets of information flying around, just waiting to be picked up by a security or intelligence service, which in turn wanted to know whether that particular piece of information could be the one that made the difference, the one that turned a defeat into a success.

"What do we know about Karim Sassi's mother?" Alex said, making Fredrika jump. "Apart from the fact that she worked at an Ericsson factory."

Fredrika opened her bag and took out a sheet of paper that she had been given by a Säpo agent before they left.

"Born and raised in Kalmar, moved to Stockholm at the age of twenty. Married young, to Karim's father, who then disappeared from the picture. She worked at the Ericsson factory in Kista until 2005, when she remarried and became a housewife in Östermalm."

"A social climber," Alex said.

"Looks that way."

A housewife—who would want to be a housewife? Fredrika couldn't understand it at all. She had been brought up by a hard-working career woman, and had never even considered the idea of not working. The very idea of putting herself in a situation where she would be dependent on someone else made Fredrika feel ill. Love didn't mean owning another person, or being owned. Not even the archconservative Spencer would come up with such a bizarre notion.

Alex glanced at Fredrika. "Don't look so bloody judgmental," he said. "You never know why people make the choices they do."

Kudos to Alex for saying people rather than women. It strengthened his argument, and made Fredrika think along different lines.

"Karim has no brothers or sisters," she said.

"No step-siblings either?"

"No."

"Grandparents?"

"His maternal grandparents are dead. I don't know anything about his paternal grandparents; they don't live in Sweden."

Alex parked outside the building where Karim's mother lived, not far from the Royal Mews. Fredrika got out of the car and inhaled the thin autumn air. She and Spencer used to see each other in secret in Östermalm, over all those years when their relationship had to remain clandestine. Sometimes she missed those days so much that it actually hurt. Their impossible love affair had been like a parallel reality into which Fredrika could disappear when life was difficult or boring. A fun interlude in an everyday existence which often seemed ridiculously dreary and gray. Everything had been so taboo, so forbidden. Not only was Spencer married, but he was also the same age as her parents, and had been her tutor at the university. Nothing was more attractive than something that went against all the rules.

Fredrika loved to think back to their initial flirting. It had been so innocent; she could never have imagined that anything would come of it. Who would be brave enough to take the first step, dare to be the person who had perhaps misjudged the whole situation? Fredrika thought she was the one, but Spencer always said that he was. It didn't really matter; it was fifteen years ago, and now they were married and had two children together.

Who is going to be my little adventure now? Fredrika wondered.

• • •

Alex led the way inside. The elevator took them up to Karim Sassi's mother's apartment on the fifth floor, and they rang the doorbell.

"Shouldn't we wait for Säpo?" Fredrika said, remembering that that was what she had agreed on with them when she was given the brief summary about Karim's mother.

"They're on their way," Alex replied just as the door opened.

Karim's mother, Marina Fager, was quite different from the way Fredrika had pictured her. She was small and thin, unlike her tall, broad-shouldered son. They had called to tell her they were coming, but hadn't wanted to say why over the phone.

"We'll wait until we get there," Alex had decided.

But Fredrika could see that Marina Fager already knew why they were there.

"I spoke to Karim's wife," she said, leading the way into the kitchen where she had coffee waiting for them.

She spread her hands wide; the despair etched on her face was painful to see.

"I don't know what to say," she whispered. "I really don't know what to say."

"Let's sit down," Alex said.

The kitchen was rustic in style, nothing like all those modern kitchens with shiny worktops and cupboard doors that could be found all over Stockholm. This was a homey kitchen, a kitchen in which to gather friends and family, not a kitchen in which to offer the police a cup of coffee when your son had hijacked a jumbo jet.

"Säpo called as well," Marina said. "They wouldn't tell me anything either; they just said they wanted me to stay at home because they wanted to talk to me."

Fredrika opened her mouth to speak, but at that moment the doorbell rang. Karim's mother leaped up from her chair and hurried into the hallway.

"We should have come together," Fredrika said. "This looks so disorganized."

"I'm not so sure about that," Alex said. "It's important that she realizes we belong to different organizations with different assignments to complete."

There it was again. The assignment.

Karim's mother returned with two Säpo officers. Fredrika recognized one of them; it was the same man who had been there when they made their first visit to Karim's house. She still didn't know his name, but presumed he had introduced himself to Marina when she opened the door. The other was a woman Fredrika hadn't seen before. They said a brief hello, then sat down at the oval kitchen table.

"How could my Karim end up in a hostage situation?" Marina said. "It just doesn't make any sense. I don't know what I'll do if anything happens to him."

"We understand that," the Säpo officer said. His voice was so calm. Fredrika watched as he almost imperceptibly leaned forward across the table, thus getting closer to Karim's mother.

"Have you seen your son lately?" he asked.

Marina nodded. "Of course. We see each other all the time—we're family, after all."

"Have you noticed anything particular recently? For example, would you say that Karim has been stressed, anything like that?"

"No, I can't say I have."

"He hasn't withdrawn? Kept himself to himself?"

"No." Marina frowned. "Why are you asking all these questions about Karim? He's the captain of the plane, not the hijacker."

As she finished speaking, she caught Alex's eye across the table. Her hand flew to her mouth in horror.

"You're crazy! Karim would never . . ."

Alex held up his hand to calm her.

"We're following up on several leads, but at the moment it does look as if Karim could be involved. We don't know exactly how or why, and that's what we're trying to find out."

The Säpo officer joined in.

"Exactly. We're not certain, but we think that Karim may be mixed up in all this. And if he isn't, then of course it's vital that we find out as quickly as possible."

Karim's mother nodded; she had settled down a little.

"Of course."

"Zakaria Khelifi," Alex said. "Do you recognize the name?"

"Of course I do," Marina said sadly. "He spent some time with Karim one summer many years ago—2001 or 2002, I think."

"How did they become friends?"

"I was working at the Ericsson factory in Kista back then, and so was Zakaria's uncle. He knew I had a son roughly the same age as his nephew, so when Zakaria came over to Sweden that summer, I asked Karim to take him out a few times. I don't know if I'd call them friends; as far as I know they haven't been in touch since then."

"Do you know what Zakaria is doing these days?" Alex said.

Marina turned and reached for a newspaper that was lying on the window ledge.

"Isn't he the same Zakaria who's going to be deported?" she said, pointing to an article on the front page.

"Indeed he is," Fredrika said. "What did you think when you read about Zakaria in the press?"

Marina put the paper down.

"The same as I thought when you turned up and started telling me you think my Karim is a terrorist. It doesn't make sense. I don't know what has happened in Zakaria's life since he was here in 2002, but back then he was a really nice boy. Hardworking and conscientious—a good boy."

"Whoever has hijacked the plane is demanding the release of Zakaria Khelifi," Fredrika said.

"And that's why you think Karim is behind this? Because they hung out together one summer ten years ago?"

It was impossible to answer that question without giving away more information than necessary, so Marina got no reply.

However, Fredrika silently ran through everything that pointed to Karim's involvement.

His fingerprints on the phone that had been used to make a bomb threat the previous afternoon.

The fact that he knew Zakaria Khelifi.

The book by Tennyson in which the photograph of Karim and Zakaria had been hidden.

The note found in the toilet on the plane after takeoff.

The doubts came from nowhere, hitting Fredrika like a blow to the solar plexus.

We're missing something here. Something really important.

It was all too simple. Everything was being served up to them on a silver platter.

"Tennyson," Fredrika said in a tone so brusque that the Säpo officer turned to look at her.

Marina Fager looked blank.

"Alfred Lord Tennyson, the poet. Do you know if he had a special significance for Karim?"

"I've never even heard of him."

"He wrote the poem 'Ring Out, Wild Bells'—the one they read out at Skansen every New Year's Eve."

Marina shrugged. "Is he mixed up in this, too?"

Fredrika suppressed a laugh. The first of the day; it would have been nice to let it out.

"No. He's been dead for a long time."

The Säpo officer had one last question.

"Where can we get hold of Karim's father?"

"I haven't a clue. Neither Karim nor I have heard from him for the last twenty years."

"According to the records, he emigrated."

"That could well be the case. Nothing that man does would surprise me."

Marina rested her elbows on the table, demanding everyone's attention.

"I didn't think you were interested in men like Karim. In a way, I'm glad I was wrong."

Fredrika had no idea what she was talking about, and she could see that her colleague from Säpo was in the same boat.

"What do you mean?" he said.

"I thought you only went after Islamists, that you assumed all terrorists were Muslims. But that's not the case."

The guy from Säpo looked as if he didn't know what to say, how to react.

"Of course not," he managed eventually.

But it was obvious that he didn't understand what this had to do with Karim Sassi, and Marina went on:

"I presume you know that Karim was born and raised by two Christian parents who only go to church on Christmas Day?"

Their expressions gave them away, and Marina immediately exploded.

"I don't believe it! You looked at my Karim and saw a terrorist, just because he has his father's name and coloring! You assumed that he was a Muslim, because that would make him fit in better in your imaginary world!"

"Listen to me," the Säpo officer said, trying to turn things around. "We haven't assumed anything, we're just trying to work out why someone is interested in what happens to Zakaria Khelifi. And unfortunately, your son knows Khelifi, or at least used to know him, and he is flying the plane that has been hijacked by someone whose only contact so far has been through a note left in one of the toilets on board."

As Fredrika listened, she thought her colleague was both right and wrong. At no point during the investigation had they put a label on the terrorists who were holding four hundred passengers hostage, but they had definitely assumed that there was an Islamic connection.

Because there was a connection in Zakaria Khelifi's case.

And there was a connection when it came to Tennyson Cottage.

A suspicion was beginning to grow in Fredrika's mind:

Karim is not the one who's behind this. At least not alone.

On the other hand, terrorism had so many different faces. Who was to say it couldn't look like Karim Sassi?

35

17:00

For the first time, Eden Lundell was standing smoking in the shelter down in the basement at Police HQ. A decision had been made to remove all smoking shelters, but for some reason the one in the basement had remained. In the past Eden wouldn't have dreamed of smoking in there. It would have been beyond tragic. Until today. It was pouring with rain outside, and she wanted to stay away from the main entrance, where reporters were hiding out in various vehicles.

She was pleased to find herself alone in the smoking shelter. If anyone had been sitting there when she arrived, she would have asked that person to leave. She needed to be on her own, to light a cigarette and think about everything that had happened during the course of the day.

It had really started the previous day, with the empty bomb threats. Eden still didn't understand where they fitted into this drama. The next thing was the bomb threat found on a flight heading for the USA. Terrorism had once more raised its head in Sweden, severely shaking the Swedish self-image, which was so pathetic that Eden couldn't take it seriously.

The image of Sweden as a country that didn't deserve terrorism. The country that trumpeted its neutrality, yet cooperated on a military basis with both the EU and NATO. The country that thought it could draw on significant reserves of international goodwill, because for decades it had been regarded as pro-Palestinian. The country that regarded itself as a role model for other nations, in every respect. Crap, all of it. Times had changed, and it was necessary to adjust expectations, to accept the reality of the situation.

She glanced at her watch. Damn it, the girls needed picking up from day care. She had no choice, she would have to call Mikael and ask him to abandon his confirmation class. National security must come first.

Decisively, she stubbed out her cigarette on the shiny surface of the ashtray. The latest information from the Americans was that they were going to ask Karim to stay outside US airspace until further notice. That sounded sensible; once he had passed over the US border, anything could happen. A plan of action began to take shape in Eden's mind. First of all, she wanted to find out what the interviews with Zakaria's uncle and Karim's mother had produced, if anything. Then she would turn every single scrap of information in Zakaria's case inside out. There had to be a link between Zakaria and Tennyson Cottage, she was sure of it. It was there, right in front of them. She could feel it in her whole body. So why couldn't she see it?

* * *

Alex Recht rarely, if ever, felt inadequate, but as he sat in the car with a female Säpo officer on the way to Traneberg to speak to Zakaria Khelifi's uncle, he could tell that his anxiety over Erik was causing him to lose his edge. He wished he could have conducted this interview with Fredrika instead, but she had gone back to Kungsholmen to write a report for her department. He glanced at the colleague who was driving, and tried to remember her name. Viola? Vivianne?

He got his answer when her cell phone rang and she answered.

"Veronika."

After a brief conversation, she ended the call.

"A colleague," she said to Alex.

"Right," he said, mostly for the sake of something to say.

After that they drove in silence. Through Kungsholmen, out onto the Traneberg Bridge. The view from up there was always magnificent, always stunningly beautiful. Stockholm was the loveliest capital city in the whole world. Alex's own cell phone rang, and he felt a warm glow in his chest when he saw that it was Diana.

"Have you heard any more about Erik?"

Her voice was thick with worry. She had lost a child herself, a daughter. If anyone knew what torment it was to lose a person you had created, it was Diana.

But we're not there yet.

"No," Alex replied. "But we're working on it."

They were "working on it." The time was almost five thirty, the plane was seventy-five minutes away from its destination, and the police were still saying they were trying to find a way to avert a disaster. But how? How were they going to do that?

He could hear her breathing at the other end of the line, and wondered what would have become of him if he hadn't met her. He had thought it would be impossible for him to love again, and had been surprised by how easy it actually was. When Diana opened her arms to him, it was as if his frozen heart thawed, and gave him back the will to live.

The car stopped; they had arrived.

"I'll call you later," Alex said. He slipped the phone into his pocket and followed Veronika up the stairs to the apartment in which Zakaria Khelifi's uncle lived.

The uncle had been interviewed by the press, and had made no secret of the fact that he was appalled by the way his nephew's case had been handled. Alex understood perfectly; he would have felt the same if he had been a relative. But he certainly didn't feel that way as a law enforcement officer.

They hadn't expected a warm welcome, but nor had they expected Zakaria Khelifi's uncle to be so openly hostile. Moussa Khelifi had lived in Sweden for over thirty years, and spoke Swedish with an almost imperceptible accent.

"What are you doing here?" he demanded. "I don't know how you've got the nerve to turn up on my doorstep!"

"We think you might be able to help us," Veronika said. "And Zakaria."

Moussa remained standing in the doorway; he didn't look as if he had any intention of letting them in.

"I came to you," he said to Veronika. "Do you remember? I came to Säpo during the trial and asked to speak to you."

"I remember. I also remember that two of our officers came down and listened to you. They gave you our phone number, and you called us later on."

"And what did I say?"

"I don't know. I wasn't on duty that day."

"I said that Zakaria was innocent," Moussa said, his eyes suspiciously shiny. "I begged you to rethink, to let Zakaria go. But you refused to lift a finger to help him."

Alex wasn't familiar with Zakaria Khelifi's case; he didn't know why Säpo considered him to be so important. But he thought he knew something about the relatives of those who had fallen afoul of the law.

"Moussa," he said. "The situation has changed. You must have seen the news—someone has hijacked a plane and is demanding Zakaria's release."

"Of course I've seen it, but it's nothing to do with me. Nothing at all."

Alex took a tentative step forward.

"Could we possibly come inside for a little while? It seems a bit silly to be discussing this on the landing."

A second passed, then another. Moussa Khelifi stepped back and let them in.

"You can't stay long," he said.

"We won't," Alex reassured him.

Moussa showed them into the living room. Alex swallowed hard when he saw the pictures on the walls, the ceramic bowls on display. Diana would have paid a fortune for them.

Veronika and Alex sat down on the sofa, while Moussa perched on a stool. It was too small, and made him look like a giant.

"Where were you working in the summer of 2002?" Veronika asked.

"At an Ericsson factory in Kista. I worked there until they shut it down."

"Do you remember a Karim Sassi?"

Moussa frowned. At first, Alex thought he was going to say no, but eventually he said slowly:

"Sassi . . . yes, I do remember him. He was the son of one of my colleagues—Marina."

"Did Zakaria ever meet him?"

Moussa thought back.

"Zakaria spent a summer with me here in Sweden before he started university. I think it could well have been in 2002. I don't have any children, and I was afraid he would feel lonely when he came over, so I asked Marina if they could hook up—Zakaria and her Karim."

"Did they spend much time together?"

"No, as far as I know they only met up now and again. Zakaria didn't speak Swedish, and although his English wasn't bad, it was nowhere near as good as Karim's. In Zakaria's family, I think it's only his sister who is really gifted when it comes to languages. She learned Swedish quicker than I did." He stopped abruptly. "Why are you asking questions about Zakaria and Karim?"

"Unfortunately, we can't tell you that at the moment, but . . ."

Moussa spread his arms in a gesture of resignation.

"I could never do your job," he said, looking Veronika in the eye. "Aren't you ashamed of what you do? Going to visit people you don't even know and humiliating yourself by asking stupid questions?"

His words took Veronika's breath away, and she didn't know what to say.

"We all have different jobs to do," Alex said quietly.

"And mine is to take care of Zakaria's interests," Moussa said. "I don't care why you're interested in him and Karim. If you don't have any more questions, I'd like you to leave."

"Do you know if they met up after 2002?" Veronika asked.

"I don't think so. I would probably have heard about it if they had."

Moussa showed them out. Their meeting had lasted only a few minutes, but he was anxious to get rid of them.

"I'm disappointed," he said when they were standing in the hall-way. "In you and in Sweden. I didn't think this could happen. Not in Sweden. What if something happens to Zakaria when he's sent back to Algeria?"

There was nothing more to say. Neither Alex nor Veronika made any attempt to explain that Zakaria was judged to be a security risk, a threat to the country, and that was why he had to go home. Nor did they comment on the fact that the threat level to Zakaria had actually been assessed; the conclusion was that it was possible for him to return to Algeria. It was part of Moussa's role as his uncle to believe that Zakaria was innocent. It couldn't be helped that Alex and Veronika had a different agenda; that was just the way things were.

They thanked Moussa for sparing the time to talk to them, and went back to the car. Alex looked up at the dark, threatening sky. Something Moussa had said was niggling away at the back of his mind, but he didn't remember what it was until they were back at Kungsholmen.

"Did we know that Zakaria Khelifi has a sister who lives in Sweden?" he said.

Veronika thought for a moment.

"I didn't take any notice when he mentioned her but, to be honest, I don't know Zakaria's case all that well."

Alex grabbed his phone and called Eden.

"Did you know that Zakaria has a sister?"

"I think he has several sisters," Eden replied.

"I mean a sister who lives in Sweden."

Eden didn't say anything for a moment.

"No," she said eventually. "I didn't know that."

Alex put his phone away.

It seemed as if they were being fed fresh information all the time, but however hard they looked, they couldn't find anything that would move the investigation forward.

36

Flight 573

When Erik Recht's mother died, Erik had found his father crying in his study. At first he hadn't known what to do, whether he was expected to turn around and walk away, or whether his father wanted some company. He had hesitated for such a long time that he eventually decided he had to make his presence felt, which he achieved by clearing his throat.

"Are you okay, Dad?" he had said.

And Alex had replied, "Everything's fine."

And that was the end of that. Erik had left his father alone with his grief. The distance between them had never seemed greater.

We can't reach one another, Erik had thought. Not even now.

Claudia had been unimpressed when Erik told her what had happened. The responsibility was Erik's, she had said. If Alex was crying, then it was up to Erik to console him. You couldn't just leave an old man in such a state.

Old.

That was what she had said, and that was how Alex could be perceived. Old and tired. However, the aging process had been slowed down somewhat by Diana, who was so dynamic and attractive that Erik couldn't for the life of him understand what she saw in his father.

Perhaps she liked his air of authority, because he certainly had that in spades. Sitting next to Karim on the plane, Erik wished he had just a fraction of his father's impressive presence. He felt small in comparison to Karim, not just in physical terms but also when it came to power.

Karim had the upper hand. In every way. And Erik didn't really understand where that impression came from. It wasn't just that Karim was the captain, and thus ultimately responsible for what happened to the plane; Erik had a nasty feeling that Karim also had additional information, that he knew better than anyone how this flight was going to end.

The police had called them again, as had the airline. Karim refused to listen to either of them. He was going to follow the hijackers' instructions, and that was that. But then they were contacted by the US authorities, and this time he did listen. They were ordered to remain outside US airspace until further notice, and Karim agreed. At least for the time being.

"What do we do when we reach New York?" Erik asked.

Karim didn't look at him when he answered. "Let's hope the Swedish and US governments have met the hijackers' demands by then so that we can land."

Erik suddenly found it difficult to breathe. "In that case, we won't be following their rules," he said.

Karim glanced at him. "What do you mean?"

"According to the hijackers, the two governments have the same amount of time to act as it will take us to use up our fuel. And that's longer than it will take for us to reach our destination."

Karim looked almost relieved. "Oh, I see. I've already thought of that. When I'm approaching Washington, I'll start circling until we run out of time. Then I'll request permission to land, as long as they've met the hijackers' demands."

Erik's heart started racing. "New York," he said.

"What?"

"You said Washington. But we're on our way to New York."

The air was so thick in the cockpit now that it was almost impossible to breathe.

"Sorry, my mistake," Karim said. "I meant New York."

No you didn't.

Tiny, glistening beads of sweat broke out on Karim's forehead.

Erik's voice was hoarse with tension.

"For fuck's sake, Karim, we have to be able to talk to one another. What the hell is going on here?"

Karim fell silent once more, and Erik just wanted to punch him.

"I'm not having this," he said. "I don't know what the fuck you're playing at, but let me make one thing perfectly clear: I will not allow you to jeopardize the safety of our passengers."

Erik got to his feet; a glance at Karim revealed that he had not reacted to Erik's outburst. Had he even been listening?

Erik quickly moved over to the cockpit door and grabbed the handle. He would call his father and ask his advice. Then he would get Karim out of the way and land the bloody plane himself.

Just as he was about to open the door, he looked over at Karim again. He was staring at the blue sky ahead, as straight as a fir tree. Suddenly, Erik knew that he was just waiting for Erik to step out of the cockpit.

If I leave now, he's not going to let me back in.

Slowly, Erik returned to his seat.

"I thought you were going somewhere?" Karim said.

"I've changed my mind."

If Karim was disappointed, he didn't show it. A short while later, he decided that the passengers must be informed of the expected delay. His tone was firm as he explained to them that because of exceptionally bad weather in New York, the flight would be significantly delayed. There was no need for anyone to worry, because there was plenty of fuel on board, and the crew would do everything they could to make sure that their journey was as comfortable as possible.

Erik hoped the passengers would accept Karim's explanation and remain calm. They didn't have time for any kind of trouble.

After Karim's announcement, silence once more descended on the cockpit.

One word lingered in Erik's mind: *Washington*.

37

Stockholm, 18:01

This day's work would never end. The realization came as a blow. Fredrika had no intention of going home until the hijacking was resolved one way or another. Spencer called her just after six.

"How are you doing?" he asked.

"Fine, but I won't be home for dinner. We can have Indian another time."

Then they talked about the children, what they should have for tea, what they should wear the following day.

How did my life turn out like this? Fredrika wondered. How did I go from a career woman with a secret lover to a married woman with two children?

Spencer's transformation was almost as dramatic: from a married, childless professor in his sixties to a remarried father of two. And yet, Fredrika had never once doubted that he would cope, or worried that he might leave her. Their relationship was as clear as if it were etched in stone. He was hers and she was his.

And that made her feel safe.

Safe. When had she ever felt safe before?

Her thoughts turned to the passengers on Flight 573. She presumed they had been informed of the delay by now. She hoped the crew would be able to continue to maintain calm and order; it didn't bear thinking about what could happen if chaos broke out. A scenario in which the passengers panicked and ran amok would be both dangerous and difficult to deal with.

The plane was now uncomfortably close to the US border. And anything could happen there. The Americans were noticeably stressed and seeing ghosts. She hoped Karim wouldn't decide to defy them.

Fredrika rubbed her hands together. There were so many dimensions to the hijacking, so many sidetracks, that she felt exhausted.

First of all, there was a North African asylum seeker who was due to be deported from Sweden, because Säpo had decided that he constituted a threat to national security.

Secondly, there was a secret US detention facility in Afghanistan.

And, thirdly, there was a man who had followed his childhood dream and become a pilot, and was now regarded as a terrorist holding hundreds of people to ransom.

The question was how these three elements hung together, because in Fredrika's mind these widely differing strands must have come from the same source. Her boss had called just a few minutes earlier and asked her to produce a written summary of all the information that had come to light so far, and to send it by courier to the government offices.

Fredrika wrote down her conclusions.

They still hadn't managed to link Zakaria Khelifi to Tennyson Cottage. It was, of course, possible that there was no connection, but in that case they must at least have a perpetrator who could be linked to both. Many people felt that Karim could be that perpetrator, and Fredrika was one of them. However, she couldn't believe that he had done this on his own.

What evidence did they have against Karim? A photograph of him and Zakaria Khelifi. A book by Alfred Lord Tennyson in which the photograph had been hidden. And fingerprints on one of the phones that had been used to make bomb threats aimed at various targets in inner-city Stockholm. The same phone had also been in contact with Karim's private cell phone.

The book and the photograph.

The fingerprints.

The telephone calls.

So incredibly careless.

She had the same feeling as before. There was something fundamentally wrong about the picture of Karim that had emerged during the course of the day. But what?

Fredrika could hear Eden Lundell's voice a short distance away in the open-plan office. She had taken off her jacket and was standing in the middle of the floor in a sleeveless top that revealed the most toned upper arms Fredrika had ever seen on a woman. Eden spoke quietly, but she was clearly annoyed.

"Mikael, I am not going to have this discussion right now. Yes, it's very unfortunate that you had to abandon your little confirmation students to go and pick up your own children while your wife tries to save the lives of four hundred innocent people, but—"

She was interrupted by the person on the other end of the line. The next time she spoke, her tone was defensive.

"I'm not being patronizing, I'm just telling it like it is. I . . . What? And what's wrong with describing your confirmation students as little? I mean, they're not exactly big, are they?"

Eden suddenly realized that Fredrika was looking at her.

"I haven't got time to talk about this now. I'm sorry you're angry, but there's nothing I can do about it."

She flipped her phone shut and put it in her pocket. Fredrika turned her attention back to her report. Eden came straight over to her desk.

"How's it going?"

Her voice was like the crack of a whip, and Fredrika felt her cheeks redden. As if it were her fault that Eden had been standing in the middle of the office conducting a private conversation.

"Fine," she said.

"We're having a meeting in a while—it would be good if you came along."

"I'll be there."

Another burst of rain spattered the window next to Fredrika. The October weather was dreadful. Soon the streets would be aflame with fallen leaves in shades of red and yellow.

Eden lingered by Fredrika's desk.

"How do you feel your liaison role is working?"

"It's good. I'm just summarizing how far we've gotten; the Justice Department has requested a report."

"Do you have any thoughts you'd like to share at this stage?"

Fredrika hesitated, and Eden read her like an open book.

"Go on," she said encouragingly.

"Karim Sassi," Fredrika said. "I don't think he's the brains behind all this."

Eden frowned.

"But surely you must believe he's involved?"

"Yes. But I don't buy the idea that he's alone."

"Me neither. Nobody could carry out something like this on their own."

"So why aren't we finding anyone else close to him?"

"I would say that's one of the major questions facing us, and I find it frustrating to say the least. There's no way he can be alone."

Fredrika had more to get off her chest: "I've been thinking about all the coincidences when it comes to Karim Sassi."

"Such as?" It was obvious that Eden was trying not to sound irritated.

"Such as the book by Tennyson, for example. And the photograph of Karim and Zakaria Khelifi. Even Zakaria himself doesn't seem to be aware that there's supposed to be a connection between him and Karim that is so strong it would motivate Karim to hijack an entire plane for his sake."

Eden pushed her hands into her trouser pockets. She wasn't wearing a watch, but she did have heavy silver bracelets on both wrists. The bracelets were covered in symbols that Fredrika thought could be Hebrew letters.

"You mean someone got into Karim's house and planted the book there?"

Her expression suggested that she thought Fredrika was crazy.

"Well, no, that doesn't seem very likely," Fredrika replied. "However, I can't help feeling it's a bit careless to leave something like that lying around. Did he want us to find it?"

"Yes, or his wife. Perhaps it was a final message to her if everything went wrong."

"So why not come out and say he's responsible for the hijacking? Why not make the demands himself instead of writing them on a piece of paper and leaving it in the toilet?"

"Because he thought, or thinks, there was a chance he might get away with it without being exposed."

"And he left the book out in case he was killed or exposed?"

Eden didn't reply. Fredrika could see that she was thinking things over.

"What if we flip it around?" Eden said eventually. "What if we assume that someone other than Karim planted the book in his house? Why did that person do it?"

"To give more weight to our suspicions against Karim," Fredrika said.

"Planting a book in a living room isn't particularly subtle," Eden said. "I mean, it would be very easy for the homeowner to say they've never seen it before, that it doesn't belong to them. And even more importantly, how would the person who put the book there know that we would suspect Karim?"

Fredrika suddenly felt immensely weary.

"I don't know," she said.

Eden took her hands out of her pockets and started fingering one of her bracelets.

"I agree with you, the business of the book seems too obvious. Almost like a kind of theatrical symbol, a specific message for the right eyes. Our eyes, for example. If it weren't for the bomb threats, I'd be on your side. In that case, the book and the photograph would be the perfect trap. But as it is . . ."

She rolled her neck, the blond hair flicking across her shoulders.

"Besides, there's intelligence that strengthens the theory that the pilot is involved. There's too much evidence to ignore."

Eden was right, and Fredrika was wrong, although Fredrika had never suggested that Karim was innocent. However, she still believed it was beyond all reasonable doubt that he could have carried out his plan alone.

How could his helpers be completely invisible?

Eden turned on her heel and went back to her office.

Fredrika stayed at her desk and tried to bring some clarity to her thoughts. What had been the point of the previous day's bomb threats? Four separate threats spread across the inner city, with no explanation, no demand for anything in return. Why? If the threats were linked to the hijacking, what role had they played?

Fredrika gazed out of the window, wishing she could reach Karim Sassi up there among the clouds.

Talk to us, she thought. Tell us what we're not seeing.

Because otherwise there's nothing we can do to help you.

•　•　•

GD had come looking for Eden while she was in the meeting with the Americans. He wanted an update, so she called him.

The meeting with the CIA agents had left her feeling frustrated. She couldn't cope with a pissing contest and battling against a head-wind in a situation like this. And then they had had the nerve to hint at that damned business in London! Eden had never imagined that her history would remain within the borders of the UK. She had actually been surprised when she was offered the positions with both the National Bureau of Investigation and Säpo, but had then decided to take this as a sign that she could put the past behind her. Which she was very happy to do. Nothing was more painful than remembering, and nothing else in her life had cost her more.

Suddenly, Mikael came into her mind. Mikael, who had had to dump his confirmation class to go and pick up the children. Mikael, whom she had snapped at and provoked, and who was beginning to get sick and tired of the hours she worked.

Eden remembered how surprised her mother had been when she told her they were expecting a child.

"You?" her mother had said. "You're having a baby?"

There was no joy in her voice, simply blank bewilderment. As if the thought of Eden having a child was utterly ridiculous. Admittedly, Eden's view of parenthood wasn't quite the same as that of many other women. They had been living in London when the baby was born, and according to the rules and regulations that applied to working women in the UK at the time, she had had only sixteen weeks' maternity leave, which was regarded as a long time. Mikael had refused to employ a nanny when the children were so small, and had stayed at home with them for a whole year. In Eden's opinion, this meant he had lost the first and most important round of negotiations over who should take the lion's share of responsibility for their daughters.

GD answered his phone. He didn't sound all that pleased to hear her voice, in spite of the fact that he was the one who had wanted to speak to her in the first place. Eden had no idea why he was suddenly so hostile, but it didn't exactly improve matters when she relayed the results of her meeting with the Americans.

"So the Germans knew about this? If that's true, it's totally unacceptable!"

Eden tried to calm him down.

"It's overstating the case to say they knew about it. And what would we have done with such a vague email?" She shook her head.

GD muttered something inaudible, and Eden moved on to a different matter: "Did we know that Zakaria Khelifi has a sister here in Sweden?"

GD sounded unsure: "I don't know. Why would it be relevant if he has?"

"I'm just thinking there could be other things that we've missed. We've always regarded him as someone who has relatively little in terms of roots in Sweden. And then we find out he has a sister here. And his uncle, whom we already knew about, of course."

Did she mean what she was saying? She thought so. They shouldn't have missed the fact that Zakaria had a sister in Sweden. Why hadn't he mentioned her himself? She wasn't included in his file with the Immigration Service, and Zakaria had never said a word about her in any of his interviews. The only sisters Eden knew about were the ones who still lived in Algeria. There had to be a reason why Zakaria hadn't said anything.

"He probably didn't want to drag her into his problems," GD said. "Nothing more sinister than that."

But Eden's brain was working overtime by now.

"It's more than that. They don't even appear to have been in touch. Or is she in our phone tap records, and we haven't realized who she is?"

"There are always unidentified individuals when we tap someone's phone."

"And the uncle didn't know he was supposed to keep quiet," Eden said, more to herself than GD. "He mentioned her as if she was an obvious part of Zakaria's life."

"I think this sounds like something you don't really need to pursue," GD said.

Eden drummed her fingertips on the desk.

"There's more," she said.

"What do you mean, more?"

"More about Zakaria's case that doesn't feel good, to say the least."

She told him what the latest analysis of Zakaria's phone records had revealed, and not surprisingly he was furious.

"Do you realize what the hell you're saying?"

"Of course I do. And believe me, I'm doing all I can to get to the bottom of Zakaria Khelifi's case."

She ended the call with a distinct feeling that she was on the trail of something that had been very well hidden. And that it was Zakaria Khelifi himself who had blocked her chances of finding it.

38

Flight 573

When Joakim was a boy, he used to think that it was possible to walk on the clouds you saw when you looked out of the window on a plane. He would press his nose against the cold glass and dream of stepping outside to play in the soft, white shapes that looked like mountains made of ice cream.

"But you can't do that, darling," his mother had said when he told her. "Clouds are just air. If you tried to walk on them, you'd fall straight through."

The very thought of plunging to the ground had made Joakim settle down properly in his seat without even glancing at the window. However, now that he was an adult he loved to sit and gaze at the clouds. They had been in the air for some hours by now; the advantage was that the distance between him and the bad-tempered girlfriend he had left back home felt immense. Joakim was certain now. When he got back, he was going to finish with her. He didn't need someone like her in his life. Not when he was moving forward, and all she wanted to do was stay in the same place.

Joakim was restless. The flight time was supposed to be nine hours and fifteen minutes, and he hadn't slept a wink. The captain had just announced that there would be a delay of several hours because of bad weather. Joakim's seat was as hard as a park bench, and the man next to him stank of sweat. Joakim fiddled aimlessly with the small TV screen set in the back of the seat in front of him. There wasn't a single film he hadn't already seen.

He picked up his rucksack and took out his camera. He scrolled through his photographs, most of which were of no interest at all.

Party pictures and photos from his niece's christening. He switched off the camera and put it back in his bag, then rummaged through the rest of the contents. Hadn't he brought a book? A guide to the world of jazz in New York—a present from his parents.

He found the book and put it on his knee. He wanted to listen to some music as well. The man next to him started glancing sideways at Joakim, obviously irritated by all this scrabbling in his bag.

You stink and I'm scrabbling. If you put on some deodorant I'll put down my bag.

After a minute or so, he realized he was searching in vain. He hadn't brought his MP3 player. He could see it clearly, sitting on the kitchen table. He had intended to bring it, but he must have forgotten. However, he was sure he'd transferred a few playlists to his new phone.

With his book and phone on his knee, Joakim dropped the rucksack back onto the floor. He turned away discreetly so that his neighbor wouldn't see that his phone was on. Lots of people had music on their phones, but they could usually switch to flight mode. Joakim didn't know how to do that; however, he had recently read an article about how someone was trying, once and for all, to get to the bottom of how dangerous it was to have a cell phone switched on during a flight. If it really was such a hazard, then why were people allowed to take a phone on board at all, the writer argued. The safety of the entire plane was left in the hands of individual passengers, with no control over how they handled that responsibility.

The article had been well written, and Joakim thought it made a good point. If it was so important for phones to be switched off, then surely people would be compelled to check them in. The thought eased his guilty conscience.

To his surprise, he saw that he had a new message. From his mother. But why? She knew he was on a plane to New York, so why would she send him a message? Or did she assume that he had his phone on?

Furtively, he turned his back on his neighbor and opened the message. If the phone was on anyway and the message had been received, surely it wouldn't make any difference if he opened it?

Quickly, he read through what his mother had written.
He blinked, shook his head. What the hell . . . had she gone mad?
He read it again.

*Joakim, I assume both your phones are switched off, but I'm
sending this anyway. Dad and I have both come home from
work and are following your journey on the Internet and on
TV. Don't give up! We love you and know that everything
will be all right! Lots of love, Mom.*

Come home from work? Following your journey?
Joakim didn't understand a word of it. Was the message really
from his mother, or someone else? He looked at it several times, but
there was no doubt.
He started to laugh. Quietly at first, then louder and louder. Suddenly he grew serious again. This wasn't funny. What were they playing at? What were they talking about? It sounded as if they thought
he was in real danger.
There must have been some kind of misunderstanding, something on the news about a plane heading for New York, and his parents must have thought it was his flight. For God's sake, there were
several flights a day to New York. Weren't there?
Joakim looked around. Everything seemed fine, and the crew
hadn't made any alarming announcements. If their flight was in
some kind of trouble, surely they would have said something? They
wouldn't just leave people sitting there, unaware that they were heading toward death?
A flight attendant was just passing his row.
"Excuse me," Joakim said.
She stopped and Joakim leaned forward so that he could see past
the smelly man.
"I was just wondering . . . Have there been any problems with
this plane?"
"No, absolutely not. You have my word."
But she wasn't smiling the way flight attendants usually do when
they speak to passengers.

"Are you afraid of flying, sir?"

Joakim forced a smile.

"No, no. I just wanted to check."

The flight attendant moved on, and Joakim felt his cheeks redden. "I just wanted to check." What a stupid thing to say. Check what? If the plane was expected to crash?

"Listen, plane crashes are incredibly rare," the man beside him said. "Driving a car or riding a motorbike is much more dangerous."

"Thanks, I know that," Joakim said.

Once more, he turned away and opened his phone, but there was no coverage. He read his mother's message over and over again. The tone and the choice of words communicated absolute despair. The more he thought about it, the more convinced he became. The flight attendant who couldn't bring herself to smile had been lying.

39

Stockholm, 18:30

They had to decide how to proceed. The plane would pass its planned arrival time in just fifteen minutes, and from then on it would be using up its additional fuel supply. Alex Recht sensed an air of indecision when he came back from his meeting with Zakaria Khelifi's uncle. It bothered him. They had to move on, take decisive action.

Everyone had gathered for a meeting in Säpo HQ, including Alex's boss and several other officers from both the National Bureau of Investigation and the Stockholm city police.

Eden began by talking about the call to the TT news agency, and Säpo's theory that whoever had tipped off the media about the hijacking was actually involved in some way.

"The call to TT was made from a cell phone with an unregistered pay-as-you-go SIM card, so that won't get us anywhere," she said. "What interests me more, however, is the fact that the person who took the call was initially skeptical as to whether it should be taken seriously."

"Why?" Fredrika asked.

"Because the caller sounded like Donald Duck."

Hjärpe, Alex's boss, let out a low whistle. "Voice distortion again."

"That's right."

Alex couldn't believe what he was hearing. What kind of a clown were they chasing here?

"So that's another dead end," he said.

"No," Eden said. "But at least we know we were right when we guessed that the caller was involved."

"Why was it so important to inform the media?" Hjärpe said.

"I would guess that the caller wanted to be sure that the plane was following the instructions in the note, and he or she can only know that if the media are monitoring the story."

The calculated execution of the hijacking made Alex go cold all over.

Eden quickly moved on.

"What is it that's driven Karim Sassi to hijack the plane he's actually flying? What's his motive?" she said.

"Have we completely ruled out the idea of other perpetrators?" Alex replied.

"We don't believe there are others, so we are assuming that Karim had help with his preparations, and that the person or persons concerned are now helping him on the ground. With regard to yesterday's bomb threats, all we know is that his fingerprints were on one of the phones. Which doesn't necessarily mean that he made one of the calls."

"Then again, there are no prints at all on any of the other phones," Alex said. "And there's nothing from the tracking to suggest that the calls were made by more than one person. All the threats were made in the same area between Stockholm and Arlanda."

"Several people could have been traveling in one car," Eden said.

Alex nodded. "True."

Sebastian, the head of analysis, indicated that he had something to say.

"I think we ought to talk about a possible motive, which you mentioned just now. What is making Sassi do this? He's not a practicing Muslim, which is very interesting. That takes out any connection with Islamic extremism, which I think we all presumed was behind this, and his motive becomes incomprehensible."

"Exactly," Eden said. "I have to admit that this worries me more than anything. *Worries* is the wrong word, but it bothers me that I don't understand what's driving him. No one close to him seems to have noticed any kind of change of personality recently, nor has anyone mentioned a burning social conscience. He has no background as an activist, and he hasn't even been a member of any voluntary organization."

"Exactly," Sebastian said. "It would have been a different matter if we'd been able to track down a clear commitment to asylum issues, for example; we could have assumed that was why Khelifi's deportation in particular had provoked him to such an extent."

"I'm meeting the German liaison officer when we're done here so that I can find out what they know," Eden said. "But they've already forewarned us that they don't have anything specific on Karim, just on the hijacking."

As Alex listened to Sebastian and Eden, his doubts grew. He couldn't understand why they thought the situation would change if they could work out Karim's motives.

Eden noticed his pensive expression.

"What do you think, Alex?"

Her voice was different from when she was speaking to Sebastian or Fredrika. Softer, as if she wanted to show that Alex was someone she liked.

"I think it's going to be bloody difficult to understand Karim's motives without talking to him," he said.

The words came more quickly than he had expected.

"Talking to him? You mean we should contact the plane and let him know we're aware of his involvement?"

"That's exactly what I mean."

In spite of the fact that he hadn't really thought things through, he carried on: "We're not getting any further, and the clock is ticking. In just a few hours the plane will either crash or be blown to pieces, if the hijackers are serious. Since it's in the air, we can't physically go in. The only thing we can do is to call the cockpit and hope we can reason with Karim, appeal to his good sense." Alex paused for effect. "Unless, of course, we want to go for the option we mentioned earlier: contact the copilot and ask him to take control of the plane."

By this stage, everyone in the room knew that the copilot was Alex's son. But that didn't matter, because they also knew that he was right.

"What if we speak to Karim and the conversation causes him to panic?" Eden said. "Since we don't know what's driving him, we don't know what values are at stake as far as he's concerned. Confronting him could put all the crew and passengers in mortal danger."

"In that case, we have to contact the copilot."

"And if he fails? The effect could end up exactly the same. Karim realizes he's been exposed, and takes drastic measures. What are Erik's chances of overcoming Karim, in practical terms?"

Alex pictured Erik in his mind's eye. As a child. Tall and thin, almost skinny. Passionate, full of ideas about how to make life more exciting. His temperament was more evenly balanced since he had grown up, but he still looked for kicks that brightened the dullness other people simply regarded as everyday life.

It doesn't get any more exciting than this, does it, Erik?

Erik was taller than Alex, but shorter than Karim. And thinner, not nearly as muscular. To be perfectly honest, Alex didn't think his son would stand a chance against his captain in a fight—unless he could find some kind of weapon to render him harmless.

"I don't think he'd be able to knock Karim out with his bare hands; he'd need to take him by surprise. Perhaps there's a fire extinguisher in the cockpit that he could use?"

Alex's suggestion aroused a hum of conversation around the table. A fire extinguisher? Impossible. Ridiculous. Eden rapped on the table to quieten everyone down.

"We haven't got time for chatter," she said. "Alex has a point; we have to decide how we intend to proceed. The fact is that we have very little chance of bringing the plane down safely with Karim at the controls. The governments are not going to meet the hijackers' demands, and the fuel will run out very soon. And then only a miracle can save us from total disaster."

"How can we get hold of the copilot without Karim Sassi realizing what's going on? I mean, they're sitting next to each other," said a Säpo investigator Alex didn't recognize.

Another burst of murmuring, which irritated Eden.

"We'll get in touch with the airline again and see what they say. We don't know enough to make a decision."

She looked at a member of her team.

"Call SAS and find out everything we need to know. Can we reach Erik without Karim realizing? And, if so, how? I'm still not sure that asking Erik to overpower Karim is the best course of action, but we need to consider it as a last resort, in which case I want to know if it's actually possible."

Fredrika spoke up: "The note said there was a bomb on board the plane; what do we think about that, now we know Karim is involved?"

"What do you mean?" Eden said.

"According to the note, the plane will be blown up if we attempt to land it or to evacuate those on board. Do we believe that threat if Karim is behind the hijacking?"

"You mean that if Karim is put out of action and Erik lands the plane without the demands being met, will the plane be blown up anyway?"

"Exactly."

Alex's heart sank. He hadn't thought about that.

"In that case we're back to what we talked about this morning," Eden said. "What are the chances that someone managed to smuggle a bomb onto the plane?"

"If the captain himself is part of the plot, then perhaps it's more likely?" someone suggested.

"Hardly. The crew have to go through the same security checks as the passengers."

Eden shook her head. "I refuse to make a final decision under these circumstances. I want to speak to the Germans first, see if they've found out anything else. And then I want to talk to our American colleagues; I want to know exactly how they're intending to deal with the plane if or when time runs out. Only then will I consider getting in touch with Karim and asking about his plans."

She had hardly finished speaking when the door flew open and a young woman Alex had never seen before came rushing in.

"Sorry to interrupt, Eden, but GD asked me to tell you that you've been called to a meeting at Rosenbad immediately."

"Rosenbad? Tell GD he'll have to go himself; I'm needed here."

"I don't think he'll accept that. It's to do with the Americans; apparently, they've contacted the Foreign Office through their ambassador and informed the Swedish government what they intend to do with the hijacked plane."

"Why do we have to go to Rosenbad to discuss that?" Eden said. "Wouldn't it be just as easy for the Americans to come here and talk us through their plans?"

"GD was very clear," the woman said. "He wants you to go with him, right now."

Eden got to her feet.

"In that case this meeting is closed. I should be back within the hour."

Alex stayed in his seat, like everyone else. His stomach was knotted with fear. The Americans had gone directly to the government rather than Säpo. That couldn't possibly be a good sign.

40

18:50

Here we go again, Eden thought. Another meeting with the cabinet office, this time at Rosenbad. It was dark outside, and a weary drizzle was falling as they drove the short distance from Police HQ to Tegeluddsbacken. There were only the two of them in the car, which felt strange to Eden.

"Do you mind if I smoke?"

GD stared at her. "In the car?"

"Yes."

"Too bloody right I mind. If you're going to smoke, you can do it outdoors."

Eden slid the packet of cigarettes back into her pocket.

"Pardon me for asking, but do you usually smoke when you're driving?" GD asked.

"It has been known."

She was too old to be reprimanded about how she took care of her health and her body, and made it clear that she wasn't interested in the conversation by staring out of the window. Why was GD behind the wheel anyway? She was a better driver than he was. All those visits to Israel and the years she had spent in London had made her the driver she was today. If you didn't put your foot down a fraction of a second after the traffic lights turned green in Tel Aviv, you were in trouble, because someone was guaranteed to drive straight into the back of your car.

Suddenly, Eden couldn't see very well. Three years had passed since her last visit to Israel. Three years of slow recovery and trying to find a sense of balance in her everyday life again. Almost everything had fallen apart back then. Things that couldn't be fixed, things she would have to carry with her for many years in the future. Had it been worth it? Could she have done it all differently?

Of course she could. There was often more than one way of dealing with a catastrophe. Her mother had once said that a person had three ways of handling things: you could go with your heart, your head, or your stomach. When Eden was in her twenties, she had added sexuality to the list, but she hadn't told her mother. And it wasn't her heart, her head, or her stomach that had sent her to the hot streets of Tel Aviv that first time. Nor all the times that followed.

The memories frightened her, and she squeezed the cigarette packet in her pocket. The interior of the car shrank; it was too small. Eden stretched her legs, tensed her muscles. They were only minutes away from Rosenbad; she told herself to keep calm. When GD stopped the car, she flung the door open and got out. It wasn't until she had lit her cigarette and taken the first drag that she realized how grim GD had looked from the minute they had set off. He hadn't said a word after his comment on her smoking. She could see and feel him watching her, looking her up and down. What was his problem?

GD strode past her, glancing at the cigarette with disapproval.

"You do know that any kind of dependency is a potential weakness in our line of work?" he said.

Eden couldn't work out whether or not he was joking.

"I don't think nicotine addiction is usually a problem," she said. "Besides. I'm not addicted. I'm in full control."

"Really?" GD looked skeptical.

"Of course. I can stop whenever I want to."

She dropped the cigarette and watched it go out on the rain-soaked gravel.

• • •

There wasn't much room behind Fredrika Bergman's desk as Alex sat down beside her.

"We need to take a closer look at Zakaria Khelifi's case," she said.

Alex hesitated, then said, "You think he's innocent?"

Now it was Fredrika's turn to hesitate. She looked around. There were still a lot of people working at their desks in the open-plan office, and several of them were sitting quite close to her.

"Come with me," she said, heading resolutely for the kitchen. Fortunately, it was empty. "I want to examine those phone records more closely. I absolutely believe that Sebastian's team know what they're doing, but there could be information there that would help us find out if the phone really did belong to Zakaria during the relevant period."

Alex poured himself a cup of coffee. Fredrika had always thought he had lovely hands, but that was yet another thing he would never know.

"If you think it will change anything, then go for it." He shrugged and took a sip of his coffee.

Fredrika suddenly felt a wave of fatigue. "What do you mean?"

"I mean what I say," Alex replied. "We're fiddling about, doing a little bit here, a little bit there. Following leads in a thousand directions and getting precisely nowhere. Like the Keystone Kops."

"Everything has happened so fast, Alex. And we have so little time."

Alex put down his cup with a bang. "We've got to decide which direction we're going in," he said, sounding agitated. "Either we save the plane and everyone on board, or we investigate the question of who's to blame. One or the other, you choose. We can't do both at the same time. And if we choose to focus on who's to blame, which is obviously what we are doing, then the plane is doomed."

"You don't think we can stop this by finding whoever is behind the whole thing?"

"We already know who's behind it; he's sitting at the controls on board the plane!"

Alex turned away.

I don't need to see your anger, Alex; I can feel it anyway.

"So what do you suggest?"

"That we forget about everything else and concentrate on one thing, and one thing only—getting that bloody plane down by letting Erik take over."

It was difficult to contradict him.

"But that's what we're doing," Fredrika said, lowering her voice as she did when she was talking to her children, trying to calm them down. "None of us believes that Karim is the only person behind all this, which means that none of us knows how everything fits together, and how best to proceed."

Fredrika was still thinking about Zakaria.

Zakaria and Tennyson Cottage.

What was the connection?

"Is Zakaria Khelifi the main focus here, or Tennyson Cottage?" she wondered.

"The bomb threats came before the government's decision to deport Zakaria."

"But the hijacking came after."

Fredrika reached for a glass and filled it with water. There was a link between Zakaria Khelifi and Tennyson Cottage, just as there was between the bomb threats and the hijacking—there had to be. And they wouldn't get anywhere until they worked out what it was.

It was like wading through glue. The investigation had been going on for less than one full working day, but Fredrika was as exhausted as if it had been going on for weeks.

"We're getting nowhere," she said.

"That's exactly what I said," Alex replied, his voice hoarse and subdued. "I don't understand what kind of breakthrough we're supposed to be waiting for. The plane has been hijacked, and the person responsible is in control of the cockpit. That's the situation, and we have to act accordingly."

Fredrika nodded and put down her glass. Alex was right, but she wasn't ready to support his suggestion that Erik should take over.

"I'll go and check those phone records."

She went back to her desk, leaving Alex alone in the kitchen. The lack of time wasn't their biggest problem. The real issue was that they had no strategy for what they were going to do when time ran out.

Trying to stop the plane from using up fuel was like trying to stop the sand from trickling through an hourglass.

• • •

It took Eden Lundell less than a minute to realize that the case of the hijacked plane had taken a different turn. They met in a windowless room at Rosenbad: Eden and GD from Säpo, the prime minister, the foreign secretary, and the minister for justice, plus a handful of civil servants from the relevant departments.

"Sit down," the PM said.

His voice was harsh and impatient, as if he had asked them several times to sit down without anyone taking any notice. Everyone immediately did as they were told. The door leading to the corridor was already closed. Eden noticed that not one but two people checked to make sure it was locked.

What the hell is going on here? And why are we on the back foot?

The PM wasted no time.

"We were contacted by the US government less than an hour ago. As expected, the hijacking of Flight 573 has caused consternation on the other side of the Atlantic, not least because of information indicating that the pilot is working with the hijackers. The US authorities have already contacted Karim Sassi to inform the crew that the plane will not be allowed to enter US airspace under present circumstances, and that they must therefore remain in international airspace until the situation is resolved. If the captain decides to attempt to land the plane within the jurisdiction of some other country, the Americans have no problem with that; the only thing they will not accept is a violation of US airspace."

Eden raised her hand a fraction, requesting permission to speak.

"What information have the Americans given Karim Sassi? Does he know we believe he's involved in the hijacking?"

"No," the PM said. "According to the Americans, they have been very low-key in their communication with the aircraft. All they've said is that under the present circumstances they regard the plane as a security risk, and are therefore instructing the pilot to remain outside US airspace."

Eden thought that sounded logical. However, she also thought the hijackers had already foreseen the US reaction, and wondered what would happen next.

Which raised the question of why the hijackers hadn't made direct contact with either the police or the government. They had heard nothing. What did that suggest? That they expected their demands to be met in full? Or the reverse—that they knew they would be rejected, and therefore didn't need any channels of communication?

This hijacking was running contrary to all previous experience. Hijackers usually lost patience, insisted on negotiations, fought for what they wanted. They would also try to speed up the process, raise the stakes in order to force the authorities to make concessions. But in the case of Flight 573, the stakes were not being raised at all. Everything was on the table already.

Over four hundred passengers at thirty thousand feet.

"So what does that mean in words of one syllable?" GD asked.

"What?" said the PM.

"The fact that the plane won't be allowed into US airspace."

"If Karim Sassi has any sense at all, he will obey their orders and stay in international airspace."

Only then did Eden realize why they had been summoned to Rosenbad at such short notice, and why the Americans had passed on their message to the Swedish government rather than Säpo.

But GD didn't get it.

"Sooner or later, the plane will run out of fuel," he said. "And they already know that the pilot is working with the hijackers, yet they still expect Karim to obey their orders?"

Eden felt as if all the air had been sucked out of the room. Without thinking about what she was doing, she placed a hand on GD's shoulder.

"Not necessarily," the PM said grimly; his face had lost all its color. "We have to understand the American perspective, even if we don't sympathize with it. It's ten years since 9/11. They will never risk such an attack happening again. Not if they have the chance to prevent it, which they believe they have in this case."

GD had nothing to say this time. When the prime minister spoke again, Eden already knew what he was going to say.

"If Karim Sassi decides to defy the order to stay away from US airspace, they will shoot down the plane as soon as it crosses the US border."

41

Flight 573

The knock on the door made both Erik Recht and Karim Sassi jump. The silence in the cockpit had been almost palpably dense since their last discussion, and Erik was deep in thought. He had to get out, but without rousing Karim's suspicions so that he would stop him from coming back in. And he had to get hold of his father.

Erik glanced at the small screen and saw Fatima. Karim pressed the release button and Erik quickly opened the door.

"It's happened," she said, closing the door behind her.

Erik immediately turned around, but it was a few seconds before Karim looked at Fatima.

"What has?" Erik asked.

"One of the passengers switched on his cell phone and got a text from his family."

"Fuck," Erik said. "How the hell did that happen? Don't tell me he's started talking to the other passengers."

"No, he came straight to me. Twice."

Erik could see that she hadn't told them everything.

"What did you say to him?" Karim wanted to know.

Fatima bit her lower lip.

"The first time he spoke to me when I was passing his seat, I lied. But then he came to find me in the galley, and this time he was more upset. He was waving his phone around, and he showed me the message from his mother. I had to be straight with him," she said.

"You told him the truth? You confirmed that the plane is under threat?"

"What was I supposed to do?" Fatima said, looking angry and

upset at the same time. "He didn't believe it was a coincidence that his mother's text arrived just after you'd said we were going to be delayed by several hours."

Erik understood that Fatima had been left with no choice, and he knew that Karim felt the same. However, Karim still looked agitated, as if he hadn't expected that one of the passengers would eventually begin to suspect that something wasn't right.

"We need to make some kind of announcement," Erik said to Karim. "More people are going to start wondering. You can't just say we're going to arrive several hours late because of bad weather."

If we get there at all, a little voice whispered inside his head.

Erik swallowed hard. He had no intention of dying. He had just become a father, and at long last he had stability in his life. He had a wife whom he loved, and a home they had built up together.

"No," Karim said. "We have to avoid unrest at all costs. I intend to wait as long as possible before telling the passengers what's happened."

Unrest.

What did that look like in a plane that was flying at thirty thousand feet? People were hardly likely to start fighting to get off first, which would have been the logical aim if they had been on a bus or in a shop that had received a bomb threat.

Erik thought it over, and concluded that he didn't agree with Karim.

"People have the right to know," he said.

"The right to know what?" Karim said.

Erik felt as if his throat was closing up.

That this might be the day when they're going to die.

"That we're under threat," he said.

"And what are they going to do with that information?" Karim's voice was so devoid of emotion that Erik broke out in a cold sweat. "If you haven't realized it yet, there isn't a damned thing any of us can do to change the situation."

What was it that Karim didn't want to reveal? What had happened that would explain his incomprehensible behavior?

"You have to talk to us, Karim," Erik said. "What's going on here?"

Karim turned away and retreated into silence once more.

Erik tried to touch his arm, but Karim moved out of reach.

"Speak to the passenger and ask him to return to his seat," Karim said. "And ask him to keep quiet. Tell him he's endangering his own safety as well as everyone else's if he starts talking."

Fatima stared at Karim's back.

"It might be a good idea if one of you spoke to him," she said. "His name is Joakim."

"I can go," Erik said. "I can have a word with the crew at the same time."

His heart was racing. At last he had a reason to leave the cockpit without it looking odd, but he still didn't trust Karim.

"You stay here," he said to Fatima, who looked confused.

Erik felt something like fear spreading through his body. If Fatima didn't stay in the cockpit, he couldn't risk going out.

"It will look odd if we both go," he said. "I'll go and speak to this guy while you wait here."

Fatima still looked as if she didn't understand, but at least she seemed to realize that her cooperation was important to Erik.

"Okay," she said.

Just as Erik unfastened his seat belt, another call came through. Judging by Karim's reaction, he was equally surprised; the voice they heard was speaking in English.

"Flight 573, respond immediately. Over."

Karim answered as required.

"Captain Sassi, this is Andrew Hoffman, US military air surveillance. Can you hear me?"

"We can hear you."

Erik didn't move a muscle. Fatima was still standing by the door.

"I am contacting you on behalf of the US Department of Defense and the US government. It is extremely important that you listen very carefully to what I have to say, and that you obey to the letter the orders I am about to give you."

Karim's face was white, his lips compressed into a thin line as he listened to the American voice.

"You have already been asked to remain outside US airspace. The following conditions apply for the remainder of your journey: you will not be given permission to cross our border at any stage. It is up to you as the captain of Flight 573 to ensure that the plane remains in international airspace, or to travel to an alternative destination outside the borders of the USA. Is that clear?"

The voice died away and waited for a response.

"Captain Sassi, did you understand what I just said?" Andrew Hoffman asked.

Karim wiped his brow with the back of his hand. "I understand," he replied.

"Good, in that case we don't foresee any problems."

It sounded as if Hoffman was about to end the conversation, but both Erik and Karim had a number of questions.

"Sooner or later, we will run out of fuel," Karim said. "Will we be given permission to make an emergency landing?"

The loudspeaker crackled.

"Captain Sassi, you just said you understood the orders I gave you."

"Yes, but when the fuel runs out, I have two alternatives: either I crash the plane, or I attempt an emergency landing. Therefore, the latter option seems the most reasonable course of action."

Erik let out a sigh of relief. He thought Karim had ruled out an emergency landing after the conversation with the police.

"In that case, you will have to do that somewhere else," Andrew Hoffman said.

What the fuck was going on here?

Karim looked almost panic-stricken, and Erik felt the same.

"What the hell are you talking about?" Karim said. "I am the captain of a plane with over four hundred passengers on board. I must have the chance to save them all from certain death."

"I'm sure you will have that chance, Captain Sassi," Hoffman said. "In some other country."

The alarm bells inside Erik's head were so loud he thought it might explode.

"You don't understand," Karim said. "I have to land in the USA."

Why? Erik wondered.

"I would advise you to change course immediately and prepare for an emergency landing somewhere other than your original destination," Hoffman said implacably. "I'm sorry, but the United States government does not negotiate with terrorists who are holding American citizens hostage. Unfortunately."

Karim looked as if he was about to burst into tears.

"What the hell is wrong with you?" he yelled. "I must be allowed to land, surely that's obvious?"

"You are allowed to land," Andrew Hoffman said. "But not here."

"What's your response to the hijackers' demands?"

"I repeat: the United States government does not negotiate with terrorists. Your flight will not be granted permission to land. If you still insist on entering US airspace, the plane will be shot down."

Shot down? Erik sat there, overcome by a kind of paralysis.

"But you must have heard what was in the note," Karim said. "You have only as much time as it takes for us to use up the fuel we have on board."

"Exactly. In which case, I suggest, as I have already said several times, that you prepare for an emergency landing elsewhere. If you want to risk it, that is."

"If we run out of fuel I won't have any choice," Karim said.

"I think maybe you should read the note again," Hoffman said. "Because, according to our information, it states that if any attempt at an emergency landing is made, regardless of whether you have run out of fuel or not, the plane will be blown up. Isn't that right?"

There was something about Andrew Hoffman's tone of voice that made Erik shudder. As if there was an implicit message in his words that only Karim understood.

When Karim didn't reply, Hoffman continued:

"Good, in that case we understand each other. Over and out."

And he was gone.

Karim looked as if he had been turned to stone.

"Fuck," he whispered.

"What's going on?" Fatima asked. "Did he say they were going to shoot us down?"

"The bastards won't let us in," Karim said.

Erik forced himself to take several deep breaths, then he turned to Karim.

"We have to do as he says. We have to try for an emergency landing somewhere else. We need to call Canada or Mexico right away, to ask if they can help us."

What the hell do we do if they won't give us permission to land either?

"I don't understand," Fatima said. "Why won't they let us in?"

Karim didn't reply; Erik's heart was pounding like a sledgehammer. Now more than ever he knew he had to get hold of his father. The Americans' stance was completely illogical. Even if you took the bomb threat into account, it still didn't make any sense.

Resolutely, he got to his feet, hoping that Karim wouldn't notice how tense and nervous he was.

"Fatima, stay here while I go and talk to the guy who got the text message."

Fatima nodded. "He's waiting in the bar with Lydia," she said, referring to the flight attendant who was in charge of the bar in first class.

Erik turned to Karim:

"I'll be back in a few minutes, and then we can decide where we're going to try for an emergency landing, okay?"

Karim didn't reply.

"I'll be right back," Erik said, passing Fatima on his way out of the cockpit.

As the door closed behind him, he forced himself to breathe calmly. He would speak to the passenger as promised, and then he would call Alex and ask why the Americans had just signed a collective death warrant for four hundred people.

42

Stockholm, 19:00

Fredrika Bergman leafed deftly through the various documents in Zakaria Khelifi's file. Extracts from phone-tap material that looked exactly the same as the police records when Fredrika was working with the National Bureau of Investigation. Surveillance notes. Copies of interviews conducted with Zakaria while he was in custody.

Fredrika spent a little time going over the interviews; Zakaria didn't dispute a single point that was put to him.

Yes, that was him in the surveillance shots.

Yes, he knew the man standing next to him.

No, they hadn't met in order to plan a terrorist attack; his friend needed some help with his winter tires.

Yes, he had made all the calls that Säpo knew about—except for the calls that had been made when the phone didn't belong to him—and no, none of the calls was about anything other than exactly what they sounded like. No coded language, no secret messages.

Someone must have tipped off Säpo about Zakaria Khelifi, because he was arrested one morning without having done anything.

But how did something like that happen? How did a man like Zakaria Khelifi suddenly become interesting to the Swedish security service and be declared a threat to national security if he hadn't done anything?

Fredrika started all over again from the beginning, and even though she knew Zakaria's history with Säpo by heart, she spotted something new. Zakaria turned up over and over again, and in the end there were just too many coincidences for any security service worth its salt to ignore. Such individuals existed not only within Säpo's area of interest, but also within the criminal circles investigated by the National Bureau of Investigation and other police authorities. Those eternal shadows that drifted from one investigation to another, always too insubstantial to grasp. Obviously, even criminals must know people who weren't on the wrong side of the law, but how were you supposed to know which was which?

There was no denying that Zakaria Khelifi had some explaining to do. The problem was that he had tried to do just that. He had answered their questions and given perfectly reasonable explanations for things that seemed strange. He insisted that he hadn't known what was inside the package he had collected. He didn't know why Ellis had said he was involved. And he claimed he hadn't made the calls that Säpo were able to link to previous investigations.

Fredrika picked up the record of Zakaria's earlier telephone traffic, which had just been analyzed again. The calls that Zakaria insisted someone else had made. How had the police coped before the age of the cell phone? In every single case Fredrika had worked on, the analysis of phone calls had been a key element. That was how they tracked down people who had disappeared, picked holes in their alibis, and were able to link them to various crime scenes and cases. On a yellow Post-it note someone, possibly Eden, had scribbled:

A comparison of the phone traffic before and after the point at which Zakaria says that he acquired the cell phone indicates that he could be telling the truth. Different contacts during the two different periods.

A long column of calls was highlighted in yellow. Where the highlighting ended, someone had drawn an asterisk to mark before and after.

Fredrika's cheeks began to burn.

What would happen if the government revised its decision and released Zakaria on the basis of the phone records? Would that bring the hijacking to an end? She was eager to find out more, but she couldn't cope with printouts; she wanted electronic access to the telephone data.

She left her desk right away and went to find Sebastian.

"I'd like access to Zakaria Khelifi's phone records."

"Isn't there a copy in the file?"

"I'd like an electronic copy, please."

Sebastian looked dubious.

"Why?"

"I want to take a closer look at them."

It wasn't really an answer to his question, but Fredrika didn't want to get into a discussion about why she was asking for the records. She wanted to carry out her own analysis, that was all.

Sebastian made room for Fredrika at his computer and opened up a new program.

"I'm sorry to disturb you," she said as she sat down.

"No problem. I've got to go and check on something anyway, and you can only access phone records from certain computers, so you might as well use mine. Let me know if you need any help."

Sebastian left the office and Fredrika gazed at the screen.

Soon her fingers were flying across the keys.

She identified the point at which Zakaria claimed he had bought the phone, and sorted all the calls into chronological order. Then she sorted them again so that all calls made to or from the same number ended up together. The phone had been in contact with roughly twenty numbers; some came up more often than others. Fredrika went through everything systematically.

Just as Sebastian had said, certain numbers came up on both sides of the dividing line, which meant that those numbers had been in contact with both Zakaria and the previous owner of the phone.

Three numbers appeared more frequently than the others. Fredrika made a note of them.

If Zakaria refused to say who the previous owner of the phone was, then surely one of the people who had been in touch both before and after the changeover would be able to help them.

• • •

Negotiating with terrorists was out of the question. Alex Recht knew that, and deep down he sympathized with that point of view.

But what if the terrorists made demands that were reasonable? For example, what if Zakaria Khelifi really was innocent, and ought to be released? Should you refuse to countenance such a demand just because it came from terrorists?

After Fredrika had left him in the kitchen, he hadn't known what to do. His daughter called him on his cell phone, wanting to know how things were progressing. Alex knew what she really wanted to ask: was he going to make sure that her brother came home? Alex didn't have an answer to that question.

He still hadn't been able to contact his daughter-in-law. In an ironic twist of fate, she was on board another long-distance flight heading for South America. He couldn't bear to think about how the news would be broken to her when she landed. They could ask the local police for help if necessary.

What was Alex's role in the ongoing investigation? Nobody knew. With only the initial bomb threats to deal with, the National Bureau of Investigation had had a clear remit, but now Alex wasn't at all sure what his function was supposed to be. No further interviews were planned, and Säpo seemed to be processing all other information themselves.

Fredrika had a point when she said there was something odd about the previous day's bomb threats. No one had claimed responsibility, no concrete demands had been made. Four separate threats, two of them targeting such widely different places as the government building at Rosenbad, and Åhlén's department store. Had they missed some underlying symbolism in the choice of targets? Did it have something to do with the subsequent hijacking? Alex didn't think so. The only link was Karim Sassi's fingerprints on one of the cell phones. Which was no bloody help at all.

Alex left Säpo HQ and went back to his own office to check on how far they had gotten with the investigation into the bomb threats, see if any new information had emerged. Not that it would change anything, but he had to keep busy somehow. He remembered their thoughts on the hijacking before they found out that Karim was involved. Either they had to get the Swedish and US governments to meet the hijackers' demands, or they had to defuse the bomb that was supposed to be on board. Or find the perpetrators behind the hijacking, thus averting the danger.

But with the captain himself involved, that last option disappeared, which was what Alex found so frustrating. There was no longer any chance of having an impact on the threat from the ground; it had to happen on the plane. And Erik was the only one who could help them.

Alex went to speak to one of his colleagues who was working on the previous day's bomb threats.

"At the moment I don't have anything useful to report," he said, barely able to look Alex in the eye. "We don't understand why Karim Sassi was careless enough to leave his prints on one of the phones, but not the others. And if we presume that others were involved, do they also work at Arlanda, or for an airline company?"

"Arlanda?" Alex said.

"All four calls yesterday were made in and around the airport."

"Yes, I remember."

"If we assume that Karim made the call using the phone he left his prints on, then we can also assume that he made that call before or after he started work. But if he wasn't the only one who called, then why did all the calls come from Arlanda?"

"Surely we must be able to sort this out, for God's sake," Alex said. "Have we listened to the recordings properly? Can't we tell if it's the same person making all four calls, or different individuals? Or does the voice distortion make it impossible to work out?"

The voice distortion, bloody Mickey Mouse. Or what had TT said—was it Donald Duck?

"I know that Säpo's sound technicians took over that part of the investigation, because we couldn't remove the distortion here. But if you're asking me, then I'd say it sounded like the same person."

Alex heard Fredrika's voice echoing in his mind:

It doesn't necessarily mean that Karim made any calls at all; his fingerprints could have ended up on that phone in a different context.

"Have we checked whether Karim has an alibi for the times when the bomb threats were made?"

"An alibi?"

Alex clarified: "Do we know whether he was in the vicinity of Arlanda when those calls were made? Have we asked his wife where he was at those particular times? Checked his cell phone, tried to fix its position? Because if he wasn't in or near the airport, then we can be certain that someone else made the calls."

They hadn't drawn the conclusion that Karim was behind the calls, but nor had they excluded the possibility. Too many loose ends were never good.

"Check that right away," he said.

The evidence was laid out like luminous stones in a dark forest, leading the police in one direction: toward Karim Sassi. It wasn't just the Tennyson book and the photograph. There were also the bomb threats, the purpose of which they still didn't understand. And the prints on the phone, and the fact that the phones had been dumped in a wastebasket in a garage at Arlanda.

Why would Karim Sassi have been so careless?

The clues he had left behind were so clear that he might as well have stood in front of the police, waving both arms and shouting: "It was me—don't you get it?"

And that was exactly what Alex couldn't understand.

It was as if Karim Sassi *wanted* to be found out.

43

19:35

She would have given anything for a drink. A long, strong rum cocktail. Eden Lundell would happily have paid an entire year's salary. Instead she defiantly lit a cigarette in her office.

I'll just have a couple of drags. I can stop anytime I want to.

The plane would be shot down if it violated US airspace. That was the news they had brought back from Rosenbad. A kind of madness she was neither willing nor able to absorb. No one would ever be able to forget the memories of 9/11. The Twin Towers collapsing, the column of smoke rising like a rocket into the sky, which just an hour earlier had carried the planes toward their destination. Events like that were bound to shape a country's policies and mental health.

The terrorist attacks in London and Madrid had had a similar effect on the UK and Spain. Rules that used to apply had become obstacles instead of tools in the quest for a safe society. To put it bluntly, you could say that security now came before openness.

The attack on Bryggargatan in Stockholm came somewhere in between. The madness had struck right in the middle of the Christmas rush, just as unexpected as a bolt of lightning in the chill of winter. The wound in the Swedish soul had healed quickly, but the scar remained, and sometimes it made its presence felt.

Flight 573 was heading toward a tragic end unless they could bring the plane down safely before it ran out of fuel. According to the hijackers, it would be blown up if it landed before the Swedish and American governments had met their demands. The same applied if the pilot attempted an emergency landing, even if he did so because he had run out of fuel. The conclusion was clear: if the demands were not met, then the plane and its passengers were doomed.

And now the Americans had said that if Flight 573 entered US airspace, it would be shot down.

Eden's hand was trembling slightly as she stubbed out her cigarette. This wasn't good news. Karim Sassi's response when both the Americans and Säpo had contacted him didn't exactly help matters. He had no intention of violating US airspace as things stood at the moment, but nor did he intend to fly to an alternative destination in order to land. When the fuel ran out, he would call the US authorities and demand permission to carry out an emergency landing.

"I refuse to disobey the hijackers' instructions," he had said.

"But you'll still be disobeying them if you attempt an emergency landing," Eden had replied.

"Yes, but if I've run out of fuel, it won't matter. I'll have nothing to lose by going against their orders. But as long as I still have fuel, I'm going to do what they want, and stay close to US airspace."

With that he had ended the call and Eden had returned to her desk to gather her thoughts.

Sebastian came in.

"Perhaps you should try knocking?" Eden said.

"Perhaps you should try giving up smoking?"

"Did you actually want something, or are you here because you're too stupid to do anything sensible?"

Eden was ashamed of herself as she spoke, partly because she sounded like a teenager, and partly because she knew Sebastian was right. At the very least she had to stop sneaking a quick smoke in her office.

Sebastian laughed wearily.

"You really are unbelievable."

Eden crossed her legs and slid her lighter under a pile of papers.

Sebastian leaned against the wall.

"Fredrika Bergman is going through the phone records."

"What phone records?"

"The ones that show that Zakaria Khelifi could be telling

the truth when he says he's only owned that cell phone for a few months."

"Let her carry on. Alex says she's really good; maybe she'll find something significant. Whatever that might be."

"I had a look at Khelifi's file myself," Sebastian said. "Even if we can't use the phone records, we still have a solid case. We don't need any historical evidence to prove that he could be involved in activities that constitute a threat to national security."

Eden went through the key points out loud:

"We think we've come across him in three preliminary investigations. In the case that led to his being charged, we were able to prove that he helped the two main perpetrators by driving them to various locations, and by picking up the package containing the chemicals that were used to make the bomb. In addition, Ellis stated in several interviews that Zakaria had been involved in the preparations."

"Allow me to play devil's advocate," Sebastian said. "Zakaria says that the phone didn't belong to him when it came up in our earlier investigations. He also says he didn't know what was in the package that he collected. And Ellis retracted his statement."

Their eyes met, and Eden could see that Sebastian was thinking exactly the same as her.

Sebastian looked surprised. His eyebrows shot up and his broad brow furrowed in a way that Eden found quite attractive.

You ought to look surprised more often.

"We need to speak to Ellis again," he said.

"Indeed we do. He and Hassan are still in the custody block, aren't they?"

"Yes—they're due to be moved tomorrow."

"Arrange an interview right away," Eden said.

Sebastian left the room.

It had been a long day for all of them, and it was going to be even longer. No one on Eden's team could go home as long as the plane was in the air. She had even made Elina, who worked part-time, stay on.

"But I have to go home and feed the kids," Elina had protested.

"Don't you have a partner who can take care of them?"

"Well, yes, but he's got his own business, and he's really busy at the moment."

"In that case, I suggest you ring him and tell him that this evening, and any other evening, a threat to national security takes precedence over his little business. And if that's not perfectly clear to both of you, then you need to find another job. In the very near future."

Just thinking about the conversation made Eden's blood boil. Sweden would never achieve equality as long as people continued to pretend that the family was the most important thing in the world. Nor would the country be safe. To think that it took a hijacking to make her realize something so obvious.

Although to be fair, it wasn't only Elina who had problems with that kind of discussion at home. As she had already discovered, Mikael wasn't too impressed by his wife's priorities.

Damn him—if he hadn't been so wonderful she would have left him and the girls several years ago.

The thought had barely crossed her mind when she was overwhelmed by such a wave of regret that she was afraid she would have to sit down on the floor. Eden hadn't cried for years, but she felt the tears spring to her eyes.

Good God, where had this come from? Adults didn't cry. Crying was a sign of weakness, not humanity.

And Eden Lundell was not, in her opinion, weak. Not after everything that had driven her from London. Since then she had chosen the only possible option: invincibility.

• • •

Logically speaking, innocent was the opposite of guilty. The only question was, who had the right to make that judgment? The responsibility lay mainly with the court, but to a certain extent with the police, and sometimes, when everything went wrong, the media. Fredrika Bergman had quickly realized that this was one of the cornerstones of the Swedish justice system.

Cleared up by the police.

This meant that the police believed, following an investigation, that they knew who was behind a crime but were unable to prove it in court, either because the perpetrator was dead, or because there was insufficient evidence. For that reason there were a number of individuals at liberty in society whom the police felt it was particularly important to keep an eye on. They didn't need a court order to do so, merely well-founded suspicions.

Fredrika didn't see anything wrong with this in principle, not as long as the system was used correctly—to keep disruptive elements under control and to prevent crimes. It gave the justice system an added dimension of security, and the authorities wouldn't start looking for another perpetrator if there was no evidence that such a person existed.

But in the case of Zakaria Khelifi, Fredrika didn't know what to think or say.

And now several hundred people were being held hostage so that he would be released. People who could die before the morning, now that the Americans had said that they intended to shoot down the plane. Eden had whispered the news to Fredrika when she came back from Rosenbad.

Which made it all the more urgent to look through Zakaria's file. If he was innocent, Fredrika couldn't think of a better time to find out. This wasn't about giving in to the hijackers' demands; this was about doing the right thing, and doing it in time.

Eden and Sebastian were heading toward Fredrika's desk; she had returned to her own workspace after she had finished with Sebastian's computer. Eden's blond hair was caught up in a messy topknot. Fredrika's hands automatically went to her own dark hair. Every strand seemed to be in place, neatly woven into a thick plait hanging down her back. Spencer had often joked that he would leave her if she ever had her hair cut.

"Come with us," Eden said, beckoning Fredrika.

She didn't stop but merely slowed down to give Fredrika time to catch up with them. Fredrika grabbed her notebook and hurried along.

In silence, the little troupe entered a glass cube with the curtains closed. Eden switched on the light and sat down at the desk in the middle of the floor. Sebastian and Fredrika joined her.

"I heard you checked the phone records. What did you come up with?" she said.

"Nothing startling."

Fredrika briefly went over what she had done and how she would like to proceed. She opened her notebook.

"I've found three numbers that were in contact with the phone before and after the time when Zakaria says he acquired it."

Sebastian got up and looked over her shoulder.

"I'll go and see if we've identified those numbers," he said. Fredrika gave him the notebook and he was gone.

"Good idea," Eden said.

Fredrika thought she looked distracted, almost as if she was having to make a real effort to hold things together.

"Shouldn't we try to speak to Zakaria's sister as well?" Fredrika said, mostly for the sake of something to say.

"We should," Eden said. "Not least because I can't for the life of me understand how we missed the fact that he has a sister who lives in Sweden."

Fredrika couldn't understand it either, but she didn't say anything.

Sebastian reappeared just as Eden spoke, having given Fredrika's notebook to one of his analysts. "I looked into the business of the sister; it's all very peculiar. Nobody in the Immigration Office knew that he had a sister here."

"So she's not an asylum seeker?" Eden said.

"We don't know. She could be, but without having said she's Zakaria Khelifi's sister."

"But why hasn't she come forward?" Eden said. "I mean, we've been in touch with everyone else who's close to Zakaria—either they've contacted us, or vice versa. Not one of them has mentioned a sister living in Sweden."

"We'll have to speak to his uncle again," Fredrika said.

"Can you take care of that while Sebastian and I see whether we can get anywhere with the phone numbers you've found?"

With that the meeting was over, and Sebastian and Fredrika went back to the investigation team area while Eden headed for the elevators.

Fredrika watched her. "Where's she going?"

"I've no idea," Sebastian replied. "You never know where you're up to with Eden Lundell."

It might have been a joke, but Fredrika could see that he was serious, and it worried her. The head of counterterrorism went her own way, usually alone.

In Fredrika's experience, that was how a person lost their way in life.

44

19:50

Efraim Kiel. Fewer than twenty-four hours ago, Buster Hansson didn't even know he existed, and now he couldn't stop thinking about him. Henrik, the head of counterespionage, had come to pass on what they had found out about the man MI5 had named as a Mossad agent.

"How's that business with the hijacked plane going?" he asked out of sheer curiosity.

"I hope it will be okay, but it's more likely to go badly wrong," Buster said. He tried to smile, but it turned into more of a grimace.

"Really?"

"Let's talk about Eden and this Israeli instead," Buster said.

"Of course."

Henrik opened the brown envelope he had brought with him and handed over a bundle of photographs.

Buster flicked through them; they showed the same man in various locations all over Stockholm. Efraim Kiel. In the foyer of the Diplomat Hotel. In a café in the Old Town. In a bookshop on Drottninggatan. At a bistro on Odenplan, together with another man whom Buster didn't recognize.

"Who's he?"

"He's the undersecretary at the Israeli embassy in Stockholm."

Buster let out a low whistle.

"That's bloody careless."

"It certainly is."

Buster carried on looking through the photographs, but there was no sign of Eden.

"He hasn't been anywhere near Kungsholmen or Police HQ?"

"No, not yet. I have to admit that I'm very doubtful as to whether this guy is a Mossad agent at all. He doesn't act like one. I spoke to surveillance at length, and he's behaving just like an ordinary tourist; he hasn't shown any sign whatsoever of being security conscious."

"Such as?"

"He always moves from point A to point B without hesitation. He doesn't take a roundabout route, or make any effort to shake off a possible tail. Of course, this could indicate that he's cool and utterly self-confident—he just doesn't expect to be followed."

"Or else that's exactly what he expects."

"And therefore, he's making a point of acting as if he has nothing to hide. Of course that could be the case. But at least we know what the Brits told you: that they were convinced he was an intelligence officer, which was why they kept him under surveillance."

"And then he was called back to Israel," Buster said. "Have you managed to dig out any more information about him?"

"No; this is a very tricky business. I daren't ask our colleagues too many questions, because I don't want them to start asking me any follow-up questions."

"Eden's name must not come into this, not under any circumstances."

"That's exactly my problem. We've got nothing concrete to put to them," Henrik said.

"In that case, you'll just have to make something up. This has to be resolved. In the very near future."

The head of counterespionage refused to meet Buster's gaze.

Buster went back to the pictures.

"I don't like this," he said, tossing them on the desk. "I don't like it one little bit. It just can't be true. Not now. Not when Eden is leading this whole business with that bloody plane. It would be a total disaster if it turned out that she was an Israeli agent."

Buster shook his head. That just couldn't happen. If Eden wasn't the person she had said she was, then she would take a lot of people down with her.

"Continue tailing him," he said. "We have to know more, we have to be sure of our ground. Then we can decide how to proceed."

Henrik got to his feet.

"I'll keep in touch with surveillance. They're not very happy, I have to say."

"Why not?"

"They want to know why they're being given so little information."

"They'll just have to be patient," Buster said.

Henrik left the room, and Buster was left alone. They would all have to be patient. He had the distinct feeling that they were still a long way from the truth about Eden Lundell.

45

Flight 573

The first-class bar on the ground floor of the plane was empty, as usual. Erik Recht nodded to Lydia, the flight attendant who was running the bar, and asked if she'd seen a young man on his own.

"He was here just now—I think he might have gone to the toilet," she replied.

Erik sat down on a barstool and rested one arm on the shiny counter. Lydia looked anxiously at him.

"Have you heard anything new?" she said, so quietly that he could barely hear her.

"The Americans are being a little difficult, but things will soon sort themselves out."

Otherwise it's all over.

"What do you mean, being a little difficult?"

Erik shook his head. "I promise I'll tell you more once I've got a clearer idea of what's going on," he said, hoping that she would be satisfied with that.

She didn't ask any more questions, but he could see that she wasn't happy about the lack of information.

"Is there much talk?" he said.

The cockpit had become a bubble in which he and Karim were enclosed. He had no idea what the mood was like among the rest of the crew and the passengers.

"What do you think? It's incredibly difficult to walk around pretending we're just circling because of bad weather."

"I do understand that." Erik's tone was vague; he was miles away.

"Can I get you something? Juice? Water?" Lydia offered.

He asked for a juice, and as Lydia served him a glass of freshly pressed orange, he thought about his father once again. He would have a chat with the guy who had received the text, then he would call Alex. For the first time in his adult life, Erik longed to hear his father's voice. He hadn't felt like that since he was a child—if even then. Erik had always felt inadequate; Alex had always found a reason to sigh over something Erik had done or decided to do. The trip to South America had been a kind of high point; after that the fight had gone out of Alex and he had stopped quarreling with his son. Was that when Erik had become an adult? He didn't know for sure.

Claudia loved to talk about their first meeting. He had been so shy, she said. So gangly and immature. Not the kind of guy you wanted to go to bed with, but more of a young boy; she had wanted to stroke his cheek and whisper: "Your day will come." Erik didn't understand it at all, but he realized that Claudia's perception of him must have changed pretty quickly, because not many weeks had passed between the first time they saw each other and the first night they spent together.

The memory gave Erik a warm glow. They had had a son, made a life together. He would never accept that all this could be taken away from him. Not now, not ever. One day, they would all die, but as long as Erik had something to say about it, that day would not come until they were old.

Suddenly he was aware that he was being watched. A young man was staring at him. Erik reflexively checked what he was wearing, and tried to remember what Fatima had said his name was.

"Joakim?" he said, getting up from the barstool.

The young man nodded, and they shook hands. Erik explained that he was the copilot, and said that unfortunately the captain was unable to come out and speak to him in person. As if that was an option they had considered.

Erik looked around; they were still alone in the bar with Lydia, so he decided they might as well stay there for a chat.

"I believe you've heard about our problems."

Joakim nodded. His arms were tightly folded across his chest, and his face was pale and tense.

"I realize everything must seem very worrying, but I can assure you that we are doing all we can to ensure a positive outcome."

Joakim didn't look convinced.

Erik went on: "It's true that we have received a bomb threat, but we have no idea whether it's genuine or not. What we do know is that all baggage on board has gone through rigorous security checks, and that it's virtually impossible to bring a bomb onto the plane."

"But can you take that risk? Assume it's a hoax?"

"Of course not. We're not taking any risks; we are following the hijackers' instructions and working with the police."

Joakim's shoulders dropped slightly.

"You've spoken to the police?"

"Absolutely—several times."

But unfortunately, the captain refuses to listen to what they say. The captain is a fucking lunatic who intends to keep the plane on the periphery of US airspace instead of looking for an alternative place to land.

Erik reached out and placed a firm hand on Joakim's shoulder.

"It would be a disaster if the other passengers found out what's happened," he said. "It's vital that as crew members we can devote all our energy to resolving this situation. If we fail, the consequences could be very serious for all of us. Do you understand?"

Joakim understood. He understood far more than Erik had put into words.

"I won't say a word to anyone."

"Thank you," Erik said. "I hope that includes your family."

He didn't want individual passengers starting to send reports back home.

Joakim looked hesitant.

"If all this takes too long, then I'm going to text my mom. She has the right to hear from me if I . . . If we . . ."

If we're going to die.

Erik couldn't argue with that.

Joakim sighed. "Although my phone doesn't seem to be working anymore."

Thank God for that, Erik thought.

"How late are we going to be?"

There was no answer to that, and Erik knew that Joakim realized that. If the plane crashed, they would never arrive.

They shook hands and Joakim went back to his seat while Erik quickly moved into first class.

He hoped to God he would succeed, otherwise he had no idea what to do next.

There were three empty seats. Erik tried to think strategically. Even if he spoke quietly, there was still a risk that those sitting nearby would hear what he was saying on the phone, and that would be stupid. Therefore, it would be best if those sitting closest to him didn't understand Swedish.

Eventually, he decided on a seat by the window, where the passengers both in front and beside him looked like Asian businessmen.

Erik nodded to the man next to him as he slipped into the seat. Nobody took much notice of him, in spite of his uniform. However, he could see that Lydia was watching him. He ignored her.

The telephone felt awkward in his hand, and he carefully followed the instructions to obtain an outside line from the plane. He could feel the sweat breaking out on his forehead as he keyed in Alex's number. Then he pressed the phone to his ear and waited as it rang out.

When Erik eventually heard Alex's voice, he felt tears pouring down his cheeks, much to his surprise.

"Dad, it's me," he whispered.

46

Stockholm, 19:55

The battle was no longer against the clock, but against those who were withholding information that could put everything right. Zakaria Khelifi's uncle wasn't difficult to get hold of, but Fredrika Bergman suspected that it would be considerably more difficult to get him to cooperate. His voice sounded weary, and for a moment she felt guilty for hassling him.

"I'm sorry to disturb you; my name is Fredrika Bergman, and I'm with the police."

Was she? Hardly. Not right now. But the truth was too complicated. If she called and said she was a liaison officer between the cabinet office and the police, the man wouldn't have a clue what she was talking about, and she would have to waste time explaining.

She reminded herself that she must get in touch with her boss at the Justice Department to follow up on the report she had sent him. She thought about the final sentence she had added before sending it via encryption software:

"There may well be reasons to question yesterday's decision on the case of Zakaria Khelifi."

She had been unable to bring herself to send the document without that addition. And before it was too late, she intended to follow it up with further supporting documentation in which she would spell out the circumstances that weakened the case against Zakaria, if such information emerged. Which Fredrika believed it would.

"What's this about?" Zakaria's uncle said. "I've already spoken to the police."

"I know that," Fredrika said. "And I'm very sorry that we need to contact you again. But it's about Zakaria, and it's urgent."

"Has something happened to him?"

The question came so quickly that Fredrika realized that Zakaria's uncle, and no doubt many of Zakaria's relatives, must be worried that something bad would happen to him.

"No, no, he's fine."

Was he? She had no idea. He might be dying of fear in his cell, facing the inescapable fact that he would be forced to return to his homeland.

"However, we are wondering about something you mentioned to my colleagues when they came to see you this afternoon," she said.

"Oh?" Moussa Khelifi's voice was full of suspicion.

"You said that Zakaria has a sister."

"He has several sisters," Moussa said curtly.

"But how many of them live in Sweden?"

She heard a sigh at the other end of the line.

"What's that got to do with anything?"

"Possibly nothing," Fredrika said, trying to hide the fact that the police were now interested in the sister who had suddenly cropped up in their investigation. "We'd just like to know her name."

And where we can get hold of her.

When Zakaria's uncle didn't reply, Fredrika went on: "It's for Zakaria's sake. We think she might be able to help us. Quite a lot."

That was what they thought, wasn't it? Why else would they want to talk to her?

"Help you in what way?"

"Unfortunately, I'm not at liberty to go into that, but I can assure you that anything you can tell us would be extremely useful at this stage."

She wished he would stop dithering, that she could convince him, because she couldn't cope with soft-soaping him much longer.

"Sofi," Moussa said at last. "Her name is Sofi Khelifi."

"Thank you. Thank you so much. Do you know where we can find her?"

"No. When she's in Sweden she usually stays with various close friends. And she's stayed with Zakaria and his girlfriend now and again."

Fredrika thought about what he had just said.

"When she's in Sweden? Does that mean she doesn't live here on a permanent basis?"

But at that point, Moussa Khelifi decided he had had enough.

"I don't know anything about that," he said. "I only see her a few times a year. If you want more detailed information you'll have to speak to someone else; I can't tell you any more."

Shortly afterward, Fredrika ended the call with a request for a picture of Sofi. Moussa agreed that they could have one, but they would have to come and fetch it themselves. Fredrika organized that, then looked at the name she had written down. Sofi Khelifi. A sister who sometimes lived in Sweden, sometimes elsewhere.

She picked up her notebook and went to see Sebastian, who was talking to a colleague.

"I'll check it right away," he said. "Come with me."

Fredrika followed him into his office, where he logged on to his computer and started a series of searches on Zakaria's sister. Fredrika peered over his shoulder, but there were no matches. Sofi Khelifi didn't exist. Or at least she wasn't visible, and that said something about her that Fredrika didn't like. It was difficult to make yourself invisible in a country like Sweden.

"Could she be using a different name?"

"That's possible," Sebastian said. "Plus, you said her uncle indicated that she doesn't live here all the time, which means that she could be based in another country covered by the Schengen Agreement and travel in and out of Sweden as often as she likes without coming to our attention."

"Can we put out a call for her?"

"I'm not so sure about that; we don't suspect her of any crime. But we could ask some of our partners if they know who she is." He swallowed and stared at the screen. "Although, of course, that means there's a significant risk that we won't get a response until it's too late."

Fredrika drew her jacket more tightly around her. Exhaustion had crept up on her, threatening to paralyze her. The investigation had no direction, it was spreading out like a fan. And now they were looking for someone who could be anywhere.

"Is Eden back?"

"No."

Fredrika thought Alex had been right: they were putting their energy into the wrong aspects of this case. On the other hand, it seemed ridiculous to ignore the reasons behind the hijacking.

Alex. Where had he gone? She hadn't heard from him for a long time.

"We ought to speak to Zakaria as well," she said. "And his girlfriend. One of them must know where we can get hold of his sister, if we think it's necessary."

Sebastian didn't move; he was lost in thought.

"That's up to Eden," he said.

So they waited for Eden to come back to the office.

The evening pressed down on Stockholm and Kungsholmen like an impenetrable lid. Fredrika gazed at all the committed souls, single-mindedly working away at the investigation. She liked what she saw; there was nothing frivolous or disorganized about Säpo. Everyone seemed to know their place, everyone fulfilled their role with something that looked like professional pride, at least on the surface. And there was something else: a warmth and a sense of community that she hadn't seen in any other workplace. Not necessarily between staff and bosses, but among colleagues. Säpo also seemed to have made significant progress when it came to recruiting civilian personnel. Someone had mentioned that they used to have a trainee program, and Fredrika remembered seeing the ads. She had considered applying for one of the posts, but had changed her mind. By that stage she had already been working for several years, and couldn't face the idea of starting all over again from the beginning.

Sebastian excused himself to go to the toilet, and Fredrika thought about Zakaria's uncle. Zakaria had a sister that no one on the investigating team had met, a sister who hadn't come forward at any stage during the legal proceedings. She could, of course, have fallen out with her brother and therefore wished to distance herself from him, but Fredrika had the distinct feeling that there was another explanation for her silence.

Sebastian came back a few minutes later, accompanied by one of his analysts.

"One of the numbers you suggested we should contact to check if Zakaria's phone used to belong to someone else is an unregistered pay-as-you-go SIM card, and can't be identified. Another belongs to a person whom we absolutely do not want to contact. But the third ought to work."

Fredrika felt something that resembled gratitude. As far as Zakaria was concerned, the key issues were his phone and his sister. And now they were getting close to an answer to at least one of those issues.

47

19:55

On the floor where GD had his office, Säpo looked somewhat different. The walls were painted in a color reminiscent of a private medical practice, and there was no open-plan office; everyone had a room of their own. Eden said hello to Henrik, the head of counterespionage, when they met in the corridor outside GD's door. He gave a start when he saw her, but smiled politely. Why the hell would he be stressed?

"I guess you're pretty busy today?" he said.

"Yes, we're under a fair amount of pressure," Eden replied as she knocked on GD's door.

She couldn't get her head around Henrik or his boring job.

GD didn't seem particularly pleased to see her.

"I presume you're here to discuss our response to the information we received at Rosenbad?"

Before she had time to say anything, he went on:

"As I see it, we ought to consider contacting Karim Sassi by phone in order to make it clear that he's not going to get away with his plan. The demands will not be met, nor will he get the chance to stage his spectacular finale by crashing the plane into the Capitol Building in Washington, DC. We no longer have anything to gain by not confronting him."

He hadn't asked Eden to sit down, but she did so anyway.

"That's an interesting idea," she said. "But there's a better option."

"Such as?"

"We ask the copilot, Erik Recht, to take over the plane and land it."

She had thought about it for a long time, and had reached the conclusion that they had no choice. The plane simply had to be brought down.

"And we can be sure that this guy is on our side?"

"Absolutely."

"What happens if he fails? That means Karim will know he's been exposed. But then, of course, he'd realize that if we called him anyway."

"Exactly," Eden said. "It doesn't seem to me that we're risking any more by letting Erik try to take control of the plane than by confronting Karim."

GD seemed to agree with her, but Eden could see that something else was bothering him. Something he didn't want to share with her right now.

She shook off her unease. There was something else she wanted to discuss, but GD was still talking about the hijacking.

"Do we think there's a bomb on board?"

"No. At least, I don't believe there is, particularly now that we know Karim is involved. A bomb seems unnecessary if the pilot is on the side of the hijackers."

"But maybe that's exactly why there is a bomb," GD said. "The hijackers might have foreseen that we would work out Karim's involvement, and therefore supplemented their plan with a bomb. Or maybe they didn't trust him."

"You mean the bomb is there to put pressure on Karim as well?"

"I'm not saying that's definitely the case, just that it could be."

"It's an interesting point of view, but I think one of the few things we can be sure about is that Karim is a part of the hijacking."

"Of course, but even the most hardened criminal can get cold feet."

And that's why there could be a bomb on board, as a kind of insurance to make sure Karim didn't pull out? Eden thought it was highly unlikely. If Karim believed there was a bomb, why was he refusing to approach a different country that would welcome him if he decided to go for an emergency landing? There was very little risk that the hijackers would know if he changed course; even if they were among the passengers, they wouldn't notice anything apart from the fact that the plane was either in the air or coming in to land.

"Actually, I didn't come here to discuss the Americans' plans to shoot down the plane," Eden said.

"You surprise me."

The tone was neutral, but Eden sensed a frustration that she didn't understand.

"Zakaria Khelifi."

GD looked troubled.

"Yes?"

Eden went over what they had already discussed on the phone, and explained how they intended to proceed. She also forewarned GD that the government might revise its decision if it turned out that the cell phone had indeed belonged to someone else. That was really why she had come to see him; they had to take this possible turn of events into account.

"The cell phone, Ellis, and the sister," GD summarized.

"We have to sort this out," Eden said. "And fast."

"Of course; if there are question marks we have to look into the matter right away. I'm just wondering why he's refusing to cooperate with us."

"You mean Zakaria?"

"Yes. If he's got nothing to hide, then why won't he give us the name of the person who used to own the phone?"

"Perhaps because he does have something to hide," Eden said; like everyone else, she had asked herself that question over and over again. "Or to protect someone. Or both."

GD got up and went over to the window. Eden wasn't sure why; it wasn't as if he had a lovely view. He stood with his back to her for what felt like several minutes. Something was bothering him. A lot.

Eden fiddled with a bunch of keys in her pocket. The keys to her house.

She wondered if Mikael was still angry. He probably was. He had never understood what was important in life. Or to be more accurate—what was most important.

Making a difference for other people, not just yourself and your family.

"Do you know why I appointed you, Eden?" GD said.

His voice was rough, as if anger was making his vocal cords contract. For some reason it made her feel nervous.

What was this all about?

"Because you knew I was the best."

GD turned to face her.

"Partly. But mostly because you had a reputation for being loyal, and for having great integrity. Integrity and loyalty, that's what I was looking for."

Eden held her breath for a moment before she replied: "And that's what you found, at the highest level."

GD nodded slowly.

"There you go then."

Nothing else. Just "There you go then."

Eden was almost angry. If there was one thing she couldn't stand, it was game playing. What reason did GD have to question her loyalty?

Without stopping to think, she said, "If you have questions about my loyalty, let me say this: my loyalty lies exclusively with the assignment we are recruited to carry out. Not with Säpo. Not with you. Not with the Americans, and not with the government. With the *assignment*. And if that doesn't suit you, just say the word. I can be out of here in less than ten minutes."

It was true, and it had happened before—when she resigned from her first summer job in a nursing home, where the staff treated the elderly residents so badly that Eden would always be afraid of growing old. And when she resigned from her summer job on a newspaper while she was a student. A newspaper where everything was about increasing circulation, whatever it took, sending Eden out on stories so cheap that she was ashamed to call herself a human being.

And when she resigned from MI5. But that was the last thing she intended to discuss with GD.

She thought she could detect something resembling sorrow in his expression.

"I definitely don't want to lose you," he said. "I just want you to do your very best to resolve this hijacking."

"You have my word on that," she said. "I'll be devoting all my time to doing my job. To the best of my ability."

GD stroked his chin as he watched her turn to walk away.

"Good," he said. "Then we're in agreement."

She hoped so, because she had been honest with him.

The assignment was the only important thing, and it took precedence over everything else. And that included freeing those who were innocent.

"I want to question Ellis again," she said, turning back. "We have to find out why he retracted his statement identifying Zakaria as a collaborator."

GD nodded in agreement. Ellis was easy to tackle; Karim was more difficult.

Eden was also thinking about Captain Sassi. How did you hold someone who was no longer on the ground accountable for their actions?

She had no answer to that question.

48

Flight 573

"Dad, it's me."

"Sorry?"

Alex sounded annoyed.

Erik pressed the back of his hand to his forehead, praying that his father would be able to hear him.

"It's Erik," he said, trying to speak more clearly without raising his voice. "Dad, it's Erik."

It took a second, but then his father spoke.

"Thank God."

It was no more than a faint whisper.

"Dad, are you there?"

"I'm here. How are you?"

Fucked.

"I'm fine. We all are. But I don't know how long I can talk."

"I understand. Where are you?"

The question told Erik a great deal about what Alex already knew. He assumed that Erik wasn't calling from the cockpit.

"In first class."

"So Karim can't hear you?"

Further confirmation that Erik had been right in his assessment of the situation.

Karim is flying us straight to our deaths.

"No. Dad, I need some advice."

"I'm listening."

I'm listening.

The words echoed through Erik's mind. Had he ever turned to

Alex for advice? He didn't think so. Because Alex never listened, he just came up with solutions to problems that Erik didn't have. Because he easily—*so very easily*—resorted to bullying tactics.

Alex had never earned Erik's trust.

Until now.

"Are you tired, Erik?"

Erik dashed away the tears.

"I can cope."

I can I can I can.

He gathered his strength.

"But we have a problem on board," he said. "Or several, it would appear. Karim isn't himself. He's been behaving oddly all day. I think . . ."

He felt sick, thought he might throw up.

"I think he's involved. I don't know how or why, or in what way, and I know it sounds illogical, but I'm absolutely certain."

The words were coming faster now; he couldn't stop himself.

"He insists on staying close to the US border and circling until we run out of fuel. If he isn't granted permission to carry out an emergency landing, we're going to crash into the sea or be shot down by the Americans."

Erik shuffled lower in his seat, hoping that the passengers weren't following the conversation, that he wasn't attracting too much attention.

"He's fucking crazy, Dad. He seems disorientated; he started babbling about Washington as our destination instead of New York."

Alex raised his voice.

"*Washington?* For fuck's sake, Erik, did you say Washington?"

Erik had heard that level of fear in his father's voice only once before. When his mother was entering the final phase of her illness, and a courageous doctor delivered the news to Alex, Erik, and his sister.

"We've done all we can," the doctor had said. "We've tried everything possible, but that's it. We're not getting anywhere. Lena isn't going to get better; she probably won't make it to Christmas."

There was nothing Erik hated remembering more about his

mother's illness and death than that dreadful day. And his father's voice haunted him night after night, long after it was all over, long after the funeral.

"I refuse to accept this. You can't just stand there and tell me she's going to die and I'll be left alone. Do something. Anything. Do something!"

But the doctor had merely shaken his head and Alex had yelled and yelled and Erik's sister had cried and cried and in the end everything was so fucking unbearable that Erik had just wanted the ground to swallow them up so that they could all die together.

That was several years ago, and this time Alex didn't need any help in order to pull himself together.

"Erik, I'll be brief," he said. "We've come to the same conclusion as you. I can't tell you exactly how we got there; that wouldn't alter your situation. The fact that you've mentioned Washington is an ominous sign. We're extremely worried about Karim's involvement and what he might do. Has he said anything about the bomb that's supposed to be on board?"

Erik really wanted to hear more about the Washington angle, but there was no time for questions.

"Several times. He seems to be completely convinced that there's a bomb in the hold, but I find that very strange. It's virtually impossible, given the security measures that apply to transatlantic flights, and Karim knows that as well as I do. And yet he still refuses to go against the hijackers' instructions."

"We have reason to believe that Karim is not going to change his mind on that point," Alex said. "We think he's going to do exactly what the note told him to do." Alex fell silent, then went on: "Do you understand what I'm saying?"

He didn't need to say any more. Alex and his colleagues knew things that Erik could only guess at, but the key point was that they had reached the same conclusion: Karim was a danger to himself and his passengers.

"I don't believe there is a bomb," Erik heard himself saying. "I think we could land the plane."

"But Karim's not going to do that," Alex said. "You do understand that, don't you?"

Erik understood everything and nothing. Almost.

"What's the problem with Washington?"

The line crackled and Erik straightened up.

"Dad?"

"I'm here, Erik. We don't have time to go into that right now."

"But . . ."

"We don't have time," Alex repeated. "You have to take over the plane. Right away. Do you hear me?"

"I hear you. And that's exactly what I was intending to do."

"Karim's bigger than you."

"I'll sort it, no problem."

"Don't hesitate, just do what you have to do. And remember, you'll only get one chance."

Erik nodded without speaking.

"Can you land the plane?"

"Of course. That's why I'm on board, after all."

Erik thought his father was smiling.

"I know, I just wanted to hear you say it."

Then their time was up. Erik had to go back to the cockpit. Overpower Karim and take control of the plane.

I'll hit the bastard over the head with a bottle of wine.

"I'll speak to you soon," he said.

"Good," Alex replied.

Erik put down the phone. If this was their last conversation ever, they would both regret the abrupt ending.

Erik left his seat; he went back to Lydia in the bar and asked her for a bottle of wine in a plastic bag. She looked somewhat taken aback, but didn't ask any questions. Erik strode up the stairs to the upper floor and the cockpit.

When he reached the door, he waited for a moment before pressing the button to request admission. This was it.

Time to put an end to the nightmare.

49

Washington, DC, 13:55

The plane would be shot down and history would be made. Bruce Johnson wasn't surprised when the news reached him from the CIA. Karim Sassi couldn't be persuaded—he was not prepared to move away from the US border, and he had no intention of landing anywhere other than the United States.

What the hell was wrong with the guy?

It wasn't that Bruce lacked ideals. There were many things he held sacred; the love he felt for his family and his country were two examples. God help anyone who came near those he held dear with the intention of harming them. The very thought made him shudder. There was no weapon on this earth he wouldn't use against the enemy who threatened those he loved.

But this. The way Karim and others like him behaved. Taking innocent people hostage, or sacrificing them in acts of violence in an attempt to change the politics or core values of another country. Killing people they had never even met, people they couldn't possibly have a grudge against. He just didn't understand it. And he really had tried hard, for a long time.

When Bruce was a child, his father had taught him that you should always try to meet the other person halfway if you had a problem.

"It's never one person's fault if two people are quarreling," he had said.

That expression had become one of the tenets that had shaped Bruce as a man and a person. His mother, a devoted churchgoer, had added the lesson of turning the other cheek. At university Bruce had written essays criticizing the Americans' unilateral attitude to the rest of the world, and the USA's inability to coordinate its foreign policy with anyone else's. Back then he had thought the USA shouldn't attempt to police the world, either on its own initiative or that of others. Instead, the USA should turn to the United Nations and seek broader international support for its policies. It was important to understand the value of establishing a firm basis for one's actions, Bruce had argued. Otherwise there was a risk that policies could become counterproductive, endangering US security instead of strengthening it.

On September 10, 2001, Bruce celebrated his twenty-fifth birthday with his family and his girlfriend. They had dinner at Bruce's favorite pizzeria, then went bowling. The next morning, he went out for a run. It was eight thirty when he set off for the university, where he was in the first year of his doctorate.

It was a day that changed him forever.

The planes that crashed straight into the Twin Towers of the World Trade Center and the Pentagon destroyed so much of everything he had believed in that he was no longer the same person when he went to bed that night. The following year he had left university and gotten a post with the FBI. He was no longer able to motivate himself to write meaningless assignments on US security policy. He wanted to make a difference, for himself and for others.

"Why don't you join the army?" his grandfather had said.

Bruce hadn't wasted any time thinking about that suggestion. He wasn't the kind of man who took up arms.

And that, it turned out, was one of the major differences between him and many of his friends and colleagues. Bruce wasn't the only one who had changed after 9/11. Loud voices screamed for revenge.

In Afghanistan.

In Iraq.

In every fucking corner of the world where they thought a terrorist might be hiding, or be hidden by someone else.

The pendulum swung the other way for Bruce. This wasn't how he had thought things would be. There had to be another way to make the world safe, other than letting the blood flow in the narrow channel of the River Tigris.

Or maybe not.

Another plane was on its way to the USA. Flight 573. With Karim Sassi in charge. A man with a secret mission: to crash the plane into the Capitol Building, once again using violence against American pride and self-esteem.

No fucking way was it going to happen again.

But to shoot down a jumbo jet with over four hundred passengers on board . . . What would they say to the relatives?

"Sorry, but we had no choice."

Was that true? Wasn't there always a choice?

Bruce went through the notes he had made during the course of a working day that already felt long, even though it was still early afternoon. He had been in touch with Säpo in Stockholm and spoken to Eden Lundell. Bruce found it incomprehensible that someone like her could have been appointed head of counterterrorism in Sweden, but what did he know? Perhaps the Brits hadn't had the sense to inform their Swedish colleagues about what kind of monster they had taken on.

However, she had had valuable information to pass on to Bruce. Valuable and interesting.

Karim Sassi was not a Muslim.

And there may well be elements that needed to be cleared up in the case of Zakaria Khelifi.

What did the fact that Sassi was not a Muslim actually mean? Everything and nothing. Bruce was one of those who was very clear about the fact that being a Muslim was not synonymous with being a terrorist, and that there were also many terrorists who were not Muslims. But in that case, what was Karim's interest in Zakaria Khelifi and Tennyson Cottage? He could, of course, be a particularly committed citizen who had lost his way due to his convictions and was now in the middle of a horrific crime, but there wasn't much in Karim's background to suggest that this was a likely scenario.

Bruce picked up a photograph of Sassi. Dark, broad shouldered, looking straight into the camera with a dazzling smile; he had the same air of assurance, the same certainty of victory as an American football player.

Who are you? Bruce thought. Who are you, and why are you doing this?

His boss interrupted his thoughts with a knock on the door.

"We have visitors from the Pentagon who would like to speak to us."

Bruce put down the photograph and followed his boss along the corridor to a spartan conference room where their visitors were waiting. Two men, one dark-haired and one fair-haired, who introduced themselves with their surname and rank. Bruce didn't bother trying to remember them. He didn't really have time for this, and hoped it wouldn't take long.

And his prayers were answered.

"We've come to talk about Tennyson Cottage," said the dark-haired man.

"We know the CIA have already been here for the same reason," his colleague went on, "but we have fresh information that we think you should be aware of."

"It's not really fresh information," the dark-haired man said. "But it is sensitive, and when the CIA came here a few hours ago, we hadn't decided whether it could be passed on to you."

"And now we've made up our minds."

Bruce looked from one to the other, thinking that the whole thing was a joke. If they kept on taking it in turns to speak, there was no way he could take them seriously.

"What is this information you've kept from us?" Bruce's boss said, sounding furious.

"We haven't kept it from you," the dark-haired man said. "We've simply been cautious with it."

Bruce linked his hands on the table in order to keep them still.

"Whatever," said his boss.

The fair-haired man looked annoyed, but said nothing. His colleague continued:

"I don't know how much the CIA told you about what goes on at Tennyson Cottage. As I said, it's a sensitive issue, even if everyone knows we have detention facilities in Afghanistan."

Yes, Bruce thought. Indeed they do.

"After the second of May everything became even more sensitive, as I'm sure you realize. We evacuated and cleared a number of our facilities. Tennyson Cottage was one of the places we decided to shut down."

Bruce blinked.

The fair-haired man smiled at his surprise.

"Pardon me for interrupting," Bruce said. "But are you sitting here telling us that Tennyson Cottage has been shut down since the second of May?"

The day Osama bin Laden was shot dead by American special forces in Pakistan.

"That's right. So you could say that whoever has hijacked Flight 573 doesn't exactly have up-to-date information."

Bruce tried to grasp the significance of what the man from the Pentagon was saying. Then something else occurred to him.

"It's possible that the Swedes might release Zakaria Khelifi; there is some suggestion that they might have made errors in the investigation that led to the government's decision to deport him."

The dark-haired man was picking at a cuticle.

"So we heard."

"And now you tell us that Tennyson Cottage is already closed? That means everything is sorted—both the hijackers' demands have been met!"

Bruce's boss cleared his throat.

"It's not quite that simple," he said.

"You mean we'd rather shoot down a plane with American citizens on board than reveal that Tennyson Cottage has been shut down?"

"He means we can't just announce that Tennyson Cottage no longer exists," the dark-haired man said. "Above all, we can't negotiate with terrorists. Just imagine what a precedent that would set. Hijackers would be lining up to get their demands met."

Bruce just had to protest.

"But there'll be an inquiry. This will never blow over. People will keep on asking questions about why it was necessary to sacrifice so many lives rather than negotiate with terrorists."

The dark-haired man gazed wearily at Bruce.

"Surely you don't think we intend to shoot down the plane if there's an alternative? Of course there will be questions afterward, and then we'll be able to put all our cards on the table. Imagine how incredibly calculating we will appear. In a positive way. The message will be very clear: forget about using violence to change the world, because it won't work. Besides, we have fresh intelligence to take into consideration."

"Fresh intelligence? From whom?" Bruce's boss wanted to know.

Bruce himself sat in silence, trying to take in what the guy from the Pentagon had said. They would appear calculating. In a positive way. Was he serious?

"From the same source as before. The Swedes will be informed as soon as they decide to hold a meeting with their German colleagues."

"And what is this new intelligence?" Bruce said.

"The Germans have received another email stating that Karim Sassi's mission does not depend on whether or not the hijackers' demands are met. He is going to crash the plane into the Capitol Building *regardless* of whether they get what they want."

It couldn't be true. There was no logic in what Bruce had just heard, none at all.

The fair-haired man clarified: "Think about what's happened today. A jumbo jet takes off from Stockholm, heading for New York. During the time it will take the plane to use up the fuel it has on board, two governments are faced with two equally impossible tasks. Even if we were to agree to their demands, we would never have time to action that agreement in the time available. The Swedes might manage it, but there is no way we could do it."

"So we were never meant to succeed?"

The dark-haired man shook his head, his expression grim.

"No."

"But now . . ."

"Now we have a very strange situation, because, yes, if the Swedes release Khelifi, then theoretically we could achieve the impossible, and meet the hijackers' demands at short notice. But the

probability that the hijackers would accept that what we say is true is
ridiculously low."

"So Sassi would crash the plane anyway?"

"That's our assessment of the situation, which is why we have decided not to release the information that Tennyson Cottage has been
shut down."

The sweat was pouring down Bruce's back.

"So what's the alternative?"

Because surely we can't shoot down the plane?

"We land the plane."

"You land the plane?"

"That's correct."

"And who exactly do you mean by 'we'?" Bruce said.

"By 'we,' I mean one of our colleagues who happens to be on
board Flight 573. His background means that he would be able to
land the plane with a certain amount of support, if he can just take
over the controls."

Bruce couldn't believe his ears.

"You have a pilot on board?" his boss said.

"Yes. But he belongs to one of our secret units, which makes the
whole thing a little delicate. And he's traveling in a private capacity;
he's been visiting friends in Stockholm."

"Does he know what's going on?" Bruce asked.

"Sassi has made an announcement to the passengers, saying that
their arrival will be delayed by several hours because of problems
on the ground in the USA. Apparently, he said something about
communication issues at the airport, which was when our colleague
pricked up his ears and contacted us to ask if we could check out the
situation. Needless to say, we then told him what was happening."

Crazy. This was a crazy story. From start to finish.

"How did he contact you?"

"He's traveling first class, so he used the phone in the armrest.
He also has a cell phone that works from time to time, though not
very often."

"But why drag someone else into this? There's a copilot sitting
next to Captain Sassi; he's perfectly capable of landing the plane, if

he can just get Sassi out of the way, which shouldn't be particularly difficult."

"That's true, but how do we get in touch with the copilot without Sassi finding out what's going on?"

The dark-haired man folded his arms.

"We believe the best option is for our man on the plane to speak to one of the flight attendants and ask her to help him get into the cockpit, where he can quickly deal with Sassi."

It slowly became clear to Bruce what kind of operative was sitting on that plane. One who was trained to "deal with" other people without hesitation.

"So he approaches a flight attendant, shows her some kind of ID, then gives her whatever information is necessary to get her to make some excuse to go into the cockpit?"

"Exactly. Because in this situation it is unlikely that Sassi will allow anyone apart from his crew through that door."

Bruce understood the plan more clearly now, and thought it might well succeed.

"What happens if there's a bomb on board?" his boss said.

"There isn't," the dark-haired man stated. "Not possible. The bomb threat was made purely to draw attention away from Sassi."

"When will your colleague act?" Bruce said.

The man from the Pentagon looked at his watch.

"We should be hearing from him at any minute."

Bruce looked down at his hands.

Zakaria Khelifi might be released.

Tennyson Cottage had already been shut down.

And soon Flight 573 would be in the hands of the Pentagon.

As long as their operative managed to get into the cockpit.

50

Stockholm, 20:10

They gathered around Fredrika Bergman's desk. They had a name for Zakaria's sister, but that was all. And the interview with Ellis, who had been convicted of terrorism offenses and had named Zakaria as a collaborator, had lasted less than ten minutes. He wouldn't say a word about why he had retracted his statement.

"Who can help us?" Eden said.

Her fingers beat an impatient tattoo against the hard surface of the desk, and Fredrika suppressed an urge to ask her to stop.

"Have you spoken to the Germans yet?" Sebastian asked.

"I've got a meeting with them in fifteen minutes. They've been waiting for this for quite some time. I'd like you to come with me."

"Okay."

"I can speak to Zakaria's girlfriend," Fredrika suggested, keen to find herself a job before Eden came up with something else. "About his sister."

"Indeed you can," Eden agreed. "But you're not employed by the police any longer, so you need to take one of the investigating officers with you. We're running out of time now, so if you could do that as soon as possible . . ."

They'd been running out of time all day; Fredrika didn't understand why Eden had said "now." The pressure had never eased.

"Why is Ellis refusing to talk?" Sebastian said to Eden.

"You tell me."

"Could he have been threatened?"

"If so, it must have happened while he was in isolation in the custody block, which suggests that the answer to your question is no."

Sebastian stroked his beard.

"In that case, it seems even more strange that he named Khelifi in the first place."

"He could have changed his mind without having been threatened," Eden said. "I've read through the transcripts; he didn't hesitate for a second when he informed on Zakaria Khelifi."

"That's exactly what I mean." Sebastian sounded frustrated. "None of us had any doubt that he was telling the truth. And he provided a lot of detail—names, events, times, again without any hesitation."

Fredrika listened to their discussion, not knowing what to say. There could be hundreds of reasons why a person would wrongly accuse an acquaintance of being involved in a crime, but considerably fewer reasons why he would then retract such an accusation. A threat was of course a possibility, but in that case how had it been communicated to Ellis?

They would never know.

"Have you told the Justice Department about the phone records?" Eden asked.

"Yes, and they were worried, to say the least," Fredrika replied. "They said they'd call me within the hour."

"They're intending to review the deportation order? Before we even know for sure whether he's lying or telling the truth?"

"I don't think so, but if we don't manage to establish the facts as far as the phone is concerned within the next few hours, they will probably feel compelled to give him the benefit of the doubt."

Eden snorted.

"And what if we find out tomorrow that it was his phone all along? Will they expect us to pick him up again? Because that's not happening."

Sebastian spoke up: "There's a great deal we don't know at the moment; let's just take one thing at a time."

The strain was showing on Eden's face.

"You could also say that we're making too many assumptions, which isn't helping us at all." She looked from Fredrika to Sebastian. "We think we might have misjudged Zakaria's background, but we don't know. We think the fact that he has a sister in Sweden could be important, but we don't know why. We think yesterday's bomb threats are highly significant in terms of what has happened since then, but we don't know how. And we think that Karim Sassi is involved, but there are inconsistencies in the evidence that haven't really been explained. Leaving that aside, we still have absolutely no idea why he's doing what he's doing."

"Plus, we don't think there's a bomb on board the plane, but we don't know for sure," Sebastian added.

"There you go, yet another thing."

In fact, there were still more things they didn't know—things that were too difficult to talk about. How were they going to bring down the plane? How were they going to rescue the passengers on Flight 573?

I can't cope with this, Fredrika thought. Not another story without a happy ending. If that happens, I'll never come back to the police.

She interrupted her own train of thought. The fact that she would never go back to the police had been self-evident since the day she left. Hadn't it?

Surely I'm not sitting here missing the most stressful job I've ever done?

"How are we fixed as far as the media goes?" Eden asked.

"We're up shit creek without a paddle," Sebastian said.

"Have we confirmed which flight has been hijacked?"

"We did that over an hour ago, Eden."

So where was I? Fredrika wondered; she'd missed that, too.

Energy. They needed energy. Otherwise they weren't going to make it. Fredrika almost felt as if the area behind her desk was a trench on the edge of a battlefield, where she was hiding away because she was too tired to fight.

"Zakaria Khelifi's phone," she said.

"Exactly," Sebastian said. "One of the numbers that has had repeated contact with the cell phone both before and after the date when Zakaria allegedly acquired it belongs to a guy called Jerker Gustavsson. He's a car mechanic, and we initially dismissed the contacts with Zakaria as being of no interest to us."

"Is he a close friend of Zakaria's?" Fredrika asked.

"I don't think so. They spoke only a few times from the point when we started monitoring Zakaria's calls, and it was always to do with Zakaria's car, or his girlfriend's car."

"How many times do you call your mechanic?" Fredrika said, never having called a garage in her life.

Sebastian laughed. "Good question. Perhaps Zakaria had a real old banger?"

"Just like the person who had the phone before him," Fredrika said.

"That's the kind of thing we need to ask him," Eden said. "We haven't got time for any guessing games at this stage. I don't care how late it is, I want someone to go and question this guy. That's more important than speaking to Zakaria's girlfriend."

Alex suddenly appeared from nowhere. His face was pale and set, his eyes blank.

Fredrika felt upset and afraid at the same time.

Are you going to have to cope with another loss, my friend?

"He called," Alex said.

His voice was so loud that others working in the open-plan office could hear him.

"Who?" Eden said.

"Erik."

He covered the last few yards in no time, and stopped by the desk.

"He called you?" Eden was unable to hide her surprise.

"From the cockpit?" Fredrika asked.

"No, from first class. He said that Karim has gone crazy."

Alex relayed what Erik had told him with such precision that Fredrika's heart ached. He had memorized every word, because if they never spoke again, he wanted to be sure he didn't forget what his son had said.

"Washington," Eden whispered when he had finished.

Alex nodded. "That means there's no longer any doubt."

It was true. It was hardly a coincidence that Karim had said Washington instead of New York. The person who had sent the email to the Germans had been right: Karim was intending to crash the plane in the capital city of the USA.

Fredrika looked away. *Shit.* She had felt compelled to question Karim's involvement, but to what purpose?

Eden changed tack.

"What advice did you give Erik?"

Alex stood there in silence.

"You told him to take over the plane."

"He'd already been thinking along those lines," Alex said. "But if he hadn't come up with the suggestion . . ."

"Then you would have done."

"Yes."

"We need to inform the Americans," Sebastian said.

"Let's wait until we hear from him again," Eden said. "Or if we think too much time has passed without any word from him. I spoke to GD, and he agreed that Erik should try to take control of the plane if there's no other option."

"One more thing," Alex said, and Fredrika could feel him trying to catch her eye.

"What?" Eden said.

He had built up their expectations by now; in just a few seconds he had been transformed into the man who knew more than anyone else.

"Karim Sassi can't have made any of the bomb threats yesterday."

"Has that been confirmed?"

Eden's voice had a sharpness that made the windows vibrate.

"I asked one of my team to check where Karim was when the calls were made from the Arlanda area. His wife says they were at a parents' afternoon at the children's nursery for several hours, so he was a long way from the airport. We've tracked his cell phone, and she's telling the truth. He wasn't at Arlanda yesterday."

Where did that leave them?

He hadn't made the threats, but he had spoken to the person who did, and for some as yet unknown reason he had held one of the phones.

"He's still involved," Eden said, underlining the one thing they could be sure of.

Karim Sassi was on the hijackers' side.

And he had been in contact with whoever made the bomb threats the previous day.

51

Flight 573

Three feet from the door to the cockpit. He had stopped there, unable to make himself go any farther. The stress surged through his body, paralyzing him in midmovement.

Erik Recht had never once struck another person in the whole of his adult life. It just wasn't part of his makeup. You didn't do that kind of thing, and that was that. A fundamental principle that marked the dividing line between right and wrong.

And now he couldn't make himself do what had to be done.

The passengers in first class watched him as he turned around and disappeared into one of the toilets. He was still carrying the plastic bag containing the bottle of wine, and he placed it on the floor before sinking down onto the toilet seat and massaging his temples.

Think. He had to think.

This was ridiculous; was there no alternative? He tried to imagine what would happen. How he would enter the cockpit, take out the bottle, and smash it down on Karim's head. Several times, if necessary. He would keep on until he was certain that Karim would be out of action for as long as necessary to allow him to carry out an emergency landing.

He missed Claudia more than ever, wanted her to be there. To take his head in her hands, look into his eyes, and say:

"You can do this, Erik."

He thought about calling his father again. Loneliness had never been Erik's thing. He had loathed it in the past, but now he feared it. He had decided not to tell any of his colleagues about his plan.

At least not yet. The conversation with Fatima in the toilet was still fresh in his mind. It would take time to convince his colleagues that Karim was involved, time they didn't have. Erik had to go back into the cockpit and take control of the plane. That was the only thing that mattered. Everything else could come later.

He thought about Fatima again. She was still in the cockpit.

That could definitely be a problem.

What would she think in the seconds before Erik managed to explain? Would she actually jeopardize the whole thing, step in to protect Karim? He didn't want to end up in a situation where he had to deal with Fatima as well.

Erik got up, turned the tap, and quickly sluiced his face in cold water. He dried himself with a paper towel. It was now or never. He wouldn't save anyone's life if he stayed here, locked in the toilet. Karim would have the opportunity to explain, but not right now. For his own sake and everyone else's, he had to be removed from the controls.

Resolutely, Erik picked up the plastic bag and opened the door. His legs were trembling as he stepped into the first-class cabin.

Now. It has to be now. Not later, now. Now.

He had taken no more than two steps when he heard a man's voice behind him, addressing him in English.

"Excuse me."

Erik turned around, not wanting to draw any more attention to himself than necessary. But it was already too late; he realized that as he looked around and saw all the passengers gazing inquiringly at him.

"Unfortunately, I don't have time to talk right now," he said. "You'll have to speak to one of the flight attendants."

"That was my intention, but then I saw you," the man said. "The flight attendant who went into the cockpit is still in there, I think."

The man gave Erik a meaningful look, as if he was silently referring to some kind of mutual understanding between them, but, as far as Erik was aware, they had never met before.

He looked the man up and down. He wasn't very tall, but even though he was wearing a shirt and jacket, Erik could see that he was unmistakably muscular; he obviously spent a considerable amount of time working out. His shirt hung loose over his trousers, but judging by the creases around the bottom, it had been tucked in until fairly recently.

When Erik didn't say anything, the man went on:

"The fact is that I'd much rather talk to you. Can you spare a few seconds?"

He was speaking so quietly that Erik was sure none of the passengers could hear him, but they could still see the two of them standing here talking.

"No," Erik said, keen to get back to the cockpit. "You'll have to wait for the flight attendant—she'll be back in a minute."

It happened so fast that Erik didn't have time to react. In less than a second, the man had stepped around him and was now standing in the aisle, preventing him from going anywhere. The man moved as close as possible, and for some reason Erik was rooted to the spot.

The man whispered in his ear:

"I know what's happened and I can help you if you just get me into the cockpit. Okay?"

Erik jerked back, involuntarily but so obviously that the man couldn't help but notice. Through clenched teeth Erik muttered:

"I don't know who you think you are, but I'd like you to do us all a favor: go back to your seat and let the crew take care of the plane."

He didn't bother waiting for a reply, but shoved past the man. His heart was pounding so hard it almost hurt. So there was more than one perpetrator on board. No fucking way was Erik about to let any of them into the cockpit. Not without a fight.

Each step took him closer to the cockpit door; only when he reached it did he glance over his shoulder to see if the man was following him. Which he was. He was dangerously close, less than two feet away.

The bottle. What if he needed to use it before he got to Karim?

Erik had no time to think. He let the man draw closer, and just as he was about to turn and confront him with everything he had, the man strode forward and pushed him up against the door.

"I'm on your side, for fuck's sake. I'm with a special unit in the US military. Don't make me do something unpleasant in front of the other passengers. Just get that fucking door open. Right now."

His voice was no more than a hiss, and it made Erik feel sick.

Why would he act like this if he was on Erik's side?

Special unit? What kind of a joke was that? If he couldn't come up with anything better, he had only himself to blame.

"Okay, okay. I'll help you."

Erik had to free himself from the man's grip in order to deal with him. He wanted to ask him who he was, who he worked for. But there wasn't time, and besides he wasn't interested in any more lies. He already knew who the man was, knew he was evil. His build and attitude conveyed something that Erik couldn't put into words. He looked like someone who was used to being obeyed and treated with respect.

But not this time.

"No fucking way are we on the same side."

As the man loosened his hold, Erik acted with a strength he hadn't realized he possessed. Without taking the bottle out of the bag, he slammed it straight into the man's temple.

Hard.

The man groaned and tried to clutch at Erik before he went down. He crashed to the floor, landing at the feet of the passengers in the front row, who screamed in terror as Erik raised the bottle to strike again; it hadn't broken.

He bent down and examined the man, who was bleeding. He was breathing, but appeared to be unconscious. Without hesitation Erik removed the man's belt, turned him over, and secured his hands behind his back. He spoke to the passengers:

"I'm sorry you had to see that. If you'd like to change seats, you're welcome to do so, but I'm afraid this man has to stay here."

He had to get into the cockpit, get Fatima out so that she could keep an eye on the man, sound the alarm if he started to constitute a danger.

Without another word, Erik got to his feet and moved over to the door. Pressed the button and waited to be let in. Pressed it again. And again.

And again.

And again.

But the door remained locked, leaving Erik standing in the aisle with the plastic bag in his hand.

Karim had no intention of letting him in.

He was going to do what he had set out to do, and kill them all.

52

Washington, DC, 14:15

Why hadn't they heard from him?

It must be half an hour since the Pentagon had instructed their man on board, and Bruce was waiting in his office, unable to settle. The man should have managed to get into the cockpit by this stage. The chances of not finding a flight attendant who was willing to help him were infinitesimal, so what could have happened?

Bruce went over to his boss's office.

"We ought to inform the Swedes," he said.

"We wait. It's better to call them with a success story when it's all over."

"They ought to have the same information as us," Bruce insisted.

"Why? Neither of us has any real chance of influencing the situation on board. It's hardly likely that they've set up a parallel operation that could jeopardize ours."

Bruce didn't agree, however.

"They were talking about trying to get hold of the copilot, to see if he could take over the plane."

"But, surely, if something like that was under way, they would have informed us?"

Bruce said nothing. If Washington wasn't keeping Stockholm up to speed, then why should they assume that the reverse was true?

"Okay, you're right," Bruce's boss said when he realized what Bruce was thinking. "Contact Stockholm and give them an update."

Bruce felt relieved. He had a feeling that poor communication had cost them valuable time, and possibly put the entire operation at risk. There was just one more thing he wanted to discuss with his boss.

"Karim Sassi?" he said.

"Something of an enigma."

"What's his motivation? He's not a Muslim. Admittedly, he had a photograph of Zakaria Khelifi in his house, but no one has been able to confirm that the two men are close, or even move in the same circles. And why the hell did he decide to include Tennyson Cottage in his note?"

Bruce's boss signaled to him to come into his office and close the door.

"Someone must be lying," he said. "There *has* to be a connection between Zakaria Khelifi, Tennyson Cottage, and Karim Sassi."

Bruce had been thinking exactly the same thing.

"Why aren't they prepared to tell us anything?" he said, referring to the Pentagon and the CIA. "They're risking the lives of hundreds of people."

"I think they're keeping quiet because they're hoping it won't be necessary to reveal whatever it might be. There's something so sensitive about Tennyson Cottage that they've chosen to play their cards like this instead of doing the right thing."

"People will ask questions," Bruce said. "They must realize that themselves; the newspapers are already crying out for more information. Regardless of whether we manage to rescue the plane or not, there will be consequences. And whatever they are hiding now is bound to come out. It's inevitable."

Bruce's boss stroked his chin.

"I agree, and I'm sure the CIA realize that, too. But I don't really understand what their problem is. Tennyson Cottage was shut down when bin Laden was killed; it no longer exists. The fact that we have so-called secret detention facilities is hardly something people are unaware of; in fact, it feels like old news."

"So there must be some other component in this case that makes Tennyson Cottage particularly sensitive," Bruce said.

His boss hesitated.

"Or there isn't, and the situation is even worse."

"What do you mean?"

"I mean there's a hypothetical chance that the reason no one is prepared to speak openly about the connection between Zakaria Khelifi and Tennyson Cottage could be that no one knows what it is. That it doesn't exist."

"How likely is that?" Bruce said dubiously.

"Not very. But it could be an explanation for what we have chosen to interpret as deliberate silence. They don't know what the link is between the two demands. Which means they don't know who they're up against."

Bruce realized his boss was right. There could be an even worse scenario than the idea that someone knew the truth and was keeping quiet about it. The thought that *no one* knew the truth.

53

Stockholm, 20:15

Being prime minister had never been easy, but Muhammed Haddad, the minister for justice, wondered if it had ever been more difficult than right now. The government had gathered for a crisis meeting less than an hour after Muhammed had sounded the alarm by informing the PM that he had received information from Fredrika Bergman suggesting that there could well be grounds for tearing up Zakaria Khelifi's deportation order. Not everyone could attend at such short notice, but the PM insisted that the meeting should go ahead anyway.

"We have to undertake a thorough analysis of the situation before we make a decision," he said. "There are countless factors that complicate matters. It's important that we reach a decision which is right not only at this moment, but in the long term."

"I agree," the foreign secretary said. "And I must express my concern with regard to how a reversal in the case of Zakaria Khelifi would be perceived by the public. This has been a high-profile affair right from the start, as we were well aware. None of us was surprised when the fact that he had been taken into custody was leaked to the press, and we knew questions would be asked. But I don't think any of us could have foreseen what happened next—the hijacking of an entire jumbo jet."

"What are you afraid of with regard to our cooperation with other countries?" Muhammed asked.

He didn't like the woman; he often found it hard to follow her thought processes, and believed she reached the wrong conclusions in many cases. This didn't look as if it was going to be any different.

"I was just coming to that, if you'll allow me to finish." She looked irritated. "If we revise our decision in Zakaria's case, and if we do it against the backdrop of an ongoing hijacking that the whole world knows about, we risk being perceived as either incompetent or weak. Therefore, others will ask themselves whether it takes a critical situation to enable us to see clearly and make sound decisions, or they will wonder whether we've changed our minds because we daren't stand up to terrorists."

"We have received new information," Muhammed said. "We have to make that very clear. The basic situation has changed, and in accordance with democratic principles, we have to review the case."

The foreign secretary was having none of it. She tugged at the scarf around her neck and fiddled with one of her dangling earrings. Muhammed had been surprised when he realized that there were men—quite a lot of men, in fact—who found her attractive. To him she was nothing more than a frigid prima donna.

"The timing is very bad. It's very difficult to see how we can change our position in Zakaria's case without being perceived as unreliable. I have been in touch with the US government, and they have made it very clear that they have no intention of bowing to the demands of the terrorists with regard to the closure of Tennyson Cottage. And they expect us to follow the same line."

"The problem is that it does actually look as if we might have reason to revise our decision with regard to Zakaria's deportation, irrespective of the hijacking," the prime minister said. "And if we are going to reverse our decision, then we ought to do it now. Not tomorrow, not next week, but now. Otherwise it will look as if we sacrificed the lives of four hundred passengers for no reason."

"We could actually wait a few days," the foreign secretary said. "Say that we'd only just received the new information. I mean, nobody would know we got it today."

Muhammed couldn't stop himself from speaking up.

"That's not only immoral, it's actually dangerous," he said.

"I agree," the PM said, looking appalled. "We can't do that."

"In that case, the question is whether we ought to revise our decision," the foreign secretary said. "To be honest, I'm not convinced that it's necessary just because Säpo have carried out a new analysis of certain telephone records. And if I've understood correctly, it's not actually Säpo who have raised the issue with us, but Fredrika Bergman."

"That's right," Muhammed said. "Fredrika did indeed raise the issue, which is entirely in keeping with her role as liaison officer. She is our ear to the ground within the police, and she passes on whatever we need to know. As far as I'm concerned, there is no problem with the fact that the information has come from her rather than Säpo."

"I agree with you on that point," the PM said. "However, I must admit that I have the same reservations as the foreign secretary. Is the information Fredrika Bergman has given us about the phone enough to warrant a review of our decision? After all, we still have the fact that Zakaria Khelifi collected the package, and was named by Ellis as a collaborator. If we change our minds because of such a small point, it feels as if we made the wrong decision in the first place, and in that case I think we need to review our procedures when it comes to security issues."

"You could well be right," Muhammed said. "But that issue is less urgent. Right now, we have to focus on Zakaria and make sure he gets a fair assessment. As far as our American colleagues are concerned, I accept that the situation is complicated, but the same applies: we need to inform them in the clearest possible terms that our decision to release Zakaria is not a question of kowtowing to the terrorists, but a logical consequence of other circumstances."

The foreign secretary let out a brief laugh. "Good luck," she said. "They'll never accept that explanation."

"Be that as it may," Muhammed said, "Sweden has been loyal in other issues that are important to them. We don't owe our loyalty to the USA when it comes to the hijacking, but to our own people. Besides which, as I said before, any decision in Zakaria's case must be seen as independent of the hijacking. Otherwise we will be in the wrong whatever we do."

"Which is exactly what makes this so bloody difficult," the PM said.

The strain was etched on his face, which in turn affected Muhammed, who addressed the others around the table. "What do the rest of you think?"

Several ministers immediately expressed similar concerns.

"If it comes out at a later date that we put American interests above our own during this crisis, then I agree with Muhammed—we will need to resign with immediate effect and call a new election," the minister for democracy said.

"We simply can't allow that to happen," the finance minister said. "It has to be clear that we did our utmost to handle the situation in a responsible manner."

By now, the prime minister was looking less hesitant. He straightened up, feeling the call of duty, and grew in stature. Muhammed had seen the same thing happen on several occasions, and couldn't decide whether he thought it was a strength or a weakness.

"I intend to ask Säpo for definitive evidence within the next couple of hours. If they can't convince me that it is necessary to deport Zakaria Khelifi, then I will order that decision to be revoked."

The foreign secretary looked less than happy, but didn't say anything.

Muhammed felt relieved; the prime minister had done the right thing.

The question was whether a review of Zakaria's case would help those who were being held hostage by Karim Sassi.

54

20:15

The Americans were going to shoot down the plane unless Erik Recht managed to take over the controls, which he was now attempting to do, according to Eden's latest report. Buster Hansson, the general director of Säpo, shuddered in his office. Why hadn't they heard from Erik? It shouldn't be all that difficult to get into the cockpit and deal with Captain Sassi. Knock him out with something or other.

Buster didn't like to describe people as good or evil. Using such terms meant moving beyond even black and white. To be evil was one-dimensional. There were no mitigating circumstances, no excuses. Therefore, a person who was evil could expect no mercy when they were convicted.

A person who was evil deserved only the worst.

After 9/11, the world had taken a dangerous turn when it became polarized, and people who had never given terrorism a thought had to decide where they stood.

You are with me or against me, you are evil or good.

God only knew what actions that particular game had legitimized.

Images from Abu Ghraib still turned Buster's stomach. That kind of behavior just wasn't acceptable. No enemy in the world should be tackled using such methods. Buster had never turned a blind eye—not once during his entire career. He had demanded order in the ranks, had refused to accept the slightest deviation from the rules and regulations. It was a question of how best to manage people's trust.

In a democratic society, the idea of a total absence of criminality was a pipe dream. The same was true of international terrorism. Buster had spent a long time trying to understand why it was so difficult for people to accept this. Terrorism was just like any other form of criminality, with the major—and critical—difference that its effects were indiscriminate. Even striking at those who normally felt secure and thought that the worst they could expect in their lifetime was to come home one day and discover that the house had been burgled, which, of course, could be pretty traumatic.

And that was why you had to be so careful in combating terrorism, because the tolerance of the methods that were acceptable was often far too great.

Buster had heard from the government just a few minutes ago. The prime minister and the minister for justice wanted what they referred to as definitive evidence in the case of Zakaria Khelifi, and they wanted it before eleven o'clock. They didn't want to say what it was about over the phone, but Buster understood. Fredrika Bergman had passed on the latest information about Khelifi's cell phone. Why they imagined Säpo had anything further to add was a mystery. And he didn't understand why the uncertainty with regard to Zakaria's phone was necessarily a point in his favor. It was as if the government was looking for reasons to change their mind. If that was all they wanted, then Buster had some sympathy with them. They were in an impossible situation.

He decided to call Eden, to discuss what to do about the government demand. It really wasn't part of the general director's remit to involve himself in specific cases, but since Zakaria's fate had attracted so much attention and had led to such dangerous consequences, it had become a matter for the top brass.

He called her office but was informed that she wasn't available.

"Of course," Buster said. "She's in a meeting with the Germans."

He ended the call, and almost immediately Henrik Theander, head of counterespionage, appeared.

"Do you have a minute?"

"Not really—what's it about?"

"Eden and Efraim Kiel, the Mossad agent."

Buster put down the phone.

"Yes?"

"He's made an approach."

Buster's stomach contracted into a cold knot. No, no, and no. They didn't have time for this. Not now. Not when hundreds of people were heading toward their deaths.

"What kind of approach?"

"He's standing outside the building."

Buster wasn't sure he understood.

"Outside what building?"

"Our building. Police HQ. He's standing opposite the entrance on Polhemsgatan."

Throughout his career, Buster had been known for his calm approach, his coolness under pressure, but this time there was too much going on all at once.

"Right, and what's he doing there? Is he trying to get in?"

"No, he's waiting."

"Waiting? Who for?"

"Eden?"

Buster pictured the scene. Sooner or later, Eden would leave work and head out into the darkness, where the Israeli was waiting for her on the pavement.

"He's not exactly being discreet."

"No."

The knot in his stomach grew, spreading upward into his chest and toward his heart. This wasn't good. Not good at all. Telling the government that they might have gotten it wrong in the case of Zakaria Khelifi suddenly seemed like a piece of piss. Explaining that they had managed to recruit a Mossad agent to run the counterterrorism unit would be considerably worse.

"What do we do now?" Buster said.

"The same as Efraim Kiel. We wait."

55

Flight 573

The man was still lying unconscious on the floor. The passengers appeared to be welded to their seats. Erik Recht was grateful for their silence, although he suspected that it wouldn't last much longer. Soon they would start asking questions, wanting to know what was going on. What would he say to them? That everything was fine, that it was perfectly normal for the captain to lock his copilot out of the cockpit? That the man Erik had just knocked out was someone who definitely deserved such treatment?

He needed to call his father again, explain the situation, tell him what had gone on. Warn him about what could happen now that Karim was alone in the cockpit.

But first of all, he had to think.

The only way into the cockpit was through a security door, built to withstand an attack by hijackers or anyone else who might constitute a threat. Erik couldn't open the door from the outside; he was dependent on being let in by someone on the inside. Several people had pointed out the weakness in this system, but that was the way things were.

He wouldn't be able to kick or break down the door. Nor would it be possible to pick the lock. Automatically, his hands went through his pockets, seeking some forgotten object that might help him. But there was nothing. Nothing at all.

"What's going on?"

A male voice came from the back of the cabin.

Erik looked around, trying to focus on giving an impression of calm competence. Which was difficult after what had just happened.

A hand shot up. "I'm the one who asked."

Only now did Erik realize that several of the passengers were crying.

A woman a few rows farther forward put her fears into words: "You have to give us some kind of information. The plane is going to arrive several hours late. And now this. What are you doing?"

She gestured toward the unconscious man and Erik's blood-stained shirt.

He searched for the right words. "We are in an extremely unusual situation. Unfortunately, I am unable to share all the details with you, because I don't have them. And I realize I am asking the impossible when I say that you must continue to be patient, but I'm afraid that's all I can do right now."

People shuffled anxiously.

"Why are you locked out?" the man at the back wanted to know.

Erik swallowed. "Because Captain Sassi is unable to open the door from the inside at the moment, but we'll soon straighten it out."

Anything else would be a disaster, although he didn't say that.

He needed help. His one-man show was over. He would start by going back to the bar and telling Lydia what had happened.

But the woman who had spoken earlier wasn't satisfied with Erik's response.

She pointed to the man on the floor. "Who's he?" she said.

Erik looked at the man he had just knocked out.

That's exactly what I'd like to know, he thought.

56

Stockholm, 20:35

Time would soon run out. The plane would have used up all its fuel within just a few hours, and Fredrika Bergman felt nothing but sheer despair.

They had called Jerker Gustavsson, who was one of the people who had been in contact with Zakaria's phone both before and after the date on which he claimed he had acquired it, and luck had been on their side. Jerker was actually at a restaurant in Södermalm, celebrating his mother's seventy-fifth birthday, rather than at home in Västerhaninge. Like everyone else, he was nervous when he heard that the police wanted to speak to him, but he certainly wasn't uncooperative.

"You're welcome to come to the restaurant," he said. "I don't want to leave my family."

"Someone will be with you in twenty minutes," Fredrika replied.

And they were. A patrol car was dispatched immediately with its blue light flashing, and time moved on inexorably.

Eden and Sebastian had been given new information by their German colleagues, who had received another email. The pilot was going to crash the plane into the Capitol Building, regardless of whether the hijackers' demands were met. No reason was given.

Fredrika felt something like physical pain when Eden told her what the Germans had said. She couldn't bring herself to look at Alex. His son would be dead within just a few hours, and there was nothing anyone could do for him. Unless Erik could save himself by putting Karim Sassi out of action.

"What's our assessment with regard to the reliability of the German intelligence?" the head of the investigation unit asked when Eden had finished speaking.

"As we established earlier, it's not possible to make any kind of assessment. The only thing we know for sure is that the original information about a hijacking taking place turned out to be correct, and it also seems likely that the captain is involved, as the first email stated. To put it briefly, we have to take this new intelligence seriously."

Alex was sitting at the table listening, pale and exhausted. Erik still hadn't been in touch, and they were now considering calling Karim, just to get some sign of life from the plane.

"Is that our next step?" Dennis asked. "Calling Karim Sassi?"

"Later," Eden said curtly.

Later? There was no later.

"Have the Germans managed to identify the person who sent these emails?" Dennis wanted to know.

"They've tried everything they can, but without success. It's as if the messages were sent from outer space."

It was obvious that everyone in the group was seething with impatience. Hour after hour had passed, and the plane was still heading for destruction.

We have to have a breakthrough, Fredrika thought. Otherwise we are going to lose both our judgment and our morale.

"Surely the person who sent the emails has to be someone who was involved?" Alex said.

"Not necessarily," Eden replied. "After all, we don't know exactly who's behind the hijacking, apart from Karim, of course. It's not impossible that someone else who is mixed up in all this couldn't help boasting about what's going to happen."

"Why would someone who's involved in the hijacking talk about it several weeks in advance?" Sebastian said. "It doesn't make sense."

A fleeting thought, impossible to catch. They were missing something, Fredrika could feel it in her whole body. The answer to Sebastian's question was right there in front of them—they just couldn't see it.

Why would someone who's involved in the hijacking talk about it several weeks in advance?

Fredrika came up with two possible answers.

"Either because he or she wants to appear innocent," she said slowly, "or the emails were sent to the Germans to make sure we don't miss what's happening."

Eden stared at her incredulously.

"I'm sorry? So that we don't miss the fact that someone is threatening to blow up a jumbo jet?"

Alex met Fredrika's gaze; he straightened up and nodded slowly. He understood what she was saying.

"That's not what she means," he said. "Think about what was actually in the emails. Details that we would never have found out otherwise."

The room fell silent.

"Go on," Sebastian said.

"I can't explain it," Fredrika said. "But . . . these messages. Aren't they just like the book of Tennyson's poetry that we found on Karim's bookshelf? Way too obvious, yet with an attempt at vagueness. The book clearly points to Tennyson, so that we won't miss the fact that Karim has something to do with Tennyson Cottage—and yet we can't find anything else pointing in that direction. Not one single thing."

Eden shook her head crossly. "Where are you going with this?"

Another idea began to form in Fredrika's mind, and this time she managed to hold on to it.

"I don't know," she said eventually. "It's just that this entire business is littered with completely bizarre elements. And I don't like these weird arrows that keep on popping up, as if someone is doing everything in their power to make sure we don't miss Karim Sassi's involvement."

"But, Fredrika, he *is* involved," Eden said. "Erik said that he happened to mention Washington instead of New York. And he refuses to move away from the US border, refuses to seek an alternative place to land."

"I know that," Fredrika said. "And I'm not saying he isn't involved. I'm just saying that someone is so determined to point us in his direction that we're forgetting to look for anyone else. I get the same feeling about this new information, telling us that the pilot has instructions that weren't mentioned in the original note found in the toilet."

Alex joined in eagerly: "Exactly. They're reinforcing an already threatening message, keeping us on track so that we don't imagine we can deviate from the original instructions."

Seconds passed, and Eden said nothing.

"So what's the aim of the person who sent the emails to the Germans?"

"To remind us that we are facing an unbeatable opponent," Fredrika said.

"Not even if we accede to the demands?"

"The hijackers know that's not going to happen."

"And why send the emails to the Germans and not to us?" Dennis wondered.

"I've asked myself the same question," Fredrika said. "First of all, I think there's a German connection that we don't yet understand. And secondly, if the first message had been sent to us, the effect would have been far too dramatic, since the plane was actually due to take off from Arlanda. The sender merely wanted to ensure that when the hijacking took place, the right information was already out there."

A German connection. But what could it be?

The only link they had seen so far was a number of calls to and from Germany on Zakaria's phone. But that was hardly a link at all, more of a vague coincidence.

Time had passed too quickly, Fredrika realized that now. There were so many thoughts and loose ends buzzing around in her head, so much that didn't make sense. Why Tennyson Cottage in particular? The USA must have several secret detention facilities, so why Tennyson Cottage? They had to find out. And soon.

And why Karim Sassi? What was the connection between Karim and Zakaria? If they understood that, then soon the jigsaw would be complete.

As Fredrika sat there, lost in thought, Sebastian and Eden moved the meeting on.

"What's next?" Sebastian asked.

"We'll wait another hour to hear from Erik Recht, the copilot," Dennis said, glancing at Alex. "Then we will need to consider other options, in consultation with our American colleagues."

"What options?" Alex said.

"We have to consider, as a last resort, confronting Karim with what we know—explaining that he's not going to be able to achieve his goal, and that therefore the best thing would be to land the plane and hand himself over to the police."

Was that really where they had ended up? With pleading as their only remaining option? Karim Sassi would get what he wanted. He would be the one who formed the dividing line between life and death.

Unless Erik managed to take control of the plane.

But why hadn't he been in touch?

Fredrika could see that Alex was suffering.

"What's our next step?" he said.

Impatient, as so many times in the past.

"We've spoken to virtually everyone during the course of the day," Dennis said. "*Everyone.* We've contacted the relatives of both Karim and Zakaria, and they all seem equally bewildered. For example, not one conversation has suggested who else might be involved apart from Karim, and that worries me, because in my opinion the idea that he could have acted alone is out of the question."

"There's still one person we haven't spoken to," Fredrika said. "Zakaria's sister."

"Exactly. And we need to find her as a matter of urgency, so that we can at least eliminate her from our inquiries, if nothing else. We're interviewing Zakaria's girlfriend immediately after this meeting; the last time we talked to her, we didn't know about the sister."

"When were we supposed to hear about Jerker Gustavsson?" Dennis wanted to know.

Fredrika glanced anxiously at her cell phone.

"It depends how quickly he can get hold of his list of clients to check whose name he has against Zakaria's cell phone number. If he needs to go back to his workshop, then we're going to lose valuable time."

Sebastian looked around. "If no one has anything else to raise, then I suggest we bring the meeting to a close."

One of the analysts raised his hand.

"We're working through lists from the relevant pay stations around Stockholm to see if we get a match on a car leaving the city and heading for the airport in the hours before the bomb threats were made yesterday, but it's a long shot. Even if we find that a known criminal or suspect drove out toward Arlanda, it doesn't prove that that person made the calls. And as you know we can't get any further with the phones that were used."

Fredrika thought about the much discussed congestion charge and the infrastructure that had been created in order to introduce it. There were pay stations around the entire inner city, where motorists were photographed and scanned so that information about movement in and out of the city could be stored, and to determine who was liable for the charge. A huge number of cars must head for Arlanda every single day.

"When do you expect to finish?"

"Hopefully, within the next few hours."

"I don't expect a match with a name we already know, but it has to be done," Sebastian said.

Of course. Everything had to be checked, every snippet of information examined in detail. Fredrika felt a fresh surge of impatience; why couldn't they get a breakthrough in this nightmare situation?

Because it hasn't even been twenty-four hours yet.

The meeting came to an end, and Fredrika stayed behind with Alex, Dennis, and Sebastian.

"Okay, so you're going to speak to Zakaria's girlfriend, and you're staying here," Dennis said, nodding at Fredrika and Alex respectively.

Fredrika accompanied Dennis. At last they were going to interview Zakaria's girlfriend, Maria. The conversation probably wouldn't change a thing, but she still wanted to see where it might lead. Because there was something missing. Her body was crying out with exhaustion, making her feel slow and heavy.

The conviction that something had escaped them floated before her like a mirage. Who was Karim's associate? Could it be Zakaria's sister Sofi?

And why would a person do what Karim Sassi was apparently doing right now?

Fredrika could come up with only two reasons. Either he was acting out of conviction, or under duress.

But how could such a thing happen? How could someone force another person to carry four hundred passengers to their death?

Her cell phone rang; it was one of the investigators who had gone to speak to Jerker Gustavsson.

"We're in luck," he said. "Gustavsson had his list of clients on his cell phone, so he was able to search for the number."

Fredrika held her breath.

"And who did it belong to?"

"Last summer, he spoke to someone called Zakaria on that number, but before that the phone belonged to a client by the name of Adam Mortaji."

And so yet another name was added to the investigation.

57

21:10

Adam Mortaji.

They had no idea who he was, where he came from, or if he still lived in Sweden. It took just a few minutes to establish that Adam Mortaji, just like Zakaria's sister, didn't exist in any Swedish records.

"Contact all our partner organizations right away," Eden said. "I want to know who this guy is, and fast."

They could ask Zakaria, of course, but that would probably be a pointless waste of time. If he had refused to tell them about Mortaji under interrogation and during the court proceedings, it was foolish to believe that he would suddenly start talking.

Fredrika sat down with Dennis and his investigator, to draw up a plan of action for their interview with Zakaria's girlfriend, Maria.

To their surprise, she was already in Police HQ when they called her. She was in reception, asking to be allowed to speak to Zakaria. When she was informed that this was unfortunately out of the question, she simply sat down on one of the benches in front of the tall windows and stated that she had no intention of moving until someone took her to see him. When Fredrika and the Säpo investigator found her, she had been sitting there for half an hour.

"I'm not going anywhere until I've seen Zakaria," she said when they had introduced themselves and explained why they wanted to talk to her.

Her expression was grim, just like Fredrika's had been on the day when Spencer called her from Uppsala and told her he was being held by the police.

Fredrika suddenly found it difficult to breathe. She still sometimes woke in the night, her heart contracting with fear. She didn't know how Spencer felt about it these days. They never discussed the matter; they simply left it in the past where it belonged.

"You can't see Zakaria at the moment," the Säpo investigator said. "But you can help him by helping us."

"I've already spoken to you; I've explained all these apparent inconsistencies. He was never a part of the terrorist plot against Stockholm—how many times do I have to tell you?"

How did she know? Fredrika took a deep breath. How could you ever be sure of something like that? The short answer is because you know the person you love.

But love could be irrational as well as blind.

You never know for sure, you really don't.

"We'd like to talk to you about Zakaria's sister," Fredrika said. She couldn't stop herself from acting as if she actually was a police officer.

"About Sofi?" Maria's anger was replaced by surprise.

"Yes."

"Why?"

"Perhaps we could go somewhere else and have a chat?"

Zakaria's girlfriend gave the suggestion some thought, then she said: "No. I'm fine here."

Fredrika and her colleague exchanged glances, then without a word they sat down on either side of Maria.

"Do you know where we can get hold of Sofi?" Fredrika asked.

"No."

It was impossible to tell if she was lying, but Fredrika thought she probably was.

"This is important," the investigator said. "We need to speak to her as a matter of urgency."

"What about?"

"We can't go into that right now," Fredrika said.

The truth was that she didn't know exactly why they wanted to speak to Sofi; perhaps because she was the only person close to Zakaria that they hadn't yet interviewed. Perhaps that was the very thing that made her interesting.

"But it would help Zakaria, as I've already said," the Säpo investigator reiterated; Fredrika thought there was a hint of pleading in his voice.

She decided to try a different tack.

"Maybe Sofi doesn't live in Stockholm?"

Maria looked tired as she picked at a fingernail.

"She lives a different kind of life from me and Zakaria," she said eventually. "Sometimes she's here and she comes to see us, the rest of the time she's all over the place."

"Have you seen her recently?" Fredrika asked.

Maria stiffened.

"No," she said, and this time, Fredrika could see that she was lying.

"Does she usually stay with you when she's around?"

"Sometimes."

"But she has other friends in Stockholm, too?"

"Not many."

"Does she speak Swedish?"

More hesitation.

"Yes, she's one of the most talented linguists I know."

"What other languages does she speak?" the investigator asked.

Good question.

"English, French, and German. And Arabic, of course."

And there it was again. Another connection with Germany.

"German?"

Fredrika tried not to sound too interested; she didn't want Maria to realize how important this could be.

"Yes."

"How come Sofi speaks German?"

At that point, Maria refused to answer, obviously aware that the situation had slipped from her grasp, in spite of her efforts to prevent that from happening.

"That's where she lives, isn't it?" Fredrika said.

Zakaria's girlfriend nodded. "That's where she has her apartment and her base. In Berlin."

"Have you been over to visit her?" Fredrika asked.

"Only a couple of times."

So, Zakaria had a sister who lived in Germany. The country from which the information about the hijacking had come. The country with which Adam Mortaji, who had previously owned Zakaria's cell phone, had close links.

The net was closing in. And now, Fredrika had even more questions for Maria.

"Karim Sassi?" she said, even though she knew that someone had already spoken to Maria about him. "Do you know him?"

"I've already answered that question."

"I know, but now I'm asking you again."

"In that case, my answer is the same as before. I have no recollection of ever meeting someone by that name. Nor do I have any recollection of Zakaria ever mentioning someone called Karim Sassi."

Fredrika believed her. With a thousand simultaneous thoughts whirling around in her brain, she tried to piece together the various fragments of information. Germany kept on coming up, over and over again, but they had been unable to find a link with either Zakaria or Karim. The link was only through Zakaria's phone, and only during the period when it had belonged to Adam Mortaji.

"Do you know a man called Adam Mortaji?" Fredrika said.

There.

A reaction so strong that Fredrika thought she would have picked up on it even if she had had her eyes closed and her hands covering her ears.

The words struck Maria like a slap in the face.

"No."

"You're lying," Fredrika said.

Maria's face went bright red, and it looked as if she had tears in her eyes. Her mouth was compressed into a straight line, and she didn't say a word.

Not one word.

Who was this man who provoked such a determined silence?

Fredrika changed tack.

"Do you know if Zakaria ever bought a phone from Sofi, or was given a phone by her?"

Maria stared at her.

"I don't think so."

"How did he get hold of the phone he's using now?" the investigator said.

"I've no idea. Before that he mostly used his work cell phone. And my phone, of course."

She looked exhausted.

Fredrika decided to take another look at the list of calls. They were onto something, she was sure of it.

"Do you have a number for Sofi?" she said.

One last shot.

To her surprise, Maria reached into her pocket and took out her cell phone.

"I think so."

Then she read out a number.

"This is the only one I have. It's Sofi's phone in Germany, but it's an old number—she doesn't use it anymore. And I haven't got the new one; Zakaria and Sofi usually Skype one another these days."

Fredrika saw Maria smile for the first time. She thought she had disappointed them with an old number.

On the contrary.

They ended the interview and went back to Säpo's offices. Fredrika headed straight for Sebastian and asked him to bring up the list of calls. It took them less than two minutes to find Sofi's number. During the period when the cell phone had probably belonged to Adam Mortaji, it had been in regular contact with Sofi's phone in Germany.

"Mortaji," Fredrika said to Sebastian. "We have to find out who he is. He's important."

"I thought that if the phone really had belonged to someone else, it would have been the sister; I thought he was protecting her," Sebastian said.

"Me, too. But it obviously belonged to someone who had been in touch with her."

"Why did the contact with Sofi stop when Zakaria acquired the phone?"

"First of all, Maria said that Sofi had changed her number, and secondly, they usually communicated via Skype. We also know that Zakaria was in the habit of using several phones at the same time."

The stress came flooding back, ruled by forces as implacable as those that govern the movement of the tide.

Four hundred people at thirty thousand feet.

A man who was due to be deported, suppressing the only piece of information that could save him.

A captain taking his passengers and crew to their deaths while refusing to say why he was doing so.

A secret detention facility that no one was prepared to talk about.

The almost tangible silence from all directions was driving Fredrika mad. So many secrets, so little time, so many victims.

But now they had something to work on: Adam Mortaji, who presumably also knew Zakaria's sister Sofi.

The only question was how they were going to find either of them.

58

21:50

There was nothing worse than silence.

Alex Recht hadn't let go of his cell phone for a second. But it didn't ring. Not once. Hours had passed since he spoke to Erik.

What the hell had happened?

In despair, he went along to Eden's office, where he found her working on the computer.

"We have to do something," he said. "I think we ought to contact the plane. Confront Karim, tell him we know everything."

Eden stopped typing.

"Sit down, Alex."

He perched on one of the chairs next to her desk.

"I can't bear it."

He whispered the words, but she heard him.

"I understand."

There was a cup of coffee on her desk, and she wrapped one hand around it. She had large hands for a woman.

"But we can't make a unilateral decision to contact Karim. We have to speak to our American colleagues first."

"Your," Alex said.

"Sorry?"

"You said we have to speak to our American colleagues. But I don't have any American colleagues; that applies only to Säpo."

Eden took a sip of her coffee, then put down the cup. It was blue, with white characters painted on it. Hebrew, Alex thought.

"I bought it in Israel," Eden said.

Alex didn't respond; he couldn't give a fuck where she'd bought the damned thing.

"Your wife died about a year ago, didn't she?"

There was a warmth in Eden's voice that he hadn't heard before, a warmth he hadn't thought she possessed, to be honest. It disarmed him, made it possible to answer the question.

"Yes. Cancer."

"And now you're afraid you'll lose Erik as well?"

He couldn't speak, and merely nodded instead.

"There isn't a cat in hell's chance that I will allow that to happen," Eden said. "Do you understand what I'm saying? Erik will get through this."

Alex stared at Eden, completely taken aback. The warmth was gone, her expression hard. Her voice and posture were utterly uncompromising.

"Nor will I allow you, Erik's father, to fall apart in the middle of all this. You can do that later if you have any reason to do so. Is that clear?"

He felt a flash of pure rage.

"Crystal clear—do you think I'd abandon the attempt to save my own son?"

A faint glimmer appeared in Eden's eyes.

"No. Just checking."

Alex wanted nothing more than to believe what Eden had said, but he couldn't understand how it was going to work, how he was going to get Erik back. Alex thought back to when it had all started. They had had a plan then. They would try to find out who was behind the hijacking, save the hostages in that way. But that was before they realized Karim Sassi was involved. Now it didn't make any difference what they found out; if they couldn't get to Karim, both the battle and the war would be lost.

Fredrika and Sebastian appeared in the doorway. Eden waved them in, and Fredrika closed the door behind her.

Alex couldn't understand why someone like Fredrika wanted to sit in some government office, rotting away. He watched her as she pulled up a chair and sat down next to him. Like everyone else, becoming a parent had changed her. The lines around her eyes gave away the fact that she probably did more than half of the household chores at the end of the working day. He had somewhat reluctantly accepted his children's view that it was unreasonable to expect women to work full-time both outside and inside the home.

Fredrika lived with a man who was older than Alex. A man of retirement age, who was looking after two small children. Obviously, he wasn't going to have as much energy as Fredrika; he couldn't be expected to provide as much help and support as she needed.

The differences between Eden and Fredrika were striking. There was so little on Eden's desk, in terms of both personal and professional items, that it looked as if she had only just started working there. Anyone who walked into her office would leave without having learned a single thing about her. He saw the glint of a wedding ring on her left hand, and suspected that things were very different in her household. Whoever her husband might be, Alex thought he probably put in as much effort as Fredrika did in order to make things work.

"We think that Adam Mortaji, who used to own Zakaria's phone, knows or is somehow linked to his sister," Fredrika said before going on to explain what they had found out from talking to Maria.

Alex listened, his anxiety as intense as a physical sensation.

They were talking too much, both to each other and to witnesses. None of this was going to help bring down the plane safely—they could do all this afterward.

Eden was listening, too, as she looked at the list of calls Sebastian had given her.

"I agree, the sister is interesting," she said. "But I find it difficult to see exactly how she fits in. Do we know anything about her relationship with Zakaria? Are they close? Could she be involved in the hijacking in order to secure her brother's release?"

Every case had its own phantom; Alex had realized that at an early stage in his career. There was always one individual who was impossible to pin down, who for some reason drifted around those parts of an investigation that lay in the shadows.

"We've been wondering about that, too," Fredrika said.

"Have we eliminated the girlfriend?" Alex asked.

"We did that a while ago," Eden replied. "We just don't believe she's capable of carrying out an operation like this. Admittedly, she might have a minor role to play, but she couldn't be the person behind it."

"This all comes back to Zakaria," Fredrika said. "Even if his sister is mixed up in the hijacking, I'm certain there's someone else who's involved, someone Zakaria is protecting."

"Adam Mortaji, for example?"

"Exactly."

Alex thought for a moment.

"So the idea that Zakaria is keeping quiet about information that could secure his release—couldn't that also be an indication that he actually is involved? Even if we're now tending to think that he isn't, do we have enough evidence for such a definitive conclusion?"

They had to get out of this Säpo framework within which every discussion so far had been conducted. Alex was sick of it. Villains were villains, whether they were bank robbers or terrorists.

The difficulties with Säpo's role were painfully obvious, and Alex thanked his lucky stars that he didn't work there. He would have gone crazy.

Eden broke the silence that followed Alex's question.

"No," she said. "In spite of intense investigative work, we can't be certain of anything at all."

Right from the start, Alex had felt that Zakaria was the protagonist in this drama, in spite of the fact that it had begun before he was told that he would have to leave Sweden. So far, Alex hadn't wasted much energy on the issue of Zakaria's guilt, but now he was starting to wonder.

What if Zakaria himself was involved in the hijacking?

• • •

Fredrika glanced at her watch. It was just after ten o'clock in the evening, but it might as well have been three in the afternoon. She was firing on all cylinders now, and her body was not aware of either fatigue or hunger. They were on the home stretch. In less than two hours, it would all be over. That thought brought her neither peace of mind nor relief, so she pushed it firmly aside.

Dennis, the head of the investigation unit, knocked on the door and yanked it open. He looked surprised when he saw how many of them were sitting there.

"I just wanted to let you know that Karim's wife called a few minutes ago. She'll be landing in Stockholm in an hour."

"She's coming back from Copenhagen?"

"Yes. She's left the children with her parents."

"Tell her we might want to see her."

"Already done."

He turned to leave, but hesitated.

"Has anything new come up? Is that what you're discussing?" he said.

"I'll be with you in two minutes," Eden assured him.

He disappeared as quickly as he had arrived, closing the door behind him. Eden turned to Sebastian.

"I want you to come with me to a meeting with the CIA shortly."

"First the CIA—then what?" Alex asked.

"Zakaria," Eden said. "Then Karim's wife."

Fredrika swallowed. She needed to update the government, but she had no idea what she was going to say.

At that moment, Eden's phone rang and she answered: "Eden Lundell."

Then she sat for a long time with the receiver pressed to her ear, saying nothing.

"It's unfortunate that we didn't discuss this in advance," she eventually said in English. "We've asked Erik Recht to do something similar." She fell silent once more.

Something similar?

Fredrika glanced at Alex, and saw that he was leaning forward in his chair, as if he was trying to hear more clearly.

"Okay, so when was this?" Eden said. "And you haven't heard from him since then?"

She shook her head, her lips compressed into a straight line.

"We haven't heard from Erik, either, and that worries me, to be honest."

She listened again, then ended the call.

"Bad news," she said in a tone of voice so sharp that Fredrika was grateful Eden had chosen a career within the police service rather than the medical profession.

"What's happened? Was that about Erik?" Alex asked.

"The Americans appear to have a whole truckload of surprises," Eden said. "Apparently, they have an operative from the Department of Defense on board, and he's been in touch with them. They've told him to get into the cockpit with the help of a flight attendant, then to put Karim Sassi out of action and take over the plane."

"So he's a pilot?" Sebastian said.

"Yes, although he usually flies a different kind of aircraft. The only problem is that they haven't heard from him and were wondering if we'd heard anything. Which we haven't, of course."

Alex sighed heavily. Fredrika could see that he was clutching his cell phone, and wished with all her heart that Erik would call.

Ring, for God's sake, ring.

"They also wanted us to know that they're sticking by their decision," Eden went on. "If we can't get someone into the cockpit, they won't let the plane enter their airspace."

An endless nightmare.

Fredrika went over the loose ends. There were a lot of them, and it was difficult to get an overview, but she had a feeling it was important not to forget about Zakaria's sister.

"Have you passed on what we know about Sofi to the Germans?" she asked.

"Yes. They didn't seem to recognize her name, or the picture we got from her uncle. Although that doesn't necessarily mean a great deal; she might use a different name in Germany.

Germany and Sweden, the USA and Afghanistan.

The world had turned into a gigantic playing field where different teams met in order to challenge each other in a competition with rules that were rewritten as they went along, rules that could usually be broken.

"What is it we're actually looking for?" Fredrika said.

"We're looking for someone who knows both Zakaria and Tennyson Cottage, and who is sufficiently wound up to hijack an entire plane," Eden said.

She was right, Fredrika thought. Whoever had written the note that had been found in the toilet on the plane hadn't mentioned Tennyson Cottage by chance. On the contrary—the person in question thought it was important for Tennyson Cottage specifically to be shut down. Otherwise he or she could have written about the USA's secret detention facilities in Afghanistan in far more general terms.

Fredrika added another factor to her analysis.

Whoever had set all this in motion was not only personally concerned with Zakaria's fate and the closure of Tennyson Cottage. But he or she also knew Karim Sassi, a man who on paper didn't appear to have a single reason to do what he was doing right now. It was equally important to find that link in order to solve the case.

And then there were yesterday's damned bomb threats. What was their significance, and who had made the calls? Fredrika sensed that it was important to find the answers to these questions. She just didn't understand why.

59

22:15

"When will you be home?"

Diana's voice was far away; Alex had to make a real effort to hear what she was saying.

"I don't know. I'm staying here until I know how things pan out."

Until I know whether Erik has died or not. Whether I'm the father of just one child from now on.

"Would you like me to come over for a while?"

Alex pressed the receiver to his ear, remembering how they had started to see one another while Alex was investigating the death of Diana's daughter. How sensitive and clandestine it had all been. And how wonderful. So incredibly liberating.

It was still wonderful; he loved to hear her voice.

"What, to the station?"

"Yes."

How many times had he been close to tears today? He blinked them away.

"No, best not."

"Call me if you change your mind."

Alex dropped the phone when they had finished talking, as if it were red-hot. He definitely wouldn't call her. There was absolutely no way that he could cope with seeing Diana until he knew for certain whether things had gone well or extremely badly.

What wouldn't he give to feel her arms around him right now?

He shook off the sense of yearning and went over to the analyst who was checking the lists of cars that had driven out of the city in the direction of Arlanda. He recognized Alex right away.

"Something I can help you with?"

Alex explained what he wanted, trying not to sound impatient. He had no right to flare up. Not here, not now. Not as long as he was in Säpo's territory. Eden had gone to her meeting with the CIA, and Fredrika had returned to her desk. She liked sitting there, on a chair behind a desk with four sturdy legs. She had worked miracles from there on more than one occasion; please, God, let her do the same again this time.

"Hang on, I'll check," the analyst said, leaving Alex alone at his desk.

Alex gazed out over the open-plan office. He didn't really know what he'd expected, but not this. Bizarrely, he hadn't even expected his colleagues from Säpo to be so pleasant. So ordinary. He had thought they would somehow seem aware of how exciting everyone else imagined their everyday lives must be, but after spending a day in their company, Alex was convinced. Working for Säpo wasn't exciting, it was frustrating.

The analyst came back. Alex couldn't work out whether or not he was a police officer, and he didn't bother to ask. The experience of working with Fredrika had taught him that it didn't make any difference whether someone was a civilian or a police officer, as long as he or she had an aptitude for the profession. And that had nothing to do with background.

The other man's eyes were shining.

"Look at this, Alex."

He passed over a sheet of paper.

"These are the cars we've highlighted as possibly of interest. Do you recognize any of the names?"

He did. According to the records, one of the cars that had driven out of the city just hours before yesterday's bomb threats belonged to Zakaria Khelifi.

• • •

This time, Eden had no intention of letting them leave the meeting room until they had given her what she wanted. She would keep her eyes fixed on them until she had all the data she needed.

It had been an incredibly long day.

She had to maintain her sharpness, her focus. If she relaxed now, everything would be lost. Everything.

The CIA agents were the same as last time. Eden chose to take only Sebastian in with her. They sat down opposite the Americans.

"Thank you for coming in again at such short notice," Eden began.

No reaction.

"Have you heard anything from your man on board?" she asked.

"No. What about you? Have you heard from Erik Recht?"

"Unfortunately not."

Silence.

"As you will understand, we have a number of questions with which we need your help," one of the agents said.

Engaging in a trial of strength with an American was pointless. They almost always won. In general terms, Eden liked Americans. They were fun to hang out with, easy to get on with in a social situation. And she sometimes envied that American drive, the constant determination to reach a little higher, get a little further. Or—preferably—higher and further than everyone else. It touched a competitive nerve within Eden that was all too seldom exploited to its full capacity.

However, she found their frequent arrogance considerably less appealing. It sometimes made them very difficult to work with, which in turn could lead to a less than satisfactory conclusion.

"I want names," Eden said.

"Names? What names?"

"The names of the internees held at Tennyson Cottage."

She was being deliberately polite. Saying "held" rather than "imprisoned" was generous.

She waited. She was aware of Sebastian's presence at her side but she didn't look at him. He knew better than to try to join in the discussion.

"No," said one of the CIA agents, "that's not possible. And as we said before—you don't need them."

"That's nonsense," Eden said. "I need a whole lot of information

I absolutely refuse to accept that shooting down the plane is a solution."

"It's not a good solution, but it's still a solution. We would be killing four hundred people in order to save thousands more. We have to have the courage to make these decisions in our job."

Really? Eden wasn't in the mood for that kind of crap. Not now, not ever.

"Not if there's an alternative," she said. "And there is."

She was conscious of the fact that she was repeating herself. Her own children had taught her the value of that particular tactic. If one of them said "ice cream" often enough, they usually got their ice cream.

It worked this time too.

"Why do you want the names?"

"To see if any of them fits into our inquiries. We have the names of several suspects."

Adam Mortaji.

The Americans came to life.

"Like who?"

"You first."

She could see that they were shocked at her boldness, but they didn't say no. She knew she was going to win.

"Okay," said the agent who had said very little so far. "This is what we're going to do. We'll give you the names of the two who were released, but that's it. Sorry, but that's as far as I can go."

Damn. It was nowhere near as much as she had hoped for, but it would have to do.

"Fine," she said. "Let's have them."

The American on the left gave her the name of the first man, who had been allowed to return home after his internment.

"An Iraqi who somehow ended up in Pakistan. Clearly of no interest to us. He was able to give us a small amount of information on various training camps in Waziristan, but otherwise he was worthless. We know that he didn't go back to Iraq, but went to stay with relatives in Jordan."

Eden made notes.

"Thank you. And the other?"

"North African, originally from Morocco. He'd also lived in the UK and in Germany. We picked him up in Pakistan, where he and his pal were busy planning a terrorist attack on a military target in Afghanistan."

Germany. Again.

"Germany seems to keep on coming up," she said.

"Yes, but this guy didn't live there for very long. We let him go in August; he headed straight back to Germany, but he didn't stay there. In May, he went home to Morocco. It was his father who was interviewed by the press and made sure Tennyson Cottage was mentioned in the article."

"A mistake he didn't repeat," said the CIA agent in the middle.

"Why his father rather than him?"

"Unfortunately, the guy is no longer with us. He killed himself last summer, shortly after he returned to Morocco."

"Could I have a picture of him?" Eden said.

The answer came after a brief hesitation.

"We can send one across. If you want to read about him, the article is online."

Eden had already seen the article. It was quite badly written, and she hadn't paid much attention to it.

"And what was the name of this guy?"

"His name was Adam Mortaji."

60

Flight 573

By this stage, the rumor had spread. The passengers realized that the crew had lied. There was some kind of major problem with the plane, and for some reason the copilot was locked out of the cockpit.

However, not many people knew about the man who was lying on the floor at the front of the plane with his hands tied behind his back, and that was the only thing Erik Recht was grateful for. The fear of what could happen if he didn't manage to get into the cockpit was mixed with the fear of what would happen if they couldn't persuade the passengers to remain calm. There were too many of them to deal with if mass panic took over. The flight attendants just kept on moving up and down, talking to anxious individuals.

Erik had gathered the crew together for a short meeting, to bring them up-to-date. He told them he suspected that Karim was involved in the hijacking, that the police seemed to be thinking the same thing, and that Erik was going to do his very best to try to get into the cockpit. Several of his colleagues had been horrified, and had demanded to know more. Surely Karim couldn't be involved? How could something like this happen? The opposition gave Erik an unexpected injection of strength. He had stated loudly and clearly that if they didn't believe him, then they should at least believe the police. Karim wasn't the man they had thought he was. He had placed them all in mortal danger, and right now he was probably holding Fatima prisoner in the cockpit. That silenced the crew, who were now giving him their full cooperation.

Erik hadn't called his father; he didn't want to worry him unnecessarily. But as the minutes passed and he still hadn't accomplished his goal, he realized that Alex must be beside himself with worry. It was more than two hours since they had spoken. Two hours outside the cockpit was a dangerously long time. Karim could have done anything, set course in whatever direction he wanted.

Erik was used to overcoming the difficulties he faced, but this time it seemed to be utterly impossible. He had tried everything, at first as discreetly as possible in order to avoid alarming the passengers, but then with increasingly drastic methods. The fucking door refused to give way, as he had known it would. Ironically, it was impossible to force the door—for security reasons. The very reasons that now drove him to work with the frenzy of a madman to try to gain access.

Erik sat down on the floor with his back against the door. Fatima. The flight attendant he had left behind in the cockpit. Why wasn't she helping him? What had Karim done to her? Erik didn't want to think about that right now; he pushed away the images of the fate that might have befallen Fatima.

He noticed that he had become disorientated, that his imagination lacked any kind of filter. He pictured the plane plunging from the sky and exploding as it hit the hard surface of the Atlantic Ocean. At other times, he could see the plane breaking in two as it hit the water, hurling the passengers to an equally violent death.

The man on the floor moved, groaning faintly.

Who was he?

And how could he have known?

He had realized what was wrong before anyone else. Could he have managed to pick up a text from family or friends?

There is something else going on here.

Erik got up and crouched down beside him. At first he hesitated, but then that barrier came down, too. With movements that felt frighteningly natural he patted the outside of the man's jacket, then his trousers. He didn't know what he was looking for or what he expected to find, but he knew he had to keep going. His hands slipped inside the jacket, feeling the rough surface of the shirt. There was a wallet in the inside jacket pocket; without thinking twice, Erik pulled it out and opened it. Various bank cards, American Express, a driver's license.

The man was called Kevin.

Erik checked the compartment containing bills, then tucked the wallet back in the man's pocket. What was it he'd said? That he knew what had happened. That he could help Erik. Fuck that. Erik didn't believe in coincidences, especially right now.

In the other pocket he found a cell phone. It was switched on, but with the sound turned off. There was no network coverage, but it must have been working at some point, because there was a message waiting.

K, mission accomplished?

Erik went cold all over.

He had been right from the start. This was bigger than any of them had thought. There were several hijackers, and they were among the passengers. Instinctively, he looked up, searching the silent faces following his every move. How many of them were involved?

How am I supposed to know who I can trust?

Resolutely, he got to his feet and moved back to the locked door.

Keep calm, for fuck's sake. The only thing you have to do is to get inside the cockpit. How hard can that be? Break open the door and bring down the plane before we all die.

A movement behind him made him jump.

"It's only me."

Lydia, who had been running the bar.

She was wide-eyed and pale. She had closed the bar after Erik's meeting with the crew, and was now working with her colleagues to keep the passengers calm. Erik knew it was no easy task.

"I've tried everything, but I can't get in," he said through clenched teeth. "I haven't a fucking clue what we're going to do."

"Fatima," Lydia said.

"I know, she's still in there with that fucking lunatic."

He placed one hand on the door, unable to look Lydia in the eye. A mounting anxiety had taken root in his body, and he couldn't shake it off.

What had happened to Fatima? Why hadn't she opened the door? That was why he had asked her to stay in the cockpit in the first place, precisely so that this wouldn't happen. And yet here he was, unable to get back in. Had Karim killed her?

The anxiety grew even stronger.

If Fatima was dead, there was nothing else they could do. Nothing at all.

61

Stockholm, 22:30

The inexorable movement of the second hand on the clock was driving her crazy. What was the best way of using the small amount of time that remained? They had an hour left now. One hour. Then the plane would run out of fuel.

Fredrika Bergman had a horrible feeling that she kept on making the wrong choices. When she was sitting at her desk writing a brief report for the department, she felt guilty that she wasn't taking part in the ongoing investigative work. And when she turned her attention to the investigation, she felt stressed because she wasn't reporting back to her employer frequently enough.

Eden wasn't back from her meeting with the CIA; it seemed to be going on for quite some time. Fredrika hoped this was a good sign.

Most of all, she just wanted this to be over. She wanted someone to call and say that the plane had landed, that the passengers had been released and everyone was fine. Then she would be able to go home at last. Give her children a big hug and go to bed with Spencer. Make love and fall asleep in his arms. Time could be a difficult concept when you lived with someone who was so much older. She had begun to hate the natural aging process and the gap it created between her and the man she knew to be the love of her life. Sometimes she wished they hadn't had children, because she knew that the day Spencer died, she would no longer want to go on living. But there were other days when she felt the exact opposite—that if it wasn't for the children, she wouldn't be able to bear the thought of Spencer dying before her. Mostly she tried not to think about it at all.

Fredrika called the department and eventually managed to get hold of her boss, who sounded stressed. The aroma of fresh coffee drifted through the open-plan office.

"We need a final decision," he said. "Do we release Zakaria Khelifi, or not?"

What was she supposed to say? Right from the start, she had felt it was wrong to deport Zakaria. What did she think now?

I haven't a clue. Is that business with the phone enough to let him go?

"We need more time," she said, as if they had all the time in the world.

"In that case, we'll review our decision. We need to decide within the next half hour, before the plane runs out of fuel. And then we have to stick to our decision. Do you understand what I'm saying?"

Fredrika understood perfectly.

"You'll have to help us explain why we reached different conclusions within days," her boss said.

"You made a mistake. A mistake that is far, far less serious than hijacking a plane full of people. No normal person would regard your mistake as an excuse for mass murder. Never. Release Zakaria Khelifi, apologize, say that new information has come to light during the day which puts a different complexion on his case. Say you are extremely sorry for the dreadful consequences of your error, and that you will be reviewing the relevant procedures in the future."

That's all you can do, she added silently to herself.

"Can't you write something we can use?" her boss said.

Did she have time?

"I can try."

"It's urgent."

"I know that. I'll get back to you."

She ended the call and put down the phone. The aroma of coffee still lingered. And the hands of the clock moved on relentlessly.

• • •

Alex's phone was in his pocket. He couldn't walk around with it in his hand all the time. Eden was still in her meeting with the CIA, and Alex was accompanying Dennis, the head of the investigation unit. They were on their way to speak to Zakaria's girlfriend, Maria, who was still in reception.

"Do you usually conduct interviews yourself?" Alex asked. He had expected one of Dennis's team to do it.

"Only sometimes, but it doesn't do any harm to keep your hand in. And right now everyone is busy with other things."

Alex thought that was an eminently sensible attitude.

Maria looked surprised when two more officers came looking for her.

This time they refused to accept her insistence that she was going nowhere.

"I want to see Zakaria," she said.

"That's out of the question," Dennis said in a tone of voice that brooked no disagreement. "On your feet. Come with me."

And she did.

Dennis took them to one of the smaller interview rooms. It had no windows and smelled musty.

"Please take a seat," Dennis said, sitting down next to Alex.

Maria sat opposite them.

Dennis wasted no time on unnecessary chat.

"At nine thirty yesterday, someone drove Zakaria's car out of the city, heading toward Arlanda. Was that you?"

Alex could see that the girl was genuinely surprised.

"No."

He believed her.

"So who was it?"

"I don't know."

Everything happened so fast that Alex didn't have time to react. Dennis leaped out of his chair and leaned across the table. With his face just inches from hers, he roared at the top of his voice:

"Do you think this is some kind of fucking joke? Four hundred people could die because you're sitting here thinking that your miserable concerns are more important than everybody else's."

He sat down again.

His outburst bore fruit just seconds later.

"The hijacking is nothing to do with me."

"We know that," Dennis said. "However, you are guilty of protecting a criminal, which is a crime in itself."

Alex searched for something to say, but decided it was best to allow Dennis to steer the conversation in the right direction.

Maria folded her arms; it was a pathetic gesture. She was on the verge of tears, but Alex couldn't have cared less. This was serious, more serious than it had ever been. Dennis was right. Her personal concerns were a drop in the ocean compared with what was about to happen to the passengers on Flight 573.

"Someone came around yesterday morning and asked to borrow the car. And I can promise you that the person in question had nothing to do with the hijacking."

"Unfortunately, that's not enough for us; we have to eliminate that possibility for ourselves," Dennis said.

"Yes, you seem to be good at that."

Alex thought Dennis was about to erupt again, but it didn't happen.

"Start talking," he said instead.

"It was only hours before you picked up Zakaria. The doorbell rang, and I went to answer it. And . . . she was standing there. She asked if she could borrow the car until Thursday. There's nothing odd about that—we've lent her the car several times in the past."

"Who, Maria? Who was it who wanted to borrow the car?" Dennis couldn't hide his impatience.

"She's got nothing to do with any of this."

"*Who was it?*"

This was something Alex had never understood, throughout the whole of his career. People who kept quiet even though everything was already lost. Why didn't they simply put their cards on the table, take responsibility for their actions? How could they justify such a course of action to themselves? How could they decide to be the difference between right and wrong, between life and death?

In the end, she gave up, after one last shot.

"I want to see Zakaria."

She was crying, which wasn't good. Not now that they were so close.

"That's not possible," Dennis said. "But I promise we won't keep him away from you for one second longer than necessary."

It was true, and it was obvious that he wouldn't lie about something like that. Maria could see it, too. She wiped away a solitary tear as it trickled down her cheek.

"It was Zakaria's sister Sofi."

62

23:00

His hair was short and unevenly cut, his face emaciated, exhausted. Eden Lundell was sitting at her computer looking at the picture of Adam Mortaji that the CIA had sent over.

So this was what he looked like. The man who had almost cost Zakaria his entire future, and who was evidently so important that he was worth risking his life for. Or perhaps he was important to Sofi, and therefore to Zakaria?

Or was Zakaria lying to protect himself, regardless of who the phone had belonged to in the past?

How was she going to find out?

Someone had clearly thought that Adam Mortaji was privy to vital information, and had taken him to a remote part of the world where he had probably been subjected to torture in order to make him talk.

God knows what he had said.

Personally, Eden would have started talking right away if anyone had tortured her. Particularly if they did something to her teeth. She would confess to anything, anything at all if they did that.

The murder of Olof Palme.

Lockerbie.

Anything, just as long as they stopped.

Eden printed off a copy of the picture and went to see Dennis.

"May I introduce Adam Mortaji, the guy who used to own Zakaria's phone."

Dennis took the picture.

"Nice one—where did you get hold of this?"

Eden perched on the edge of Dennis's desk.

"From our American friends. And he's not only the guy who used to own Zakaria's phone. He's also the link between Zakaria and Tennyson Cottage."

She relayed what the Americans had told her to Dennis, who was briefly lost for words. Then he exploded.

"They knew right from the fucking start that there was a guy in Sweden who'd been in Tennyson Cottage, and they didn't tell us?"

"I don't think they were lying. I think they believed he lived in Germany, and didn't have any connections with Sweden."

"But surely the Germans must have known who he was?"

"I'm sure they did. But that doesn't mean they followed his every move. It's not exactly difficult to travel from Germany to Sweden without any of the authorities taking any notice. And if I'm reading the call lists correctly, he's spent a lot of time in Sweden, both before and after his internment."

Dennis pulled up the lists on his computer.

He looked at Eden with admiration.

"A lot of things seem to be falling into place," he said.

"There's also a great deal that worries me," Eden said. "We know that Sofi has been in contact with Adam Mortaji, and I think that could partly explain why Zakaria wasn't prepared to give us his name. But it concerns me that Sofi has kept such a low profile throughout Zakaria's trial, and that she has never, ever come forward. I think she must have her own reasons for behaving in that way."

Dennis ran a finger over the picture of Adam Mortaji. God knows what he had endured during his time at Tennyson Cottage.

"Is Zakaria's sister the brains behind everything that's happened?"

"It's possible, don't you think?" Eden said.

"And I'm sure Adam Mortaji has been a great help to her."

Eden bit her lower lip.

"That's the thing," she said. "Mortaji died in June."

Dennis was clearly shocked.

"He's dead?"

"He killed himself. The Americans didn't say why, but I'm guessing it had something to do with his imprisonment."

"Which could explain the demand that Tennyson Cottage specifically should be shut down."

Eden nodded.

"What I still don't understand is how Karim Sassi fits into all this."

Eden knew that her tone was a little too matter-of-fact, but she had neither the time nor the energy to become personally involved in the tragic stories that were unfolding. There was a limit to how much misery a person could absorb in one day.

Dennis shook his head slowly.

"Me neither," he said.

He looked at the sheet of paper in Eden's hand.

"More surprises?"

Eden looked at the printout. It was the article about Adam Mortaji that she had found on the Internet after a thorough search. She passed it to Dennis.

"Mortaji isn't mentioned by name," he said after a moment.

"No. His father was afraid for both himself and his son, and chose to remain anonymous. But of course the Americans realized who he was."

"And you said he died in June?"

"Yes. Apparently, Mortaji left Europe in May, and returned to Morocco. He died soon afterward. His father was terribly upset that his son's girlfriend didn't get there in time."

"In time for what?"

"You can read it for yourself," she said. "But if I remember rightly, the girlfriend was on her way to Mortaji's parents' to be reunited with her lover, but for some reason she was delayed, and didn't arrive until the day after he died."

She shrugged.

"It's a very sad story, but right now we need to get this picture out as quickly as possible. Send it to the Germans, and distribute it to our own staff. I want to know everything there is to know about Adam Mortaji."

She swallowed hard. Wanting to know everything was something they often wished for but rarely achieved.

The nasal voice of her British boss echoed in the back of her mind: *Go, Eden, for God's sake, just go.*

Memories from a time gone by, a time she didn't want to think about.

"I'll give the picture to one of our operatives," she said, reaching out to take it from Dennis.

"Hang on," he said, looking more closely at the image.

He pointed to Mortaji's chest, which was partly visible because he was wearing a vest.

"He's got a tattoo there," he said.

Eden looked. Dennis was right; she hadn't noticed it.

"What does it say?"

"I've no idea; something in Arabic, I think."

"I'll ask Sebastian," Eden said.

She found the head of analysis at his desk.

"Can you get this translated?" she said, showing him the tattoo.

Sebastian opened a drawer and took out a magnifying glass. Eden burst out laughing.

"Bloody hell, Sebastian—you keep a magnifying glass in your drawer? Does that improve your analytical skills?"

Sebastian gave her a wry smile.

"Watch it, Eden."

She remembered the discussion when she had referred to his colleagues as so-called Arabists, and tried to assume a serious expression. It didn't last long; she was soon laughing again. The magnifying glass was covered in greasy fingerprints, and looked like something that had been stolen from a museum.

"Come with me," Sebastian said.

With the picture in one hand and the magnifying glass in the other, and Eden following on behind, he went over to one of his colleagues.

"Can you read this?" he said, handing her the picture.

The girl screwed up her eyes and peered at it.

"It's a bit small."

Sebastian gave her the magnifying glass, and she smiled.

Eden coughed into the crook of her arm to suppress another giggle. Who would have thought a laugh could be so liberating.

"It doesn't say anything in particular," the analyst said, and Eden's high spirits turned to disappointment.

Of course it didn't; why had she thought otherwise?

"But surely it must say something?" Sebastian said.

"It's just a name. It could be his girlfriend or his sister. Hard to tell—there's only a forename."

Sebastian was equally disappointed.

"Okay, thanks for your help," he said. "So what's the name of this girlfriend or sister?"

"Sofi."

63

Flight 573

She was woken by an excruciating pain. At first, she couldn't remember where she was, or what had happened. She cautiously moved her arms and legs, but stopped immediately. The source of the agony was in her head. The smallest movement made her want to scream. The pain came in waves; the only way to keep it under control was to lie absolutely still.

Fatima blinked. Once, twice.

The floor was hard against her cheek. Hard and cold. And there was a constant banging sound all around her. She closed her eyes. She had to think, try to remember.

Slowly, the memories began to surface.

She was still on board the plane. She didn't know how long she had been unconscious, but she realized they were still in the air.

More memories.

Erik Recht had gotten up and left the cockpit. She recalled Erik's face and the message in his eyes before he walked out:

"Make sure you stay here until I come back."

The next recollection was from the toilet, where she and Erik had locked themselves in so that they wouldn't be disturbed. Erik had been agitated, talking loudly about Karim's odd behavior. She had stuck up for Karim, hadn't wanted to hear such nonsense—how could Karim possibly be involved in the hijacking?

And now she was lying on the floor of the cockpit, knocked down by the same man she had defended just hours earlier.

The realization of the dilemma in which she found herself almost took her breath away. She was terrified. She was still in the cockpit, which must mean that Karim was there, too.

Please, God, don't let him notice that I've come around.

When had he hit her? The details were unclear, but she thought her problems had begun when Erik rang the bell, wanting to be let back in.

"Leave him out there," Karim had said.

And then, when he saw first surprise and then resistance in her face, when he saw her reach for the button that would open the door, he had leaped to his feet and grabbed hold of her.

"For fuck's sake, don't you understand what I'm saying? I don't want him in here—if you let him in, we're all going to die."

Fatima remembered what she had seen when she looked Karim in the eye, trembling with shock:

Despair.

Unmistakable despair in those beautiful dark eyes.

"But what's happened?" she had said, wanting to try to understand what lay behind his irrational determination to keep Erik locked out of the cockpit.

He hadn't replied. At the same time, Erik started hammering on the door, and she knew he must have realized what was going on.

Karim had no intention of letting him back in.

She didn't know how long Karim had held onto her. It had felt like an eternity, and suddenly Erik had stopped banging on the door. For a brief moment, she had thought the danger was over, that Karim was going to let her go.

Not that she knew where she would have gone.

And he had, in fact, let go of her, told her to sit down on the floor. She had done as he said, because by now she understood that something had gone terribly wrong.

Karim had moved toward the door and, at first, she had believed he was going to open it. When he turned around, he was clutching the fire extinguisher. She heard him say something she couldn't remember, then he lifted the extinguisher and . . .

It was as if her head had suddenly been reminded that it was hurt, and she forced herself to squeeze her eyes tightly shut to stop the hot tears spilling over and giving her away.

Shit, there was no way she could fix this on her own.

The tears were caused by the pain, which felt like needles piercing her eyeballs. She didn't have time to cry. She didn't want to cry.

But what was that noise, drowning out all the normal racket of an aircraft?

The door. Erik was out there again. Or had he been there all the time?

Fatima gave a start as Karim yelled:

"Stop it, for fuck's sake, just stop it! You're not coming back in, you hear me?"

There it was again, the echo of despair. It was unmistakable; she was absolutely certain she was right. Something was terribly wrong. Something more than the fact that the plane had been hijacked.

Karim, what have you done?

Eventually she had to open her eyes a fraction in order to work out where she was in relation to Karim. The light was blinding, and she instinctively closed them again.

Fatima tried again, and this time it was easier.

She was lying behind the seats, not far from the door. Karim was sitting with his back to her, his shirt sticking to his skin with perspiration. He was sweating as if he had just completed a ten-mile run. He was raking his hands through his hair, repeating over and over again:

"I can't cope with this, for fuck's sake. Stop banging on the fucking door. Please, please let this be over soon."

She tried raising her head. It went better than she had expected. The fire extinguisher was next to Karim. She couldn't think of any other weapon within reach.

She would have just one chance, she knew that. If she reached for the extinguisher, she had to be certain that she could get to her feet in the next movement and bring it down on Karim's head. If he had time to react, she was screwed. He was far stronger than her in purely physical terms. One chance. That was all she would get. And it would be over in seconds.

Fatima waited a little while longer. Erik carried on hammering on the door. Surely it had to give way soon? Should she wait?

No. It was a security door, designed for exactly this kind of situation. It was built to withstand extreme pressure from the outside, in order to protect the crew, and thus the passengers. Which meant there was a problem if the threat was on the wrong side of the door.

She sensed that Karim was about to do something really stupid, something that wasn't part of the plan. The noise from the door was obviously distracting him, which was good. She had to try to gather her strength.

Then an alternative course of action occurred to her.

The button that would unlock the door—could she reach that instead? Erik would be inside in no time.

By now, Karim had his hands over his ears, and his head was drooping.

It was now or never.

The button or the fire extinguisher.

She counted silently to herself.

One, two, three.

Then she saw it. Just inches away.

A fork.

Not a plastic fork like the ones they handed out to the passengers in economy, but a real fork made of stainless steel. The kind you got if you were traveling first class. Or if you were a member of the crew.

Slowly, Fatima reached out and grasped the shiny metal.

She had to act right now, because she wouldn't have this opportunity again. She would try to reach the button, then hurl herself at Karim. And say a prayer that Erik would move fast.

She closed her eyes and took a deep breath. Gripped the fork as tightly as she could and felt the pain in her head roll backward and forward like ocean waves.

She was ready now.

Now.

Now.

64

Stockholm, 23:05

A sister and a brother. A woman and the love of her life. Unbreakable bonds and an act of desperation. In one way so simple, in so many others completely incomprehensible. And still so many missing answers to the questions they wanted to ask.

In any other investigation, everything they had found out over the last couple of hours would have been regarded as a breakthrough, but not this time.

The passengers were still in a hostage situation up in the sky, and the Americans were still intending to shoot down the plane. And they were almost out of time. It was a matter of minutes rather than hours before the disaster would become a reality.

"Please don't let there be a bomb on board," Alex said as he stood beside Fredrika, looking out of the window.

Darkness and rain. Not a glimmer of light. Nowhere.

Fredrika took Alex's hand.

"It's going to be all right," she said.

"Do you really believe that?"

No.

Nothing was as it should be. The government had recently issued a statement saying that it had revised its decision to deport Zakaria Khelifi, and this had unleashed a storm of questions and reactions in the media. And in the middle of this inferno, the plane continued its journey toward destruction.

"Absolutely."

"But how can it be all right, Fredrika? They'll run out of fuel in half an hour."

"We still don't know how Erik has got on."

Our last hope.

Alex glanced over his shoulder.

"The others will think we're an item if we carry on standing here like this."

She squeezed his hand.

"Who cares. We're police officers, after all. We're supposed to screw around more than other people."

Alex's jaw dropped, and Fredrika smiled.

"Don't you remember Peder saying that?"

Alex pulled his hand away when she mentioned the name of their former colleague.

"I remember."

The strain felt like a physical pressure in Fredrika's chest. That was one of the reasons why she had left the police—the fact that the job demanded such terrible sacrifices. All the time. Nonstop.

Forgive me for deserting you when you had already lost Peder, but I just couldn't cope anymore.

"Is Spencer at home with the kids?" Alex asked.

The question surprised Fredrika.

"No, he's in Café Opera, drinking himself under the table."

Alex laughed quietly.

"Sorry. I'm old and stupid. Of course he's at home with the kids."

Spencer had called not long ago, and Fredrika had rejected the call. She didn't have time for him right now. Nor for the children. God knows what state she would be in when a new day dawned, bringing the drama to an end one way or another.

"Am I interrupting something?"

Eden was standing behind them. Fredrika got the feeling she had been there for a while.

"No," Alex said.

Eden asked them to come along to one of the meeting rooms, where Dennis and Sebastian were already waiting.

"I heard back from the Germans," Eden began. "They said they definitely have no knowledge of Sofi."

Dennis adjusted his collar. He was wearing a khaki shirt that Fredrika thought would have suited Spencer.

"In that case, I can only conclude that they've missed what this girl has been up to, because you don't embark on an operation like this unless you know what you're doing. If she is involved, of course."

This could well be true, and there were other aspects of what they had learned that frightened Fredrika.

"It doesn't matter whether or not they know who she is. Sofi lives in Germany. The man we assume was her boyfriend was held in an American detention facility in Afghanistan after traveling to Pakistan to attend terrorist training camps. And the Swedish government recently decided to deport her brother Zakaria," Eden summarized.

All day—*all day*—Fredrika had been on Zakaria's side, but now she didn't know what to think.

They had to get hold of Sofi. Without delay.

"How are we going to find her?" she said.

"We contacted the airport police and they found Zakaria's car in the long-stay garage, on the same level as the wastebasket where the cell phones were," Eden said. "Do you know where it was parked?"

"You just said it was in the long-stay garage," Alex said.

"I meant more specifically. It was also on the same level as Karim Sassi's car."

"But how the hell did we miss it, in that case?" Dennis said. "We were there, for God's sake, taking fingerprints from Sassi's car!"

"Yes," Eden said. "But at the time we didn't know we needed to look at the cars nearby, did we?"

"Could that have been where they met?" Fredrika said. "Is that how she got Karim's fingerprints on the phone?"

Eden made a note on the pad in front of her.

"We don't know that, and at the moment I don't think we should waste any time on finding out."

Eden's phone rang, and she answered.

"I haven't got time to talk now, I'll call you later."

Fredrika guessed it was a personal call, and this was confirmed when Eden went on:

"Well, if she's got a temperature, give her some Alvedon. Seriously, Mikael, this will have to wait until I get home. No, I have no idea when I'll be back. If I'm not going to make it before morning, I'll call you. 'Bye."

She ended the call and slipped the phone back in her pocket.

Fredrika couldn't take her eyes off Eden. There was something about her posture and her tone of voice that sent shivers down Fredrika's spine. It wasn't just that Eden was under pressure; she sounded as if she couldn't give a damn about her children. But surely that couldn't be true. Could it?

"However, we do need to find out how Karim Sassi fits into all this," Eden said.

At last.

"That's the only major question we don't have an answer to as yet," Dennis said.

"And, ironically, it's the only one that interests us right now," Alex said.

"There's something else I find strange about all this," Fredrika said. "The timing. There's no way the person behind the hijacking only got to work yesterday. This has taken an enormous amount of preparation."

"Exactly," Alex said. "And the Germans received that email several weeks ago."

"I think we all feel the same," Eden said. "And I'm wondering if this is what happened: the hijacking was originally planned only as an act of revenge, with the aim of getting Tennyson Cottage shut down. But then Zakaria was unexpectedly detained, and the perpetrator then set the wheels in motion earlier than he or she had intended, with the aim of securing Zakaria's release as well."

Fredrika could accept that explanation; it seemed pretty credible.

"But what about Karim Sassi?" Sebastian said. "*How the hell did he end up in this mess?* I mean, Sofi is the one who obviously has a reason to do something like this for her brother. But where does Karim fit in?"

"He's the one who's executing the whole thing," Dennis said.

"Yes, but why?"

Fredrika couldn't keep quiet any longer.

"Could it be that he has no choice?"

Eden put down her pen in frustration.

"How is that possible, Fredrika? I hear what you're saying. You think Karim is a victim rather than a perpetrator. But the fact remains—it's Karim and no one else who constitutes the greatest danger on board that plane right now. If he's not doing it of his own free will, what kind of pressure has he been subjected to?"

Fredrika had no answer to that question. She had asked it herself, over and over again. What would it take to make a man sacrifice the lives of hundreds of people, including his own, against his will?

She didn't know, couldn't come up with a sensible explanation.

At that moment, Alex's phone rang.

It was Erik.

65

Flight 573

At first, he hadn't been able to work out what was wrong. Everything had happened so fast. So incredibly fast.

The fork.

The fork in Fatima's hand, dripping with blood when she opened the cockpit door and fell into Erik's arms. Lydia had to step back quickly.

"Oh, God, I think I've killed him."

Fatima's voice was no more than a faint whimper, but Erik heard every word. He let her sink to the floor, took the fork out of her hand, and stepped over her body into the cockpit. Lydia knelt down beside her.

Karim was lying on the floor clutching his neck as the blood spurted out across the carpet. Erik hesitated before bending down to check if he was conscious. He gripped the slippery fork as he touched Karim's shoulder.

Karim raised his head and looked at Erik. He was weeping.

"Forgive me, Erik, please forgive me. I had no choice."

Erik felt the rage explode in his body.

"No choice? Are you crazy?"

His voice belonged to someone else. It was deeper and louder than it had ever been before.

"My family," Karim whispered. "They said they'd kill my family. It was them or me, so of course it had to be me."

Erik didn't understand what Karim was saying. He could hear the words, but they didn't mean anything.

"Who said that?"

Karim coughed and choked. His head sank back.

Erik looked at the wound, then straightened up. Resolutely, he got out the first-aid box and found a dressing. The wound looked horrible, but he didn't think it was life threatening.

"*Who, Karim?*"

"Forgive me, I had no choice."

Karim's voice was fading. Ironically, he looked calmer than he had done all day—as if he had found peace.

"But I do," Erik said, applying the dressing with rough hands.

Karim groaned.

"Just so you know, I'm taking command," Erik said. "We'll be landing shortly."

"Forgive me," Karim said again. "I'm so sorry."

But Erik had neither the desire nor the capacity to forgive him. Not here, not now. He found a short strap in one of the lockers and bound Karim's hands behind his back. Lydia appeared in the doorway.

"Is everything okay?" she said.

It was a stupid question, but Erik thought he knew what she meant.

"Yes," he said. "Everything's okay now. Get someone to take care of Fatima, then come back in here. Close the door behind you."

When Lydia had left the cockpit and closed the door, Erik bent down so that his face was close to Karim's.

"Answer me," he said. "Who told you your family was going to die?"

"I don't know. They're being held hostage."

"Your family?"

"Yes." His speech was becoming disjointed. "Don't know where. You have to do as they say, Erik. Don't divert away from Washington or my family will die."

Was he out of his mind? Did he really think Erik was going to let hundreds of people die, himself included, in order to save Karim's family?

"No chance," Erik said. "Absolutely no chance."

He slipped into Karim's seat. So they were close to Washington,

DC; if he had to make an emergency landing, it would have to be there.

Karim managed one last sentence before he lost consciousness.

"She said it was for Flight TU003."

Erik was barely listening.

"Who said what?"

But Karim was gone—and soon, Erik realized that he had fresh problems.

Big problems.

"This can't be happening," he whispered.

Someone rang the bell; Lydia was back. Erik let her in and yelled at her to keep an eye on Karim.

"Are we going to land?" she said.

"Too bloody right we are," Erik said. "We're almost out of fuel."

The color drained from Lydia's face as Erik made an emergency call.

"Mayday, Mayday, this is Copilot Erik Recht."

The words came automatically, almost as if he had pressed Play on a recording.

A flight controller in Washington, DC, responded.

"Erik Recht, we have received clear orders to deny your flight permission to land."

"I know that," Erik said. "But Captain Sassi is no longer in command."

"Where is Captain Sassi?"

Erik hesitated.

"He's lying on the floor, seriously injured."

Silence.

"I will pass on what you say to a higher authority," the voice said eventually. "Until you are given permission to land, your plane is still not allowed to enter US airspace."

"Hang on, listen to me! We have hardly any fuel left; you have to give us permission to land right away!"

"I'll get back to you."

And the voice was gone.

Erik tried to keep his fear and stress in check. Then he addressed the passengers and crew:

"This is your copilot speaking. For various reasons we have experienced a considerable delay, but it now appears that we will be landing very shortly. I would therefore ask all passengers to return to your seats immediately and fasten your seat belts."

How much time did they have?

A jumbo jet with no fuel could glide a very long way, but Erik didn't want to end up in that situation. Attempting to land with failing engines would end in disaster. They had to land now, without delay. Anything was better than an emergency landing.

The loudspeaker crackled into life:

"Copilot Recht, you are speaking to Andrew Hoffman, US military air surveillance."

It was the same man who had called earlier, the one who had said they didn't have permission to land.

Erik answered.

"I understand that Captain Sassi is no longer in command."

"That's correct."

"Are you alone in the cockpit at the moment?"

"The answer is no, I have a flight attendant by the name of Lydia with me. And Captain Sassi, but he's unconscious."

"No one else?"

"That's correct."

This was followed by silence, and Erik realized he hadn't given Hoffman the answer he wanted.

"Copilot Recht, I repeat: is there anyone else in the cockpit apart from yourself, a woman called Lydia, and Karim Sassi?"

"No."

What the hell was this all about?

"How did you get back into the cockpit?"

Erik was in despair. He didn't have time for an interrogation.

"Another flight attendant who was in the cockpit with Captain Sassi managed to put him out of action, then she opened the door for me."

"Did anyone apart from yourself try to gain access to the cockpit at any stage?"

Fuck. The American Erik had knocked out.

"Yes, a man. He was behaving in a threatening manner; he said he would help me if I could just get him into the cockpit, but for a start I couldn't get in there myself, and secondly, I didn't know who he was."

"I understand," Hoffman said. "Where is this man now?"

"He's lying on the floor outside the cockpit door."

"He's lying on the floor?"

"Listen to me, we're almost out of fuel and I must—"

The voice that interrupted him sounded like a clap of thunder.

"You are not calling the shots here, Copilot Recht. All you have to do is keep calm and await instructions. Why is the man lying on the floor? Is he hurt?"

"I knocked him out. I had no choice."

Erik could hear Hoffman breathing heavily.

"I'm sorry—you knocked him out?"

"Yes, sir."

"And now you claim you're in command of the plane? That a flight attendant managed to put Captain Sassi out of action all by herself, then opened the door for you?"

This couldn't be happening. For the first time in his life, Erik experienced something close to sheer panic.

"Please, you have to listen to me. I—"

"Copilot Recht, I have no reason to distrust you. But tell me one thing. Given that you've just said that an operative of the US Defense Service is lying unconscious on the floor, how am I supposed to know that everything else is in order?"

An operative of the US Defense Service?

Erik shook his head.

"I didn't know he was telling the truth," he said. "And I couldn't take the risk."

The fuel gauge was dangerously close to zero. Erik couldn't take his eyes off it. When the fuel ran out, the engines would die. And then the situation really would be critical.

"In that case, allow me to clarify my question: How do I know that Karim Sassi hasn't, in fact, taken you hostage, and is forcing you to talk to me and say the things you're saying?"

There were no words. Erik sat there in silence.

The voice went on: "As you must realize, it is not possible for us to revise our earlier decision merely on the basis of what you're telling me now. If you need to effect an emergency landing, then you will have to contact an airport outside the USA and hope you have better luck there."

"But we're all going to die!" Erik roared. "We're out of fuel, I can't change course and go somewhere else!"

Hoffman's voice was ice cold and crystal clear when he replied: "You are not landing on American soil. Do you understand?"

Then Erik heard himself repeating the words Karim had spoken not so long ago: "I'm very sorry, but I have no choice."

After a brief silence, Hoffman said: "In that case, I must unfortunately inform you that neither have we."

And he was gone.

It took Erik a few moments to grasp the significance of what he had just heard. He got out his cell phone, which was working now that they had lost height, and called the only person in the world that he knew for sure would listen to him.

"Dad, it's me again. I'm in a hell of a mess."

66

Stockholm, 23:20

Lights were showing in only a few windows in Police HQ. It was a cold night. Eden Lundell realized she should have put on a jacket.

She hadn't actually gone out for a smoke. Someone had called her cell phone, but then the coverage suddenly dipped inside the office. She'd lost count of the number of times she'd mentioned this problem; something was interfering with telephone traffic in the building, and it was bloody inconvenient. Particularly right now, as Erik Recht approached the US border with hardly any fuel, and still without permission to land. In spite of the fact that he had managed to deal with Karim Sassi.

So Eden had rushed outside to allow the call to come through. And lit a cigarette. She'd give her phone another fifteen seconds, then she would have to dash back inside.

She didn't hear him until he said her name.

"Eden."

It couldn't be true.

The ground disappeared beneath her feet. For the first time since the drama of Flight 573 began, something else filled her thoughts. Completely.

The voice was right behind her, and she suppressed the urge to turn around immediately. Instead, she dropped her cigarette and stamped on it. In silence, she watched the glow disappear; only then did she turn.

"I thought we'd agreed not to see each other anymore," she said.

Her voice sounded so thin, and her heart was pounding.

"That's strange. I have no recollection of any such agreement."

It was several years since they had met, but the memories were as clear as if it had been yesterday.

They stood in silence on the pavement outside the main entrance of Police HQ on Polhemsgatan. There wasn't a sound or a movement nearby. Everything was quiet. But inside Eden there was only chaos. Memories she didn't want to acknowledge burst into life and faded like stars against a dark sky.

"We've been waiting for you to get in touch."

"In that case you've been waiting in vain."

The expression in his dark brown eyes was serious, and she wished he was a little farther away so that the difference in height wasn't so obvious. She was shorter than him; the top two buttons of his shirt were undone, and she could see the gold chain around his neck. The one he had inherited from his grandfather, who had died fighting for his people and his new country.

It was far too late in the day for this kind of encounter. She was worn-out, and knew that she didn't have the capacity to be strong.

Eden was fragile.

"Go away," she said, pushing past him.

She heard him say something just as her cell phone rang again. As soon as she saw the number, the feeling of vulnerability was gone. She answered as she always did.

"Yes."

She had been longing to hear Bruce Johnson's voice. Suddenly she was no longer alone on the pavement.

"I believe Erik Recht has been in touch with you, too."

She had been waiting for this.

"Yes."

She held her breath.

"Sorry, but nothing has changed. The supreme commander is sticking to his decision. We can't risk letting Flight 573 enter US airspace. It's just not possible. We have information which clearly indicates that the captain is intending to crash the plane into the Capitol Building, regardless of whether we meet his demands. And Erik Recht can't prove that he is in control."

Eden heard the words, but she couldn't process what she was

hearing. They had had the chance to avert a disaster, and now that chance was gone. But she had clung to hope. Desperately. Mostly for Alex's sake, she realized.

"Your decision is incomprehensible."

"To you, perhaps, but not to us."

"That's crap—you're on our side. You think this is crazy, too."

Bruce didn't say anything, but Eden stuck to her guns.

"Is there anyone we can call? Anyone we can pressurize?"

What could he say to that? Of course there wasn't anyone they could call. The decision had been made by the US supreme commander, the president himself. It was as close to a pronouncement from God as you could get these days. The plane would be shot down. According to American logic, this would cost hundreds of lives, but save thousands.

"I'll call you later when I know more," Bruce said.

Then he ended the call, and Eden was seized by uncontrollable rage.

He would call later.

Later.

But there was no later, for fuck's sake!

The hostages would die and the perpetrators would achieve their goal. Didn't the Americans get that? If they shot down the plane, they would be doing the terrorists a favor. They would be fulfilling the mission Karim Sassi had been unable to complete.

Eden had reached the doors now, completely focused on calling the next person to whom she must pass on the latest news: Alex. How could he possibly deal with what she had to tell him?

We still don't know how this is going to end.

Efraim waited while she spoke to Alex, then caught up with her.

"I'll be back."

She looked up.

"That's not necessary."

"I don't agree."

Then he walked away. Eden stood there, with one hand on the door and the other clutching her phone as she watched him go.

Why did it have to hurt so much? The pain was actually physical.

It felt as if someone had reached into her chest, pulled out her heart, and thrown it down on the pavement along with her fucking cigarette butts.

She tried to cling to the image of Mikael, the man she had loved for so long and betrayed so badly. But over and over again, he was pushed aside, and it was Efraim's face she saw instead.

Efraim, taking her hand and leading her back to his apartment in the heat of a Tel Aviv summer.

Efraim, winding her hair around his fingers as she cried out with a combination of guilt and desire.

She was almost fascinated to realize how easily he had punctured the protective bubble inside which she had chosen to live her life. Eden was no longer invincible. During the minute it took her to get back to the office, she cried more than she had cried in her entire adult life.

• • •

The plane was going to crash, and all those on board were going to die. The US government had chosen the option they had all thought was unlikely, and now there was no way back. That was what Eden had been told. The fact that Erik insisted he was in control of the plane made no difference. They wanted proof. And there wasn't any.

Fredrika Bergman pretended she was calling her boss in the Justice Department because of the passengers, because the world would become a dark and evil place if the plane was not allowed to land.

But deep down in her heart and soul, she knew she was fighting for one thing only: the survival of Alex's son.

"We've tried everything," her boss said; he had just spoken to the minister for justice. "The prime minister has contacted the White House personally to express his concern, but they refuse to cooperate. Unless they have proof that Erik Recht is in command of the plane and that Karim Sassi is out of the picture, they will not let them cross the border."

"But what kind of proof do they want?" Fredrika said. "Pictures—can we ask Erik to send pictures?"

"That won't help. They could be staged."

Eden came back smelling of smoke, and Fredrika thought she looked as if she had aged fifteen years during the few minutes she had been away. She even looked as if she had been crying.

As if they could afford more secrets right now.

After the calls to the cabinet office and the Americans came silence.

Alex's face was gray.

"What can we do?" Eden said.

It was a rhetorical question. She wanted them to say they had come up with a fresh approach, a new strategy for dealing with the problem. They hadn't. The absence of words was as palpable and troubling as the smell of smoke surrounding Eden.

"He's got to bring him around," Alex said.

"Who?" Eden said.

"The American he knocked out. He's the only one who can convince them that the plane is no longer in the hands of the hijackers."

"But he's unconscious," Eden said. "That's why we're in this mess."

Alex shook his head.

"As long as he hasn't killed him, which he hasn't, he's got to try to bring him around."

"But how?" Fredrika said, knowing that they were all thinking the same thing.

"I don't know. But we need to contact a doctor right away, get advice from someone."

Sebastian was the one who reacted most quickly.

"I'm on it," he said, running to his desk.

The ground beneath their feet was on fire. The situation had never been more urgent, and yet Fredrika felt as if time was standing still.

Then a call came through from Rosenbad.

Eden took it.

Erik had entered US airspace.

67

Washington, DC, 17:22

Since the decision to shoot down the plane had already been taken, Erik Recht's emergency call stating that he was entering US airspace did not lead to any lengthy discussions. The Department of Defense had been informed, and the White House was now closely monitoring developments. Bruce had left his office an hour ago and had been transported at high speed to Dulles International Airport. Nobody expected that the plane would be allowed to land, but if it did happen, it would be at Dulles, and his boss wanted him on the spot.

Bruce didn't like what was about to happen. There was a risk, or a chance, that Erik was telling the truth when he said that he was now in sole command. If that was the case, then to deny the plane the opportunity to land, saving all those on board, would be unforgivable.

He had lied to Eden when they spoke just a few minutes earlier. Of course he was worried, just as she had said. But like the loyal colleague he was, he opted for an appearance of solidarity. Eden was not the kind of person Bruce wanted to confide in.

The discussions in the White House must have been turbulent. In Bruce's opinion, the president was taking a risk. A huge risk, in fact. Because the problem was clear: once the plane had crashed, and the dead had been brought home and the wreckage salvaged, they would find the black box. There was a considerable danger that the box would contain recordings confirming what Erik had told them: that Karim Sassi had been removed from the picture.

What would the president say to his electorate then?

Bruce shared his thoughts with a colleague who had also been sent to the airport in haste.

"So what do you suggest?" the other man said. "That we allow the plane to fly in, and risk the lives of even more US citizens?"

That was out of the question. Bruce knew it. It was politically impossible for the president not to show that he had the capacity to take action.

"How long will it take?" he said instead. "To shoot down the plane, I mean."

His colleague ran a hand through his hair. His forehead was beaded with sweat.

"I don't know. It's only about a minute since he breached US air-space. I imagine we can take him down in less than sixty seconds."

A minute.

Bruce swallowed hard.

He wondered what Erik Recht had said to his passengers. Had he prepared them for what was to come?

"Ladies and gentlemen, this is your captain speaking . . ."

One of the air-traffic controllers spoke up.

Erik Recht had been in touch with them again.

He believed he had some information they would want to hear.

68

Flight 573

They had tried everything, but the American whom Erik Recht had knocked unconscious, and who apparently worked for the US Department of Defense, refused to come around. A call from Stockholm informed Erik that they had contacted Karolinska Hospital, and that one of their emergency doctors would try to give some advice.

But Erik was doubtful. Several doctors among the passengers had already tried to help, but they were all in agreement about the man's condition. He had probably suffered a severe concussion, and even if the injury was not regarded as life threatening, it was impossible to say how long he would remain unconscious.

However, Erik immediately called the US authorities and asked for a respite.

"Just let us consult a doctor," he said. "I only need three minutes at the most."

When there was no immediate response, he went on: "For God's sake, it has to be in your interests not to have to shoot us down!"

He was begging, more than he had ever done in his life.

He was begging to be allowed to live, to be able to see his family again.

And he was begging for his crew and his passengers.

They gave him three minutes, but made it clear that they wouldn't wait any longer.

Erik was so stressed that he could hardly breathe. The emergency doctor from Karolinska was put through, and quickly reached the same conclusion as the other doctors when he was told what had happened to the American, and what they had done to try to bring him round.

There was no magic wand. The man was unconscious, and that was that.

Erik had never felt so alone as when the emergency doctor's voice disappeared.

"In that case, there's nothing else we can do," Lydia said.

Unlike Erik, she hadn't shed a tear all day; she was standing in the middle of the cockpit, pale and stiff.

"I'll tell the others," she said. "How long do we have left?"

Erik looked at the clock but found it difficult to focus. His vision was blurred, and he was ashamed of his own weakness.

"I don't know—two minutes at the most."

Lydia left the cockpit, and Erik was alone with Karim. He allowed the plane to lose height, as if he was going to land, and wondered whether he ought to tell the passengers what had happened. Or what was going to happen. That he couldn't wait any longer, that he had to try to land, otherwise they would crash into the sea. That they were going to die anyway, because the Americans were so afraid of terrorists that they would rather shoot down a plane carrying their own citizens than risk making the wrong judgment call in favor of the hijackers.

Erik closed his eyes. He wouldn't call his father; they had already said everything there was to say. The only person he wanted to speak to was Claudia, but he couldn't get hold of her.

He leaned back against the headrest.

I'm coming to join you, Mom.

Someone rang the cockpit doorbell. Erik blinked, glanced at the camera, and let Lydia in. Her voice was so shrill that at first he couldn't make out what she was saying.

"He's awake, Erik! He's awake!"

But it was too late. There was no time left. The information he had received from the Americans was unequivocal: the order to bring down the plane had already been given. Erik felt a terror so powerful that it almost ejected him from his seat. His roar must have been heard right through the plane.

"Listen to me, for fuck's sake! He's conscious!"

He didn't stop shouting, he just kept on repeating the same words over and over again, louder and louder.

Lydia and a colleague dragged the man into the cockpit. He was weak, hanging limply in their arms. But Erik looked at his eyes, and they showed a strength and resolve; if he could just get to the microphone, he would be able to speak to his fellow Americans.

The man on the other end of the line was also shouting to make himself heard.

"So where is he, then? If he's conscious, why can't we talk to him?"

When Erik paused for breath, he could hear the racket in the background on the American side. It sounded as if at least a dozen people were standing there, yelling at one another.

The American reached him.

It didn't make any difference, Erik realized. If the order had already been given, they would all die before a new decision could be made.

The man was slumped on the floor, but he reached out, and Erik gave him the microphone.

"This is Kevin Davis speaking. I can confirm that Captain Sassi is no longer in control of this aircraft. If that's not enough, I demand that you put me through to the Pentagon so that I can confirm my identity."

That was when Erik spotted them on the right. Two planes. Strike aircraft, without a doubt.

An airborne death squad.

Erik gave up.

Kevin Davis was still talking, but Erik knew that it didn't matter. His words had reached the Americans too late. There was no time to divert the strike aircraft.

Or was there?

Kevin Davis was silent now, listening to the person on the other end. Then he spoke to someone else, introducing himself once again. Erik saw his face suddenly relax.

Erik quickly turned to look at the two planes. They were still in position.

Kevin Davis tapped his arm. Erik looked at him.

And Davis said the magic words:

"We have permission to land."

Erik didn't react.

"Didn't you hear what I said? Get us down, for fuck's sake!"

Only then did Erik understand. As if in a trance, he turned his full attention to the task ahead.

Landing the plane.

Bringing the passengers and crew to safety.

Erik headed toward Dulles airport, where he had been told to land. There was just enough fuel, but there was no margin for error.

The strike aircraft accompanied him every step of the way.

And when the wheels of Flight 573 touched down at long last, the planes soared away into the sky and disappeared into the darkness.

Wednesday, October 12, 2011

69

Stockholm, 00:11

It was the longest night of the autumn. At least, that was how Eden Lundell would remember it. She would also think of it as the night when the past made a fresh attempt to catch up with her.

She assumed that she would win, as usual.

They were receiving bulletins from the Americans at intervals of less than a minute. First of all, the plane was going to be shot down. Then came a message that Erik had called to say that the man he had knocked out with a wine bottle had finally regained consciousness.

Then nothing.

Midnight came and went.

After seconds so long they felt like months, another call came through. At one minute past midnight. Kevin Davis had been able to confirm that what Erik said was true. Captain Karim Sassi was seriously injured and was no longer in command. One minute later, they were given permission to land at Dulles airport, and as soon as the plane touched down, Bruce called Eden.

To her surprise she was shaking with rage as she listened to what he had to say.

"They could have *died*," she said. "Do you understand what you've done?"

"They could," Bruce replied. "But they didn't, and I think we would prefer to focus on that."

Eden didn't waste time arguing; she slammed down the phone and turned to Alex.

"They've landed. They're all fine."

Alex's shoulders dropped and his face lost the strained expression he had been wearing all day.

The battle for his son's survival was over.

"Thank God," he said.

Fredrika was sitting next to him; she was equally relieved, and placed a hand over his.

It had been so close.

So horribly close.

There had been so little time left when Erik landed the plane. The fuel levels were so low that he had been prepared for an emergency landing with the engines shut down.

Bruce had called the touchdown "impressive."

Eden still thought of it as extremely dangerous.

"What happens now?" Fredrika said.

Eden looked at the phone and tried to remember all the information Bruce had spewed out during his call.

"There were no other planes on the tarmac when Flight 573 came down. The emergency services were waiting for them on the runway. The media were banned, but of course they realized what was going on. The Americans are issuing a press release, and they will be holding a short press conference, where they will answer the most important questions."

She shrugged.

"And the government?" Fredrika said. "Our government, I mean."

"They were contacted at the same time as us. I'll get in touch as soon as we're done here."

"Me, too," Fredrika said.

Alex got to his feet. "I'll go and call my family," he said.

Eden, Fredrika, and Sebastian stayed put. Bruce called again.

"Karim Sassi is in bad shape, but he's going to make it," he said. "The flight attendant stabbed him in the neck with a fork."

Eden could see it in her mind's eye. The fork penetrating his flesh, the blood spurting out. She felt nothing. Karim Sassi had endangered the lives of hundreds of people. If she hadn't been so keen to find out what had driven him to do such a thing, Eden would have been quite happy to see him die.

"And Kevin Davis, the guy Erik knocked out?"

"He'll be fine, too. He's got a severe concussion; he'll have to spend a few days in the hospital, and I think he'll be off sick for a while. He seems to have some problems with his vision and his memory."

Eden was worried for Erik. The Americans were world leaders in holding people responsible for the most bizarre occurrences.

"Bruce, Erik couldn't possibly have known that he was one of you."

"I'll leave the DA to decide that," Bruce said tersely. "If he'd just listened to the guy instead of trying to kill him, things would have been very different."

"Yes, but—"

"I have no intention of discussing this with you, Eden. That's not why I called."

Always that illusion of superiority.

I have no intention of discussing this with you, Eden.

Who the fuck did he think he was?

"I'm calling because Karim Sassi became hysterical when they carried him into the ambulance. Well, you know what I mean. He's extremely weak, but he was showing clear signs of stress. He says that his family are being held hostage, and that they're going to die."

Eden shook her head.

There was no possibility that this was the case. They couldn't have missed something like that.

"He says that's why he did it," Bruce went on. "Could there be any truth in this? If so, there's very little time, because the news that the plane has landed without the hijackers' demands being met is already out there, as you know."

Eden pressed the receiver to her ear, trying to suppress the warning bells in her head.

She could feel the others staring at her.

"He's lying," she said. "Not a shred of doubt about it. We've spoken to Karim's wife several times. She and the children traveled to Copenhagen yesterday morning, and now she's back in Stockholm. We've been to see her."

Or had they?

Dennis had come over to her desk; he caught her eye and nodded in confirmation.

"In that case, I've no idea what he's talking about," Bruce said. "I just wanted to check that there was no truth in what he said. I'll get back to you on that."

"Please do," Eden said. She thought for a second, then added, "That doesn't necessarily mean he's lying."

"What?"

"Karim Sassi. Just because his family hasn't been kidnapped, that doesn't mean he couldn't have believed that was the case. Which was why he helped the hijackers. Because he thought his family would die if he didn't."

Her brain was functioning on autopilot, and she suddenly realized how everything hung together.

"How could something like that happen?" Bruce said, his voice dripping with skepticism.

"It would only take a phone call," Eden said.

A call from one of the phones that was used to make the bomb threats on Monday.

For fuck's sake, they had been led by the nose all the way along.

A wave of nausea came over her; she broke out in a sweat, the perspiration running down her back. The bomb threats had had one aim—to consolidate their suspicions against Karim. The person responsible for the hijacking, most probably Zakaria's sister, had pointed them in the direction of Karim and away from herself. In spite of the fact that they had worked out Sofi's role in the drama, they had missed the fact that Karim was merely an instrument for her malevolence.

It was such a significant failure that Eden could feel herself blushing.

"Surely no normal person would carry four hundred people to their deaths to save their family just on the basis of a phone call?" Bruce said. "I mean, wouldn't you call your family to check if they really are being held hostage?"

Eden shook her head.

"I haven't worked out all the details," she said. "I just know that what he's saying is relevant. You have to talk to him. Soon. Tonight, if possible, so that whoever is behind all this doesn't have time to get out of Sweden. Ask the right questions. Find out what he has to say, and I'll work on it from my side."

She could sense Bruce's doubts in his silence.

"You can't seriously believe he's telling the truth?"

"I don't believe anyone would do something like this without a really good reason. And I've spent most of my time today trying to understand what motivated Karim. I came up with jack shit."

"Okay," Bruce said. "If you're buying the kidnapping angle, then perhaps you'd like to hear part two of his mixed-up story. He mentioned a flight number to the copilot before he lost consciousness on the plane."

Eden frowned. "What flight number?"

"Flight TU003. He said that was what it was all about, or something along those lines."

Eden didn't know what to say or think.

"We'll check it out," she said, without any real conviction that it would prove useful.

Alex interrupted her.

"Ask him about Erik."

"What's happening with Erik Recht?"

"We're holding him and the rest of the crew. We'll be questioning him shortly."

Eden avoided looking at Alex.

"And that other matter we were discussing? Will you be prosecuting?"

"Eden, this has been a hell of a day, if you'll pardon my language. I can't possibly answer a question like that right now."

Eden ended the call, feeling extremely irritated.

"What did they say?" Alex wanted to know.

"They'll be questioning Erik shortly."

"Good," Alex said. "In that case, he'll soon be home."

Eden thought that was unlikely, but she didn't say anything.

They had an awful lot of work ahead of them. It had been a long day, but it was going to be an even longer night. Eden had no intention of going home. She would stay at work and tackle one thing at a time.

She was still spooked by the encounter with Efraim.

No, she definitely wasn't going home. She wouldn't stand a chance of getting to sleep anyway.

Sebastian seemed to read her mind.

"I'm staying," he said. "What do we do now?"

Eden gave him a grateful look.

"We start with Karim's wife."

70

Washington, DC, 21:15

It was several hours before the doctors would allow them to carry out an initial interview with Karim Sassi. He had undergone an operation to stop the bleeding in his neck, and the anesthetic had made him very tired.

"I don't really know how much help he'll be in his present condition," the doctor said. "But you're welcome to speak to him for a little while."

Karim's eyes were cloudy when Bruce and his colleague walked into the room. He listened as they introduced themselves and explained that he was suspected of being involved in the hijacking of Flight 573, and of attempting to blackmail the US government, thus breaking the United States laws on terrorism.

"How do you respond to these accusations?" Bruce said after his colleague had read Karim his rights.

At first, they didn't think they were going to get an answer. It looked as if Karim wanted to say something but was having major problems in actually speaking. Bruce was just about to go and fetch the doctor when Karim spoke:

"My family."

It was no more than a whisper, but Bruce heard what he said. So Karim was intending to stick to his story, claiming that his family had been kidnapped.

Bruce was about to tell him that his family was okay, and that they had other matters to discuss, when he changed his mind.

"They're still missing," he said.

His colleague was staring at him as if he had lost his mind. Of course the family were okay—they always had been.

Bruce prayed that his colleague would keep quiet.

Karim's reaction was totally unexpected. With a groan, he tried to sit up and get out of bed. A stream of whispered words came pouring out, but Bruce didn't understand a thing because they were all in Swedish.

With firm hands he pushed Karim back down.

"You're going nowhere," he said.

"You don't understand," Karim said, speaking in English now. "She's still got them. She said they'd die if I broke the rules."

He began to cry, in a way that Bruce had never seen a man cry; it was deeply disturbing.

Bruce took a deep breath and tried to find the right words.

"Karim, listen to me. It's obvious that something terrible has happened, but we can't help you if you don't talk to us. Do you understand?"

Karim wiped his face; he looked gray and exhausted. If the doctor came in, the interview would be over.

"I understand."

"Good. Start from the beginning. How did you come into contact with these people?"

Once again, Karim had difficulty speaking.

Patience, Bruce thought. This situation requires patience, which unfortunately I don't have.

"Just one. She's alone."

"Who is alone?"

"The person who did all this. The woman who took my family."

More tears, and by now, Karim Sassi's chest was rattling so much that Bruce discreetly gestured to his colleague to close the door, so that he couldn't be heard out in the corridor.

"They're gone," Karim whispered. "All gone."

Bruce had seen more liars than he could count. Over the years, he had become highly skilled in seeing how lies altered a person's face, small details that might escape the untrained eye, but which he noticed immediately.

He could see none of these signs in Karim. Not one. Perhaps it was because of the anesthetic, perhaps because he was exhausted. Or perhaps he was actually telling the truth, in which case Bruce assumed he must be going through the torments of hell right now.

"We're looking for them," he said. "We won't give up until we find them."

They had to move on. He was happy to provide reassurance if it calmed Karim down.

"She's always one step ahead, all the time."

"Do you know who she is?"

"No."

"She didn't tell you her name?"

"No."

"But she must have had other people helping her?"

"I don't know about that."

But what about you, Karim? You were one of those people, weren't you?

As far as Bruce was aware, it wouldn't change Karim's situation even if it turned out that he had actually believed his family had been kidnapped. A compassionate judge would regard it as a mitigating circumstance, but nothing more. You couldn't endanger the lives of over four hundred people in order to save just three.

"So you don't know this woman who took your family?"

"No."

"How did she get in touch with you?"

"She rang me. The previous night. She rang and left a message on my voicemail. Although it wasn't really a message, just a long silence. So I called back, mainly because I was curious. I thought whoever it was must have left a message, but for some reason it hadn't recorded. She said she'd got the wrong number. Asked about someone I didn't know; I said there was no one of that name in our house. I didn't recognize her voice."

Karim fell silent.

"Then what happened?"

Karim closed his eyes, and Bruce thought he had fallen asleep. He gently nudged Karim's shoulder, and his eyes flew open.

"Then what happened?"

"She called again. This morning."

"You mean yesterday morning?"

"Before we took off. She called me before we took off. Said she'd taken my family, that I would be given a task to fulfill, and that I must follow my instructions to the letter. *To the letter.*"

Karim's chest rose and fell.

"And what were these instructions?"

"She told me over the phone. Told me to write the demands on a piece of paper, then stick it to the wall in one of the toilets."

"You were the one who wrote the note?"

"Yes."

Bruce thought for a moment. This was all too weird; he couldn't take it in.

"Okay, let's just rewind here. For a start: how did you know that she really had taken your family?"

Fresh tears trickled down Karim's cheeks. "She let me speak to my daughter."

Bruce felt his pulse rate increase.

How was this possible? How could Karim's family have been taken hostage without anyone missing them? They'd been in Denmark all day, hadn't they?

"And what did your daughter say?"

Karim turned his head so that he was gazing at the window and the black night sky outside.

"She said she wanted me to come home, that the girl was stupid."

"Was she upset?"

Karim nodded, and whispered, "It was so short. Much too short."

"How long did your conversation last?"

"Less than a minute."

"So you never met her?"

"No."

Bruce began piecing the information together, and with the help of the reports he had received from Stockholm during the day, an unpleasant picture began to take shape. There was Karim's contact with the phone that had also been used to make bomb threats targeting various locations in Stockholm's inner city. And there was the information from the neighbor who had seen Karim's youngest daughter speaking to a girl in the street.

Is that how it had happened? Had someone used such a simple ruse to convince Karim that his family had been kidnapped?

"Didn't you try to call your wife?"

"Yes, but she always has her cell phone on silent, or switched off. This time I couldn't get through at all."

The doctor came in, and when he saw Karim's dull expression and heard his labored breathing, he was far from happy.

Bruce cut him off before he could say a word.

"We're almost done."

"Two more minutes, then I'm afraid you'll have to leave."

Bruce turned to Karim, desperate to finish asking his questions.

"What further instructions did you receive? Apart from the ones you wrote in the note?"

"None."

"So why did you fly to Washington instead of New York?"

Karim turned back to face Bruce, his expression almost one of surprise. As if he had been reminded of something he had forgotten.

"Sorry, my head's all over the place. You're right, she told me that I wasn't to land in New York under any circumstances; I was to head for Washington, DC."

"And where did she tell you to land?"

"At Dulles airport."

"Nowhere else?"

"No."

"She didn't tell you to crash the plane, regardless?"

Karim's gaze sharpened.

"What do you mean?"

"You heard what I said."

"I don't understand."

"Then let me ask you again: you weren't told to crash the plane, regardless of whether or not the hijackers' demands were met?"

Karim looked as if he still didn't understand the question, even though he had heard it twice.

"No," he said. "No, definitely not."

And then he said something that made Bruce stiffen.

"How could you think that I would have accepted something like that? I love my family, more than anything in the world. But I couldn't take the lives of over four hundred people for their sake. It would have been a terrible decision to make, but . . . She said there was a bomb on board, but I didn't believe her."

He shook his head.

"So you wouldn't have done it?" Bruce said.

"No, I wouldn't."

Of course he wouldn't. That information had been given only to the security services involved, to deter them from opposing the hijackers' demands. Or possibly to provoke a stress reaction.

Which was exactly what had happened.

We were so close to damning ourselves forever.

The doctor cleared his throat behind Bruce.

"Your time is up," he said.

"Of course."

Bruce had just one question left; the rest could wait.

Karim looked anxious when he realized that Bruce and his colleague were about to leave.

Bruce got in first.

"Just one more thing. Why you?"

Silence. It was obvious that Karim had asked himself that same question.

"She said it was because of Flight TU003," he said.

Bruce didn't understand.

"What does that mean?"

"Don't you think I've asked myself the same question? I have no idea."

Bruce didn't know much about planes or airline company employees, and wasn't quite sure what to say next.

"Have you ever been captain on a flight with that number?" he asked eventually.

"I certainly have," Karim replied. "Just once, back in May. A flight from Copenhagen to Rabat. I stood in for a colleague. It's the only time apart from today when I've had to carry out an emergency landing."

Bruce didn't comment on the fact that Karim hadn't actually landed Flight 573.

"What happened?" he asked instead.

"There was a fight among a group of passengers. The crew couldn't manage to break them up; I decided they were a danger to other passengers, so I landed in Munich."

Bruce instinctively thought that this information could be important, but he didn't know what to do with it.

"Were any of the passengers particularly upset because you were landing in Munich?" he said.

Karim coughed and brought his hand up to the wound in his neck, as if he was afraid it might burst open.

"Not as far as I recall. Apart from the guys who were fighting, of course, but that was only to be expected. The problem was that it took almost eight hours before I was allowed to continue the journey. During the time it took to land and get rid of the troublemakers, a terrible storm came in over the city. Gale-force winds, hail, thunder, and lightning. It was positively apocalyptic. They shut down the whole airport for several hours, and then, of course, there was a line when we were able to leave."

Bruce made a note of the flight number, then caught his colleague's eye. Time to end the interview and head back to the office.

Just as they were about to leave, Bruce heard Karim's hoarse voice once more:

"Promise me you'll try to find my family. I don't care what you do with me, just make sure you find them. I have to know what's happened to them."

Bruce hesitated for no more than a second.

"Karim, they're fine. They were never taken hostage."

71

Stockholm, 05:06

It was five o'clock in the morning, but Fredrika Bergman didn't feel at all tired. Alex had gone home a few hours earlier to be with his family; Fredrika and Eden stayed on, along with Dennis and Sebastian. The night was dark and cold, and Fredrika was happy to be indoors.

She updated her employers on the hour and every half hour. Once the media had grasped the fact that no one was seriously hurt, and had managed to pass this on in a range of articles, anxious relatives stopped calling the police.

It didn't take long before it became known that the police suspected Captain Sassi of being involved in the hijacking, and at the same time there was a flood of questions as to why the government had revised its decision to deport Zakaria Khelifi. After that, Fredrika didn't have a minute to herself.

She spoke to her boss at the Justice Department and provided him with the basis of a statement to the press. Zakaria's deportation had been reviewed due to a comprehensive reevaluation. The government simply couldn't risk getting such an important decision wrong, and it was better to be safe than sorry.

Fredrika looked at what she had written down.

Why was she still not happy about this?

She had gotten what she wanted, after all.

Zakaria Khelifi would be allowed to remain in Sweden.

There was nothing but emptiness inside her. She knew she ought to go home and go to bed, get a few hours' sleep. Instead she went to find Eden.

"How's it going?"

Eden glanced up. She didn't look in the least bit tired.

"It's going well. I've put out a call for Zakaria's sister Sofi."

Zakaria's sister, who was probably the person behind everything that had happened over the past few days. Please don't let her leave the country or go underground. It would be a nightmare to lose her, knowing that she was still out there in the field as an opponent.

"What if we don't find her?" Fredrika said.

"We'll find her."

She could hear from Eden's tone of voice that she didn't want to discuss the matter any further, but Fredrika was worried. Someone who had worked out such a detailed plan wasn't going to leave her own disappearance to chance. And all they had to help them track her down was a name no one recognized and a picture from her uncle that was several years old.

Fredrika remembered that Eden had assumed that the person behind it all was a man. Jumping to conclusions. The world wasn't black or white; it was usually gray.

"The government is going to release Zakaria for good," she said. "There's absolutely no chance that they will review their decision again."

"I know," Eden said.

"What do you think about his case, in the light of all that's happened?"

"I don't think anything. I know. Zakaria is up to his ears in shit."

Information had come flooding in over the past few hours. Karim's wife had confirmed parts of his story; someone had called his cell phone and left a silent message on his voicemail. Karim had mentioned it to his wife, then called the person back. She hadn't seen her youngest daughter speaking to a girl over the fence, but the child had told her about it.

Eden had sent two officers over to Solna even though it was the middle of the night, and they had shown the neighbor a picture of Sofi. The woman had shaken her head and said that she hadn't really seen what the girl looked like.

"I just remember her hat. She was wearing a big blue woolly hat."

The Americans were skeptical about Karim's story and the explanation for his actions. Fredrika and the others had no doubts whatsoever. It was totally illogical to believe that someone would risk so much without a very good reason.

Fredrika had sat in on the interview with Karim's wife, who had asked several times what would happen to her husband now and wanted to know when he would be coming home. They had tried to sidestep her questions and had answered evasively that they would have to wait and see. Karim was injured, and was in need of care first and foremost. They told Karim's mother the same thing when they contacted her to tell her that her son was safe.

But they all knew the truth: Karim wouldn't be coming home. Not for a long time, perhaps never.

The thought made her so sad that it was unbearable.

Any one of us would have done the same thing in his situation.

What also made her sad was that she couldn't for the life of her see how they were going to connect Sofi to the crimes they suspected her of.

"We don't have a shred of evidence," she said to Eden.

"Don't we?"

"No one has seen her; we have nothing to prove that she was involved, apart from the fact that she drove a car to Arlanda. And that she spoke to Karim, but the courts will never accept an identification solely on the basis of someone's voice."

Eden finally looked up from her screen.

"You can't think of any other evidence Sofi has given us, without realizing it?"

Fredrika sensed a trap, but chose to walk right in anyway.

"No."

"Two things," Eden said, holding up two fingers. "First of all, she must have made sure Karim's fingerprints ended up on the phone. We can only guess how it happened, but I'm going to ask the Americans to ask Karim whether he's used anyone else's phone over the past few days. My guess is that Karim met her, probably in such an everyday situation that he had no reason to suspect anything was wrong. But with a bit of luck, he'll remember what she looked like."

Of course. Monday's bomb threats had had one purpose and one alone: to point the finger of suspicion at Karim.

"And the other thing?"

"Flight TU003," Eden said, turning the monitor so that Fredrika could see it. "Do you remember the article in which Tennyson Cottage was mentioned? Adam Mortaji's father said that his son had killed himself, and his girlfriend didn't get there in time. Sofi could have been clever and gone for any pilot, but instead she chose to make it personal."

Fredrika leaned forward; there seemed to be a passenger list on the screen.

"Karim flew from Copenhagen to Rabat in May," Eden said. "I'm absolutely certain that Sofi was on board, under a different name. The flight was delayed for so long that she arrived too late to see Adam, the love of her life. By the time she finally got there, her boyfriend had already killed himself."

Fredrika felt that sensation of emptiness again. She realized Eden was right. Hopefully, it was only a matter of time before they worked out Sofi's alias.

"It was very convenient for her that Zakaria actually knew Karim," she said.

It took a while before the extent of the damage Sofi had deliberately caused Karim became clear. She had made absolutely certain that he would appear to be involved in her plan. While he defended his actions on the grounds that his family had been held hostage, the police would be able to confirm that this had never been the case. The question was how the Americans would choose to judge him. Harshly, in all probability. Very harshly indeed.

"It doesn't look good for either of them," Eden said, as if she knew what Fredrika was thinking.

No, it certainly didn't.

"What about the recordings of the bomb threats?" Fredrika asked. "Did you get anywhere with trying to remove that stupid voice distortion?"

Eden pulled a face.

"It wasn't quite as stupid as we thought, but we're working on it."

In Fredrika's opinion it probably didn't matter all that much. She was convinced it was Sofi's voice they would hear if they managed to remove all the interference.

"She must have broken into Karim's house," she said.

"To plant the Tennyson book, you mean?"

"Yes. It seems strange that they didn't notice anything."

Eden's cell phone rang, and she picked it up off the desk.

"She could have had people helping her. Skilled people. And the book was only lying on top of the others on the shelf, after all. If nothing else had been touched, why would they notice an extra book among all the rest?"

That was true, of course. And it might not have been there for long.

"So you don't think she was working alone?" Fredrika said.

"On something like this? No, I don't."

How would they find out? Fredrika had no idea. Reluctantly she had to admit that she'd run out of energy. She just wanted to go home.

"There was something else I wanted to talk to you about," Eden said. "Sebastian has started looking for another job; he feels he's ready to move on. We'll be needing a new head of analysis; would you be interested?"

Fredrika was paralyzed with shock.

"Me? Head of analysis? Here?"

She looked around at the world outside Eden's glass cube, in an open-plan office so cut off from the rest of the world that she thought she would go crazy if she came to work here.

"What do you think?" Eden said.

Eden, who would be Fredrika's boss if she said yes.

"It's not for me," Fredrika said. "But thank you for the offer."

Her shift with Säpo was over, and she didn't feel as if she wanted to come back.

• • •

It had been worth a try. Fredrika Bergman had many of the qualities Eden looked for in a new recruit.

Integrity.

Analytical skill.

Intellect.

But if she didn't want it, she didn't want it, and that was the end of that.

What was more difficult to deal with was the fact that her own employer was keeping secrets from her. She had seen it when she went outside to get a signal on her cell phone, and Efraim turned up. At first, she had thought she was just being paranoid, but after a minute or so she was certain. There were two surveillance officers sitting in a car on the other side of the street, and it was obvious that they were there because of Efraim. He had presumably seen them as soon as they started following him.

But how could Säpo possibly know about Efraim?

She knew it couldn't be a coincidence. And she remembered how stressed GD had been whenever she had met up with him during the day. Something had happened, that much was clear, but for the life of her Eden couldn't work out why it had happened right now.

Of course the Brits had come calling; she was wise enough to realize that. The question was, why had they decided to pass on information to her new employer at this stage? Eden would never have gotten the post as head of counterterrorism if they had known from the outset. It was that simple. For a while at the beginning, she had wondered whether to take preventative action, to devalue the information by going to see GD and putting her cards on the table.

I made a mistake.

I allowed myself to be led astray and embarked on a clandestine relationship with an Israeli who turned out to be a Mossad agent.

I swear I didn't know who he was, and I also swear that as soon as I realized the truth, I ended the affair just as quickly as it had begun.

The only damage done was to me personally. I betrayed my husband, and believe me, I pay for that every night when the guilt keeps me awake.

But she couldn't bring herself to make things so simple. Instead, she had allowed the time to pass, and that had been another mistake.

The Brits knew that she wasn't a spy. The very idea was ridiculous. But it was a good story to sell to others, which was what they had done. To Säpo as well, no doubt. Just to discredit her. And all because when she had realized what Efraim's agenda was, she had chosen to end their relationship rather than reporting it to her superiors and beginning to play a double game.

"Do you realize what an opportunity you've thrown away?" her boss had yelled. "You could have carried on seeing him, pretended to let him recruit you, and gained a unique insight into Mossad, for fuck's sake!"

The problem was not that Eden didn't realize, but that the price was too high. She would never forget that night when it all ended, and she got back late to the apartment she shared with Mikael.

"We have to move to Sweden," she had said. "I no longer have a job."

And then came the tears. The regret. The despair. She didn't know whether Mikael would have stayed with her if he hadn't had his God. If he hadn't been such an expert when it came to forgiveness.

I'm the only one who can't forgive, Eden thought.

She hadn't forgiven her former boss, or Efraim, and she definitely hadn't forgiven herself. The shame and embarrassment set her heart on fire. She clenched her fists in her lap and forced herself to breathe calmly. It had been so horrible, seeing Efraim again.

It's not so much that I hate him, more that I still want to go to bed with him. Just once more. Mikael, my love, forgive your wife for being such a cheap creature.

They were flowing again, those bloody tears. Didn't she deserve something better than tears after a day like this?

In fewer than twenty-four hours, she had led an investigation where the team had managed to work out the story behind a hijacking that could have had such dire consequences that Eden didn't even want to think about it.

Resolutely, she dried her eyes. Enough. For several years.

She had a job to do and family to take care of. And she had decided to do what she should have done right from the start.

GD picked up on the first ring.

"Please don't tell me you have more bad news," he said, referring to the hijacking.

"This is about something else," Eden said. "Are you still in your office?"

"Yes."

"Good. I'll be there in five minutes."

She hung up.

Hopefully, she could get rid of the problem if she revealed as much of the truth as possible.

As far as the hijacking was concerned, she was reasonably happy, but not satisfied.

All their questions had been answered.

All their questions apart from one:

Where was Sofi?

November 2011

72

She could still recall the lighting in the room where her fate had been decided, and she realized that she was going to get away with it. The light itself was almost a shade of blue. The man sitting opposite her, evidently an agent with the federal prosecution service, followed her gaze as she looked up at the ceiling, and shook his head.

"You're not the only one who finds it unpleasant," he said.

She gave him a disarming smile.

"It's fine."

He laughed.

"It's pretty miserable working in a place where even the lighting is crap."

She laughed, too.

His expression became serious once more.

"So, Lydia, you want to go home, preferably within the next few days."

"Yes—tomorrow if possible."

"Naturally, we have no intention of standing in your way. You've been enormously helpful, and we trust you to come back for the trial. Your evidence will be very important."

She nodded firmly.

"Of course, I'll help you in any way I can."

The agent made a few notes on the papers in front of him, then he put down the pen and looked her straight in the eye.

"If no one else has done so yet, I must thank you on behalf of the United States government. You and your colleagues showed great courage in a very difficult situation."

"Thanks," she said, although that didn't feel like the right thing to say at all.

"I hope this terrible episode won't make you look for a new career. Individuals like Karim Sassi are few and far between, thank goodness."

"No—I love my job, and I intend to carry on flying."

Weak, pathetic people. That stupid bastard Karim couldn't take the pressure. He was going to get us shot down by some shabby fucking American missiles, and I had no intention of dying that way. Even though I was definitely prepared to die.

"Amazing," the agent said, and she could see tiny beads of sweat forming on his fleshy upper lip.

She tried to curb his enthusiasm.

"I don't believe I'm any different from my colleagues. We all intend to carry on flying."

Ten minutes later, she was standing on the pavement outside the prosecutor's office, breathing in the cool autumn air. All the relevant documents had been signed, and she would be leaving the USA the next day.

For a while, she had thought she'd had it. They had released her name and photograph to the press, but the picture was several years old, and Sofi knew that even if she bore some resemblance to the girl in the photo, it would never occur to anyone that it could be her.

Apart from Zakaria, their uncle, and Zakaria's girlfriend, Maria. And they would keep quiet until the day they died.

It was love that had brought Sofi to Europe in the first place. She married a man who had a residence permit in Germany, and at first, she had thought she was in love with him. Until she met Adam. She had waited just long enough for the authorities not to regard her marriage as a sham, then she had wanted to file for divorce.

But Adam said no.

It would be easier for both of them if the bond between them remained a secret, and she agreed with him.

By this time, he had shown her the right path. She had been so blind before she met him, allowing so many injustices to go unchallenged. But not any longer. In Adam's company, her hatred toward the USA and every other country engaged in the so-called war on terror grew and grew. A war that apparently legitimized any insanity whatsoever.

It wasn't right.

They had been well aware of the risks they were taking, and had acted accordingly. Her marriage broke down; that was inevitable. However, the structure of her relationship with Adam didn't change. They didn't start seeing each other more frequently, and when they did meet, it was as discreetly as possible. When Adam was finally arrested, they knew they had done the right thing. No police officers came banging on Sofi's door, no one wondered whether she might have been involved in the crimes of which Adam was accused. He was never charged. Twice they picked him up; twice they had to let him go.

The third time was during his trip to Pakistan.

Sofi hated recalling the uncertainty, the fear.

Why hadn't she gone with him?

No one knew where he was, no one knew what had happened. And there was no one she could ask.

Then one day he came home, but by then the Americans had already broken him.

It was Sofi who in turn had shown Zakaria the right path. Since she had acquired a residence permit in Germany using false documents and was known there as Lydia, she didn't tell anyone she had a brother in Sweden. Zakaria did the same; hardly anyone knew his sister in Germany, who came to visit him from time to time. Sofi didn't know how much he had told Maria, but she did know that Maria was loyal, and that was enough.

At first, Zakaria had been unsure; he had taken plenty of time to make up his mind. In the end, he had agreed, of course. Sofi had come up with so many persuasive arguments. Something had to be done; they couldn't just stand there watching. They had to *act*, make a stand. And they had quickly discovered that they were not alone in their struggle. They found support in both Germany and Sweden. Sofi would be eternally grateful to the person who had helped her by calling the TT news agency. Calling from the plane was out of the question, so she had needed backup.

They had also helped to take Adam to Sweden when he returned from Pakistan. He needed rest, peace, and quiet. But Adam got neither. Zakaria kept his distance, didn't want to be seen anywhere near him if either he or Adam were wanted by the police, and all Sofi heard was that Adam was getting worse and worse. One day, he went back to Germany, then traveled home to his parents.

If only she'd gotten there in time. If only she'd been able to speak to him.

She had made her decision at Adam's funeral.

It was lucky that she happened to be a flight attendant; she had virtually unlimited opportunities to travel. There was absolutely no reason for the security services to question her movements around the world.

She could speak Swedish, so it wasn't difficult to get a job with SAS, the Swedish airline. The conditions weren't good, but it was the same everywhere. It wasn't a permanent job, but that wasn't what she needed anyway. She appreciated the fact that she was flexible and could fly out of several different cities.

She had bumped into Karim Sassi purely by chance one day. She had made a point of remembering his name after that disastrous flight to Rabat, when he had landed in Munich for no good reason. After that the plan had almost written itself. She made sure she was on several flights with Karim, and when she wasn't working, she spent her time alone in the apartment that Maria had helped her to rent.

Although she had been so careful, Sofi was still surprised that she had gotten away with what she had done. At least for the time being. She thanked her god that everything had gone so well. She had managed to get to Karim's house after he had left for the airport and persuaded his daughter to say a few words to her daddy on the phone, to convince him that his family were being held hostage. Then she had made it to Arlanda in time to get on the same flight. Thank goodness Erik Recht had been just as late as she was; Karim hadn't said a word about her poor timekeeping. He had had plenty of other things to think about by that stage.

She wouldn't be coming back to the USA for the trial. No way.

Sooner or later the authorities would realize, or begin to suspect, how everything hung together.

It didn't really matter.

The mission was accomplished. Zakaria had been released the day after the hijacking, and apparently, Tennyson Cottage had been shut down months ago.

Sofi had resigned from her job with SAS and returned to Germany, where she had dismantled her life in less than a week. A friend had promised to take care of her mail.

Now she was on safe ground, waiting for what would happen next. She was convinced that it was only a matter of time before they worked out who she was, but by then she would be far away.

Zakaria had emailed her from a secret address that they had long ago agreed to use only in emergencies.

"We need to lie low for a while," he had written. "Our next contribution to the campaign will have to wait."

Sofi was happy to wait.

She had all the time in the world.

They both did.

Afterword

*H*ostage is a work of fiction.

Shall I just repeat that so that everyone feels safe?

The book you have just read is fiction. As far as I know, it bears no resemblance to actual circumstances. If it does, this is completely unintentional. I usually say that I write primarily to entertain my readers, and that is the case here, too. If I decide to do anything else, I will let my readers know.

However . . .

In January 2011, I moved to Vienna, to take up a post as senior terrorism analyst with OSCE, the Organisation for Security and Co-operation in Europe, only weeks after a suicide bomber had blown himself up on Bryggargatan in Stockholm, and only months after returning from my posting to Baghdad. I couldn't let developments in the outside world pass Fredrika Bergman by. Just for once, she had to get involved in a case that touched on one of my more professional interests. I also felt that after *The Disappeared*, I needed to give her and Alex a new kind of challenge, and therefore, I decided to write a book that differs from my earlier novels in a number of ways.

Besides, it was only a question of time before the urge grew too strong for me: the urge to write a book linked to one of the two places in the world that I love and find fascinating, namely the USA. It is a country to love, and sometimes to question. A true friend cannot be uncritical. Even an author who writes with the aim of entertaining the reader has the right to spice up her work with important dilemmas and problems that the reader will hopefully consider afterward.

My books usually write themselves, and that was also the case on this occasion. I made use of all the sources around me. Sweden, after experiencing its first suicide bomber. The world after 9/11. One of the questions raised after the terrorist attack in Stockholm echoed in my mind for a long time: "The guy was on Facebook and wrote about his views there. So why didn't anyone notice?" I was astonished. Did people really think that the Swedish authorities had nothing better to do than sit and read everything that's written on Facebook? Didn't they realize what the consequences of such an approach would be? And didn't they realize how many people express various kinds of frustration and sometimes pure hatred through social media, both in Sweden and abroad? Are we to bring in all these individuals for questioning, interrogate them about their visions and plans? Do we fine them? And if so, by exactly how many thousand percent would the forces of law and order need to be increased?

I am often asked how much time I spend on research, and when it comes to this book the answer is: many, many hours. Given my background, it was very important to me that the context in the novel could be perceived as factual, and could also be found in sources that are accessible to all. For example, it is no secret that the USA has, and has had, so-called secret detention centers in other countries, and it is no secret that Sweden has laws that mean that a person's permanent residence permit can be revoked under certain circumstances. However, both Tennyson Cottage and Zakaria Khelifi are products of my own imagination. Even someone who has worked in security policy for several years has the right to make up stories.

And terrorism is a productive subject, if you want to write exciting books. That may be crass, but it's true. Having a vivid imagination and a never-ending desire to tell a story is also a great help, of course. To a certain extent, I had great fun writing *Hostage*. You have to love Eden Lundell, don't you? She became such a delicious part of my literary excursion to my former workplace, the Swedish security service (Säpo). Many crime writers before me have tossed Säpo into the mix, and many will do so in the future. I don't know what makes it so difficult to do Säpo justice. I don't know why it's so hard to work out what they do and don't do, what they're allowed to do and what they're not allowed to do. After plowing through their home page in my quest for publicly available information, I discovered a wealth of interesting details about what our country's security service actually does. All you have to do is take a look. As I did.

One of my early readers was horrified by the ending of *Hostage*. The guilty parties, the terrorists, get away! But why should that be so surprising? It's a cornerstone of our justice system that if there is reasonable doubt on the question of guilt, then it's better to be safe than sorry. Which sometimes inevitably leads to the fact that those who are guilty will get away with what they have done. And who says the story is over when it comes to the hunt for Sofi Khelifi? All I have said is that I am letting her rest for the time being. While Eden Lundell lights another cigarette and wonders whether she really has got over Efraim, I will allow Sofi and Zakaria to bide their time and make plans for the future. They won the first round in their battle, and they might also win the next, but sooner or later even the most successful bad guys have to pay the price.

Acknowledgments

As usual when I write my books, I have received fantastic support from Piratförlaget. Warm thanks to everyone who works there, and special thanks to my publisher, Sofia, and my editor, Anna. Without you, things would often come to a standstill and end up much worse.

Thank you also to everyone at the Salomonsson Agency who continue to ensure that my books reach readers outside Sweden's borders. Special thanks to my agent, Leyla, who puts such an enormous amount of energy into promoting my books overseas.

Thanks to Johan for his opinions and nonopinions on my manuscript.

Thanks to Karl-Henrik for taking the time to answer all my questions about airline security and routines.

And thanks to Sofia E. for once again reading my book and coming back to me with wise comments.

And finally, thanks to my fantastic family and all my wonderful friends who continue to think it's cool that I write books, and who are always there when I want something else to think about, or when I simply want to call them and tell them the latest news about my writing.

Thank you.

Kristina Ohlsson
Stockholm, Winter 2012

About the Author

Kristina Ohlsson is a political scientist and, until recently, held the position of Counter-Terrorism Officer at OSCE. She has previously worked at the Swedish Security Service, the Ministry for Foreign Affairs, and the Swedish National Defence, where she was a junior expert on the Middle East conflict and the foreign policy of the European Union. Her debut novel, *Unwanted*, was published in Sweden in 2009 to terrific critical acclaim, and all her novels have since been bestsellers. Kristina lives in Stockholm.

About the Translator

Marlaine Delargy has translated works by many writers, including John Ajvide Lindqvist, Åsa Larsson, Anne Holt, Michael Hjorth/Hans Rosenfeldt, and Johan Theorin, with whom she won the CWA International Dagger in 2010.

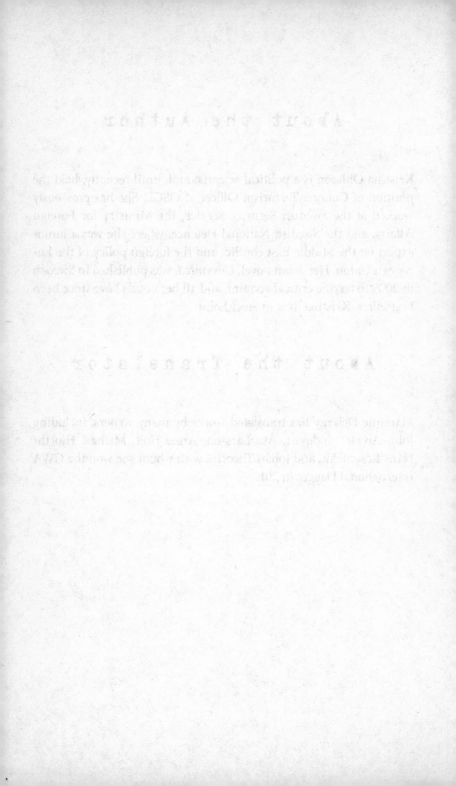

About the Author

Kristina Ohlsson is a published scientist and, until recently, held the position of Counter-Terrorism Officer (OSCE). She has previously worked at the Swedish Security Service, the Ministry for Foreign Affairs and the Swedish Political Intelligence. She was a terror expert on the Middle East conflict and the foreign policy of the East Asian Union. Her debut novel, *Unwanted*, was published in Swedish in 2009 to critical acclaim, and all her novels have since been bestsellers. Kristina lives in Stockholm.

About the Translator

Marlaine Delargy has translated works by many authors, including John Ajvide Lindqvist, Åsa Larsson, Anne Holt, Michael Hjorth, Hans Rosenfeldt, and Johan Theorin, with whom she won the CWA International Dagger in 2010.